WHAT WE GIVE,
WHAT WE TAKE

WHAT WE GIVE, WHAT WE TAKE

A NOVEL

RANDI TRIANT

SHE WRITES PRESS

Published 2022

Printed in the United States of America

Print ISBN: 978-1-64742-405-3
E-ISBN: 978-1-64742-327-8
Library of Congress Control Number: 2021916156

For information, address:
She Writes Press
1569 Solano Ave #546
Berkeley, CA 94707

She Writes Press is a division of SparkPoint Studio, LLC.

For Fiona

"People should not become their losses."

—Howard Norman, *Northern Lights*

Part One

DICKIE

Chapter

ONE

I was fifteen years old when my mother left me for Vietnam. I want to believe she did it for me. Fay was good at lying, though, and she didn't lose any sleep over it. Unlike me. I lost my ability to lay my head down, close my eyes, and drift off to dreamland bliss. I lost my name too. Not right away. That would come later.

What I wouldn't give to have my real name again. To start over at forty, living a life where people actually know you, a life in which you can sleep a solid eight hours per night. But I can't. I continue to go by Pete Smith, the name I took out of precaution and self-preservation. They're not qualities to brag about. They're both born of fear. But they keep me out of trouble in Province-town, Massachusetts, where most of the residents—the artists, the drug addicts, the drag queens—have one philosophy in common: To hell with the past. All you have is the present. Deal with it.

Provincetown is as far east as you can get without falling into the ocean. Because the Cape is shaped like an arm curled around, what you would ordinarily think was the west end of Province-town is actually the east end and vice versa. Without your ordinary compass, a sense of vertigo prevails. Nothing is as it seems. A man with a fake name and dark circles under his eyes can easily disappear into a place like that.

Still, I worry that my disappearing act will come to a close as quickly as it began twenty-five years ago. Those are the nights when I end up letting myself back into the PO so I can surround myself with the calm of sorting through envelopes and packages that haven't been collected. I like to keep my hands busy; if they're moving, I tend to stare at them less. I make a pot of coffee, sit in the back, and allow myself one of those packages. I don't just choose it willy-nilly. I have my rules. The package has to be unclaimed for over thirty days. There are more than you'd think to choose from. It has to be one of the small ones. Those packages have an intimacy I'll never have. Small boxes can hold objects that require forethought or a deep connection, like an engagement ring.

One night I found two packages addressed to the same woman from the same man. I couldn't help it, I opened both, making sure that I could easily reseal them without the woman knowing. I eased off the tape by holding each to my desk lamp. If you're ambitious you can pick up some useful talents being a postal clerk. The first box held a stone. That was it. A common river stone that looked like it had been worried by someone's thumb for some time. It was speckled black, smooth, and slightly sloped inward from the pressure. Inside the other box was a scrap of paper. "Come home," was all it said. Nothing else. I felt like I'd seen an animal get hit by a car.

The next day I kept an eye on the rental boxes, waiting for Dorothy Smythe to come in and collect her mail. When I finally saw a woman slide a key in box 185, I opened the Dutch gate and went over to her. She was a tall, slightly paunchy woman with her hair tied back in a bandana. Normally she'd be exactly the type of woman I'd try to pick up at the A&P. But not this day. This day something else came over me.

"Excuse me," I said in a low voice so that no one else would hear what I was about to say. "But you have two packages waiting for you."

Dorothy Smythe stared at me as if I'd slapped her. She was just like me, wanting her anonymity and her life of not knowing anyone. It was my own worst fear of what could happen to me, and here I was doing the same thing to her. She ducked her head as if she didn't want me to be able to remember her facial features. I knew the gesture well.

"I'm sorry," I murmured. "I won't bother you again."

She didn't say a word, just turned around and left. She never came back. Her stack of mail grew too large for the single box she'd rented. We never got a change of address card. Eventually, her mail stopped coming to the Provincetown PO. Dorothy Smythe was somewhere else now. Someplace where a minimum-wage postal clerk didn't bother her with reminders of what she'd left behind. Someplace safe.

Earlier in the evening before my mother left, she and I had been sitting on the scratchy plaid couch in the living room of our mobile home in Key West. The evening news with Walter Cronkite was on the black-and-white television that had a bent clothes hanger for an antenna. It was April 19, 1967.

"Those poor boys," Fay said.

"Who you talkin' about?" Fay's boyfriend asked. We'd moved to Key West with Johnson three months before. He was like an animal that had been caged too long: He chewed the inside of his mouth constantly, and his blue eyes seemed smaller than they actually were. Now he leaned against the archway into the galley kitchen, holding a half-eaten beef jerky. To the left of the living room were two small bedrooms separated by a spit of a bathroom with a shower stall the width of your waist. That was the extent of our home, a word I use loosely.

Fay pointed at the television. "There. Look."

Walter Cronkite was standing in front of a map of Vietnam

with a pointer in his hand, like a schoolteacher. "American forces in Vietnam have now topped the four hundred thousand mark," he told us. "And forty-five thousand more troops are on their way."

"There's no end in sight," Fay said, leaning as far toward the television as she could without falling off the couch. I tried to look interested, but every night the news showed the same footage of our soldiers trudging through thick bushes with huge packs on their backs and rifles in their hands. They always seemed to be walking in circles, like a bunch of Boy Scouts on a badge mission. Sometimes there were clips of Bob Hope and a couple of beautiful girls in bikinis on some stage, with thousands of soldiers cheering them on. Vietnam was another universe, though. I couldn't get worked up about some guys I didn't know in some country where it rained constantly, and the grunts were up to their eyeballs in mud. There were far too many things right in that mobile home I needed to worry about.

Johnson waved at the air with his beef jerky. It looked like a flattened turd. "Hey, remember me?" he asked Fay.

She shushed him, turned up the volume on the TV, and sat back down on the couch next to me.

"Ginny's over there now," she said when the news went to a commercial. Ginny was a contortionist in the Amazing Humans Show, a carney that also featured Fay in a water tank escape routine. The year before, the Humans show had folded. Peace-loving hippies didn't want to see someone swallow a sword or stick a head in a vise. But Ginny was still my mother's best friend. I hated watching what she could do with her legs. She called Fay "babydoll," although they were almost the same age. One time—I was four or so—I caught her kissing Fay in our trailer. She was holding my mother, but Fay's hands were down alongside her own thighs. Even at four years old I saw what Fay would give and what she took.

"Ginny says it's beautiful over there." Fay turned to me.

"That right?" Johnson said. He cranked up a transistor radio he was holding in his palm. Baseball season had just started. He wanted to show Fay who was boss. He stood there, leaning against the wall, listening to that aquamarine-colored radio. Fay had bought it for me for fifty cents at a tag sale. Most of what came out of its quarter-sized speaker was static.

"Ginny's in Vietnam?" I asked. I took every opportunity I could to show my mother I was better than Johnson—in this case, a better listener.

"Chuck's got some line on the army. They're willing to pay big bucks for the entertainment value. He's already sent Ginny and a few of the old gang over for a couple of weeks to put on a show for the boys."

Chuck was the owner of the Amazing Humans. He only smiled when he was causing someone grief. One of his front teeth was missing, but that didn't stop him from smiling a lot. If Fay wasn't around, he liked to hide my crutches whenever I put them down, and then he made me play a stupid hot/cold game, always shooting that gap-smile at me. I had a rotten time walking without my crutches. When I was two, I got polio. I wore leg braces and needed crutches for balance—what I called my sticks. The polio had paralyzed the nerves in my legs, especially in my shin muscles. My calf muscles overcompensated, tightening as if they were cramping, and pulled up my heels so badly that my toes permanently pointed to the ground. Under the strain, my ankles rolled inwards. The braces locked in my heels and kept me from walking on my toes. They made it possible to walk, but without my sticks I could only manage three steps before I pitched forward to the ground. My sticks were my rudders. Each of them had an aluminum cuff that gripped below my elbow, while my hands gripped the worn rubber handles. I no longer need the leg braces, but I still depend on those crutches.

Sometimes I'd be a hand's length away from where Chuck had hidden them, and he'd lie and say, "Colder, colder, cold." He loved seeing me stumble around like when Frankenstein first stood up from the operating table. You'd think it'd be hard to hide two metal crutches, but Chuck was resourceful: underneath a tent flap, between a couple of hay bales. He made the most of whatever was at hand. And though he loved to torment me, he never laid a hand on me. "No harm, no foul," he'd say.

That wasn't the case with Johnson. Soon after we arrived in Key West, he'd tripped me on purpose one day when I was jimmying past him in the living room. I'd gotten up from the couch in a hurry to switch the TV channel and left behind my sticks. For short distances, it was too much of a pain to deal with them. The television was only two steps away. But Johnson stuck out his foot and I went down like a shot water buffalo, as he would've said, and I almost broke my nose on the threadbare wall-to-wall. I knew I was too big to cry, knew I'd be in deeper with Johnson if I did, but the sheer pain of it caused my eyes to water. I angled my face away so he wouldn't see. Fifteen years old and I was lying on the ground like a big baby, hoping to God that Fay would come out of the bathroom, where she was taking a shower, and see what kind of shitty mess she'd landed us in this time. My fingers picked at the shag rug as I willed myself not to cry and hated myself for wanting to.

"Get up," Johnson snarled at me. "Stop screwing around." He dug the toe of his work boot into my thigh until I struggled up.

After that, whenever Fay was doing her afternoon solo show on the pier, something inevitably made Johnson mad—I hadn't tightened the ketchup lid enough, or I was watching too much TV—and he'd slap me across the face, ordering me not to cry.

"I'm doing you a favor. You better toughen up, boy," he'd say. "Cryin's for sissies. They're gonna beat the crap outta you at school. You're in the big city now."

By the time Fay left for Vietnam, I'd learned how to do the exact opposite of whatever my natural physical reaction was every time Johnson started up his cryin's for sissies routine. I'd built a vault of steel and locks and bolts, a vault no one could get out of, not even my mother, the master escape artist, and into this vault I stuffed my tears, shoved them in and stomped them down to make room for more. With each stinging cheek, I'd imagine the back of a garbage truck, the metal wall slamming down, crushing milk cartons and soup cans and cereal boxes into a flat nothingness. I imagined Johnson in there too, a look of horror smeared across his filthy face along with the rotten tomatoes as the metal wall shut him up. In some ways a slap is worse than if the person just hauls off and clocks you one. A slap is something a girl would do, but somehow it made me feel like *I* was the girl, not Johnson. You let someone punch you every day, well, that can be seen as a sign of your strength. You can take it. It shows what you're made of. But a slap? A slap means you're a lightweight. A wimp.

Sometimes I wondered, though, if Johnson *was* doing me a favor. I'd look down at my legs and see them for what they were: a weakness to take advantage of. I wasn't like other fifteen-year-old boys at Key West High School in more ways too. They wore their dirty hair down to their shoulders, for one thing. Mine was always in a brush cut, the blond giving off a bristly sheen. It gave me a look of innocence, an altar boy ready to pass around the Sunday basket. Corduroy bellbottoms clung to the other boys' hips, and their shirts had large kidney shapes that reminded me of the paramecia we studied in science. My standard outfit was a pair of Boy Scout shorts, a white underwear T-shirt, and a pair of old men's oxford shoes. The other boys talked about screwing girls and getting high. I'd never really talked to a girl, let alone screwed one. Girls seemed untouchable because they were always giggling in the hallways about some secret joke that only they knew the punch line to, and I worried that the punch line was me and my legs and my crappy mobile home. I'd see them in the distance, huddled shoulder to shoulder, as impenetrable as a chain-link fence, and I'd wonder if Fay had been like them in high school, although if I stopped to think about it, I had no idea if Fay even *went* to high school. I knew nothing about Fay and her childhood. The one time I asked her what her parents were like, she said the past didn't mean diddly-squat.

"What's important, Dickie, is today and tomorrow. They're the only things you can fix. If the past is broken, it's shot to shit. Pack it in and move on."

I never told Fay about Johnson using me as a slap bag. I could see that she still thought of the Amazing Humans as her family and that she missed them, and I worried that the friction between Johnson and me would make her leave us both. If I complained about him, she would be forced to choose sides. His beef wasn't with Fay, it was with me. *You're not his kid*, I'd tell myself after another episode with him. *You're in the way.*

And now the Amazing Humans was in Vietnam, and Ginny was sending postcards that invited Fay to join them. For years I'd lived in fear that my mother would leave me behind. Sometimes she had, with her boyfriend of the moment, but not for long, a couple of days at most, just until the Humans set up in whatever new town I was about to become briefly acquainted with. But one day, when I was ten, I'd overheard Chuck telling Fay that as soon as he could, he'd sell the Humans and buy one of those charter fishing boats—that was the life. Tourists would pay anything for the thrill of landing a four-foot marlin.

"You're out on the ocean all day, catching a tan, and getting paid for it," he said.

"Sounds good to me," she replied, surprising me. I'd never

forgotten it. I stored that memory in my vault as well, sandwiched in there with all the tears and the slaps.

Now, sitting on the couch next to me, my mother rested her hand on my thigh. Her body was compact, all muscle. In Key West, she did two hundred sit-ups a day and swam a mile off the pier and back. "To control the mind, you have to control the body," she told me. Every time she said it, I'd look down at my legs. As a boy, I couldn't tell if she knew the effect her body had on people, especially men. Now I know better, especially if she sat right next to you, the cool skin of her arm touching yours, her long blond shag so close you could blow on it and feel the ends tickle your mouth.

Johnson was still pretending to listen to the game on the transistor. All I could hear was static, the buzz of a drill.

"I could earn twice, maybe three times what I make here. We need the money," Fay said, standing up. "I want to get you a new pair of braces. Those are all banged up."

"They're fine," I said right away.

Fay glared at me. "No. They're. Not. I'm the worst mother in the world, letting her son go around in those things." She walked across the small living room and disappeared behind the thin kitchen wall. I heard her open a cupboard and pull out the shoebox where she kept all her handcuffs and lucky picklocks and keys. She came back to me, extending an envelope that held a letter from Ginny. I opened it. "There's a man here," I read aloud, "who'll pull your teeth out for ten cents. Is that why more Americans pile in every day? Chuck says he can get you on a plane with the Red Cross, he's got some deal going. They'd really love your act, Babydoll."

"I hear they eat their own dogs," Johnson said, staring at the transistor like it was showing a movie.

"You don't know what you're talking about," Fay said.

"Mom?" I pushed up on my sticks to a standing position. "What does Ginny mean about—"

Fay quickly put her index finger to her mouth, glaring at me again. I shut up, though I knew exactly what Ginny had been saying. What I was dumb enough to believe was that my mother would take me with her. It was so far she'd have to take me.

She walked over to me and clamped her arm around my shoulders. Johnson rushed over, grabbed the letter out of my hands, and tore it in two, letting the pieces fall to the stained carpeting. I wanted to slug him with a stick. Then he stepped back across the room, closer to the screen door, as if he intended on blocking it.

"You're going to leave me for a bunch of people who only come to see you because you're half-naked?" His hands clenched at his sides.

Fay bent over, picked up the letter halves. "Don't," she said, fingering a torn edge. Letter in hand, she folded her arms across her chest and stared him down. The sounds of a truck rumbling by came through the screen door. A group of kids passed the front of our house. Fay kept looking at Johnson. Slowly his fists unclenched, and then his face got less cruel-looking, as if all the tension was being ironed out of him.

"Just tell me what you want me to do," she said, standing next to me, with her eyes fixed on him.

"Fay . . ." Johnson stared down at his cracked work boots.

She held up her hands. "You tell me how to make it right. That's all I want."

When he didn't say anything, I said, "He just wants to complain."

Fay jerked her head back, shooting me a hard look. "Stop giving him lip when I'm at work. We're lucky he'll have us." Suddenly I felt like I did when I fell flat on my face in front of Johnson. As soon as she said it, though, Fay looked down the skinny hall that led to our bedrooms. "You want a real home, don't you? You want to get better?" she said so quietly only I could hear. I didn't know what to say. Part of me, of course, wanted just that. But I didn't want her to leave either. While I was thinking this over, she went and put the ripped letter back in her shoebox.

"Fay . . ." Johnson said again. But she wasn't having it. Giving him a wide berth, she walked out of our mobile home and stood at the curb out front, staring at the passing cars. Johnson didn't move. I went and joined him at the screen door. We watched her, afraid she'd hop in one of those cars and leave right then. Fay put her hand in the pocket of her miniskirt and pulled out what we knew would be a quarter. Holding up her left hand, she maneuvered the coin across the top of her knuckles by moving her fingers as if she were playing the piano. It was a favorite exercise of hers. She worked the left hand, then the right. After a few passes, she was concentrating so hard on the silver blurring across her hand that a truck could've come within inches of her and she'd never notice. "You lose your concentration and you drown," she told me once.

"She only leaves because she doesn't want to hurt my chances of getting better," I finally said to Johnson as we stood there.

He turned toward me. "What're you talking about?"

"Forget it. You don't understand."

"I understand. I understand you can't avoid making mistakes in life. But that's something your mother doesn't understand, I can tell you that. She'll still be here, no matter how far she goes." He kept talking, but I stopped listening. In my mind, Fay came back in and asked me to join her in my cramped bedroom. She said, "I'll get our things together, Dickie." She packed my Boy Scouts and my T-shirts. She packed her flip-flops, her worn-out sequined show outfit, her shoebox of picklocks and handcuffs. I saw us leaving at nightfall, when Johnson was asleep. I saw it all.

I saw nothing.

Chapter

TWO

I said we *moved* to Key West, but that word has a finality that wasn't part of our lives. Before Johnson, Fay and I had usually traveled from place to place with the Humans, from Enid to Detroit to Millinocket, setting up a camping trailer for no more than two weeks at a time. Fay's philosophy was "The next place will be better, you'll see." I tried to believe her and for a week or two I did. But children are nothing but eyes; they notice everything. It's not what's under the Christmas tree that matters, it's what isn't.

We weren't so poor that we had to eat leftover pizza out of dumpsters, but there were telltale signs that we weren't doing so well, especially when we finally stayed put in the Keys. Hoping to cash in on the Florida tourist trade, my mother got a county license to set up her water tank on a pier in Key West. The tank, a cylinder of Plexiglas standing upright, was a little over six feet tall. At the top, a wooden ledge ran along the circumference; my mother could perch there if she wanted. The water was as warm as the Floridian weather.

Fay's routines involved a heavy linked chain wrapped around her body, except for her arms and hands, which were hand-cuffed in front of her. Twice a day, she performed the Chinese Water-Torture Cell. Houdini called it *the old upside down*. With the chain wrapped around your body, you're lowered headfirst into the tank. At the top, your ankles are clamped in wooden stocks. What the audience doesn't know is that the water is at just the right level so that when you drop in, your weight forces the water to rise, which in turn pushes open the clasps on the stocks. Fay's ankles would be released, her back toward the audience. She kept her lucky pick in a tiny pocket inside her bikini bottom. Blocking the audience's view, she slipped the fingers of her cuffed hands into her bathing suit bottom and retrieved the pick. The handcuffs sprang open, the chain unraveled easily. She surfaced within two minutes.

Without the chaos of traveling with the Amazing Humans, everything about us was thrown into high relief in Key West. Fay wore the same clothes almost every day: a boy's white cotton T-shirt that came in three-packs from Kress's in Miami for a $1.29, a jeans miniskirt or velour hot pants, and flip-flops. I was usually in another Fruit of the Loomer from the same three-pack and a pair of Boy Scout shorts. Fay had found a whole slew of the shorts at the Salvation Army in some town in Jersey when we'd been passing through with the show. The khaki color was slightly off regulation—it leaned more toward pea soup than evergreen—and the shorts swam on me. I looked nine years old in them, not fifteen.

"You'll grow into them," Fay said.

I wouldn't. Below my waist it looked like the bottom half of Howdy Doody's body, useless marionette legs that needed positioning. Two thick, ruler-sized pieces of metal ran from a rubber cuff under each knee to stirrups bolted to my shoes. By the time I was fifteen I was wearing a pair of coffee-colored oxfords, another Salvation Army bargain.

"They're old man's shoes," I complained.

"What do you mean? They're so cool. You look like James Bond." She winked. I stared down at them as she was tying the laces and tried to imagine I was James Bond tracking down Gold-finger. They still looked like old man's shoes.

When I contracted polio, the Amazing Humans show had been doing a few weeks in Philadelphia. At first, Fay thought it was a simple flu because on the fourth day I seemed to recover and was back horsing around with Tina the Sword Swallower. But a few days later, Fay woke up to find my body twitching violently next to hers, as if I were being electrocuted. Four hours later, I was weak from my knees to my toes. She rushed me to the hospital, but it was too late.

After my legs became paralyzed, Fay began having trouble with her escape routines. At least that's what Ginny the contortionist told me years later. Fay started taking longer to pick the handcuffs. A couple of times, she dropped her lucky picklock before unlocking the handcuffs. Then there was the time we went to the E.J. Spiniff Home for Crippled Children in Fallsview, Connecticut. Fay took me there after hearing it was the best place in the country for polio therapy. The Amazing Humans was doing a show in the parking lot of a boarded-up Catholic school in nearby New Haven. We were living in a small trailer that we hooked on the back of our asthmatic station wagon whenever the Humans traveled to the next show. We hadn't met Johnson yet. I was seven years old and Fay was worried about me. Over my hideaway bed, I'd pinned up a full-page magazine ad that showed the March of Dimes poster child, Delbert Dains, walking with his braces and crutches. I had the same ones. Delbert was wearing a little blue suit, with shorts instead of pants so we could see his braces better. Maybe if I were on a poster, I'd be famous and Fay would want to settle down then. We could live in a home where the kitchen table didn't become another bed at night. Delbert gave me hope for that. But after Fay saw the Delbert Dains poster, she headed for the payphone two blocks away.

"Getting you better is 90 percent attitude, 10 percent luck." She dialed the number for the Spiniff Home.

"Looks like a country club," she said, smiling, as a taxi drove us up the main drive to a mansion. The station wagon had quit that morning. We'd left Ginny, who was as handy with tools as she was with bending her limbs, to fix it. Fay paid for the taxi using our food money for that week. She was always making decisions like that: big on inspiration, short on logic. We didn't talk about how we'd actually pay for me to get the therapy. We passed rolling green lawns and white, pink, and blue hydrangea bushes that looked like the fireworks I'd seen at county fairs on the fourth of July. There wasn't a child anywhere in sight.

As soon as we were shown the rooms where the patients got therapy, everything changed. Fay took one look at a child in an iron lung and we were out of there, me struggling to keep up with my sticks, my leg braces squeaking as her flip-flops slapped down the linoleum hallway.

"Someone should report those people," she fumed as she opened the waiting taxi's back door. The whole way home she stared out her window and didn't look at me once.

The night Fay left she came to me on my cot. Lying next to me on top of the sheet, she whispered, "There's people who fully recover from polio. It's just a matter of time and money. I told you about this new treatment in New York, right? They say it's all about the heat." Her voice was so soft I missed words here and there. It didn't matter, I knew them by heart. "You believe I want what's best for you, don't you?"

"Yes."

"Okay then." She bolted up as if she was going to leave.

"We should've moved here sooner," I said, to keep her there. When we'd moved in, the mobile home still had signs of its previous tenants, members of a motorcycle gang: stains and burns in the Pepto-Bismol wall-to-wall, a couple of cracked windows, pizza boxes everywhere, crumpled squares of aluminum foil in the bathroom. But Fay at least made it clean and it didn't have wheels on it.

"Are you kidding? It's awful," she said now. As soon as she said it, I noticed how dirty the Venetian blinds were and that they were missing some slats. My cot from the Salvation Army seemed harder than usual.

She swung her legs over the side of the cot, her back toward me.

"It isn't good for you if I'm here all the time." Her voice was as cold as the ocean after a storm. Then she turned to me. "You have to believe you can get better, okay? You've got to believe 100 percent. That and the big bucks and you just don't know." Her face softened. "We might be able to cure you yet."

She didn't wait for me to answer but walked out of my room, toward her bedroom. What she'd said made me nervous. Was she really thinking of leaving me with Johnson? He practically ignored me when she was around, but the minute Fay went to the pier for her daily show, he was on me.

"When you gonna start bringing in some money?" he'd say, or something like it.

"I go to school, remember?" I'd say every word with a snideness that I glazed with an extra-wide gleaming smile. Johnson could never figure out if I was smart-talking him or not.

"Lotsa kids get a job after school."

"I can't exactly stock shelves." I'd raise my sticks for effect.

"People like to support the unfortunate. I seen it all the time. There's that young girl at the packy. What's her name? The one who bags your stuff up, always talks so loud."

"She's an idiot for God's sake!"

Not that Johnson was bringing in much money either. The only job he could land in Key West was a night gig on the Big F, a fishing boat. During the day, the Big F took groups of tourists out for sport fishing, but at night it brought in marijuana. The pot bales were loosely covered in plastic. Johnson, who'd been a farmer before he met Fay, figured it was as near to pitching hay as he was going to find down there.

I couldn't believe that she would leave me with *him*. The thought of him being able to slap me whenever he wanted spun around inside me and I felt dizzy and nauseous. Maybe she hadn't been talking to me, maybe she'd been talking to herself. She couldn't be around me if she couldn't fully believe I was going to get better. I trusted then that if she was going to leave me, she'd only do it because she absolutely had to, because she felt herself slipping into doubt. I trusted she didn't want to hurt my chances of recovery. I trusted she wouldn't be gone for long.

Fay had picked Johnson out of an audience in Buffalo, New York. She told me later she could see he'd cleaned himself up to come to the show. His hair was slicked back with witch hazel, and he was wearing his only blue suit, which had a cigarette burn on the arm. The cuffs didn't quite reach to his wrists. His cheek moved up and down to the rhythm of his gnawing.

"I need someone strong to help me out with what I'm about to attempt," Fay called out to the audience. "No wimps need apply." She pretended to look over the crowd, like she was hell-bent on picking the absolute strongest person. But she always went for the weak ones. She crooked her index finger Johnson's way, and that was that. Within a week of the show's closing, Johnson was driving his pickup to Key West with us next to him in the cab.

"For God's sake, let's go somewhere warm and green," Fay

said. Her empty tank sat like a miniature corn silo on the truck's rusty flatbed.

"Sounds good to me," said Johnson. He was tired of the hard winters up in Buffalo anyway. He leaned forward and smiled past me at Fay.

"Let's go to Florida," she said without hesitating. "Warm weather's gonna be good for you," she murmured. "I'm going to fix it right down there."

Johnson whooped and batted at the driver's wheel. "Goddamn. Florida it is." He thought the farther away he could take Fay, the better his chance of keeping her. Sometimes he was so dumb it killed me. At first, I believed he was like one of my mother's boyfriends, Roger. Stupid, but harmless. When we'd moved into Roger's apartment above a noisy game arcade on the boardwalk in Atlantic City, Roger had said, "I bet you never thought you'd be living in beachfront property." The boardwalk was a long thread of taffy stores, bars, strip joints, game arcades, and boarded-up storefronts. At night, I was kept awake by the outside banter of prostitutes and the pinging of mechanical cowboys shot down by Gatling guns. We lived with Roger for two weeks before the Amazing Humans picked up again and we hightailed it for upstate New York. While Fay packed up the station wagon, Roger cried quietly, leaning against the car's back fin.

I felt sorry for Roger. He wasn't the sharpest tool in the shed, as Fay often said, but he'd given us a home and had never raised a hand to me. "She doesn't like that," I told him, and forked my fingers in the air toward his eyes. He snuffed hard, but still his tears kept coming.

Now we were driving to Florida with Johnson, and the longer we drove with him the more I began to think that he wasn't like Roger at all.

"Florida it is," Johnson repeated, and this time slapped my

leg. I was wearing my shorts, and the hard smack of his palm hitting my skin drew Fay's attention away from her opened window. Already there was the pink blurry outline of his hand.

"Hey!" she said. Reaching across me, she swatted at his arm.

"I barely touched him!" he cried.

"Jerk," I muttered.

Fay shot me a hard look. "Pull the car over! Now!"

"He's all right," Johnson said nervously, glancing past me at Fay again but not slowing down.

"I don't have the time or the energy to be your referee." She angled her body toward her open window. I didn't know if she was talking to me or Johnson. I was so mad I almost punched him. We'd only been with him a week and already he was causing trouble between Fay and me.

"You two work it out right now or I'm getting out," she said into the rushing air. A passing highway sign said Ham Hocks and Towels. Pete's Barbeque Pit. Best in the South. Five hundred yards.

"He's all right," Johnson repeated. "Just a little exuberance, that's all." He snorted. "You're tougher than that, right, boy?"

"You bet," I said, sitting up straighter. I turned my head to Fay. Tapping her on the shoulder, I waited for her to look my way. When she finally did, I gave her a wink. "Couldn't feel a thing," I said, smiling.

How stupid I was that day. How unbelievably stupid.

Chapter

THREE

The morning after Fay showed us Ginny's letter, she was gone. When Johnson and I woke up we found a note on the Formica table saying, *I'll be back*. I felt as if I had crushed a baby bird in my hands.

"She ain't coming back," Johnson said. He punched the lever down on the toaster, although there wasn't any bread in it. "She ain't coming back," he repeated, louder. He hit the lever again, but it stuck and wouldn't spring back up. He stared at me, as if I had broken it.

Don't look at him, I thought. Mrs. Henderson started up her old Buick in her car park next door. She waved at me through her open car window, and I wondered if she'd heard him. I worried all the time what the neighbors thought of us. Mrs. Henderson's mobile home was the same model as ours, but it looked better. She had a lineup of rose bushes out front that hid the foundation's ugly cement blocks. She was always weeding the flowerbeds that were nearest to our house.

I'd known we were different from other families for a long time. Once, when I was eight, Fay took me to a public library. The Amazing Humans had just arrived in Lake George, New York, where it looked like we'd be staying a few months as part of a summer-long festival of fun. I'd been reading since I was five, comic books that Ginny brought to me weekly, that she helped me through a few times and then I read over and over. They weren't about Superman either. One had a cover with a woman who stared in shock at a coffin under the Christmas tree while her husband raised an ax behind her. *Tales from the Crypt* was one of Ginny's favorites.

Fay, though, was dead set on getting me a proper library card now that it appeared we were settling down for a while. The Lake George librarian—brown beehive, tight face—looked up as if she was startled to see people in her library, especially us. In seconds she took us in, a skinny boy with metal braces and sticks and a mother dressed in a tube top, velvet hot pants and pink flip-flops.

"May I help you?" she asked in a syrupy voice.

"We'd like a library card," Fay said.

"Would you like a lollipop, dear?" the librarian asked me in a loud voice, pushing a large jar of jammed-in Tootsie Roll Pops in my direction. *If I put my hand in there*, I thought, *I'll never get it out again.*

"No, thank you, ma'am," I said.

It was as if I'd recited the Declaration of Independence. A grin the shape and size of a half-moon stretched across her face.

"We're in kind of a hurry," Fay told her. "Is there a form we need to fill out?" Fay was scheduled to perform within the hour.

"I have to type it out for you," the librarian said, slightly irritated at the interruption. "I'll just need your driver's license." She took out a yellow form and rolled it into her typewriter.

Fay smiled the smile she gave to men that she was about to dump. "Oh, it's not for me. It's for my son here—Dickie."

The woman got a pained expression on her face. "Oh. Well, then. I'll need to fill out this form here then." She ripped the yellow form out of the typewriter, threw it back in a drawer, and placed a blue one on the desk instead. "We have some nice picture books in the children's section."

Fay and I both must have appeared confused then, which the librarian probably took as further evidence that I looked younger than I was. I *was* small for my age, but still.

"He's eight years old and he's been reading since he was five," Fay informed her, picking up the blue form that the librarian had placed on the desk. She handed it to her. We watched as the woman painstakingly typed in my name, our temporary PO box address—lots of white-out and "darn its" under her breath. I shifted my feet a little. I wanted to borrow some books, but not enough to go through this. Fay didn't like it when people looked down on us.

"Mom," I whispered, tugging on her T-shirt.

"Hmm?" Fay's eyes were still on the woman, who made yet another mistake and let out a sigh as big as Niagara Falls.

"Mom, let's forget it," I whispered.

"Dickie, we're getting you a card. This is important," Fay replied, loud enough that the woman heard her. Of course, then I wanted the card more than anything simply because she wanted it. I looked around at the shelves crammed with books. There were more books than I could read in a lifetime. I wouldn't have to read the same old comic just because it was the only one I owned. I could read a book a day and still not have read a quarter of the books there.

When the librarian was through, she went to hand the card to me, but my mother stepped in between us. "You know what, Dickie?" she said, not looking at me. "We don't really need a card for you with Daddy buying you all those nice books." She stared at the librarian, who was starting to look very unhappy with us. I was too. My heart had taken an immediate nosedive. *What daddy? What books?*

"Thank you anyway," Fay told the librarian, and holding on to the back of my head, steered me out.

"But I wanted those books," I whined as we walked down the cement steps outside.

"What books?"

I couldn't answer that. I had no idea what books there were.

"See?" she said, pushing me down the street. "You don't even know what books you want. I just saved us a huge waste of time."

We never went back there again.

Now Fay was gone, and Mrs. Henderson's Buick drove away from our two homes that were alike but so different, a swirl of sand dust following her like bad exhaust.

"I'm going out," Johnson said, and grabbing his old farm coat off a nail, he threw open the screen door. That coat was the kind I imagined a railroad man would wear, a grimy denim coat with big square pockets and a dull plaid inside that looked like a blanket. He hadn't worn it since we'd moved to Florida. It was eighty degrees outside.

I looked at the wind-up alarm clock on the kitchen counter. We moved that clock from town to town as if we were afraid of missing an important appointment, or a minute of our stupid lives. Eight o'clock in the morning. He could get a solid twelve hours in at Sloppy Joe's, a bar on Duval Street, before heading out for the night shift on the Big F.

My mother's confidence didn't stop her from asking me several times a day how she looked. "How's my hair?" she'd ask, running her hands through it.

"Fine." I'd give her the no-teeth-showing smile she was fond of.

"No, really. Does it look okay? Can you see my split ends?"

"You look great," I'd reply. But to no avail.

"Too much Aqua Net, right?"

Fay was funny that way: One minute she was sweet-talking a man up on stage, in full command of every move he made—Johnson would've licked the linoleum floor if she ordered him to—and the next minute she was asking me ten times if the canned tomato soup she heated was hot enough. "Does it need some salt? It does, doesn't it?"

I always said no even if it really did need some salt. That didn't stop her, though, from saying, "You sure? I want it to be right for you."

One afternoon, after another round of back and forth, I took the salt.

"I knew it," Fay said, her face a mask of disappointment. Then she stood and, grabbing the full bowl away from me, turned to dump it into the sink. It seemed like she stood there forever, my lunch hovering over the drain.

"No! It's fine," I pleaded with her. "Honest." If I didn't have the soup I might go hungry until dinner.

"No, it's not edible. You said so yourself." One hand still held the bowl in the air, the other tucked into her hip.

"It's great. It's perfect." Some days this worked, and I got the soup or whatever it was back. This day it didn't. She poured the soup down the drain, but as soon as she did, she shook her head and said, "I should be shot." She looked over at me then. "I can't even make you a can of soup right. You deserve better."

"I'm fine," I said, rising from my chair.

But she waved me back down. "No. No. I'm going to make you lunch. You sit there. You have to keep your strength up, Dickie."

When Johnson slammed out of our kitchen, he didn't go to Sloppy Joe's. He was back within an hour. The whole time I hadn't moved from the kitchen table. I read Fay's note over and over as if I had the intelligence level of that girl who bagged up our groceries. I was still in my pajamas.

"*Dis*-charged before I was even charged," Johnson muttered when he barreled through the door. Immediately, he took down the cigar box from the top of the fridge where we kept our food and rent money.

I stood, grabbing my sticks. "Where'd you go?"

"The recruitment office." He jabbed his finger at my chest. "You're a ball and chain around my neck, boy." He spun around in the small space and I automatically ducked. But he only opened the fridge door and stared into its empty shelves.

"You tried to enlist?"

Johnson slammed the fridge door and poked his finger at me again. "Hey, do I answer to you?" he said. "Do I?"

I took a step back against a cabinet. "No."

"Then shut up." He kicked the garbage can out of his way. "I'm a free man, mister. I don't answer to you." Then he stormed out again, this time without his coat.

I hung around the house all day and into the night, flipping through old copies of *Eerie* and *Creepy*. For ten minutes I stared at the first page of one of my favorite stories called "What Unspeakable Evil Is Found in the Summer House?" when I realized I hadn't read a word and then suddenly I was ripping the magazine in half, shredding the pages until there was just a pile of confetti on the table. Then I watched fuzzy show after fuzzy show on the TV. Jack LaLanne performed a series of nifty tricks on parallel bars, swinging his legs straight, then scissoring over the bars into the opposite direction, his biceps bulging as his hands shifted from front to back. By the time the local evening news came on, the reality of Fay's leaving was so crushing I was on the couch in a fetal position, my leg braces scraping on top of one another. The nighttime spring air smelled heavily of Mrs. Henderson's roses.

"We begin tonight's news with an update on Vietnam," the local anchor said. I immediately sat up. Vietnam. *Stop feeling sorry for yourself and listen.*

I watched as stretchers were rushed to a waiting helicopter, the sounds of the chopper and gunfire almost drowning out a young reporter as he tried to interview one of the injured men on board the chopper. "We tried to dig in, but they were all around us. Our flanks were surrounded," said the injured man. When the reporter asked how many wounded there were, the guy repeated the same thing, "We tried to dig in, but they were all around us." The program went back to the anchor for a second, showing him writing something at the news desk and then immediately switched to a Mr. Clean commercial. A cartooned tornado swept across every countertop and left everything gleaming.

"Shit," I said out loud, miserable again. *Surrounded? When did it get that bad? Was Fay there? She couldn't be. Ginny said it was beautiful. They were probably with Bob Hope. Bob Hope would never in a million years be surrounded. They had to be in a different part. Maybe she hadn't even gotten there yet. How big was Vietnam?* I cursed myself for not knowing more about its geography. I didn't even know where Vietnam *was.* I promised myself I'd go first thing in the morning to the library and find an atlas. I tried not to think about Fay, tried to focus on the next movie, *One Million Years B.C.,* and Raquel Welch and how pretty she looked. But it was no good. For one thing, Raquel was a blond also. Fay kept creeping back in. My eyes welled up and I rubbed roughly at them. *I'm just mad, that's all. Mad she didn't take me along. If she'd taken me, though, that would've meant one more mouth to feed. She needed to go by herself. This way she could send more money home. Maybe come home sooner.*

Fay has a plan. She always does. What's your plan? I asked myself. *What if she strolled through the front door at this exact moment? She'd be so disgusted.*

Hoisting myself off the couch, I got dressed and left the house. I clicked my way down Duval toward Sloppy Joe's. It was one thing to have Fay gone, another to worry that Johnson might leave me too. He'd already tried to enlist an hour after finding out she'd left. I didn't want to end up in a foster home where a mob of kids played dodgeball on the cement driveway and tried to beat the crap out of the handicapped kid.

He wasn't at Sloppy Joe's. I ordered a Coke and slid onto a stool at the bar.

"Johnson been in here?" I asked Jeff the bartender. I busied myself with a Coke, swirling the swizzle stick around so that the plastic marlin on top looked as if it were swimming.

"Been and gone."

"Can't believe they didn't take him." I scratched at my head.

"Well, they ain't gonna take nobody with a heart condition." Jeff grinned at me. "What'd your mama do to your old man, kid?" he asked, loud enough so everyone sitting at the bar could hear him.

I slid off my stool, grabbing my sticks. "He ain't my old man," I corrected him.

Jeff winked at someone to the right of me. "She practice some of that circus voodoo on him?" he asked, laughing. "Hey, come on, kid, I'm only kidding. Come back."

That was the night I started my kitchen counter routine. If I was to stay there with Johnson, I needed to build up my strength. If Jack LaLanne could do it, so could I. I held myself up between the two counters in our galley kitchen and by rotating my hips, swung my legs back and forth. Two minutes later I was spent. I swung myself on to one of the skinny counters, breathing hard. As Fay would've said, this was not a job for wimps.

After a few weeks, my arms got stronger. I learned how to control my hips to get a solid momentum going, to use my stomach muscles. When my arms got too tired, I lay on the linoleum, doing sit-ups, building up to two hundred a day, just like Fay. If I worked hard at it, I could get ready. I'd show her how strong I am. It was 90 percent attitude, 10 percent luck.

Night after night, on my bed I imagined what she'd say if she walked in right then. "Let me tell you something, Dickie," I imagined her saying. "People who think life *does* things to them are losers." She'd rap me on the chest. "You're working on your upper body. That's where a real man's strength is, anyway. By the way, how's my hair look?"

After Fay left, I stopped going to school. Johnson didn't care. When I failed to show up for a few weeks, since we didn't have a phone, the district sent a woman in a blue dress with a wide cinched belt to our home. She was carrying a vinyl portfolio. Johnson wasn't home. I was on the couch and saw her coming, although I mistook her for one of the women who sometimes had stopped by to see if Fay was interested in buying any Tupperware. So, I met her at the door.

"I've been real sick," I told her, when I found out who she really was, hanging my head down, so I wouldn't have to look at her standing on our steps. I adjusted my stance on my sticks, wincing for good measure.

"I'd like to talk to your mother," she replied, pushing the bridge of her cat eyeglasses.

"She's out, getting me medicine." I forced myself to look her in the eye. "She should be back soon, but she said something about stopping at Gearson's to get something for dinner."

The woman opened her portfolio and extracted a business card. "Please give her this. I need to speak with her."

The next several times she came I made sure to duck into the kitchen or hide on the floor so she couldn't see me through the windows. After she'd bang on the door for a few minutes, I'd hear her heels clicking away. I didn't really like it that someone was keeping tabs on me, but I didn't want to go to school either. Kids always find out what you're hiding. I didn't want anyone knowing that Fay had left me. It was bad enough I didn't have a father and we lived with Johnson.

Every night while he was at his job, I kept up with my kitchen counter routine. I had no idea how important that routine would become. A few weeks later, by chance Johnson sat next to a doctor at Sloppy Joe's. I was on the other side of Johnson, drinking my nightly Coca-Cola before he headed off for work at the docks. Most afternoons I spent at Sloppy Joe's on a stool next to him. "Where you can't get into any mischief, boy," he was fond of saying. At five thirty or so, I'd go home again where I'd wait to watch Cronkite, eager to hear any news of the war. Then, I'd swing myself stupid for as long as I could hold myself up.

"The kid needs water immersion therapy," the doctor said as he bit off the leafy part of the celery in his third Bloody Mary. As he spoke, I could see the celery leaves being mashed by his teeth. He looked like a dinosaur in a Japanese monster movie.

"Water?" Johnson said.

"Wa-ter im-mer-sion ther-a-py," the doctor repeated. He glanced down at my polio-wasted legs and deformed feet, his forehead crinkling. "Muscle function's been compromised. Just put the boy in water three times a day."

Since we didn't have a bathtub, Johnson fixed up Fay's old tank. It still sat outside in a sandy strip between our mobile home and Mrs. Henderson's car park. One day, he carried me up the steps to the top of it and lowered me in. "Swim around in there now, Dickie. See how you like it," he said in a voice that told me he didn't really think I'd like it anytime soon.

I didn't.

The water was freezing. He'd filled it with the garden hose. Although there was a shelf that I could hang onto to keep my mouth and nose above water, that first time, with the shock of being in the tank, I forgot that. When I slipped under the water, I panicked and tried to claw my way up the glass.

"Grab the shelf, Dickie," Johnson shouted through the glass. "The shelf. Goddammit, boy, the shelf!"

At first staying in the tank wasn't easy. If I moved my elbows off the shelf, I went under. I had trouble getting back to the surface using my legs. I hadn't yet learned to use my hands to walk up the glass sides, or to propel my body using my thigh muscles. The sides were also too close for me to move around very much. Within a matter of days, I realized the easiest way to pass the time in the tank wasn't to move any of my body parts. I willed my elbows to stay on the shelf. The tank was a straitjacket. Once I finally understood that, I began to settle down.

"How about you go visit the tank," Johnson would say every day, plopping me in. He picked me up easily and did with me as he pleased, especially if my braces were off. The bottom half of my body was still thin, like one of those starving kids in Vietnam I'd see on the evening news, running from a bombed rice paddy.

But in the tank I was the fastest mover you've ever seen. I closed my eyes, and I was out of our dingy mobile home and running across fields of sand, flying over palm trees and the Florida Keys and fishing boats, like the Big F, that weren't too far from where we lived—only three blocks away—but were in another universe. From there it was minutes before I landed in Vietnam.

•••••••

One night, Johnson spooned out our dinner from a blackened cast-iron pan: canned spaghetti and meatballs. He never heated our food long enough, like he was in a hurry even though he wasn't going anywhere.

"What's wrong? You like pasta," he said. He speared one of the meaty gumballs on my plate with his fork and popped it into his mouth. We were sitting at the pull-down kitchen table.

There was no right answer to this. If I said, "I like pasta," he'd say, "Well, how come you're not eating *my* pasta," and then it'd be another visit to the tank. If I said, "I *never* said I liked pasta," it'd be another visit to the tank anyway. He didn't see many options. The tank had become pretty much his answer to everything that stumped him. I wasn't his kid. He was lost without Fay. The rubber band, taut between us, had stretched so thin you could see through it.

I looked out the living room jalousie window. It was a beautiful night, dark blue sky and warm as a bath. "We don't deserve this weather," Fay told me once on such a night. We were sitting on the makeshift steps leading up to our front door. "Well, you do," she added, giving a soft knock on the metal band below my knee.

It'd been two months and I hadn't even gotten a postcard. Where was she at that very moment? I was keeping up with my kitchen counter routine, and the tank was becoming like a second bedroom, but still. Where *was* she? A few nights before, Cronkite had shown Martin Luther King speaking to thousands of people in Central Park. They held signs that said things like, "Don't drench the jungles of Asia with the blood of our sons." People wanted the war to end. Did Fay?

I closed my eyes and sucked up a waterlogged strand of spaghetti. Johnson lit a cigarette, turned away, and stared out the same window. I could tell by the way his face relaxed that he was thinking about Fay too. He was the kind of man who was gentle only with farm animals and women. At the table I watched as he slipped away from me, his mind elsewhere. After all those years of tractor riding, he too could pretend to go to some other place. With Fay. Just like I did when I was in the tank.

Chapter

FOUR

Fay was gone for over four months when Johnson came up with a money-making scheme. He said we needed "capital" to pay for gas to get back to Rushford, his hometown in upstate New York. The only reason he'd take me was that I was the one chance he had to see Fay again. He started wearing his pants cuffed on purpose to his job on the Big F. Every night when he came home from the docks, he stood on a newspaper, unfolded the bottoms of his pants, and gently tapped them. Marijuana sifted to the floor. He could get two joints every couple of days that way, and he sold them in the bathroom at Sloppy Joe's. He kept the dollar he got for each joint in a cigar box with his original ticket to the Amazing Humans show and whatever we had for food money and rent at the trailer park.

"I could get killed for this, you know," he told me. "I hope you appreciate what I'm doing for you." He looked away as if he was talking to someone else in the room.

One night he lit a joint and passed it to me on the couch. I didn't feel anything right away, not until the joint was almost burning my fingers as I held it to my lips.

"We're like them hippies on TV," Johnson said.

It felt like a dead weight had been placed on my chest, but then that lifted. When my usual defenses began to fall away, I made a mistake. I decided to show him my kitchen counter routine.

"Damn, boy, you could be on the Olympic gymnastics team," he said and laughed as I swung my legs. He sat at the fold-down kitchen table, tipping back on his chair's hind legs.

"You think so?" I started to laugh along with him. "They're going to Mexico City next year."

"That right?" He watched me swing back and forth. My feet almost touched his shoulder.

"Yeah, they were talking about it on TV the other night. I guess I'll have to learn Spanish. Si, senor," I said, laughing uncontrollably from the pot.

Johnson didn't think it was funny. He let the chair fall forward. The front legs slammed down onto the linoleum.

"What're you fixing to do? Huh? What are you planning?" He leaned forward on the chair. I swung myself onto the counter, and busied myself with turning on the water, intent on washing my hands. I could feel his gaze fixed on me. I lathered my hands and my arms, making a big show of it, the way that doctor at Sloppy Joe's had showed me in the men's room. "Germs, son, are the number one killer of mankind," he'd told me. To sidetrack Johnson, I repeated what the doctor said.

He didn't say a word and picked up one of my sticks from where it was leaning against a wall. He turned it upside down, balancing it on the metal cuff that usually wrapped around my forearm. It teetered for a minute. The pole wobbled, making little circles in the air. Then he touched it with the tip of his boot and the crutch crashed to the ground. He picked it up.

"I thought it was accidents that were the number one killer." He leaned the crutch against the wall and gave it a little pat. "I'm gonna have to keep a closer eye on you. Make sure you don't come to no harm."

I stared at my hands, afraid to move a finger.

"All that swinging—it can't be good for you," he said.

This made me look at him, incredulous. "It's making me stronger."

Johnson shook his head. "You could fall down when I'm not here."

"No, listen, Fay would want me—"

"Fay asked *me* to look after you. I don't want to catch you swinging no more. I couldn't live with myself if you got hurt." This last bit confused me, almost convinced me that he was really worried about me. But then he grimaced as if he'd twisted an ankle. His mouth was working overtime. "I want you to promise," he said louder.

Something in his voice stopped me from arguing with him any further. "Okay," I said, making a silent promise to continue practicing when he was at work.

The pot didn't bring in enough money to get us to Rushford or even to Miami.

"My paycheck's barely keeping us in hotdogs," Johnson complained one morning. "We need to be in the big leagues. Not in the farm leagues."

Two days later, he was grinning at me from across the kitchen table.

"What?" I asked, suspicious.

He slid a piece of paper across to me that had the same smudges my mimeographed tests would have when I used to go to school. It was a death certificate. I quickly scanned it, suddenly feeling queasy. In the space for the deceased's name it listed Fay's. I felt like I was going to throw up. My coloring must've changed because Johnson stood up and, reaching out, quickly grabbed the paper back.

"Hell, boy, it ain't real," he said, sitting down again. "I paid someone to get me it. Cost me a whole week's pay, but this here"—at this he waved the certificate in the air—"is going to get us some real cash. You got to give a little to get a lot."

I must've been staring at him blankly because he went on. "You think I'm taking care of you because I like you? Shoot." He waved the paper again. "This is your meal ticket, boy. You and me, we're going to take a little ride to the Social Security office, and next thing you know we'll be getting what they call SSI checks real regular-like."

"I can't do that," I said, surprising him. I couldn't. It would've been betraying Fay. She wasn't dead. She was alive somewhere and she was going to come home.

Johnson shoved back from the table. "You'll do what I tell you," he said, staring hard at me.

By the afternoon, we were in his old truck, driving up to Miami. It was three hours to the district office. Johnson drove slowly, as if we had plenty of time to get there.

"We want to arrive fifteen minutes before the office closes." His left arm dangled out the window. He had on a pair of my mother's big bug-eye sunglasses because he'd forgotten his. I couldn't take him seriously with those glasses on. They made him look like an alien. Part of me kept hoping that it was all a hoax, a test he was putting me through.

"See, they want to go home at quarter to four," he continued. "They're through for the day. Sick and tired of the place. You get 'em then, and they don't look over everything as much." He glanced over at me. "Then they take one look at you, and bingo . . . they don't question anything, see?"

At the office, there was a large woman who was wearing a too tight sweater set and eating a Hershey's bar at her desk. A man in a dark suit was already packing up his briefcase for the night. The woman let out a sigh when we walked through the glass door and waved us over, impatiently. As we moved toward her, she took in my braces, just as Johnson had predicted. She lowered the half-eaten chocolate bar to her desk, the candy still in its folded brown wrapper.

"We're almost closed," she said. She touched the corner of her red lipstick to wipe away some leftover chocolate.

Johnson flashed her a smile and nudged me in the back, so I smiled also.

"I'm truly sorry, ma'am," he said. "We drove all the way from the Keys and the truck overheated." He slid the death certificate onto the desk and sat down in the orange plastic chair across from her. He jerked his head toward a chair next to him. I sat down.

"It was *her* truck," he lied and pointed at the paper. He shook his head convincingly. "I know I should get rid of it, but he's attached." With this he placed his hand on my shoulder and squeezed as hard as he could. I almost yelped. Instead my eyes filled, which is exactly what Johnson wanted them to do.

The woman looked over at her coworker who was slumped at his desk, his briefcase perched on top, ready to go.

"Go on, Jimmy," she said. "I can handle this."

She opened one of her file drawers and took out a blank form from a manila folder. "You fill this out, and I'll take care of the rest." Then she winked at me.

The whole way home, Johnson was insufferable, singing to the staticky radio, tapping on the dashboard. I shot him glances every so often, stunned that he'd pulled it off. I realized I really had no idea who I was dealing with. Every day he did something that was worse than the day before.

The only check I ever saw was the first one. I was lying on the couch, watching *The Jack LaLanne Show* and marveling at how many push-ups he could do, when Johnson, who was at the kitchen table, whistled. He waved an envelope in the air and then kissed it. When he opened it, though, his face hardened.

"Your mother's life is only worth a one-time funeral payout of a hundred and fifty dollars and sixty-eight dollars every month after this. Goddamn government is screwing us every which way." He glared over at me as if I were to blame.

"It's enough to buy some food with," I said, shrugging. I still felt bad about the whole thing, like it would somehow jinx Fay.

"Shut up," Johnson snapped. Then he stood. "I'm going to Sloppy Joe's." When I started to get up, he held up a hand. "No, you stay here. I've had about enough of you for one day." He shoved the check in his back jeans pocket and slammed the screen door on the way out.

It wasn't long before we started to smoke some of whatever he brought home every night. Sometimes when he was working, he ripped a hole in the plastic wrapping and stubbed his boot on one of the bales so a chunk of buds fell off that he could quickly tuck into his cuff.

"This is our secret, you hear me? They find out about this, I'm gonna end up on the bottom of the ocean with bricks tied to my ankles." At the kitchen table he tenderly wrapped a bud in tissue and put it to bed in the cigar box. "You'd probably like that, huh?" He looked at me on the couch, waiting for me to say one wrong word.

"I don't know what you're talking about." I turned my attention back to the television. *Twilight Zone* was on and a man who really was an alien was being tied up. Fay could've gotten out of that rope hold in twenty seconds.

Johnson walked over and practically sat on me on the sagging couch.

"What're you watching?" When I ignored him, he turned and slapped me across the face. Hard. My head automatically leaned with the force of it, but nothing else shifted on me. I knew better.

I stared at the TV. *Don't cry. Don't cry.* My cheek stung, like I'd burned it with a clothes iron.

"What'd I tell you about cryin'?" he asked and jerked his hand up as if he was going to hit me again. It was a bluff. He did it to see if I'd flinch. If I did, it would be met with another smack. "Huh? What'd I tell you?"

I sniffed hard. "Crying is for sissies."

He stared at me, his hand still hovering in the air within striking distance. "I'm getting tired waiting for you." His other fingers drummed on his pants leg. "You gonna answer me or not?"

"*Twilight Zone*," I told him, my voice quivering. "It's a good one."

He sat there for a long time, so close that I could smell the marijuana dust leftover on his fingers. He kept glancing at me, missing most of the show. I blinked maybe three times during the last ten minutes of the program.

The first time Johnson put me in the tank out of anger, I'd gotten stoned by myself while he was at work. When he got home, he took one look at me, lying on the couch in my pajamas, eating that night's dinner of pork and beans, cold. The next thing I knew, he was sliding me through the top of the tank, pajamas and all, and then walking away. Thankfully, I didn't have my braces on. When he reached the screen door, though, he rushed back and yanked me out. He brought me in, deposited me on my bed, and pulled my covers up around my wet clothes. Finally, he collapsed on the floor, like he was having a heart attack.

"I'm a dangerous man," he said. "I should be locked up." He held his wrists out as if I were the one to lock him up, then dropped his hands on his lap.

I shivered with cold. My pajamas were sticking to me. My nose was running. But I didn't move. Johnson was all I had.

"You want me to get Fay's old handcuffs out of the box?" I finally said. He started laughing hard. I noticed that when he helped me out of my clothes, his hands were gentle, his fingers slowly lifting off my wet shirt as if he were removing a stubborn Band-Aid.

Recently, I was walking home from the PO, along Commercial Street in Provincetown, and some teenage girls passed me. They'd been swimming in the bay with their clothes on. Their T-shirts and designer jeans stuck to their skin. The sight of them made me remember that night with Johnson. Remember it the way it really happened, not some adolescent story I'd dreamed up and convinced myself had happened. He hadn't pulled me immediately out of the tank. He left me in there. He didn't come back for close to an hour. I could've pulled myself out, but then what? Thrown myself onto the hard-packed sand? By the time he came back, my arms ached from perching on the shelf. Johnson clawed at my wet clothes, yanking at them as if he couldn't stand to touch them.

The end of September we finally received word from Fay. It was a landslide: an entire batch of postcards wrapped in a rubber band, curled like a tube. Maybe she'd sent them more regularly, but we got them all at once. The ones she sent Johnson leaked just enough hope to make him think twice about leaving me, or Florida, behind. Fay wrote to him: *You're a good man.* Or: *It won't be too long now. Patience is a virtue.* I read mine aloud to him, not that he'd asked. Mine were all the same—they gave hints about how Houdini escaped under water—but I liked seeing Johnson, his face darkening, a sign that his mind was scrambling to work out what her messages really meant.

"Goddamn government probably thinks your mother's a spy, sending you some kind of secret code," he said.

Houdini could hold his breath for three minutes, said the first postcard. *Make sure your handcuffs are light,* said the next one. *English spring-loaded are best. Hit them against a hard surface and they snap open. Chubbs are good in a pinch. Their levers aren't made to close. Hairpins are lifesavers.* Another one read: *The bigger and longer the chain, the more slack you have to move in. Handcuffs AFTER you're chained. Once you're out of the cuffs, you're home free.* Some of the cards were funny. In one, Fay wrote: *Underwear only. Diverts your audience.*

"Houdini was a psycho," Johnson said, but he didn't think her postcards were about Houdini at all. It was killing him that he couldn't put it all together.

He wasn't the only one either. Logically, I knew they were simply facts about how to be a successful escape artist. But, as the months went by, I reread them like they were a difficult crossword, at first hoping that if I examined them one more time I'd see something I hadn't seen before, the one word that could open it up, solve the puzzle. When I couldn't fill in the blanks, I'd end up feeling disappointed—in myself. Why wasn't I good enough? Not only to figure it out. Why wasn't I enough for Fay to come home? Did she think about me sometimes? At all? I was fifteen and hadn't given her any trouble. I hadn't been to school since she left, but when I had gone, I'd known some kids who were even younger than me who had caused their mothers all sorts of heartache. Tommy Maloney. At twelve he was still in fourth grade. Rumor had it that he was responsible for the obscene graffiti that kept magically reappearing on the brick walls of the school after it was sandblasted off. Or Rob DelVecchio. Fifteen and he'd already gotten one girl, a promising senior, pregnant. And I could've gone on. All I'd ever done was travel around the country with Fay, attending school whenever she let me, and sticking close to her. The only girl I'd ever looked at was her. I didn't have any *friends* to speak of, had never brought someone home. Hadn't once asked her to cook up a batch of brownies or to put up with boys fighting and chasing each other around the house. How could I have? We never had a home until Key West, and I sure as hell wasn't going to have someone meet Johnson. I was a good son, wasn't I? Where had I gone wrong? And then invariably, I'd glance down at my legs and see the answer. Maybe if Fay wasn't coming home yet, she had her reasons. Maybe we'd talk about it when she did come home. I still hadn't given up hope that she would come home. I couldn't. To do so would've made me accept that I'd be stuck with Johnson forever and that thought I couldn't stomach. Fall would be coming soon. She loved the fall, said it cleared out the dead wood.

Every night I went to sleep believing tomorrow, tomorrow will be the day she walks through that door and says, "So, what have you been up to all these months? Driving the girls crazy, I bet. I bet you've forgotten all about your old mother, right? Those shorts look too tight. Do you need new ones? What do you think of my new haircut? I think she went too short. Poor thing didn't understand a word of English. Has Johnson been treating you all right? I must be the worst mother on earth, leaving her baby boy for such a long time. Can you forgive me?" I imagined I smiled and nodded my head, giving her the divine forgiveness she ached for.

And every morning I waited to hear the screen door slam and when it didn't, I turned over on my cot and stayed there, face down, until I heard Johnson get up around noontime.

Those postcards. I can still see them. The one with the lone carriage being drawn down a dirt road by a Vietnamese boy no older than me. The one with the long white building with shutters and a veranda the length of a football field. It looked so peaceful. Like she was at a vacation resort. Right after Christmas we got only one postcard, and it didn't say anything about locks or keys or underwear. It was addressed to me. *When it's time, it's time,* she'd written. On the front was an illustration, half of it bright orange and the other half blue, and over that there were two tanks aimed at each other, one with the Communist flag, the other the flag of South Vietnam. It was the last one I'd receive, but I didn't know that then.

I kept that postcard under my pillow. When I heard Johnson snoring, I took it out and, with a flashlight, read that one sentence over and over. I was like him now, looking for the real message behind her words. I thought she was telling me something. She'd be home soon. She'd had enough. *When it's time, it's time.*

Chapter

FIVE

n the tank I learned to hold my breath underwater for longer and longer. It had become Johnson's ready-made babysitter, his handy punishment. I was glad. If I was in there, he wasn't near me, needling and poking, or something worse. One night after getting exceptionally high, I asked him to take me outside and put me in.

"You wanna drown?" he said and stubbed out the roach on a Spam can lid.

"I want to show you something."

"What? Some kind of water ballet thing?" He laughed at his own joke. When he was stoned, he thought he was the funniest person in the world. "You trying out for the high dive?" He bent over, laughing harder. His cackle was like when the wicked witch laughs in *The Wizard of Oz*, and you know Dorothy is in for it.

"Just put me in." I removed my braces.

He straightened up quick. "It's your funeral. I can be on a bus tomorrow," he said and, lifting me up, carried me out to the tank and lowered me in.

"You have to time me," I said.

"Time you?"

I released my fingers on the perching ledge and drifted down.

Crouched on the bottom of the tank, I could see his mouth moving like a fish. I motioned toward my wrist like I was wearing a watch. With each passing second, he held up another finger. I started to feel light-headed. The water took on a grayish look. When he'd gone through both hands six times, I pushed off the sides and burst to the surface. Sixty seconds.

He let out a whoop and pulled me out. "God damn, God damn!" Sitting me on the steps, he eyed me with what I thought was confusion, as if I'd asked him to help me with homework.

"It's not that big of a deal," I said. "Houdini could hold his breath for *three* minutes."

Johnson wouldn't let me brush it off that easy. When he brought me to Sloppy Joe's that night, he bragged about it to everyone seated at the bar. The place was jammed with old timer fishermen and tourists lured by their travel guidebooks informing them of Hemingway's frequent drinking bouts there. He glanced over at me, giving me a tight smile. He'd never smiled at me before. *He's proud of me*, I thought. It *was* the longest I'd ever held my breath. I didn't tell anyone that. The only person I wanted to tell was in a country where you could pay someone ten cents to pull out your teeth. It was the first time, however, that Johnson said I could do anything. Clamping a hand on the back of my neck like he was a loving father, he squeezed as he whispered in my ear, "Go on, drink up," forcing me to take a sip of his beer. And then another. He ordered pitchers of beer for everyone at the bar. When he paid for the beer, I realized he'd been using our SSI money. That's when I knew something wasn't right.

"Hey, is that our—"

One of the regulars perched nearby, a fisherman nicknamed Whiner, piped up. "We're in Key West, for cryin' out loud!" He slurped his beer. "People are born with gills here."

"Bet you fifty dollars he can escape from handcuffs underwater," Johnson said, surprising the hell out of me.

"What?" Whiner bellowed. He slapped the bar. "You're on!"

Before I could say, "Don't listen to him," Johnson upped the bet to a hundred bucks. Then everyone jumped in, drunkenly yelling out whether I could do it or not. It'd gone too far for me to stop it. With my index finger, I grabbed the metal band below my knee and lifted upwards until I thought I'd sever the finger right off. I wanted Fay to stride through those wide-open doors. I wanted her to say, "I'll take it from here, Dickie." I wanted her to run through her tank escape routine, wearing only her bra and underpants. No one would've remembered I was still in the room.

At the bar, Johnson clapped me on the back. "I'm gonna enjoy every minute of this." He squeezed my shoulder until I thought it was going to snap.

They set the date for two weeks later.

"I can't do it," I tried to tell him the next morning at our kitchen table. We'd hardly slept. Sometime after midnight, realizing that he wasn't leaving his bar stool, I'd finally passed out in a rusty beach chair in back of the bar. We'd straggled home at dawn, hangover tired.

In the kitchen we tried to focus on any object that wouldn't move. Everything about Johnson looked tight that morning, like he was afraid to move a muscle because it would *ping* off and fly a hundred feet as if he'd stepped on a land mine. It was pouring outside, a storm front had moved in. The kind of front that bombarded the town really fast only to disappear quickly, even before the steam from the pavement evaporated, like Walter Cronkite told us the B-52s did in Vietnam.

He stared into his freeze-dried coffee.

"I'm not doing it," I said, shaking my head. "No way."

"Don't push me, boy." His eyes were slits. "How you think we're gonna get another car so we can get outta here? That piece of shit out there won't get us even to Georgia. The goddamn SSI checks ain't enough. I bet everything we had last night."

"I've never been in handcuffs," I yelled at him, and then immediately wished I hadn't because he shoved back from the table and dashed over to Fay's discarded shoebox on top of the fridge. There was nothing in there except an old pair of police-like handcuffs, the kind you could buy in any of the sex shops in town. He slammed them down on the table.

"No way!" I reached for my sticks, but I wasn't fast enough. Johnson grabbed me, one arm slipping around my neck in a head-lock, the other lifting my butt, and hurdled us through the screen door. I had my braces on but that didn't stop him. He'd reached his limit, as Fay would've said. The end of the line. The hand-cuffs gouged me in the neck where his hand held me tight. My fists tried to bat his head, but he tightened his forearm grip on my neck and squeezed, cutting off my air, so I gave up. It was no use.

At the tank's steps, he suddenly stopped. Then he dropped to the ground so hard my braces rattled. I immediately curled on my side with him half-sitting on top of me, his arm still firmly wrapped around my throat.

"You like that? Huh?" he said, his locked forearm choking me. "Look at you, crying like a baby." His hold tightened. I could feel his shoulder digging into the side of my head. "What you think I am? Day in, day out. I'm here. Won't be too long. You still wait-ing for me? Huh? Huh?" With each "huh," he squeezed my neck. I was crying and hating him and my useless legs, hating Fay for sending him those postcards, hating the rain that threatened to drown us, hating the tank. I started to black out, thinking *he's going to kill me.*

"You're gonna earn your keep for once," he said, shifting his body. I started to yell at him that it was because of me that we got any money at all when one knee came down on my rib cage, squeezing the breath out of me, his rough hands pinning my arms down in front of me so he could lock the handcuffs on my wrists. I screamed, hoping that maybe Mrs. Henderson could hear me on the other side of the carport. But she didn't. She and everyone else in the mobile park were already at their jobs, changing beds in motels, mixing Bloody Marys for the breakfast crowd that in the stormy weather couldn't sign up for a charter boat to go barracuda fishing later on.

Johnson grabbed me up again and carried me up the steps, one hand vised over my mouth. The rain was pelting us. "You're gonna get us the hell out of here," were the last words he said before the tank's water hit me.

The water cleared from the swirling bubbles and waves. Almost immediately his fist came toward me in the water; the key to the handcuffs was sticking out of his balled-up hand. He'd forgotten to give the key to me. He wanted to help. He was perched on his knees on the wooden rim of the tank, his face skimming the top of the water, one shoulder in the water so he could get the key to me. His other hand gripped the tank's lip, for balance. His fist shook again, causing tiny waves to move through the water, as if I were in a bathtub and we were playing submarine. I could hear his muffled voice. "Take it! Take it!"

I closed my eyes. The water moved again, and I could feel his arm snaking closer to my face. *Wait*, I told myself. *Wait*.

I imagined Fay was there. Her hand went up to the glass, and mine went up on the other side. We matched finger to finger, palm to palm. And then we both reached up, and with two hand-cuffed hands, we pulled on that sunovabitch's wrist as hard as we could.

Part Two

FAY

◆●•••••●◆

Chapter
SIX

Batlike, the plane descends in total darkness. It feels its way without sight, relying on a sixth sense, a kind of telepathic radar. The pilot has warned them, his voice scratchy from lack of sleep and intercom static: "Threat of enemy fire requires us to land under cover of darkness. Fasten your seatbelts."

But nothing prepares them for the actual thing: the interior lights off, no illumination on the runway, not so much as the light of a stubby candle. It's as if they're free-falling through a dark elevator shaft. As the airplane plummets, closer and closer to the hidden tarmac—*solid ground*—Fay hears someone praying in a low monastic drone, the engine smothering the words.

There are thirty people on this military plane, a C-141 that smells of tiger balm, upset stomachs, things gone awry. Most of the passengers are Red Cross volunteers, girls who look barely old enough for their proms, here to cheer the troops, to play checkers and slamboard with them, to serve their country. When they land, they'll be called chopper chicks, or Kool-Aid kids when they're helicoptered in to dole out the stuff to the men. Men who before their one-year tours are up will be hooked on horse. The sugary drink will never taste so good.

Blindfolded by the darkness, the C-141 drops again. Suddenly—Fay's not quite ready for the jolt—the wheels miraculously bump the runway. Jesus. The girl on Fay's right starts to cry. Across the aisle another Red Crosser, her blond hair perfectly flipped at the ends into hairsprayed checkmarks, throws up. The man on Fay's left, the owner of an American construction company, is happy. He will make the sale. He will pave over the entire country before he returns to the States three years later.

"Welcome to Saigon, ladies," he bellows. A soldier hisses at him. It's immediate, threatening. *Shut the hell up, mac.*

An arrow of thought pierces Fay: *We're not in control here. Anything can happen and probably does.*

When the doors open, heat surges in like a crowd at a one-day sale. In the grey darkness of night fading, Fay is overwhelmed with nausea from fatigue and the smell of gasoline and oil. As she steps out of the plane, she can only make out the shadowy outlines of giant palm trees off to the left of the runway. The heat is too thick, like nothing Fay has ever encountered, not even in Key West in July. Dizzy, she hesitates on the top step. To steady herself, she fixes her gaze on the trees, which seem to sway in the nonexistent breeze. She feels faint. Her lungs clamp with the 110-degree temperature and 100 percent humidity.

Immediately Fay is shuffled onto a DC-3, the plane that will take her nearer to her final destination: Qui Dao. She finds a seat even as she's thinking, *You could just end it here, turn right around and go back to Key West, Florida, and no one would be the wiser.* She thinks of Dickie and how she'd be able to take him to a specialist in New York if they only had some money. She reminds herself that's why she's here. She read in the papers about a new polio treatment that involves hot lamps and daily massages. It's expensive, requiring a specialized round-the-clock nurse. Fay hates that the rich have access to medical options that the poor don't. Her father was a small-town doctor and if he got two phone calls in the night, one from the Hudsons, a wealthy family in town, and the other from the Skeets, a family of ten that lived in a prefab in the woods, he told the Skeets it would have to wait till morning.

On the DC-3 she focuses on the fact that she can make money in Vietnam, more than she can back home. She won't. She'll barely break even every week. She doesn't know that yet, though.

Fay remembers how she sat with Dickie on his cot last night, after Johnson's snores came as steady as rain.

"I bet we'll make a ton of money there," Dickie whispered to her in the dark.

Fay ignored the "we" of it. "Yes, that's what Ginny says." Ginny was why she was on this plane to Vietnam. A year ago, Fay had left the Amazing Humans. She'd had no choice. She'd left thinking Johnson was her ticket away from Chuck, but Johnson was nothing more than a dead end where an angry mob waited. At night Fay would lie in her bed in Key West, imagining what Ginny and the others were doing in Vietnam. She didn't need to imagine what Chuck was doing. She knew. But the others. The year she'd spent away from them had sharpened her fond memories and softened the bad ones. Maybe things would be different with Chuck now that she'd been with Johnson. Chuck always knew when his winning streak dried up, when there was no more to be gained. He knew when to walk away from the craps table.

Ever since she received Ginny's letter, Fay has imagined the Humans in an exotic city in Vietnam, playing cards late into the night, drinking Mai Tais with miniature umbrellas, eating fortune cookies until they got a fortune they could live with. She sees herself performing in front of appreciative grunts who tip her extravagantly.

Now, on the plane, she thinks again of poor Dickie, convinced he was coming with her. Sitting with him on his cot last night, she'd rubbed his bristly hair back and forth, a habit from when he'd been very young.

"You have to do what you have to do, right?" Dickie said. It was something Fay said repeatedly. To Johnson. To Chuck. Whenever she wanted them to feel bad about something they'd done. She said it to give them a hard time, although Dickie wasn't giving her a hard time—he never did, did he?—and he hadn't done anything wrong. He was doing his best to make her leaving him work. Sometimes she wished he wasn't so understanding.

"I haven't been a very good mother, have I?" Fay asked. She straightened the thin white sheet across his chest, noticing that his upper body was finally getting some muscle, the result of thirteen years of using the leverage of crutches to yank his metal-clad legs along.

Though it was something she said every week, Dickie never lost patience with it. More than anything else, he wanted to please. Dickie had thrown his arms around her neck. "You're the best," he'd whispered in her ear.

Having gotten what she came for, Fay kissed his forehead. "See you in the morning, then," she told him, although she knew she wouldn't.

On the DC-3 that's about to depart Bien Hoa air base in Saigon, Fay stares out through the oval window at the fringe of lemon rising at the bottom of the horizon. There are no lights on in this second plane either, nothing but the rustling sounds of the plane being loaded and people finding their seats. What is she doing here? She's a water tank escape artist, a possum-belly queen who lost her virginity in the well of a semi traveling from one poor excuse of a town to the next.

Fay has one talent: She can hold her breath underwater. In Qui Dao, she's supposed to perform the Chinese Water-Torture

Cell once a day for the grunts. The old upside down is nothing more than a trick. She once believed that she led a life of danger, but now, on this plane, it occurs to her that maybe it was all a lie, that maybe her life, like the old upside down, always had an escape hatch. It was all a matter of knowing what was behind the trick, knowing the back way out of a burning building. But this time the doors and windows have been nailed shut.

On the DC-3, she buckles herself in with a seatbelt that's unraveling at the edges. It tugs on her halter top, revealing more of her right breast. She smooths her miniskirt. There is no air conditioning, and the cotton material feels like a winter coat. Crossing her legs, Fay kicks the seat in front with her platform shoe.

The Red Crosser in the seat turns around and peers over the back—big teased hair, horsey smile. "Could you stop kicking my seat please?" she says, smiling as if they're best friends. "I'm a bit of a nervous traveler."

"Sorry," Fay says, her foot stopping in midair. She tries passing a quarter over her knuckles, a habit that normally calms her, but it's no good. The quarter keeps falling off onto her lap, and each time she doggedly puts it back between her index and middle fingers. *Come on, come on,* she says to herself as if the coin is what's holding the plane up.

Next to her, Construction Man sings softly under his breath: "Rocket City, Rocket City." It makes Fay think of a child hiding in a closet, an adult's voice nearby, whispering, "Come out, come out, wherever you are."

When the DC-3 lands at the airport in Da Nang, the sun is fully rising, and a mob of begging children greets them. Most of them are missing something: an arm, a leg, a tiny hand. Dickie is everywhere. Dickie surrounds Fay. When she breathes, it's Dickie's breath she takes in. When she walks through the plucking hands, it's Dickie she moves aside. There are tens of Dickies. Crying. Pleading with her to give them something. To Fay, whose Vietnamese is nonexistent, the words spoken in such high voices sound like a cartoon.

Breathe. Breathe. You must get out of here.

One of the children, a girl, latches onto Fay's wrist and yanks with all her forty pounds. "Please miss," she says, though it comes out Pea mith, as if she has a lisp. The girl is emaciated. Her face looks twelve, but her body is a kindergartener's. Nevertheless, she holds her own against the other crowding children, shoving them away from Fay with her free hand and her hips. Fay is hers. When she jabs another child with a hip, they look as if they're doing a popular American dance called the bump.

Fay looks around helplessly for the other people from the plane. *Where the hell are they?* There's a bus somewhere that she's supposed to get on, a bus that will take her to Qui Dao. She sees the bus in the distance. Somehow, she's been separated from the rest of the group. A line of Red Crossers is ribboning into the bus. But the children have formed a ring around her that grows tighter and tighter, their plucking fingers more insistent despite the girl's best efforts to keep Fay for herself. Fay glances in the direction of the bus again. It seems farther away. The line of Red Crossers is shorter. "I need to go now," she tells the children, but they don't stop trying to grab her. *Damn it!*

The girl repeats the same words, tugging more impatiently on Fay's wrist as she keeps shoving the pack away. Fay tries to shake her hand loose, but the girl holds on. Fay's other hand is holding her pocketbook, a black metal lunchbox, the kind a construction worker would have on the job. She'd covered it with a shellacked collage of magazine cutouts, glossies of women with perfect bodies in skimpy bikinis. Fay tightens her fingers on the metal handle.

"Let go!" she says, her voice strained. There are about ten Red Crossers left. *Shit!*

Again, a stream of words. It's like that's the only sentence the girl can say.

"I don't understand!" Fay says, but she does. She knows when someone wants something from her. She's used to *that*. She tries pushing her way through the mob. Her clothes are sticking to her like she took a moonlight dip in a lake. Fay glances nervously at the bus: *Don't leave.*

One of the other children, a stick of a boy, slips in on the far side of Fay's miniature security bouncer and pushes his hand into Fay's pocket. At the same time another boy tries to snatch her lunchbox.

"Stop it! Get away!" Fay shouts. She yanks her lunchbox hard and startles the two boys into dropping their hands.

The girl lets out a torrent of words then. Fay doesn't understand a single word, and for a brief moment she forgets about the bus and feels a strange sense of relief. She's watching the girl get more and more agitated, but it's not Fay's responsibility, not her fault, not her problem. *I don't owe them a thing.* For the first time in a long time, Fay doesn't feel responsible. Maybe it's the thirty-hour plane ride behind her. Maybe it's not understanding a word of what the girl is saying. Maybe it's finally being away from watching Johnson pick on Dickie more and more each day. She's made a good decision after all. She is simply here to perform her act for the army. To make some money. The godawful trip was worth it if this wonderful sense of freedom is what she ends up with. *There's nothing like a new town to make you feel as if you can start over.* She wishes she'd done it sooner.

As Fay pushes her way through the groping hands and small bodies, the girl makes a move for the lunchbox. She's still screeching in Vietnamese, only now Fay can tell the words are different.

This immediately changes the scene. It's all been an act. The girl has pretended to be Fay's protector, and when that doesn't work, she adjusts her plan. Although Fay can't understand her, she can tell right away that the girl's encouraging the others to close in. Fay is their mark. Small hands pinch and poke her body everywhere, her legs, her thighs, her waist, her arms. Three Red Crossers left. *I'm not going to make it*, she thinks.

Then her wrist is no longer in the girl's hand. Instead, it's grabbed from behind by a larger hand. Fay automatically jerks away, but the hand holds on and yanks her so hard she's whipped around to crash into Construction Man. He's gripping her wrist as if he's just bought her at a slave auction.

"Dickhead!" the girl yells in English.

"Get lost!" he bellows, turning to Fay. "This way." He plows his way through the pack, swiping each clamoring child aside. They're nothing but leaves on a windshield.

"Don't hurt them!" Fay cries even as she senses that Construction Man is on a mission. She's an American like him. He's the type who believes these natives must be taught who is in charge. It disgusts her. He punches a boy who has come too close, shoves another to the tarmac, and maybe they all realize there's nothing to be won here, no dong to be received. The group slacks off. Construction Man and Fay are suddenly free of them. He begins to run, dragging Fay toward the bus. She looks over her shoulder and sees a girl—is she the one who attacked her first? The children are standing close together. The girl stretches her palms out, pleading. As Construction Man and Fay get closer to the bus, the girl looks smaller and smaller. Although she's surrounded by children, she seems alone, and Fay realizes she was wrong: She will not be free here. Not at all. Whatever relief she'd felt before has evaporated as quickly as the children disappear into the glare of the unmerciful sun. *I'm here for the money*, she reminds herself in order to

60

feel better, to have something to hang on to. It's barely a shoelace, though.

When they run up to the bus, Fay notices that its windows are covered with wire. It's like they're prisoners to be transported to a new facility. Construction Man keeps his hold on her wrist as he pushes her up the steps.

"Back off," she says, wrenching her hand free. She walks down the aisle past the Red Crossers piled against each other in their row seats.

"Are you okay, honey?" one of them asks. Fay ignores her.

"Phew," Construction Man says when he plops down next to Fay. He shakes his head, but his slicked-back hair stays firmly in place. Slipping his hand inside his button-down shirt, he says, "My damn heart is pumping like a twenty-five-dollar whore."

Chapter

SEVEN

F ay doesn't tell anyone that she's made a mistake by leaving the States and coming to Vietnam. Who is there to tell? One of the Red Cross chicks? Construction Man? She knows what he'll say: You've made your bed, now lie in it. Fay knows other things too. She can't admit them yet. Can't admit that sometimes she turned away when Dickie approached her, dragging his legs along, deliberately placing one stick in front of the other, his face hardened into a rigid smile as he concentrated on reaching her. Each click of his braces mimicking a ticking clock. She can't admit that she's turned away from him now when he's needed her most. She's left him with a man she probably shouldn't leave with a dog.

She knows also that tonight when she falls asleep, she'll be wrenched out of a cave of darkness by one ceaseless question: *Why?*

Why didn't she sign him up for the vaccine?

Fay was sixteen when she had Dickie. A year and a half later, it was 1954 and the polio vaccine had been discovered. But by then Fay was listening to Walter Winchell every Sunday night on the radio while traveling with the carnival. What people don't know about living on the road is how much downtime you have, especially on Sundays when crowds are thin due to church services followed by pot roast dinners. Those are family events; they've never been part of their lives. Dickie's father had been gone since her first trimester. Fay had no money, just what she earned from her act. She wasn't doing the old upside down yet. Her act was simpler: Her wrists were locked into English spring-loaded hand-cuffs, she was thrown into a pool of water, and the handcuffs fell open as soon as she hit them against anything.

But no matter how much money Fay didn't have, there was always Ginny's Motorola portable radio to bring them the news. It perched on a banged-up crate that smelled of sour milk. Six of them huddled around it, like a game of craps. On April 4, 1954, Walter Winchell began his weekly program with words that made her shush everyone in Ginny's trailer.

"In a few moments I will report on a new vaccine. It may be a killer," Winchell said. After the commercial, he reported that mon-keys had died from the vaccine and doctors were lining up little white coffins. Fay looked down at Dickie, sitting on the floor, two years old and playing with the only toys he had, a small dented pot with a lid. She was eighteen years old then. She made her choice. As a parent you do the best that you can, but what do you do when you find out that was the worst thing you could've done?

She remembers one of the doctors telling her at the hospital, "The damage to the neurons may be permanent in both legs. We just don't know yet. Sometimes it takes ten years to correct itself." He paused. "Usually in children we see it only in one leg. How long did you say he's been like this?" Fay felt like she'd murdered her son. She didn't cry, though. At least not *there*, not in the hospital. As soon as she could, as soon as Ginny ducked out to find a bathroom, how-ever, she ran to the safety of the station wagon and she wept, her head down on the front seat so no one would see. In the time it took to snap her fingers, everything had changed for her and Dickie.

Thirty minutes later, Ginny found her.

"I've been looking all over for you," Ginny said, as if that was an unbearable thing in itself.

Fay sat up, wiped her cheeks.

"Slide over, Babydoll," Ginny told her through the open driver's window. When Ginny got in, she slid her hand along the dashboard as if looking for dust.

"Listen," she said. "You did what you could do. Even the doctor said so."

"When?"

"When what?" Ginny turned and looked at her.

"When did he say that?"

Ginny looked away, focusing on the dashboard. "You did what you could," she repeated and started the car.

At first, after Dickie recuperated, Chuck felt like a savior to Fay. Now she knows he was just waiting for her to lower her guard. Waiting for the *right* moment.

"You've had enough hard knocks, Chiquita," he told her within a few months. "Let me take care of things for a while, gracias." Chuck sprinkled his vocabulary with words he thought showed that he was fluent in other languages. Fay wasn't enamored. She thought it was comical. He pronounced it grass-ee-us.

He did take care of everything. He moved Fay and Dickie into his larger Streamline, gave them a real bed instead of a converted kitchen table. Fay no longer had to worry about where the next can of Chock full o'Nuts or Quaker Oats was going to come from. She no longer had to perform twice a day. Chuck brought her home presents: a bottle of Jean Naté, cans of Aqua Net, a silver ID bracelet with an etched *Fay* in scrolled letters and matching silver necklace. A toy fire truck for Dickie from the local Texaco station.

There were telltale signs, though, that something else was brewing. Chuck would constantly readjust that thin silver necklace around her throat or tuck her hair behind an ear. He began to tell her what she should wear, how she looked prettier with longer hair. That a hamburger should be cooked for exactly four and a half minutes on each side. Did she know that the correct way to make a bed was hospital corners first then fold down the top of the sheet? He slipped such suggestions into the middle of a conversation like he was sliding a love note under her door.

"I'm thinking the Humans might be ready for Atlantic City come the spring," he told her one day. "By the way, I found some forks in with the spoons. What was your thinking there?"

Whenever Fay found herself bristling after he told her what to do, she talked herself down. *He's here, isn't he? Taking care of you and a three-year-old that's not his. It's more than Dickie's own father did. So what he tells you how to sweep the floor? It's a small price to pay for what he gives you.*

He never touched her either. For a month he slept on the converted kitchen table bed. Then one night he didn't show for dinner. Darkness settled in. At midnight, pinning Dickie to her hip, Fay searched the other Humans' trailers, stopping first at Ginny's.

"Goodbye and good riddance is what I'd tell him. Maybe we'll hit the jackpot and he'll drive off a cliff," Ginny said.

Fay didn't know why Ginny hated Chuck so much. She wasn't sure she wanted to know. She had a good thing going. Why talk about something that had caused the bad blood between those two? Their past had nothing to do with her.

Not finding him on the carnival grounds, she returned to the Streamline. It was late. Maybe he was scouting out another location. Tickets sales hadn't been so good lately. She lay on the bed with Dickie, who, half-asleep, nestled into her belly. The next thing she knew, Chuck was in the trailer, switching on the Coleman lights, slamming the refrigerator door, and cracking open a beer with his teeth. He pulled out a vinyl-covered chair, turned it backwards, and sat down facing her, his stubby arms dangling, one hand gripping the neck of the beer. Fay still remembers that she felt as if she'd swallowed a stone. Not a pebble. A stone. Rough and jagged. It was so quiet she could hear Dickie sleep-breathing next to her.

"Stand up," Chuck said quietly.

The stone shifted. "What?"

"Stand up. Don't make me tell you again." He spoke the last words slowly as if she was stupid. Maybe she was. This certainly wasn't in her book of knowledge.

Chuck began to rap the bottle slowly against the back of the vinyl seat like a metronome. It made a soft thumping sound that seemed to grow louder as she hesitated. She wondered if she should play along with whatever was in his mind or put the kibosh on it before there was no going back.

Finally, she leaned over, and tucking Dickie in closer to the jalousie windows, she did what Chuck told her. She slipped out of the bed. It was a cool evening, and she shivered, her nineteen-year-old body visible in her translucent nightgown.

He flicked his fingers at her in an upward motion. She didn't move, suddenly feeling like she did when she was seven and her wraparound skirt came untied as she raced across the school playground, her Fruit of the Looms blazing in the sunlight.

"Don't make me say it again." *Though he hadn't actually said it*, Fay thought. *He hadn't actually said the words. Maybe she should mention that. No, better not.*

He raised himself from his chair, his face hardening.

"Okay, okay," Fay hurriedly told him, and in one motion took the nightgown off over her head. She held on to it, though. Could feel the polyester material cool against her leg.

"Lie down on the floor," Chuck said.

When Fay did, he walked over to her. Before she could do anything about it, he was suddenly sitting on her stomach, his knees pinning her arms down. He leaned toward her face and she smelled his beer breath. When he tried to kiss her, she angled her mouth away, but that only made him laugh. Not a good sign, Fay knew that. Knew this was something she hadn't expected, hadn't counted on. That she'd made a big mistake. Still, it surprised her when instead of kissing her, he licked her cheek sloppily. She let out a wail, "Stop!" She started to thrash underneath him. Chuck growled, "Don't wake him up," and leaning close to her ear, whispered, "You're mine now."

Construction Man's name is Tom Thorne and he's come to Vietnam so that his dump trucks and vibrator rollers can lay down asphalt and rubble everywhere.

"Even over the fucking paddies," he tells Fay on the bus ride from Da Nang to Qui Dao. She wishes he'd shut up. After what happened at the airport, she doesn't want anything to do with him. The Red Crossers gave him earnest smiles as he walked down the aisle; they'd watched him save her. Fay doesn't see it like that. If he hadn't shown up, she would have given those poor children a few coins. That's all they wanted. He made it into something else. She was fine with those children before he got there and all hell broke loose.

"Even over the fucking paddies," Tom Thorne says again. Fay notices he has the annoying habit of repeating himself like most men who are in love with themselves. He snorts. "Why the hell not? They won't need 'em." He laughs nervously. Fay imagines him cracking his corny jokes everywhere he goes. This is just one more convention of pile drivers and crane operators to entertain. He's going to bring down the house.

The sweltering bus barrels on, the bumpy road is half gravel, half dirt through tiny villages surrounded by rice fields, overgrown trees, and bushes that look like they could swallow you whole. It reminds Fay of that movie she watched with Dickie one rainy morning on Sunday Horror Theatre, *Day of the Triffids*, she remembers it was called. The out of control plants ended up taking over an entire house from the outside, suffocating the people inside.

The sunlight is glaring, made worse by the dense green that Fay sees everywhere. The intense color seems to reflect the rays on every leaf and blade of spiky grass at her. A rivulet of sweat hasn't stopped drifting down the center of her chest since she landed. With the windows open, the hot air rushes in, making it difficult to breathe. She had no idea that Vietnam would be so hot. She'd seen the film clips on Cronkite every night, the filthy grunts trudging through swamps and woods, but she'd separated them from the Vietnam where she was going. She'd imagined noisy streets smelling of fish, with balconies and bars lit up by neon signs, and thousands of grunts on R&R, just looking for someone to blow their wallet on.

Occasionally, the bus speeds past a rice field with oxen and two or three farmers bent over, their cone hats shielding their faces from the bus, followed by a village of small houses of stone with thatched palm roofs, the vegetation on every side a protective wall.

The bus somehow picks up even more speed, moving so fast that the only way she can stay in her seat is by grabbing the top of the seat in front of her. The Red Cross volunteers are sitting together in the first eight rows, each couple with their arms wrapped around each other, trying to shore one another up. Trying to get *prepared*.

"Oh joy. Looks like we're in for another goddamn round of *Kumbaya*," Thorne shouts in her ear over the bus's rumbling.

"At least they're not here to screw somebody."

"Don't be too sure of that." Thorne smiles. He likes confrontation. Fay has seen his type a hundred times in the front row of county fairs, doing their utmost to get a free look up something. He's as ordinary as day-old milk.

"What's that song you keep singing?" she asks. "Rocket City, Rocket City?" The question is meant to give her something to cling to, a piece of everyday conversation. The best way to rectify a bad decision is to go about your daily business. Vacuum the house, wash the laundry, unload the groceries. Before you know it, you've forgotten what it was that got you in trouble in the first place.

Thorne's teeth line up. "Da-nang," he says, drawing out the second syllable like a bell that's chimed. "Home sweet home for the next year or more if I have anything to say about it. More fireworks than the fourth of July. Where there's missiles, there's road damage."

"Incoming or outgoing?" Fay asks sarcastically.

Teeth again. "Bada boo bada bing," Thorne shouts. "Incoming."

For a second Fay can hear Johnson's nasal voice saying, "Asshole." It makes her smile. Johnson. He's probably sitting at the kitchen table, her note in his hands, still not sure if it's a trick. She hadn't said where she was going, only that she was. Who knew what his love would fuel him to do? She doesn't want to be followed. She wants to *disappear*.

When she'd picked Johnson out of the front row in Buffalo, New York, and he'd smiled up at her, Fay worried that she hadn't applied her makeup well. That the blotch of purple under her right eye would be noticeable. It was the first time she'd ever been hit by anyone. There'd always been the threat from Chuck. Never the follow-through, except for the night before. Once was enough. Fay didn't want to go through a repeat performance. It was time to leave and she saw Johnson as her ticket out. A rube that she and Dickie would dump as soon as they had put some miles between them and Chuck.

When her performance was over and her wet feet touched the stage again, Johnson was there. So was Chuck. He looked small next to Johnson, stocky but small. She'd chosen well.

"This your boyfriend?" Johnson asked, shooting a thumb in Chuck's direction.

Taking a deep breath, Fay took a gamble and shook her head. "The owner."

Chuck took a step toward her, but Johnson stopped him short, holding up his hand while he stared at the right side of Fay's face. For a minute no one said anything.

Then Chuck said, "We got to get you home." He clamped a wide hand on her wrist. "Thanks for coming to the show," he told Johnson.

Johnson stepped in front of them both. "There's an all-night diner nearby. You're probably hungry."

"No thanks," said Chuck.

Then Johnson put his hand on Chuck's chest and said, "I wasn't talking to you, asshole," and Chuck averted his eyes. Fay knew he was measuring the odds. Was it worth it? The Humans were pulling out of Buffalo that night. By morning they'd be in another town. Another town where there'd be another sixteen-year-old like she'd once been, a slip of a girl interpreting possessiveness as love, as a safe harbor, as anything but. Chuck weighed the plus and minus of taking a stand, released his grip, and walked away.

But she hadn't chosen well. Within a week, on their way down to Florida, Johnson had shown his true colors, slapping her son's leg for no reason. She'd immediately done the right thing, had slapped him back, yelled at him to stop. She'd blown it, though, when she'd turned on Dickie just because he'd back-talked Johnson. Sometimes she felt she couldn't stand another minute of her life. Dickie had made it worse, telling her he couldn't feel a thing, smiling at her as if it was all a big joke. Fay wanted him to stand up for himself for God's sake. She wanted to tell him: You're not going to have me around forever. The truth of it was every time Dickie smiled, Fay knew he was a better person than she was. How could anyone live with that every single day?

Qui Dao, Fay's destination, is a hospital compound for amputees and burn victims. Three hundred beds for five hundred patients, and 90 percent of them are children. The armed forces have Bob Hope, Miss America, the USO. Occasionally, Wayne Newton helicopters in on what everyone calls a flying crane. The Chinook lands and hundreds of grunts cheer as the chopper chicks hand out more grape Kool-Aid and Cheetos.

The troops get Hope and Newton, Qui Dao the Amazing Humans. They're a mishmash of genetic accidents and bad childhoods: Lucy the Wolf-woman, Guppy Boy, Funnel Head, Tina the Sword Swallower. They put on a show meant to inspire. You may be down but you're not out. Look what we can do. For the first time in their lives, Jimmy and Timmy, Siamese twins who are attached at the chest and do a tango number, look at the Qui Dao kids and think they have it good.

When the bus pulls up to the entrance for the hospital compound, Fay can see through the bus's wired window that Chuck is waiting. She freezes. Where is Ginny? She hadn't expected Chuck. Not alone. Well, she's here now.

"I'll be fine. Don't you worry about me, sweetheart," Tom Thorne calls after her as she follows the Red Crossers down the aisle and out of the bus. "You take care now."

Fay doesn't say goodbye. Thorne is staying on, traveling deeper into the napalmed areas where his construction crews are already waiting, the engines of their dump trucks and vibrator rollers revving, eager to get on with rolling out the blacktop.

The napalm and Agent Orange have already done the hard work, scorching and leveling hundreds of years of vegetation and history in minutes.

As soon as Fay steps from the bus, the doors swing closed and the bus pulls out. There's only two more hours before five-thirty curfew. The driver, a South Vietnamese man, must deliver Tom Thorne before he can make his own way home. He steps on it.

"Hey there, Chiquita," Chuck says to Fay, like it was yesterday when they parted ways. He looks out of place, standing in the middle of the compound, with his western shirt and its snap pockets and his motorcycle boots. He moves to hug her, but she steps back. He's too quick. His skull and crossbones belt buckle presses into her stomach. She squirms out of his hug.

"Hey. We're good, right?" he says. "No harm, no foul."

"Where's Ginny?" Fay asks, looking around, unsettled from the trip over, the number of children she's already seen, and now Chuck. Ginny hadn't mentioned children in her letter. She'd just said, *Come. You can make big money. I'll take care of everything.*

"She's getting your digs all set up." Chuck smiles and Fay notices that the space where his front tooth should be is filled with a gold stud that is too small, leaving a tiny gap on either side. His words have a faint whistle to them now.

"You're gonna love it. I got you a new tank," he tells her.

That stops Fay. She's always had to provide her own tank. She figured he would scrape up some secondhand one for her. Maybe Ginny had been right. Maybe it's better here. Maybe this is a sign. People can change.

Chuck claps his hands. "Come on. Everyone's waiting." Lifting her one suitcase, a battered, dirty white Samsonite, he walks away. There's nothing to do but follow him, Fay's metal lunchbox clunking against her leg with every step.

Chapter

EIGHT

The Red Cross volunteers and the rest of the Amazing Humans are housed in hootches, small huts made of plywood, corrugated tin, and other war leftovers. It's as if Wendy and the Lost Boys have constructed a village. The hootches are in a red dirt field that everyone calls the Pit. To the left is the main compound comprised of the surgical hospital, rehabilitation clinic, and the workshop where they make artificial limbs. The buildings form a U of white two-story structures with verandas and pillars surrounded by palm trees, reminding Fay of Key West. Except these buildings are a work-in-progress. The Pacifists for Change (PFC) built and run the whole shebang, funded through the generous endowment of a Midwesterner who made his fortune in brass PEX pipe. Although the hospital compound has been technically designated a "safe zone," wayward missiles sometimes set them back months. Sandbags dot the roofs. A pair of monkeys the size of toddlers sit atop the sandbags like sentries, chattering and screeching warnings whenever someone walks across the compound.

The PFCers wanted some entertainment for the children, something that would take their minds off the fact that they no longer had their right hands or that they had burns over 20 percent of their bodies. One of the nurses who'd arrived with the first team after the compound was built told the hospital director about Chuck and the show. "It's nothing big, but they were pretty popular at the county fair when I was growing up. They're called the Amazing Humans."

The director liked the name. That's what most of their patients were. Amazing humans. They'd somehow survived the daily destruction and death and ended up here.

As if they're at an all-night supermarket checkout, the new patients and their parents line up at the compound's front entrance by a handwritten sign that reads in Vietnamese:

No Weapons Please
90 percent of the patients in this Center
have suffered injuries caused by weapons.
Please leave yours outside.

Each of the waiting patients is a child, an amputee from a land mine or missile. Fay doesn't know where to look. There are so many amputated limbs there's too much open space, like when woods are suddenly leveled for a split-level development. These are the patients who have somehow walked twenty or more miles from villages in the highlands.

In front of the rehab center's porch lie the guts of a shot-down military airplane wing, dragged here so that the metal can be reused as hinges and brace hardware for the artificial limbs. Nothing is thrown away. Lives must be salvaged.

Fay takes it all in. *Jesus, it's a morgue. I can't stay here.*

Chuck doesn't take Fay straight to what will be her hootch. Instead they go to his, where they find Ginny, Tina the Sword Swallower, and Siamese Twins Jimmy and Timmy waiting with a bottle of Jim Beam and Dixie cups. Jimmy and Timmy and Tina wave at her from a rickety card table they're sitting at, playing high card wins. Ginny is playing too, although she stands as soon as Fay walks in. Chuck quickly strides over to the card table and pours himself a drink and, downing it, sloshes out another. He wipes his mouth with the back of his wide fist and sits down in Ginny's vacated folding chair that has one leg shorter than the other three. It keeps making a thumping sound every time he shifts his weight. Still reeling from the trip, Fay cues into that sound. It reminds her of something. She can't put her finger on it, not when she's so jet-lagged.

"Hey Babydoll," Ginny says, smiling. She hands Fay a small paper cup full to the brim.

Her stomach is still cramping from the plane, but Fay takes the drink anyway. She needs something to level her out. The thumping sounds from Chuck's chair add to her feeling of everything being off-kilter. Where has she heard it before? She downs the cup in one gulp and motions for Ginny to fill it up again. It warms her throat like a scarf she's wrapping around her neck.

In spite of the heat, Ginny is, as usual, wearing her red cowboy boots that match her red-orange hair. The consistency of it comforts Fay. Whenever Ginny walked toward you on the street, you felt as if a beautiful fire was coming at you. Like something you'd want to curl up in front of in a living room. Ginny has had those boots for years. They've been resoled five times. An orphan, she refers to her boots as "the parents."

"They keep me on the straight and narrow," she told her once. She makes Fay laugh more than anyone else.

Fay wants more than ever for Ginny to crack a joke now.

"So, you survived," Ginny says as she raises her own paper cup to her lips. "Kool-Aid chicks treat you alright?"

Fay doesn't know the term, but assumes she means the Red Cross gals.

"They weren't the problem. I sat next to some construction jerk."

"He's not the only one. Everyone wants to make a buck."

Fay wants to tell her, "That's why *we're* here, isn't it?"

"There's money to be made in them hills," Tina cracks. In her act she swallows a fake Samurai sword that she swears is the real deal. But anyone can see that the handle is loose, allowing the shaft to be collapsed, shoved up, and hidden. Barely nineteen, Tina wears a pageboy silver wig to hide her mousy brown frizzy hair. Her eyelids are usually lined in thick black kohl that's offset by the white lipstick that she perpetually freshens to match her white go-go boots. Her most startling feature is a small tattoo on her right cheek. It's a blue Japanese wave that seems to ripple when she laughs. Tina looks like she could be the girlfriend of a Hells Angel, but Fay and Ginny know she's lambswool underneath the costume. She, like them, is from a speck of a town with one zip code.

Fay can't believe they're having this conversation. It's too normal, as if they'd just run into each other after a performance. *Show go okay? What an asshole in the front row, huh?* After the jarring plane trips and the scene at the airport with those kids, after her year-long absence, she expects something more than the business as usual greeting that the Humans are giving her. But what did she expect? A banner saying CONGRATULATIONS! YOU MADE IT!? The Humans have never been demonstrative toward each other. They're like a family that has lived together for too long in a one-bedroom apartment. It's every man for himself at the dinner table. She can't, though, get past the image of that line-up of injured children with their small bloody stumps and dirty faces, waiting outside the compound. She'd assumed there would be no children here. She'd only imagined hundreds of soldiers. She wants Ginny to clear up the misunderstanding, to assure her that those children will be nonexistent wherever it is they're putting on their show.

"Some kids tried to roll me at the airport." She sits on a cot next to where Chuck had left her suitcase. She sets her pocketbook lunchbox on the plywood floor.

"I swear to God those kids are more reliable than the planes," Ginny says, shaking her head. She walks back to the card table. "You're in my seat," she tells Chuck.

"You're in my hootch." He thumps the short leg down.

Ginny grabs onto the back of the chair and tilts it, prepared to dump him out.

"Come on," she says. Chuck waits a beat then stands. He grabs a beer out of a nearby mini fridge and, carrying his whiskey cup in his other hand, he joins Fay on the cot. She shifts as far as she can to the end.

"Throw me over that church key, will ya, Ginny?" he says.

Ginny throws him a bottle opener. Fay feels a sense of disorientation again. She's two steps behind everyone else.

He shrugs. "When in Rome . . ."

"Are those kids I saw runaways?" Fay asks.

"You have to have something to run away *from* to be a runaway," Jimmy says. He and his brother cut the deck and show a four of clubs to everyone at the table.

"Shit. You keep cutting like this," Timmy says to Jimmy, "and we won't be able to get our shoes shined."

"I'm not cutting, you are," Jimmy replies. "Don't blame me for your mistakes."

"They sure do love the show though, don't they?" Tina says, startling Fay. She can't get a grip on the conversation. Tina picks up the deck of cards.

"Who's 'they'?" Fay notices Ginny is biting her lower lip, pretending to concentrate on Tina cutting the cards. She takes another sip of her drink.

Tina shoots her a look of surprise. "The kids."

"Our wonderful audiences," Jimmy and Timmy say in unison.

"Stifle it." Chuck downs his beer in one long draft and then wipes his mouth.

Fay feels a trickle of sweat roll down her neck.

"We're performing for kids," she speaks slowly. Between Chuck and the kids, she doesn't know what to grab on to. It's like she saw a pileup on a highway and swerved for the nearest exit ramp, only to end up in the middle of a race riot.

"I told you that," Ginny says. "In my letter." She holds up the top third of the deck. It's the queen of diamonds. "Read 'em and weep."

"No, you didn't."

"What's the problemo?" Chuck asks, standing up so fast that Fay automatically flinches. But he only walks over to the card table where he picks up the bottle and motions with it to Fay. She doesn't say anything.

"Kids are the easiest marks in the world," he says. He waves the half-empty bottle in the air. "Every day is Christmas to them," he adds.

Ginny finally looks over. "I told you," she says softly.

Fay wants to scream at her but suddenly she's overwhelmingly tired. She feels as if she could fall asleep that minute, sitting up, paper cup in her hand.

"Did you bring your flip-flops?" Tina asks, looking at Fay's feet that are still in their pink platforms. "The showers are full of leeches."

Fay feels her eyes well. She shuts that down fast. Only Ginny has ever seen her cry. She's tired, that's all.

"You need another drink, Babydoll?" Ginny asks. Before Fay can answer her, Ginny waves in the air. "Christ, Chuck. What does the girl have to do to get a drink around here?"

Around Fay's fifth cup of Jim Beam, Chuck slides a piece of

paper on her lap like it's a napkin. She's still sitting on Chuck's cot, watching the others who have switched to five card stud. High card was getting monotonous.

"You need to sign this," he says quietly, handing her a Bic pen with the plastic end chewed down. She takes it, her hand starting to tremble a bit. She's made a mistake, she can see that now, but she's afraid to open the door and make a run for it. Something even worse could be out there. Once you're locked into the car on the roller coaster, you have to go for the ride, see it through. Something deep inside her, though, tells her not to sign anything Chuck gives her. His intentions always have ulterior motives.

"Babydoll, come here and help me with this hand," Ginny calls to her. She shimmies over on the chair, giving Fay a place to sit, but Chuck stabs at the air with his hand.

"Focus on the damn cards, not something that don't concern you," he spits out.

Ginny winces. She crosses her legs and slaps a card face up on the pile.

"What's this?" Fay forces herself to ask and swallows the rest of her whiskey. He's too close to her, towering over her. She glances at Ginny, but she has her eyes pinned on the fan of smudged cards in front of her face. Everyone looks slightly farther away than they are. The whiskey is hitting Fay hard. She hasn't slept in thirty hours. From a distance, though, Ginny has started to look good: tan and rested. Her normally wavy hair is frizzy, and on her face, sweat glistens. She looks ripe. Like she's just come from a sauna or had a heated sexual tryst with someone. Fay runs her hand down her own neck to wipe away the sweat trickling down.

"There'll be enough time for that, later. Just sign it," Chuck says quietly. Again, Fay is confused. *Time for what later? Playing cards? Or something more? No way he's thinking that she and Ginny*

. . . Christ, that hasn't happened in years. And it was only those two times. I was lonely, that's all. Nothing more.

It started one night, late, right before she moved in with Chuck. She and Ginny had drunk too much and been *without* too long. Just two times, but each time Ginny went down on her, she hadn't moved with any great speed. Her tongue and mouth had lingered on each part of Fay, from her mouth to the arch of her neck. Her shoulder. That small indentation in her neck that could serve as a resting place for a pendant if she'd ever owned one. Ginny was hell-bent on melding their two bodies into one. Fay didn't want to stop what was happening. Nothing could've been further from her mind. For a second, Ginny's tongue found a spot right below Fay's belly button. Her hand slipped between Fay's legs and then underneath her, lifting her slightly. As Ginny's mouth continued its downward drift, her wrist and forearm suddenly pressed into Fay's wetness and slowly began to rock her back and forth. Fay could barely stop herself from screaming out loud.

It had been Fay who had showed up at Ginny's the very next night. The first time had been a fluke, its intensity born from the novelty of it all. Fay was sure that she wouldn't feel the same way the second time around. She did. What was more, Fay heard Ginny say, "I love you," after Fay finished coming. When Ginny got up to put her clothes back on, Fay had the overwhelming urge to grab her, to pull her back down and start all over again. It unnerved her.

The third night Ginny came to Fay's trailer. Fay met her at the flimsy screen door. The aluminum doorframe was bent so much that it didn't close right. Fay didn't invite her in.

"I'm all for a good time, you know that," Fay said, picking at a torn metal thread on the screen. Behind her, Dickie was playing with a bunch of toothpicks on the chipped vinyl floor.

"What are you so afraid of?" Ginny said it so low Fay almost didn't hear her. Ginny rested her hands on her hips. Her miniskirt barely covered her pubic bone. As Fay took in Ginny's legs, she felt a bullet travel from her throat south. She didn't want to hurt her. Ginny was the only one who took care of her when she first joined the show. But this, this Fay couldn't allow. While it was happening, she loved it. But afterwards she felt like she'd been blindfolded and taken somewhere, someplace she couldn't get to on her own. She hated the feeling of dependency. She hated knowing that the ache she carried around with her the day after could only be alleviated if she went to Ginny's trailer. Hated the sense that she'd be at the mercy of someone else for that feeling.

"There's nothing to be afraid of," Ginny said.

"It's not about that," Fay lied.

"God, Fay. I won't say it again, okay? I was caught up in the moment." Ginny raised her hand so that the tips of her fingers pressed against Fay's fingers, still picking the other side of the screen. Fay felt it in her knees this time. "You were so *there*," Ginny added softly.

The sharp metal thread pricked Fay's finger then. "Shit!" She stuck her finger in her mouth and sucked on it.

Ginny started to open the door as Fay backed up, saying, "I can't," and tried turning away from the door when Ginny caught her and, clamping their bodies together, locked on to Fay's mouth. Fay nearly dropped right then and there. Somehow, she managed to push her away.

"I can't," she said loudly. "I've got Dickie to think about." She didn't know why she'd said that. Fay had never let him enter her decision-making before, so why would she have said that to Ginny? She knew it was something else that stopped her from going further with her, but it was too much to sort out at the time.

Whenever she thought about those two nights, she still, ten years later, felt that stabbing ache between her legs.

Now in Chuck's hootch, Jimmy and Timmy throw down three aces and two jacks at the card table and Ginny yells, "You cheating scum."

Fay wonders if Ginny's said something to Chuck. But this confuses her further. Ginny barely tells Chuck anything. Was Ginny trying to stop her from signing the paper Chuck has given her? Suddenly she isn't so sure. She wishes she hadn't had so many shots of whiskey. Ginny is refusing to look at her, shuffling the cards repeatedly into a collapsible bridge. Fay needs Ginny to tell her what to do, she always has.

Chuck is in front of her again, pouring more whiskey into her empty cup. He nods at the paper on Fay's lap. It's a bogus contract that requires Fay to perform once a day for one year. If she doesn't hold up her end, Section XXI(a) states that Chuck can seek damages for lost revenue in the amount of twenty-five thousand dollars. Fay starts to read the first line even as she can't decipher the words, they're blurry from too much whiskey and lack of sleep.

Suddenly, Chuck grabs her shoulder and squeezes, hard. So hard that all Fay wants to do is sign the fucking piece of paper, get it the fuck over with. Now. Her legs have started that tiny trembling they used to do when she'd stand naked in the kitchen.

"No need to take the time to read it a-whore-a," Chuck says, dragging out the last word. "It's a military form, that's all. Everyone signed. Says you understand you're in Vietnam. That I'm responsible for your room and board."

"Well it ain't Hollywood, that's for sure," Fay says weakly and laughs, her nerves speedballing because of Chuck.

"Right." He lowers the almost empty quart of Jim Beam on to the floor. "Good girl," he whispers in her ear.

Fay finds the line at the bottom of the form and signs her

name as best as she can, her hand shaking so badly she must steady it by placing her other fingers on its wrist.

"One more thing." Chuck swigs his drink. He wipes his mouth with the back of his hand. "All the patients here are thieves and they'll do anything to get their hands on a passport. Especially an American one. They sell 'em on the black market for the price of a house." He takes another drink and swallows. "Just to be on the safe side, you should give me yours. I've locked everyone's up."

Startled, Fay says, "On the plane they told us to carry our passports at all times in case we ever got stopped by police."

He waves his hand in the air. "The white mice aren't interested in us, trust me." Chuck smiles and once again, Fay fixes on his shoddy dental work.

"The white mice?" She feels as if there are two languages she'll have to learn: Vietnamese and the slang everyone whips out.

"South Vietnamese pigs," Tina says, and giggles drunkenly, confusing Fay once again.

"Police," Ginny explains.

Fay looks at Ginny again. "Did you give him yours?"

Before Ginny can answer, Tina says, "Everyone did."

"Okay, I guess." Fay opens her lunchbox, sorts past the Indian bead change purse that Dickie made for her, her dime store sunglasses, and a small pair of scissors that is deceptively sharp. Removing her passport, Fay hands it over.

"Let's get you settled," Chuck says.

Chapter

NINE

Fay's roommate, Carol Perkins from Nodaway, Iowa, has covered the four plywood hootch walls with polyester comforters she brought from home. She's set up a folding stool as a night table next to her cot. It has one object on it: a photograph of her boyfriend, Johnny Ray, in full military gear. The frame has red-hearted quilted material stretched over the sides.

"Thank goodness for Sears Montgomery," Carol says, retacking a corner of a gingham printed comforter. She is Red Cross. Their motto is *A touch of home in the combat zone.* In the weeks ahead, Fay will find out that Carol spends her off hours tacking and retacking the corners of her comforters. She has made their hootch look like a gentler version of a locked-down ward in a mental hospital, padded and dark. Surprisingly, it's almost peaceful. You'd have no idea they're surrounded by destruction and death.

Carol is nineteen. "That's your bed over there," she says over her shoulder. She picks up an old can that says Eight O'clock Coffee on it and, reaching in, pulls out another tack. She could be at college, telling her new roommate which side of the room is hers. Fay is only rooming temporarily with her until Chuck supposedly gets it sorted out. The center isn't prepared to house an entire carney. They want the diversion, but not the responsibility. They've got too much responsibility as it is. Five thousand people have lost at least one limb so far. Every day someone loses a foot, a hand, or both. Demand is outweighing supply.

"There. That looks better," Carol says, standing back to admire her work. Then she walks to the comforter and jabs a tack in the lower right-hand corner.

When her shifts end, Carol from Nodaway, Iowa, brings stories home to Fay. "One mother poisoned her child after she took him home," she tells her the second week. "He was a stomach with a head. She just couldn't deal." She pauses, tack in hand. "There now. That looks better, doesn't it?"

There is something not quite right about her roommate, Fay thinks. But then, she can tell already that there's so much wrong about this place. Where do you draw the line between who's really crazy and who is faking it? How do you know if Carol is simply trying to blend in so she can get through the one-year tour slightly unhinged, but unnoticed and unharmed? She might not be so insane after all.

Every morning in Qui Dao, Fay writes out a postcard to Dickie. The first one has a carriage being drawn down a dirt road by a Vietnamese boy no older than Dickie. For five minutes she stares at the blank square, struggling with what to write. *Having a good time* is a downright lie. But she can't bring herself to tell him she'll be home soon either, or that she misses him. She hates it here, but it's better than where she was. She doesn't miss the anxiety of waiting for Johnson to give her an ultimatum: It's him or me. Or worse, having to step in between him and Dickie at every turn. She did her time with Chuck. That was enough. She's tired of being the fixer, of always having to think of the way out.

The postcards all end up the same—they give hints about how Houdini escaped under water. Dickie was always interested in her act; he'll like these short tips that she sends him. He'll get a good laugh out of them. Smiling, Fay writes out the first one: Houdini could hold his breath for three minutes. She writes out a few to Johnson too, telling him things she knows will make him think twice about leaving her son.

She doesn't mail them. She can't. She's in hiding. She's entered the witness protection program. Writing them every day eases whatever nascent longing struggles to surface and tamps it down again. Those postcards are her penance and her absolution all rolled into one.

By the end of the first week, Fay understands that war is an insomniac. In Vietnam, the rockets start up at midnight every evening, an alarm clock that isn't needed because everyone is still awake, waiting. Outgoing artillery sounds different than incoming. There's a boom, like a cannon, so loud that it shifts Fay on her cot even though the howitzer is a quarter mile away. If you hear a hissing, spitting sound, however, that's incoming and you best be running your ass to the nearest hole in the ground. Because they're a hospital they're supposed to be safe, but occasionally a stray rocket hits inside the compound. They can't take any chances; they must take precautions when the bombing begins. From the bottom of their beds they grab flak jackets and helmets, arranged like bathrobes for a chilly morning. They race outside for the bunkers, swampy holes filled with water snakes and leeches and sometimes rats. Bugs called *bo gao*. They lie in the bunkers, wondering what would be worse: getting hit by a missile and becoming a fourth degree or getting typhoid. Some nights they argue the points in favor of each, but typhoid always wins out. Fourth degrees are the patients burned all the way through, down to the muscle. They wait for one thing: the infection to set in and finish them off.

One night, Carol breaks rank. "I'm not going," she tells Fay.

She pulls her flimsy mattress down onto the floor and crawls underneath. With the mattress on top of her, she wiggles under her skeletal bed frame. Fay does the same, surprised because she's never been a follower before but relieved that she won't be salting down leeches later on. They spend the night like that, somehow dozing off and on despite the noise because they're used to it and so exhausted from not sleeping every night. At least the dirt floor is dry and there's nothing crawling on their ankles. Fay expects Carol to say, "There, now. Isn't that better?"

The military is everywhere. Jeeps noisily barrel down the street ahead of truck convoys. Grunts with M16's strung over their shoulders like pocketbooks stroll the street in front of the compound. They're not allowed on hospital grounds. A PFC staffer tells her, "This is a place of peace, of healing." Still, they patrol right outside the gate. In the turmoil, Fay tries to focus on her show. The tank has always been her savior, her release from the rest of her wrecked life. No matter what was going on she always had the daily show to perform. The old upside down will pull her through this. But the tank is not her sanctuary now. The tank's dull, scratched Plexiglas tells her right away that Chuck was lying, this tank is older than Dickie. The water is too hot from the suffocating heat. Forty-eight hours after Fay fills it from a rare water hose, the water is murky. There are too many bugs here. Every morning there's a fresh layer of heavy black beetles as round as walnuts and hummingbird-sized mosquitoes. Fay flicks them out after breakfast at the mess, but they leave a milky residue that drifts through the water, like oily gravy. Water is scarce at the compound. Fay can't refill the tank every time the bugs start to pile up. She must make do.

"You're in 'Nam, sweetheart," Chuck tells her. "Not some fancy schmancy resort. Five maynutos to showtime, Chiquita."

●······●

She must do one show a day at two o'clock. Her tank sits on a makeshift stage made from plywood and discarded two-by-fours. There is a ladder that leads from the stage to a small platform at the top of the tank. After climbing up, Fay picks up the heavy chain that lies coiled like a snake on the platform's floor. She hands it to Ginny, who handcuffs her wrists and wraps the chain around Fay's body starting with her shoulders and working down. There's enough chain left at her ankles for the end link to be pulled upwards where it's lined up with the starting link on her chest. A padlock is pushed through both links, joining them together, and then clicked shut, its keyhole facing Fay. Ginny leaves room when wrapping the chain to allow a little give for Fay to wiggle within. She needs to be able to reach her favorite pick tucked in a tiny pocket inside her bikini bottom. When she's locked in, she hops to the platform edge and jumps into the water.

The children sit in rows in front of the makeshift stage. There are bamboo roofs over the stage and the children's area for the monsoon season, expected to start in June. The children who can, sit up on thatched mats or on a few folding chairs; the rest lie down on the hard clay dirt. Fay used to take a minute to let her eyes roam over her audience, but now she closes her eyes before submerging herself, not just because the water is always foul. She can't stand looking at the children. They attend the shows every day until they get a limb fitted and learn how to walk again or can pick up a tin cup with a hook.

During the performance they yell out their critiques in Vietnamese. With her limited three-week vocabulary, Fay can now understand a few phrases. "Don't do it!" or "Escape! Escape!" It sounds to Fay like an accusatory rabble and she ends up wanting to escape from *them* rather than the tank. This wasn't the easy money Ginny had promised. Not by a long stretch. Still, she's not in that mobile home in Key West. Not waiting for the human tornado, for the seams to split.

One day Fay begins her usual two o'clock show and sees a boy in the front row who was in the same seat the day before. His newly bandaged stub where his knee and the rest of his lower leg used to be is a beacon to her. He's an A-K, an above the knee amputee. One of his hands is missing and a bandage covers the end of that wrist ending in nothingness. Surrounded by other children who have arms and legs missing, he could've easily blended in. But, yesterday while most of the children yelled over each other, this boy was silent. He locked his eyes on Fay as the chain was wrapped around her and then as she dropped into the tank, as if he were studying to become an escape artist himself. Afterwards, when the Red Crossers walked up and down the rows handing out candy corn and Kool-Aid to the other excited children, this boy still didn't take his eyes off Fay. He watched her silently as she stepped off the stage.

Seeing the boy on a second day in a row slightly disconcerts her, but not as much as when he suddenly opens his mouth and, over every other child's jabbering, shouts out what her next move should be. "Wrap the chain!" he yells in Vietnamese. "Tighter!"

Ginny, her assistant for this show, turns to see who is shouting these instructions. "Who's he think he is? Ed Sullivan?" she says, an inch away from Fay's face. They're so close it would hardly take any movement for Ginny to kiss her.

"He was here yesterday."

"Oh goody. A fan." Ginny begins to lift the chain from Fay's ankles to her chest.

"Lock her up!" yells the boy, his one fist pounding the air in rhythm to each syllable. The bandaged wrist is raised also like it can't help itself. "Lock her up!"

"More like a stalker," Fay mumbles. "Why the hell did you tell me to come here?" she blurts out to Ginny, surprising them both.

Ginny stares down at the plywood flooring. "I thought it would be good for you."

Before Fay can respond, a girl sitting next to the shouting boy repeats what he says in a piercing yell. She's a B-K, her below the knee artificial limb ends in a painted replica of the brown Mary Jane on her real foot.

"Hurry up, will you?" Fay's spooked by the girl joining in. Ginny quickly tries to marry the last link with the first link against Fay's chest, but she has trouble matching the openings together. She hasn't paid enough attention, she's wrapped the chain too loosely, and left too little by Fay's feet.

"Faster!" the boy screams.

"He's just excited," Ginny says. "Can you blame him?" She's serious, but Fay laughs from the tension. Finally, Ginny clicks the padlock shut. She winks at Fay.

Closing her eyes, Fay plunges into the tank and submerges herself. Underwater, she breathes, blowing a steady stream of bubbles away from her face to divert the audience's attention. She angles her body away from the audience, especially that boy, and with handcuffed hands, slips her fingers into her bathing suit bottom, retrieves the pick, and unlocks the cuffs, freeing her hands to move within the encircling chain. There is only the one padlock left blocking her freedom. She can hear muted shouting coming through the Plexiglas and the water.

There's no place like home, she thinks, trying to ignore them. In the last three weeks, it's become her mantra.

Then, she falters a bit with the pick in the padlock's gate.

Shit. Come on.

The pick isn't quite in. It's angled too much. Instead of going strictly by touch, Fay's forced to open her eyes and redo the pick.

The padlock springs open. She's been in the tank for over a minute. She can go up to two and a half if she must, still the delay unsettles her. As her shoulders shirk the chain off and her hands come free, she looks at the audience—something she has for seventeen years steadfastly refused to do because if you look, you lose focus, and if you lose focus, you drown. Through the semi-cloudy water, she sees the boy, his face and body distorted by the murkiness, that stumpy arm waving in the air a reminder, especially as she frees her own hands, a reminder of what she has and he *does not*. The gulf between them overwhelms Fay. It's the same feeling she'd get when she'd be at home too long with Dickie. The thought hits her again: *How much did Ginny know when she sent me that letter?*

As soon as she's out of the tank, she grabs her towel and climbs down the ladder as fast as she can.

"Hey Speedy Gonzalez," Ginny calls, but that doesn't stop Fay for a second.

The money isn't as good as promised. Whatever Chuck's getting from the PFC, Fay sees only twenty-five dollars a week from it. "You're getting free room and board," he tells her. "What more do you want?"

"I have to send *something* to Dickie," Fay snaps back. She has no intention of sending Dickie anything yet. She needs it for herself, to get back to The World. That's what everyone here calls going home to the States. Who knows if she'll return to Key West? At least not right away. She now needs a vacation from this vacation. The point is she has to get out of here, away from these kids.

"Not my fucking problem!" Chuck waves his hand in the air as if he can make her disappear. "Tell that candy ass you left him with to get a job."

That night she's downing beers with Tina and Ginny in their hootch. The hootch has two cots, a couple of beat-up traveling trunks full of clothes, and a large poster with a picture of Tom Jones. Tina and Fay are sitting on one cot, Ginny on the other. There's a clothesline running below the center of the tin roof with Tina's pink lace underwear. They get a mildew smell from drying inside, but the one time she tried to leave them hanging outside she lost most of them to thieves. Now she's not taking any chances. Like birthday party streamers, bras and panties perpetually hang over the cots.

Fay shifts uncomfortably on her chair. "Fucking Chuck. How the hell am I supposed to live on twenty-five dollars?"

"We're all in the same leaky boat," Tina tells her. She shakes her head in consolation.

"You could've told me," Fay says as if she's speaking to the two of them, although everyone knows it's aimed at Ginny. Fay doesn't want to come on too strong, but she needs to know if Ginny purposely kept things from her. She said Vietnam would be good for her. *Maybe she simply made a mistake. There is that possibility. She shouldn't leap to conclusions. Ginny's never led her wrong before.* She wants to believe that Ginny would've warned her if she'd known before she'd mailed Fay the letter. *Maybe she hadn't been in the country long enough. Wouldn't Ginny have stopped her from coming if she could've?* Another idea keeps worming its way in, however.

"I tried to tell you," Ginny says, tilting her beer can into her mouth. She swallows. "We should go to Ly Son Island this Sunday. Someone told me it's got beautiful beaches with white sand. We need to take advantage of our one day off. You need to relax, Babydoll."

Fay's jaw clenches. She starts to tap one of her flip-flops on the ground. "When exactly did you tell me that this place is a shithole? In your letter?"

Ginny pretends to read the side of the can. "No wonder I'm getting fat."

Tina says, "You're not getting fat, you're getting curvy." She walks over to one of the trunks and takes out a bottle of cheap tequila and a few tin cups. Fay stares at them in disbelief. First Chuck ignored her and now her best friends are no better. She feels her anger swelling up. The beer aftertaste is bitter.

"Let's have a toast," Tina says. She fills the cups and passes them around.

Before Fay can stop herself, she takes her cup and throws it as hard as she can at Ginny. The cup hits the mark, the tequila drenching Ginny's T-shirt that says *Beauty is in the eye of the holder*.

"Jesus!" Ginny yells, jumping up and wiping off her shirt. "Goddamn it, Fay! I thought I was doing you a favor! Did you really want to spend another day with that farmer?"

"Oh, come on. Let's all kiss and make up," Tina says, holding out her cup as a peace offering.

Fay stares at the hanging lingerie and fights an overwhelming urge to rip every bra and pair of panties down.

"I wish that letter had never found you," Ginny mumbles.

"Now, come on, Fay." Tina rubs the lip of her cup against her tattooed cheek. "We're in this together." She walks over to Fay's cup on the dirt floor and, wiping it off on her miniskirt, pours Fay another and holds it out to her. Fay doesn't budge from the cot. Instead, she focuses on digging the inside of her palm with her nails.

Ginny takes a step toward her. "Look, I know you're upset. It'll get better. I promise. It'll be like old times."

Fay hesitates, split between smacking the living daylights out of her and moving on. *Maybe it was simply a mistake. Maybe Ginny hadn't meant it to be this bad. It was just poor judgment on her part.* The stone in her stomach softens. She needs to believe that

Ginny simply made an error. That she wanted to see Fay so much that she didn't see how bad it was here. *How many times has she saved your ass? One fuckup and you're ready to trash the only friendship you've had?*

Reluctantly, Fay takes the cup, stands, and knocks tin against tin. The sound is hollow and empty.

"Here's to those who wish us well, and those who don't may go to hell," Tina says.

Fay's eyes find Ginny's. Ginny has been the one certain thing in her life. But it's as if Fay has jumped out of an airplane with only a sheet attached to strings fluttering behind her as she hurtles to earth, and Ginny is the only one there to catch her. Sighing, Fay downs the tequila in one gulp and realizes too late that she's swallowed the shriveled-up worm too.

······●●

Chapter

TEN

By the end of her fourth week the tank has become Fay's prison. With each passing day, the children's shouts and squeals seem louder and more biting. *Look at us! Look at us!* they appear to say as they wave their stump arms in the air. It's critical that she stay focused on the pick, the chain, escaping, but she's started to let her mind wander lately, imagining those kids stalking her, or Dickie in their mobile home spending never-ending days in his pajamas on the couch, watching out the window for her return like a PI on a stakeout.

She must get out of here. One day, unable to bear it any longer, she makes a beeline for Chuck's hootch.

"I can't do it anymore. I want to go home."

"That'll be difficult," Chuck says. He's sitting on a wood box, busily attacking his fingernails with a pocketknife.

"All I'm saying is I need to get out of here." She forces herself to add, "I'll make it up to you."

Chuck's pocketknife pauses mid-scrape. Staring down at his hand, like he's inspecting it, he smiles, the gold tooth gleaming. Then he looks her up and down. "Chickie, whatever it is you're selling, I don't want it."

This throws Fay.

"You said you wanted to come here, right?" Chuck scans his nails again. A thin shaving drifts to the floor. "You couldn't wait to leave that son of yours." He pauses. "I guess motherhood isn't all that it's cracked up to be."

Fay's hand twitches, she wants to smack him so bad. He's closer to the truth than she can bear. He's always worked her guilt. All that stuff about their needing money, about Vietnam being a gold mine, about getting Dickie that expensive treatment—was it just fancy gift wrap on a cheap present? Fay feels as if she's punched her own stomach, low and hard. Is she really here because of something else? Is she really here because she couldn't spend one more minute watching Dickie click through the house? One more minute thinking about the mistakes she'd made? Maybe it was simply because she missed Ginny. Fay can't sort it out, can't remember clearly the reason why she came here anymore. It's like when you argue with someone and weeks later can't remember what the hell the quarrel was about.

Fay runs her hands through her hair. It hasn't been washed in a week. Showers aren't a luxury, they're something to avoid. Her hair only gets wet every day in the tank's oily water.

"Well?" Chuck says. His pocketknife hangs in the air.

Fay finger-combs her hair back again, although it had stayed in place the first time checked by dirt and oil. *It doesn't matter*, she tells herself. She can make things right. She simply needs Chuck to give her a ticket out. She doesn't have the money herself. She closes her eyes, measures her breathing like she does in the tank.

"I didn't know it was going to be like this," she says, opening her eyes. "I made a mistake."

"Not my problemo," he says, this time waving the knife in the air. "Besides, you and me have a one year contract." Wincing, he digs at a hangnail.

"Yeah, right. And this is the Hilton."

Without a word, Chuck walks over to a battered trunk with a big padlock on it. Fishing out a bullring of keys, he makes a show of going through them until he finds one that he slides into the padlock. There's something so deliberate in his movements, the silence hovering over them, that Fay senses immediately that something's wrong. Something she hadn't counted on. Chuck trawls around in the trunk and pulls out a thick envelope.

"Here we go," he says. He hands her a form that looks vaguely familiar. She sees her name scrawled at the bottom. She stares at this paper with her name on it, this fake contract that allegedly locks her in for three hundred and thirty more days, and she's about to rip it into shreds when Chuck eases it from her hands.

"You better get going. Show starts in an hour."

"I want my passport back," Fay demands. She's not going to leave empty-handed.

Chuck smiles. He returns to the trunk. Sliding the contract back into the fat envelope, he throws the envelope in, slams the lid, and clicks the heavy padlock, pocketing the keys. He turns around and looks at her. "I can't do that."

"What do you mean?" Fay can feel her heartbeat quickening, her face getting warm.

"What do you need it for? You're not going anywhere."

Without thinking, Fay picks up one of his folding chairs and flings it across the hootch. It smacks a plywood wall, splintering part of it with a tiny venous crack.

"Hey!" Chuck cries. He steps toward her. Fay runs out before anything more can happen. Halfway back to her hootch, she notices her hands are tightly clenched into small white balls.

Inside her hootch, she paces back and forth, a POW in solitary confinement. Chuck owns her again and Ginny sold her out. *Why? Damn it!* She grabs a grayish towel and heads for the showers. The showers are nothing more than plywood walls with a couple of rusty showerheads a foot above your head. There's a women's shower and a men's, but without security, who knows if everyone will stick to the rules? Fay thought that a shower would make her feel better. How often had she gone for revitalizing swims off the pier in Key West whenever she was mad at Johnson? But, as soon as she turns on the water, she knows it's a mistake. It's too warm, even with the cold faucet fully cranked. It's a slap in the face. Leeches are in a mud puddle by her feet. She hops around underneath the steamy water. How many more days can she live like this?

The next morning Fay is out of the hootch as the sun is rising. Carol is still sleeping, her sheet pulled up tightly around her neck. If Fay can get to the airport maybe she can get on a seven-eleven, a military flight that leaves every morning at seven and arrives in Saigon four hours later. Every day they allow a handful of American civilians on board. She doesn't have a passport, but she's an American, for God's sake. At least she'll be allowed to go to Saigon. From there, she'll have to come up with a plan. The important thing is to first get out of Qui Dao.

She hitches a ride from a couple of grunts in a deuce and a half—a two-and-a-half ton truck that will pick up incoming supplies at the airport. Sitting between them, Fay can smell the bitter, earthy smell of pot from the driver. One of his hands is loosely on the steering wheel, his other rests on the top of the seat behind her. The grunt on her other side keeps hitting his thigh with his hand as he hums a fast jazz tune.

"Kind of early to be out, isn't it?" the driver asks her. He's young, maybe eighteen. His face is skinny and too angular. When he smiles he grimaces like he has a toothache. He looks down at her tanned thighs, smiling. Fay has the urge to tug at her hot pants, to try to cover her legs. She wonders if maybe she's made a bad decision getting into the truck with these two.

Jazz Boy is ratcheting up the beat a little. The humming has turned into full-fledged scatting with some yowls thrown in for good measure.

"I'm catching the seven-eleven," she shouts over Jazz Boy's medley. "I have to get to Saigon. My husband's been wounded. Badly." Immediately, Jazz Boy falls silent and then lets out a soft, "Bummer, man."

Fay rubs one of her eyes with the heel of her hand. "You boys are doing God's work today," she says quietly, laying it on thick. "Giving me a ride like this, I mean."

The driver squirms in his seat and, removing his arm from behind her neck, places both hands on the wheel in the ten o'clock, two o'clock position. The rest of the trip is dominated by silence.

"Good luck," the driver mumbles at Fay as she jumps out of the truck at the airport entrance. After Jazz Boy hops back in, she hears him say, "That chick bogarted my buzz, man. No more hitchhikers. It's too fucked up."

There's a crowd in the airport despite the early morning hour. Fay threads her way to a line of ten Americans who have the same idea she has. They're in front of a makeshift table that has a couple of NCOs—noncommissioned officers—manning it. For a second Fay wonders if she can somehow cut in up front, somehow slide in without anyone noticing. Maybe she should pretend she knows someone, greet them like they're old friends and then just remain standing there as the line starts to move. How many will get seats? She's heard they only take a few civilians. Through the plate glass windows the plane outside on the runway is big, a DC-3, like the one she arrived in.

Everyone has their passports out. They look sleepy or happy, already imagining how they'll spend their time in Saigon. They have *their* documentation so there's nothing to worry about. *Shit. Think. Tell them you forgot it back at the hospital. Just blend in, walk with everyone.* Fay hears the *thwack* of an NCO stamping another passport and his, "Have a good trip." A woman and a man, missionaries holding Bibles, get their passports stamped and they're waved on. The line inches forward. Fay frantically wonders if she should try the same made-up story she told the truck driver about the badly wounded husband. Then again, they might have records right there of who is officially wounded, and they'll catch her in the lie. Another person walks toward the plane, a bounce in his step from relief. There are only three people left in front of Fay. She must settle on her excuse and stick with it. She has to be confident. But when the next man is told, "Have a good trip," she still hasn't made up her mind about what she'll say and starts to panic. *Goddammit. Just pick something.* As that thought hits her mind, she simultaneously hears the words, "That's it for today, folks. Sorry."

Without hesitating, Fay rudely pushes past the two people in front of her. "Look. I have to go. It's an emergency," she loudly tells the two NCOs who have already started to gather together their paperwork.

"Ma'am, everything here is an emergency," one of them replies stiffly. His closely shaved head has a bald spot the size of a baseball where a scar is laced across.

"No, you don't understand," Fay insists.

"Come back tomorrow. We'll see if we can get you on then." With that, the two officers walk toward the glass doors. Fay follows them, going all the way to the tarmac. She only stops when they turn around and order her to go back inside. Reluctantly, she returns to the waiting room, watching them hand paperwork to the NCO at the bottom of the steps leading into the plane and as they climb and then disappear into the plane itself, the propellers already moving in a grey blur. The cabin door closes. The plane inches down the runway and then begins to pick up speed, fast. The nose tilts upward. She watches until the plane is a black spot in the sky.

She won't go back the next day or any other day. Why bother? Her original thought that she'd just show up and get a seat seems naive now. Once she isn't selected the first time, her adrenaline evaporates and by the time she walks all the way back to the compound, she's convinced that without a passport she'd only be kicked out of the line. She was foolish to think it would be otherwise.

"There are two ways out of here," Ginny tells Fay a week later on their way to the mess for lunch.

"I'm not interested in the one involving coffins," says Fay. They kick up clay dirt clouds as they walk through the Pit that make her bare feet in their flip-flops look rusty. Although Carol tells her every morning that the monsoons are going to start soon, the wretched sky is clear.

Ginny laughs. Her red boots stride along like they're on a Texas range. "Neither am I. Only other option is to do the time." She slides her arm around Fay's waist.

Fay scowls, moves away from her hold. "I don't need to be told something I already know," she snaps. She's sure now that Ginny was in on the whole thing: the one-year contract, Chuck controlling their passports. She hesitates to confront Ginny. What would that gain her? She needs at least one person on her side. Why, though, would Ginny do such a thing? Fay realizes she doesn't really want to know the answer. The whole truth may be worse than what she knows already. Instead, she tells herself that Ginny was too afraid of Chuck to stand up to him, knowing full well that Ginny has never been scared of anything in her life.

The smell of *nuoc mam*, fish sauce, permeates the air the closer they get to the mess. The PFCs try to fit in; every day there's one Vietnamese and one American food selection, but everything ends up tasting like fish. Even the mangos. The mess hall has long metal tables packed with PFC employees, volunteers, and Red Crossers on benches. Everyone looks as if they could use a month-long R & R.

Lunch is almost over. The lines leading up to food service are short at this hour. Fay takes two slices of greasy Spam over a bowl of plain rice. She and Ginny find a small space to share on one of the benches. The rest of the table has American PFC staff speaking to each other in Vietnamese. Fay remembers when she used to sit in her elementary school's cafeteria and the girls and boys around her would speak in what they called pig Latin. She never could correctly switch the syllables herself, however, and would often be silent for the entire thirty minutes.

"Sorry, do you understand Vietnamese?" the young woman next to her asks. She looks like she's barely legal. Fay can tell she's a volunteer by what she's wearing: civilian clothes—a light yellow button-down shirtdress—as opposed to medical whites.

Fay smiles. These PFCers always try to include you in the mix. Whenever she happens to sit next to one in the mess hall, she's thrown by the contrast with the Humans' philosophy of it's a dog eat dog world.

"Some," she says, and slices a corner of the Spam. The poor-tasting food and her loss of appetite have caused her to lose seven pounds of muscle in the last two months. With no fat to speak of, her body has focused on what's left for the picking, her muscle. The Spam has the flavor of the griddle it was cooked on. Today it's fried eggs.

"We were just talking about a platoon that had to be evac'd out this morning." The woman clears her throat. "They were on a search and clear, but they ran into an alpha alpha." Every time someone speaks Fay imagines they're all members of a secret society. The woman looks down as if she's dropped food on her lap. She smooths her shirtdress. "Only five of them made it out."

"That's too bad." Fay lifts a forkful of rice and mechanically chews. She doesn't know what to say when they tell her such news. She doesn't know what the hell a search and clear is, or an alpha alpha. It doesn't matter. It all ends up the same: gurneys and coffins being evac'd out. Next to her, Ginny busies herself with her corn beef hash like it's her last supper.

"Forty of them . . . gone like that," the woman says, snapping her fingers. "You have to ask what's it all for."

"We're not here for the politics, Jane," a bearded man across from them pipes in. He looks like one of those Amish people except he's looped his stethoscope around his neck like a daisy love chain that hippies wear.

"I know, I know," Jane murmurs. Chastised, she stares into her bowl and, using her chopsticks, plays with the mixture of fish in *nuoc mam* and rice. "At least five of them are on their way home," she adds, giving Fay a thin smile. "Wounded, but on their way home."

Fay grins at her. Not because she's happy for the five who through luck and good fortune haven't been killed. No. Ginny was wrong. There are *three* ways out of here.

But how to go about it? It could mean the difference between a chopper ride and a pine box. How do you make sure you're shot, not killed? Injured, not maimed for life? Fay doesn't want to end up an A-K for God's sakes. She also isn't sure how to take the first step, how to put herself in harm's way. She could simply, she supposes, go for an extended walk after curfew. No one is allowed on the streets after five thirty every night. What if she's found, however, by the wrong people and isn't shot? Instead she's taken somewhere to be beaten and raped. She needs to control the situation. She imagines a clean shot through her thigh in the front and straight out through the back. Something that will get her choppered out and then on a plane home. Something she can recover from quickly. That will leave barely a scar. She could talk Carol into letting her go into the field with her, then what? The idea of convincing a group of grunts to take her out into the jungle hoping for enemy fire is ridiculous. Her persuasive powers are good, but not *that* good.

She doesn't own a gun. Wait, she could get one. The idea of shooting herself . . . does she really have what it would take to do it? She has to test what she's willing to do somehow. Yes, that's what she has to do. Put herself—what she is capable of *doing*—to a test.

Fay chooses a day when Carol is out in the field with other Red Crossers. She takes out her scissors from her lunchbox pocketbook. Slipping her hot pants off, she sits on her cot with her feet on the ground, her legs wide apart in front of her like a Playboy pinup. She opens the small blades and douses them with some whiskey. Searches her left leg up by where the thigh intersects with her pubic hair. Up here a scar won't be noticed in her act. She's not worried about the kids; it's Ginny who doesn't miss a thing. Fay lowers the flat side of the scissors to her warm skin. The hootch is its typical sauna. Sweat drips from her wrist to the salty dew on her thigh. Although the blades feel cool against her tan skin, the room's temperature seems to rise. She lets out a slight gasp as she rubs the flat side slightly from left to right. Can she really do this? *Don't think*, she tells herself and tilts a blade so it's in the cutting position. She's never hurt herself before. No matter how awful her life has gotten, she's never seen the sense in making the pain worse. There are so many people waiting in line that want to hurt you in this world, why add your own name to the list?

She presses down slightly and rakes the blade across. Not enough to draw blood. Enough only to leave a white line trailing across her tan. Her fingers tremble as if someone is stroking her in all the right places. She goes back over it. *God, that hurts.* An exclamation point of blood appears. *Shit.* The sight of the small scissors in her hand and the trickle of blood stop her. *What am I doing? How can I shoot myself anyway? There's no gun. I don't have a gun.* She hangs her lack of courage on this logistical problem. It's easier than believing she doesn't have what it takes to get out of Vietnam. If she can't sacrifice this measly part of herself, what hope does she have?

Chapter

ELEVEN

Two weeks later, around their third drink at Happy Bar, Fay turns to Tina and Ginny and says, "I've figured it out. All I have to do is kill Chuck." She's partially serious. Since that day when he refused to return her passport, her anger has grown exponentially, like those math problems that Mr. Hodges, her high school math teacher, used to write up on the blackboard. They seemed like something you could never fence in.

Happy Bar is in the center of Da Nang. The balustrades on the buildings that line the streets remind Fay of home, even as the scent of overripe mango borders on sickening, like someone wearing too much perfume. Bicycles, ridden by adults, dart in between the traffic. A lot of the children have been hurt from mines, grenades, booby traps. Bicycles are too tricky. You need feet and hands for a bicycle, so the kids weave in and out, straddling Honda motorbikes.

This morning the monsoons finally began. To celebrate, they drove into Da Nang in a Citroën Trois Chevaux they borrowed from a PFC social worker. Its two-cylinder engine made it about as fast as Dickie's go-cart. They passed a couple of drenched Vietnamese women with long bamboo poles straddling their shoulders, each end tied to a large woven basket full of potatoes.

After the car was parked on the street, they speed-walked through the puddles to the bar, avoiding the eyes of the shoeshine boys sheltering in large cardboard boxes turned on their sides, their hands clutching small blackened cotton balls. There's something about those cotton balls that saddens Fay, how they're worked down to the smallest of fuzz and still not thrown away, how overworked they look. At the bar, the three women folded up umbrellas and ordered sloe gin fizzes and Mai Tais. Happy drinks at Happy Bar.

At first, they talked about when they would be leaving. When they would be going back to The World. When they'd be leaving on what everyone calls a freedom bird. *Soon*, they lied to each other. *Any day now.* They've been here for months. They don't have the kind of money it takes to buy off Chuck. They don't even have enough to buy a forged passport. To pay off someone who will pay off someone who will pay off someone to get them seats on a freedom bird. The US government's planes, what everyone calls Air America, are strictly for CIA business, government workers only. Sometimes the PFC hospital staff rides for free, but that's it, no one else. Air Vietnam has long waiting lists, the tickets are expensive. Besides, there's Chuck and they don't have their passports. With that facing them, Ginny and Tina convince Fay that the best thing they can do with their money on this particular day is buy sloe gin fizzes and Mai Tais. At least then they can forget about Chuck and Air Vietnam.

They're sitting in low white chairs at a low table with a white cloth. A Vietnamese woman in a red minidress is dancing alone nearby, doing the swim and the pony while two uniformed boys urge her on as they drink their fifteen-cent beers. The boys are so young they look like they're dressed up for Halloween.

There's something about the definitive way Fay says she'll kill Chuck that catches Ginny' attention.

"Listen," she says to Fay, leaning in over the table. "We're surrounded by so much crap you're not thinking straight." She lights up a cigarette, eyeing Fay. "Did you know they rip off fuel from the Air Force and sell it as cooking oil?" she says, switching topics. "*Cooking oil.* You light a match anywhere near it and you're fried." Ginny sucks on her Pall Mall as if for the strength to go on. "Imagine doing that to your own people? That's crazy."

Tina motions to the bartender for their fourth round. "Crazy? I know crazy," she says. "Did I ever tell you about my Aunt Cesspool? That wasn't her real name. Her real name was June. Like the bug. Just about everything that came out of that woman's mouth was filthy."

It's ten o'clock in the morning. Their next show is in four hours. The day stretches ahead of them, unraveling, like a thick roll of gauze bandages.

The fourth degrees don't make it to the Humans' daily shows outside in the Pit. One day Ginny talks Fay into visiting them in the hospital ward. "They never get out. They're all wrapped up like mummies. It won't bother you as much to look at them." When Fay still balks, Ginny adds, "You have to start *somewhere.* The sooner you get used to it, the better. We're here for eight more months, Babydoll."

It's overwhelmingly hot in the burn ward. You'd think the rains would cool everything off, yet it feels even muggier. Today the electricity isn't working, the fans are on strike. The electricity has the mind of a promiscuous teenager: It decides when and if it wants to put out. There's a small body on Fay's right that she'd think was dead except for eyelashes that blink every so often through the two round holes in the bandages wrapped around its face. Fay can't tell if it's a boy or girl, although she thinks it must be a girl because the black lashes are so long. And there are the lips, strangely unmarked, perfect, moving and forming words Fay doesn't understand.

"Ginny, come here," she says slowly, but Ginny is already on the floor, her legs hooked over her shoulders, and she's doing a kind of crab walk with her hands, trying for sheer entertainment. Some of the kids on the cots begin to laugh, but laughing stretches what's left of their skin, and they end up moaning. Ginny stops, unfolds her body, and stays on the floor, her head resting against one of the gurneys. She's worn out.

When it's time to leave, Fay touches the girl's mitted paw. "I'll come back," she tells her.

The next day, when she does, a nurse greets her with her head shaking. The gurney has someone else on it, a boy with half of a smooth face showing, the other half is covered with Silvadene cream.

Immediately, Fay retrieves a xu from her pocket and starts to move it across her knuckles. Despite the trembling, she manages to keep the coin going for a few passes. How long before that child is gone and another is in its place? And then another? The unrelenting death in this country is too much. She has an overwhelming urge to clamp her body onto someone else's living skin, to be taken so completely that thought is an impossibility. She hasn't really thought about those two nights with Ginny in years and lately it seems she can't get them out of her mind. She wants that kind of oblivion. She wants to scream her head off.

The new boy says something to her in Vietnamese. Fay looks to the nurse for help. She only has four months' worth of routine vocabulary: Hello, thank you, see you tomorrow.

The nurse turns to Fay. "He wants to know if you can juggle."

Later, in her hootch, Fay counts her money again, piling up coins in towers that inevitably topple over and shuffling dong, Vietnam's paper money with its green buildings and block letters. She's done in seconds, the time it takes to pour a shot of tequila, throw it back, and swallow. It's eleven in the morning.

●·····●

Fay wasn't always an escape artist. As a child, she didn't lock her-self in a discarded refrigerator. She wasn't preoccupied with how long she could hold her breath in the backyard pool. Her parents might or might not have been the reason she ran away. Fay never thought much about it or them after she left. Her parents had adopted her when she was three years old, but it never took. Her mother had wanted a loving, cuddly child. Instead she got Fay, a skinny, jumpy girl who'd push away whenever she tried to hug her, as if she were being strangled. "Let go!" Fay would cry out, squirming against her mother's wrapped arms.

The girl didn't think right, according to her mother. The first time she caught Fay jumping off the garage roof with her doll's parasol, it was chalked up to her being a spirited six-year-old. The second time she did it, Fay overheard her mother telling her father in their bedroom that night, "That girl has the common sense of a bat. Do you think there's something wrong with her? How many times can you break an arm before it sinks in that you need to change direction with your way of thinking?"

"I'm a doctor, Eleanor, not a psychologist," Fay's father replied. "Maybe she's just adventurous."

By the time she was twelve they no longer romanticized her behavior. One afternoon after school, she ran through the front door and breathlessly told them that there was a man in town who'd stopped her and told her he wanted to take her to Hollywood. He was waiting for her to pack her bags at that exact moment.

"A man? What man?" her mother shouted and ran to the win-dow expecting to see the man on their stoop.

"He's waiting for me in his car by the playground," Fay said in an irritated voice. She was clattering up the stairs to her bedroom when her father's voice cut her short.

"What'd I tell you about talking to strangers? You're not going anywhere, least of all Hollywood."

Fay stopped on the fifth step. "He isn't a stranger. His name is Tom Wheeler."

"How dumb can you be?" her mother said, shaking her head.

Until she was fifteen, she felt like one big disappointment to everyone around her. It was then that she became an escape artist out of love. Fay doesn't know who in the Amazing Humans first called him Darwin—it was before she'd joined—but it stuck. His real name was Adam and there were times when she thought that name fit him better. Times when he acted like he was the only man on earth, God's gift to women. He looked exactly like the Marlboro man, the rugged cowboy with the long hair and a thick moustache. Fay found out later he often lied and told girls he was the actor on the billboards.

When she was fifteen, she saw Darwin for the first time on a stage. He was billed as the Mind Reader. He'd do this bit called Bag of Money that the Amazing Kreskin had already made famous and could probably do better, but a housewife in Duluth didn't know that. There were five paper bags on a table in front of Darwin along with a bottle of Scotch and a glass. He pretended to put a hundred-dollar bill in one of them and crunched down the tops. He mixed up the bags. Then he selected four people in the audience to come up on stage. Darwin pretended to concentrate really hard, pointed at two of the audience volunteers and, handing them Bic lighters, asked them to set fire to two of the bags. After the bags went up in flames, he asked the two other marks to torch two more bags. That left one surviving bag on the plain wood table. The audience had started to become his now. They wanted to believe he had the right bag in front of him. That he knew from the get-go where the hundred dollars was. They didn't care that it was his hundred dollars. A hundred dollars is a hundred dollars. They didn't want *him* to lose any money. Jesus.

"Humanity is a beautiful thing to cuckold," he used to tell Fay. And the Bag of Money trick was proof of that.

On stage, he'd sloshed out a drink. He cocked his head as he stared at the last bag, as if he were taking the bag's measure. Drew the moment out as long as possible. He was good at making people wait for things. Finally, with the air saturated with the electricity of nervous anticipation, he grabbed the bag and tore it open, only to find nothing in there, the ripped pieces falling to the table and the floor. He pretended to be slightly rattled then. He called out to the four marks, pleading with them to check their pockets, even asking them to pull those pockets inside out. Again nothing. The audience was solidly his now—they had no choice. They didn't know where he'd hidden the money, but they hoped to God he had. How the hell was he going to get out of this one? they wondered. Darwin stepped down from the stage. He reached behind someone's ear in one of the first two rows and pulled the hundred dollars from the air.

Here's the trick: The whole time he'd been palming the money. He faked putting it into the bag. He held it tucked up against his palm, hidden, until he was ready to show it.

This was all preamble though. The warm-up act.

After the clapping died down, he picked out a pretty young girl in the audience and asked her for a five- or ten-dollar bill. He liked this part best. Liked seeing her smile at the thought of being included in the act. Liked grazing her fingers as she forked over the money and watching her get uneasy when he began the whole act all over again, only this time with *her* five dollars. Sometimes Darwin teased her before he made her money appear again. Told her to say "please." Practically got her to go on her knees. By then she wasn't doing it for the money, she did it because he wanted her to and she felt that. She was drawn into the act and she liked it. She liked the attention, his concentration on her alone, a hundred people looking on. She'd never had that much attention. It wasn't that she'd been ignored before this moment. She'd just been overlooked. She was living in Dent, Indiana. She wanted out. Fay was fifteen when she was *discovered*. When she was asked for that five-dollar bill. She'd always wished for something more, something adventurous.

It's funny the ways Vietnam reminds her of Dent, Indiana. The way people here screw in the smallest places possible. A supply closet in a ward will do, or the restroom at a bar. Sometimes there's a grunt jacked up on black beauties who will offer himself to you right on the street. *Come on baby, light my fire.*

In Dent, Indiana, it was the possum belly of a semi, the truck that had brought Darwin and the whole Amazing Humans crew into town for ten days. The small compartment underneath the cabin usually held tent stakes and poles, but it was empty when Darwin and Fay used it that first time. This was right after the show in which he'd picked her out. It was rough going on that metal floor. *No worse than the flatbed of a pickup*, Fay consoled herself. Oddly, she felt safe, as if they were in a special pod headed for another planet. By lying down with him in that confined place, she became what the carney calls a possum belly queen. At fifteen she liked the sound of that. It was as close to royalty as she'd ever gotten. Possum belly queen. Who knew where that would take her? It sounded like a novelty act in the Amazing Humans Show. Something wild and mysterious. Something never before seen.

Carol shakes Fay awake. She's hunched over, perched on Fay's cot. "Listen!" she whispers.

At first Fay can't hear a thing, other than the usual sounds from the surgical ward: a child crying and what always seems like aluminum pans dropping onto linoleum. Then Fay hears it. A man's voice, shouting in English, "Where's my boy? Where's my boy?" Carol and Fay edge over to the wall and gingerly lift a corner of a comforter, uncovering the square that is their open window, a hole in the plywood.

"Army," Carol says conspiratorially.

He's twirling around in the middle of the Pit, stopping every so often to jab his M-16 in the air and scan the sidelines for what's out of range from his peripheral vision. What's in the dark. "Where's my boy?" he shouts again.

"His son isn't *here*, is he?" Fay asks, incredulous. She's seen only Vietnamese kids in her audiences.

"Some of them have 'boys.'" Carol's voice is distant, as if she's sleepwalking. "They carry their rifles. Their packs. Give them backrubs. Get their beer."

"That's disgusting," Fay replies, wondering if Johnson is forcing Dickie to get him beers.

Carol shrugs. What can you do?

"Isn't it weird how oil is the only thing that stops the burning?" she asks, confusing Fay. In another month Fay won't be puzzled anymore by Carol's non sequiturs. She'll *understand* them.

"You'd think that water would help, you know?" Carol continues. "Like you should run into water to get it off. To stop the burning," she adds as if by way of an explanation and lowers the comforter back into place. The peace of darkness descends again in their hootch.

"Get off what, Carol?"

Carol turns and looks at her. "The napalm, silly. Oil's the only thing that'll stop the burning. Isn't that weird?"

After the next show, Fay finds Carol from Nodaway, Iowa, building a fence, *a picket fence*, around their hootch. In the middle of the monsoon. She's hammering scrap wood into the dirt. The rain and heat have soaked her T-shirt flat against her body. With her blond hair, Carol looks like a prom queen who's been conned into entering a wet T-shirt contest. When Fay sidles up next to her, she doesn't look up or stop the hammering.

"Those boys at the battery really came through this time. They were supposed to use all this for some sort of bonfire. Some stupid Shake 'N Bake thought we should have a Hawaiian luau thing. Can you imagine?" Carol pounds another stake into the ground. "Their priorities are all out of whack over there," she snorts.

Fay is stunned that Carol is making fun of an army officer, even one fresh out of officer school with no combat experience— that's what they call a Shake 'N Bake. Carol holds the army up as nothing less than saints and saviors. Lately, however, she's noticed that Carol has been saying things she wouldn't have said two weeks ago. The other morning at breakfast someone inadvertently bumped into her and she dropped her tray and yelled, "Fuck me and the horse you rode in on!"

"Carol, stop." Fay touches her on the shoulder. "It'll only wash away."

Carol acts as if she doesn't hear her. Next to her there's a small pile of scrap wood that she's obviously cut down using the rusty saw that lies abandoned in the mud, like a child's broken toy. She retrieves another jagged piece and though it's too big, she hammers it in anyway.

"*Carol.*" Fay stubs the rubber sole of her flip-flop against one of Carol's soggy pickets.

"You know what they want me to do? They want me to start flying out, you know, programming in the field?" Carol gives the wood another whack and then points the hammer at Fay. "They're gonna chopper me in with some other girl. We're supposed to stick a rubber band on some grunt's pinkie and thumb and tell him to try and get it off without using any other part of his body. That's what the Cross wants me to do for entertainment." She pauses and, holding the hammer, swipes her drenched bangs off her wide forehead. "That's what they think will get the poor bastard's mind off the fact that there are only so many times you go out there and you don't come home again." She fixes her eyes on Fay's as if she's somehow responsible for this.

"That's it. I'm out of here," she says quietly. She scratches her cheek with the head of the hammer. Carol says this knowing she's not going anywhere—she's still got two hundred and five days left in her tour and she's not a quitter. Her boyfriend, Johnny Ray, is stationed in Cam Ranh; he'd enlisted, and Carol had followed him, only to be sent by the Red Cross to Qui Dao. Every week she sends off a letter to her superior asking to be transferred to Cam Ranh, but the Red Cross isn't in *The Dating Game* business.

Fay bends over the woodpile. Finding the straightest piece she can, she hands it to her. "We don't belong here," Carol says, and, taking the wet wood from her, goes back to work.

Fay can't stand watching her. She finds the nearest wall of sandbags under which she sticks her bare toes. Folding her umbrella, she begins. Around the hundredth sit-up, she's totally drenched, the tops of her naked toes have blisters and she's forgotten about Carol from Nodaway, Iowa, her picket fence, and whether they belong there or not. The only thing she concentrates on is how she's going to get out of there.

In the morning they wake up to find that half the fence is gone. Things disappear around the center: metal bed pans, food from the mess, bed sheets still smelling from the rice water that the Vietnamese orderlies use to wash them. Some claim it's relatives of the patients; others argue against the American grunts. Looking through the rain at the empty space where the fence had been, Carol's face hardens. "They'd steal your hair if it wasn't attached to your goddamn head," she says.

"I caught someone once trying to sneak off with my sword," Tina tells Fay and Ginny after Fay recounts the story about Carol and the fence. They're at Happy Bar again, it's becoming a daily morning habit, drinking happy drinks that cost fifty cents and with every sip make them sad.

"It was Jimmy and Timmy, for Chrissakes," Ginny says, scowling. "They were only borrowing it for their act, and you know it."

Ginny turns in her seat so she's facing Fay, blocking Tina out. She tugs at the new sling that now cradles her right arm to her chest. Fay can tell by the tugging that Ginny's really pissed off at herself; she has to take it out on someone. Yesterday Ginny lost her concentration during her contortionist routine—some kid in the front row looked as if he'd been burned all over with a cigarette, but it was from artillery fire. Focusing on him, Ginny ended up dislocating her right shoulder. She won't be able to do her act for four weeks. Fay wishes she'd thought of doing the same thing herself.

"Yeah, well, it *felt* like someone had stolen it," Tina mutters. Happy Bar has become a nursing home now, its residents carping and biting at each other when their lunch is delayed. Ginny motions impatiently to Van the bartender to bring them another round. The Mai Tais arrive and they sip on them, wincing because Van always adds too much Curacao. They each drain their glasses, hating and not saying a word about the sweet taste.

"I know," Tina says finally. "Let's go back and build a fence for her." She stands up from the table, propelled by the sheer excitement of the idea, teetering on her go-go boot heels.

Ginny scowls. "That's the stupidest goddamn thing I've heard." That makes Tina sit right back down. She swipes her face tattoo like she's wiping away some spray from the waves.

"Shut the hell up, Ginny," Fay snaps. She's irritated that Ginny has found a way out. *She won't have to see those kids for weeks. What's she so mad about? She won't get paid, but who cares? She won't face those poor kids every morning.* Taking out a xu, Fay moves it back and forth over her knuckles before Ginny grabs it and, raising her good arm, pitches the coin across the room.

The three of them stare at the black and white tiles where her lucky xu hits with a clink. It was the first one Fay got when she arrived. Van appears at their table and puts the next round down. None of the women touch the glasses. They're at the juncture of plain ugliness or something deeper, more lasting.

Tina speaks up first. "The damn sword isn't even real. It's just a gimmick. Everyone in the audience knows it's fake." She pulls peevishly at her fake silver bangs across her forehead.

Ginny points to her arm in the sling. "I couldn't do another show," she admits wearily. "I couldn't face those poor kids." And then quickly, before she can stop herself, adds, "I *wanted* to break something so I wouldn't have to see them for weeks." She looks down into her drink.

They've started on the truth game, something the three of them only resort to when they're really trashed and can't separate themselves from what's happening around them enough to joke about it. Fay knows it's her turn to speak, but she hesitates. She wants to go back to how they used to be, to telling stories about the Vietnamese, topping each other with how bad it was for other people. Not them. Never them. They've gone off track here. They've left the DMZ. What the troops call, *leaving the perimeter.* Tina adjusts her wig. Ginny, eyes down, taps her cowboy boot against a table leg. Fay watches the toe hit the metal leg. Together, separate. Together, separate.

Ginny looks at her. "Go on," she urges gently.

If you're going to enter the game, be prepared to play. Darwin used to tell Fay that whenever she'd start to argue with him. "I'll tell you one thing," Fay says now. "I don't miss having to pick up after Dickie every damn day." She tries to sound like she means it, but Tina is staring at her as if Fay's got three weeks to live.

"You try living with him for a month! No, a week," Fay snaps at her. "You couldn't last three days!"

"He loves you," Ginny replies quietly and tries to cover Fay's hand with her own, but Fay pulls hers back. She can't have anyone touch her, not now. Especially Ginny.

"I put him exactly where he is. Didn't I?" The words tumble out of Fay's mouth, like a rockslide, stunning all three of them. "Shit."

Ginny glances away toward the bar, which Van is polishing in wide circles, wiping down the bar as if he has patrons to clean up after. Busy work to make the chaos sane.

Tina forces a cough. "Let's play strip poker," she says, although there isn't a deck of cards. Between her fingers, she nervously twirls a silver strand. It looks like a thin ribbon of tinsel.

"I did, didn't I?" Fay repeats to Ginny.

Ginny turns and stares at her. "No."

"Now you're going to lie?" The thought of Ginny lying to her—*God*. She reaches in her jeans pocket for her lucky xu only to realize it's on the floor. Maybe it wasn't that lucky. "Dammit." Her fingers, still in the pocket, scratch obsessively away at the material like they're trying to dig their way through to her skin.

Ginny faces Tina. "Building that fence sounds good to me now."

They end up talking a Vietnamese nurse at the clinic into giving them five wooden tongue depressors that they stick crookedly into the ground. Still, they feel satisfied. There's something about doing this for Carol from Nodaway, Iowa—a woman none of them would probably even like in The World—that makes them feel good.

"Ain't that something," Tina says, pointing at a wild dog that has come over to lift his hind leg and relieve himself against one of the depressors.

When Carol returns from programming in the field, she doesn't mention the new fence. She's riled up about some Marine who apparently broke a plywood board.

"He-broke-the-slamboard," she says to Fay, enunciating each word as you might to someone who doesn't know English. She sighs loudly and sits down on her cot. She tells Fay that she and the other Red Cross programmer play this game called slamboard with the troops. There are teams, and each team is given small cards with preprinted answers on them. A square of black Velcro is on the cards' backs. Carol and her sidekick ask questions—what is Ringo Starr's real name? who wrote "I'm a Believer" by the Monkees?—and the guys rush up and slap the right answer card on a plywood board that also has little swatches of Velcro. First one there gets points. Points are good.

"Except this guy smashes the slamboard to bits. On *purpose*," Carol adds.

"Maybe he was working out some aggression," Fay tells her, but Carol doesn't see the humor in it. Fay wishes she had a slamboard of her own to unleash *her* frustration.

"I'm sick of giving these jugheads the benefit of the doubt. They're not exactly making my job easy." Carol gets up, moves to the doorway. Suddenly, she stiffens, like someone has jammed a gun in her ribs and she's afraid to move. "What the hell. Some jerk stuck popsicle sticks where my fence was."

Chapter

TWELVE

F ay ended up with Darwin every night for one year in the possum belly of the Humans' semi. It was the only place they could be together. Darwin was bunking with Funnel Head and Fay was in with Ginny then.

On their one-year anniversary, Fay persuaded Ginny to let her use the camper for the entire evening. Ginny didn't like Darwin, but she gave Fay the camper anyway. This was years before anything would happen with Ginny, yet Fay knew even at sixteen that she could get Ginny to give her anything she wanted.

Fay boiled up a pot of canned chicken noodle soup on the portable Coleman, but she added in too much water. At sixteen, her imagination didn't run to the gourmet side of things. Whatever it was, it had to be quick. There was never time for anything else. And then there'd been her stomach. Lately, nothing seemed to settle quite right. It was as if her clothes were made from cheap wool. Something was off.

"Soon we won't be able to recognize you," Tina had said one day, patting Fay's stomach, but when Ginny had glared at her, Tina had changed the subject, asking them, "So, if Jimmy and Timmy masturbate, does that mean they're homosexual?

In the camper, Fay found a knob of a red candle rolling around in a shoebox that held bent forks and knives. She stuck it on a paper plate and lit it, and then she sat down at the fold-down eating table and waited. She knew Darwin had had a show that afternoon, that it usually ended around six o'clock. An hour passed. Then another.

Around ten or so, the aluminum door banged open into the camper as if a tornado was passing through. "What's this?" Darwin said. "Trying out a new act, honey? Spooky." He fluttered his fingers in the air. "Séances are tough," Darwin said, popping open a beer. He stared at it but didn't take a sip. Instead, he put it down on the countertop as if he'd had second thoughts and wanted to keep his wits about him. "The dead aren't the most reliable, you know. And the marks . . ." He sighed dramatically. "The marks always want to be forgiven by the person you're supposedly raising from the dead." He waved his right hand. "But we're not in the forgiveness business, are we?"

He leaned against the countertop and folded his arms across his chest in a serious way. Fay knew then he had something to say and it wasn't going to be good news either. Nevertheless, she was hoping that maybe he'd gotten cornered into a game of cards with Chuck and some of the others. He'd had a few. Maybe he'd just lost track of the time. He'd forgotten it was their anniversary. She wasn't ready yet for what was coming. She'd turned her back on her parents, on Dent, Indiana. Didn't he know that?

"Let's put the little fella out of its misery," he said, and blew out the candle.

They were in total darkness then. They couldn't see anything for a moment. Instead Fay smelled something familiar and threatening. Jean Naté. The perfume of choice among girls her age who had money. As soon as Fay's nose sussed out the evidence on Darwin's clothes, Tina's prediction came true: Fay became a woman, losing in the time it took to blow out that candle her childish way of trusting everything and everyone.

By week's end Darwin was gone with his Jean Naté teenager,

hooking up with another carney and performing an act in which he shot an apple off the girl's head, or tried to, with mixed success. Within a few months Fay's clothes didn't fit at all because Darwin had left her pregnant. Her compact body became too swollen to do her act, her feet and hands too bloated for handcuffs. Instead, every afternoon Chuck had Fay hand out flyers to mothers waiting for their children on the street corners of elementary schools.

"They trust you. They see you and that fat tummy of yours and they believe that it's a family show," he informed her, another valuable lesson in Fay's education.

Dickie was born a month early during a scorcher in a small hospital outside Memphis. He was small because he hadn't stayed inside Fay long enough. Holding him easily on one arm, she counted his toes and fingers. "Don't you worry," the nurse told her. "He's gonna grow up to be a handsome, strong man." Maybe Chuck was right when he taught her that it all comes down to what we want to see, what we want to *believe*. Fay believed the nurse that day. Part of it proved true at least. Dickie would be handsome, towheaded, and blue eyed. But strong, no. Any chance of that Fay took away from him.

The full force of how the *yes* of her son's life was strangled with her one unlucky *no*, the force of the utter responsibility for that decision that she has for years tamped down so carefully, seizes her breath now in Qui Dao, as if she's stepped onto a third rail.

Once, right before Fay came to Vietnam, Dickie asked her what she thought about when she did her act, when she was shackled and submerged under water with no apparent way out.

"You're dead if you think," she told him.

"Oh," he said, smiling. "I get it." He was so pleased with himself. He often was whenever he learned some trick of how she escaped. Dickie was talking about the tank, though, and Fay wanted to teach him a life lesson. How much easier it would've been for him if he'd just adopted her way of life. She didn't tell him enough. She didn't elaborate. She always cut too much to the punch line. She should've told him it's not hard to escape. The trick is doing it before you think about it, before your will to live conks out. Fay should've told him it's not hard to lose yourself either. The trick is *staying* lost. You always end up, eventually, in a place that you recognize. A place that you'd thought you'd left behind. But the whole time you've only been driving around in circles. Wherever you go, there you are, as Johnson would've said.

One day in September, Fay scribbles out a postcard to Dickie, and it doesn't say anything about locks or keys or underwear. *When it's time, it's time*, she writes. On the front is an illustration, half of it bright orange and the other half blue. There are two tanks aimed at each other, one with the Communist flag, the other the flag of South Vietnam. Dickie will get a kick out of the tanks ready to blow each other to kingdom come. She'll mail this postcard, as well as all the others now. She doesn't care anymore if Johnson tracks her down. Let him. She needs to tell Dickie that she's thinking of him. She knows that much.

Fay licks a stamp and places it squarely on the right-hand corner. Before she can rethink her decision, she's bundled all the stamped cards together, and she's out of the hootch and heading for the compound's mailbox.

Chapter

THIRTEEN

The week after what would've been Thanksgiving, at a Humans show, Fay sees construction man Tom Thorne in the front row. She *knows* Thorne. He thought he was her savior once, at the airport. Maybe he'd do it again. Thorne claps his hands when Tina swallows her sword and laughs loudly at all of Jimmy and Timmy's knock-knock jokes.

He brings Fay to the Flamingo where, just like in Happy Bar, they sit on low white chairs at low tables covered with white cloths. Seeing those tables reminds Fay that she's trapped. Two grunts on leave huddle in the corner with a Vietnamese girl who's crying as she drinks her sloe gin fizz. She looks thirteen. She's probably ten. One of the grunts keeps pretending to find a xu in her ear, which seems to only make the girl cry more, but that doesn't stop the grunt from performing his magic.

"Ain't this something?" Thorne says as he chinks Fay's champagne glass. "God bless America." His face is badly sunburned, his forehead peeling.

They could be in Topeka, Kansas, after the last show at the State Fair. Thorne could be a farmer, astounded by his luck of getting her to go out for a celebratory drink. And maybe, he's thinking, for *more*. She doesn't care what he thinks as long as he helps her.

"I have a son," Fay begins. "I need to get to him." The words seem startlingly new, like she's just given birth. As soon as she says them, she realizes it's true. She needs to find Dickie.

"Don't worry," Thorne says, covering her hand with his on the white tablecloth. "I'll find him. If he's in Vietnam, I'll find him."

Fay starts to laugh then, which only confuses him. He removes his hand. She can't help herself. She laughs louder until Tom Thorne starts to laugh too, more out of nervousness than anything else. As soon as he starts to laugh, Fay stops, leaving him dumbfounded and uncomfortable. The bottom line is she needs him, but she doesn't like Tom Thorne. It wasn't his fault that he sat next to her for the whole plane trip here, but there it is. When you get food poisoning, you usually avoid that particular food again; its association is too strong. He reminds Fay of every bad decision she's ever made. He reminds her of soiled mattresses and towns with streets named after local politicians. Of shows that have gone horribly wrong. Plattsburgh, when a group of drunken college boys relentlessly shouted obscenities at Ginny, her ankles tucked behind her ears. Detroit, where Marjorie, half woman and half man, was beaten up till her sex was unrecognizable.

Thorne stands, stretches. All his muscle is in his legs. His torso is paunchy. No upper body strength. He's used to running, not standing his ground and fighting. Fay knows exactly how his legs will feel, every muscle, every tendon. Every man she's ever ended up with has had those legs.

"Well, I'd like to stay, but I gotta get back," he says.

Tom Thorne is all she has. He must know someone who would do what Fay needs done. Fay's not even sure what has to be done, it's a jumble of fragments involving finding her passport, forcing Chuck to let her go, a plane ride. The how is still undefined. An image of Chuck on his knees and a hooded person bending Chuck's fingers back the wrong way drifts into her head.

"Shit, so soon?" She tucks a blond strand behind an ear.

Thorne smiles. "Don't worry, I'll be back."

My don't worry man. My I can fix anything. My savior.

"I can hardly wait." Fay showers him with her best show smile.

He walks away a few steps, but then something, a *thought*, makes him turn back around, altering his course. "Your son," he says. "Where did you see him last?"

If this was Judgement Day, Fay knows how it would sound if she says that she'll do anything now, whatever it takes, to get back to The World. That she'll make the most of Tom Thorne and his devil pact connections, that she'll smile as she lifts his wallet and steals whatever dong is in it as she uses him up and spits him out and makes him think he's enjoying every bit of it. She knows how it would sound: too little too late. For once, she shuts off that voice in her head.

To stop him from walking out now she says, "Things aren't good at home. I have to get back to my son. He needs me. I made a mistake." There's honesty in the simplicity of it. Her breathing even slows down. She waits a beat and then adds, "He has polio."

Immediately, Thorne returns to the table. As if it's been in the back of his mind the whole time, he suggests that maybe Fay should give a private show at the Long Bihn officer's club. "It'd give you enough moolah to get home. Those boys are sitting on a pile."

When he tells Fay this, she laughs out loud.

"What? What's so funny?"

At the very least she expected he'd offer to *pay* for her plane ticket or to reserve her a free seat through his construction connections. *That was the easy part, remember?* She hasn't even told him about killing Chuck yet. Point B now seems impossible. She's wasting her time with Tom Thorne. She wants a diamond and he's given her a mood ring.

Fay downs her drink and stands.

He waves his hands, says, "Now wait a minute." He tells her there are thirty officers in Long Binh connected with USAEV, United States Army Engineers Vietnam, and they want some entertainment—that's where Fay comes in.

"They're under a lot of pressure," he says.

"Yeah, blowing up bridges can be stressful," Fay replies, irritated with him but mostly with herself. How could she have believed that *he* could help her? She's asked a garbage man to design a new house.

"You could take their minds off things," he says quietly, leaning across the table. "I understand they're willing to put up some major cash."

The way he says *major cash* unexpectedly gives Fay a thrill and nauseates her at the same time. It's the same feeling she gets when she clicks the handcuffs shut in her act. *Goddamn it, I won't do it.* Who knows what could happen with thirty detonation experts? She'll get the money somewhere else for the ticket and whatever else has to be done to get home. But whom else does she have? Other than Ginny and Tina, there's no one else. Ginny would give her the small amount she's saved, but it wouldn't be enough. Besides, Fay already feels as if she's indebted to Ginny for something she can't name. And Tina lives from week to week.

Thorne is it at the moment. He's all she has. She has to keep him invested somehow. *You pick your mark and you stick with him.* How many times had Darwin told her that? You have to appear flexible, easygoing, like there's nothing at stake. Sometimes the hardest ones to turn are the ones who ultimately give you exactly what you want.

"You think me escaping from a pair of handcuffs will do the trick?" Fay knows full well that won't be enough for the Army Engineer Corps.

Thorne looks off to the side, feigning interest in the table of grunts. "Lose the bathing suit and you're on to something," he says lightly as if he's told her the weather.

If she does this, she might be able to go home. She could go back to Dickie. That's what a good mother would do. That's what *she* should do.

"What exactly are we talking about major cash-wise?" She pretends to herself that it won't hurt to hear how much they're willing to pay for some ass.

Thorne grins. "Two bills."

"You'll want a front seat I suppose," Fay says, settling into the rhythm of the deal. This she's familiar with. Her initial disappointment and irritation have been thrown aside by the easier feelings of control and manipulation. Two bills is chicken feed, but she can shake him down for more.

He nods and then licks his lips. "They want a round eye," he says simply. "They miss home. It's the holidays."

She doesn't want to remind them of their girlfriends or wives, their fantasy! She doesn't want them getting any ideas that they can *touch* her! She wants more between them than a tank of glass and water. She wants what she's always had, the barrier of the unknown. She's *different* from their girlfriends. Every time she's climbed out of the tank unharmed, her wrists and ankles free, the mystery of it has separated her from anyone watching. People, especially men, stay away from what they can't understand. They end up thinking that for all they know she could lock *them* up. That's how it should go.

Fay instantly sees herself as those officers will see her in Long Binh. They'll see nothing more than an American woman, a good-looking *chick*, with a tight, small body, in handcuffs and shackles, fighting for her every breath. Exposed, vulnerable, helpless. The months of blowing up bridges and men, women, and children will have taken their toll on these bridge and tunnel guys. Their bodies feed on explosives. Adrenaline and anger and revenge course through their veins along with oxygen and blood. They're no longer the men who cut lawns on Sunday afternoons and fall asleep in their Barcaloungers. Those men are dead and long gone.

"Now wait a minute," Thorne says quickly, searching her face. He's made his fortune picking up on signs that a deal is about to go sour. Making sure those signs are rerouted, dispensed with. "We'll fly you in and out on a C-130, easy as pie. I've got a load of asphalt coming in. We dump that, throw in a few seats and your tank and we're off. Four hours later I'll have you back home, safe and tucked in."

Fay hesitates.

"You want to see your boy again, right?" His saying it so matter-of-factly, almost like a challenge, reminds her why she's still here with him.

"Four," she says, fixing her eyes on his.

"Yeah, that's what I said. Four hours, I'll have you back."

Fay shakes her head. "No, four *hundred*. And you'll have me back in three hours."

"Okay." He sighs.

Fay knows no matter how she twists it, there'll still be thirty pairs of eyes devouring her every move, imagining exactly what they'll do to her. It's a small price to pay though. She consoles herself with the idea that they won't have a clue about what's swimming around in her head. How she'll secretly be despising them and everything they stand for. When it comes down to it, she'll be one step ahead of them no matter what. I'll just close my eyes and blot them all out. Every fucking one of them.

"Don't do it," Tina says when Fay explains Tom Thorne's idea. They're at Happy Bar with Ginny. Today the place is full of journalists who've suddenly realized there's a human story to be found here in Da Nang. There are children living in cardboard boxes on the streets. There's a burn ward at maximum capacity. Stories galore that can bring home the war to The World.

"You're going in naked?" Ginny stubs out her cigarette.

"Look, you have to give to get," Fay says. "I have to get out of here. I need the money. It's not like I haven't done it before."

"I thought you'd never strip again for nobody. Remember that?"

"Rules don't exactly apply here."

"What about Chuck?" Ginny lights another cigarette.

Fay shakes her head. "Don't worry about Chuck."

Ginny frowns. "That piece of paper we signed when we were drunk off our asses isn't going away. He isn't going to let you go. He'll get some MPs to haul your ass back here. You won't get past the ticket agent." She sucks on her Pall Mall. "I hate that man." She yanks impatiently at her sling. Her shoulder has taken longer to heal than expected. She's got two more weeks to go before she can do her act again. Fay knows that the sling has suddenly turned into a cement block tied to her neck. Ginny has too much time on her hands. She ends up watching the shows every day anyway, especially Fay's. It's either that or drink alone.

"I'm sorry I got you into this," she tells Fay.

"You're not responsible."

"That's what I've been saying about her for years," Tina says. It's a stupid joke, but it's enough to lighten the situation, sort of.

"Fuck Thorne and the plane he rode in on," Ginny says morosely and drags on her cigarette.

"I was on that plane," Fay replies. "And trust me, there was no fucking."

Ginny blows out a fistful of smoke and smiles. "Were you expecting some?"

As soon as the words are out of Ginny's mouth, Fay blushes. She thinks she probably meant nothing by it. Carney talk has always been a free-for-all of dirty sexual innuendo. Fay's not sure, though. After she rejected Ginny that last time at her trailer, Ginny never brought it up again. Not even a hint. *It was her pride*, Fay thought at the time. Looking down now, she's mesmerized by the sight of the pointy toe of Ginny's crossed-over cowboy boot gently bobbing in the air as if to a beat. Maybe Ginny was protecting herself then. Why ring the doorbell again when the door's been slammed in your face? Ginny's been left too many times, starting with the orphanage. Maybe she's waiting for her to make the next move. Fay fiddles with her drink glass. She hasn't thought about Ginny for weeks, not since she's kept her mind on getting out of there. She doesn't want to start again. Stay focused. Think about Dickie. She motions to Van to bring them another round although her drink and Ginny's are untouched. Her news about doing the Long Bihn show has momentarily left a bad taste in their mouths that they don't want to compound by Mai Tais. Tina has been downing hers though, no problem.

"Whether you do the show for those bridge and tunnel assholes or not, there's no way Chuck will let go of you," Ginny says again, softly.

"Let me go let me go let me go, lover," Tina drunkenly sings off-key, massacring the Peggy Lee hit.

Fay concentrates on Van walking toward them with the fresh drinks. "Stop worrying about it," she tells Ginny and finally throws back one of the drinks lined up in front of her. "Who *are* all these people?" Fay asks, looking around. She has to steer Ginny away. She can't talk anymore about Chuck. Fay eyes the newcomers as if they're trespassing. They don't have much, but Happy Bar is theirs, damn it.

But is it? As Van puts their drinks down, Fay is struck by how little she knows about him. Not once has she or Ginny or Tina asked him one question about himself despite all the hours that they've spent with him. They don't even know who owns Happy Bar for that matter.

"Hey Van," she says, stopping him before he turns away. "How long have you worked here?"

Ginny stares at her suspiciously, but Fay goes on. "Do you like working here?"

"Happy Bar is mine," he says, and looks around the bar with a serious expression that Fay can't tell is from astonishment or pride. "One day it will be my son's." He turns and points to the wall behind the bar where there are several pinned up snapshots. They're too far to see from the table where they're sitting, but Fay knows they must be of his son. Or maybe he was saying sons—plural. She feels like she's been kicked in the stomach. How often had they sat at that bar and she hadn't even seen those photos, let alone asked about the people, Van's *family*, in them? For the first time she wonders how much else she has missed seeing in Vietnam. How she really knows nothing about anyone or anything outside of the Amazing Humans and where they are living. How maybe her entire perception of this country is full of holes. How maybe Ly Son Island isn't the only beautiful thing to acknowledge in this vast country. How instead of focusing only on the homeless shoeshine boys with their blackened cotton balls, she could've noticed the people on their way to work at the bustling restaurants or the white-walled hotels with their floor-to-ceiling vintage French shutters, the businesses that were still open and thriving on that same street despite the war. Instead of believing that the kids in her audiences were all the same—an endless demanding, yelling horde—she could've admitted that as the weeks went by she'd noticed that each had his own personality, like the boy who brought his teddy bear to every show; or the girl who reached over and covered the bear's eyes as soon as Fay went in the tank.

But if your perception has been bullshit, where does that leave you? Fay thinks at Happy Bar. What can you count on?

"Who are all these people?" she repeats, rattled now.

"Bad people," Van says, staring straight at the reporters. "They steal *everything*." He stands behind Fay and Ginny's chairs as if to show everyone in the room whose side he's on. And Fay is surprised again, this time by Van's generosity, his willingness to draw in the three of them as if they are his family too.

Tina and Fay lift their drinks then, pretending to raise them to the bad people. "*Ginny*," Fay pleads, desperately wanting now to be reconnected to the one thing she could depend on in the past. She motions her glass toward Ginny's. Ginny reluctantly raises hers. The moment of separation has passed. They're in this together again. There are three days before Fay gets on a C-130 with Tom Thorne. A lot can happen in three days. Maybe Chuck will have a heart attack, one of those one-shot deals. Here today, gone tomorrow.

"May we kiss who we please . . ." Tina says, clinking her glass against the others. "And please who we kiss . . . Ain't that the damn truth."

For a long time, Fay believed Chuck loved her. Despite his stalking her every move. When she washed the dishes. "You missed a spot there, Chiquita." When she ironed the pocket flaps of his western shirt so they'd stay flat. "See that? That, right there. Do you need glasses? It's curling up. Who taught you to iron? It's a good thing you have me, Chiquita. Who knows where you'd be. Give me the fucking shirt. Well, do it right this time."

He watched her most intently at night, when Dickie was asleep. Made her stand naked in front of the refrigerator, with the door open. Not every night. Just when he was *in the mood*. He leaned back on a folding chair, his legs splayed, a drink she'd made him in his fist, a rum and coke, or a Harvey Wallbanger. Made her stand there through two more drinks—he'd make those himself—while she held herself as still as possible so he wouldn't say the words she dreaded most: "You moved." Because if he said that, it might mean she'd stand there all night. The refrigerator air was cold in summer and positively unbearable in February.

"You moved." She came to hate those words. They settled into her stomach, acidic, diseased, a bottle of rat poison. She wanted to cry out then. She wouldn't. She learned to shut that down fast. Crying wouldn't end this. Wouldn't allow her to go to bed any sooner.

She came to hate other things. "Don't wake him up." She hated that too. Like her moving a toe on the linoleum would do that. *Dickie*, she'd tell herself, her hands and feet starting to tingle from the not moving. *I'm doing it for Dickie.*

Afterward, after they had had sex, after Chuck fell asleep, snoring next to her, she'd slide out of bed, inch by inch so that she wouldn't wake him. Some nights it took her the better part of a half hour to get her whole body out of the bed. She'd pad silently to the kitchen and, leaning against the counter, light a cigarette. She'd look over at Dickie, still asleep on a bed made out of the dinette banquet, his face warm and rosy and peaceful, and in that moment, she honestly couldn't say if she loved him or hated him with all her heart.

Hours after Fay returns home from Happy Bar, a bout of heavy shelling goes down in the darkness somewhere outside the compound. Fay automatically falls off her cot onto the floor and rolls smack into Carol.

"Criminy!" Carol says. "You're under my bed!"

"Sorry." Fay's head is pounding. The hangover from the drinks with Ginny and Tina has now come on full blast. She rubs her forehead, which seems to make it worse. Rolling under her own cot, she curls into a fetus. Maybe if she squeezes herself tightly, she won't feel so hung over.

"You have no idea how much my head hurts right this second." She can hardly make out Carol's face in the darkness.

"That's what you get from hanging out with the wrong crowd."

"Don't lecture me, Carol."

The shelling pauses and then starts up again, like someone nodded off at the switch for a second.

"They're having some kind of hippie dance thingamajig this Friday at Camp Beecher," Carol says in between the blasts. "Wanna go?"

Fay laughs out loud at the absurdity of it. The exertion sends a spear of pain through her forehead like she's eaten ice cream too fast.

"What's so funny about that?"

Fay's eyes adjust to the dark. She can see Carol's face is scrunched up. She's sick of Fay making fun of her.

"I can't. I'm doing a show for some bridge and tunnel guys."

"What show?"

"An extra. They want me to perform. I need the money."

Gunfire heats up in the distance. It reminds Fay of the caps that neighboring kids used to shoot off near her mobile home in Key West. The tinny-ness of it haunts her.

"Rule number one," Carol says. "Never go anywhere alone. You can't trust them. You can't trust *anyone*." It sounds so unlike her, but before Fay can say anything in response, an explosion goes off somewhere nearer to the compound. It seems so close they both shut up and cover their heads as if the roof of their hootch has been hit and is raining down on them.

"What do you need the money so much for anyway?" Carol finally asks.

"I've got to get home to my son," Fay blurts out. This is the first personal thing she's ever told her. Carol had no idea that she even has a son. With her head hurting and the gunfire and the incoming, Fay's filter is shot to shit.

"How much you got?" Carol scrapes her feet on the dirt, adjusting.

"Not enough."

"*How much?*"

"One hundred eleven dollars and thirty-three cents."

"When was the last time you counted? Maybe you missed—"

"I don't need to count, Carol. I *know.*"

Outgoing rocket fire starts up. They listen to the boom of it leaving the main street in front of the compound. Who knows if it will find its Communist target miles away, or hit an unsuspecting family sleeping on the dirt of their own hut?

"Jesus, I've got to stop drinking," Fay says, massaging her temple.

"Uh-huh." Tapping her index fingernail against her front tooth, Carol tells her, "Listen, if it'd help, I can give you maybe a hundred."

This so startles Fay that she breathes in too deeply and dirt gets into her mouth and throat. She starts to choke and cough like she's tubercular. The idea that Carol—Carol, whom Fay had secretly ridiculed to Ginny and Tina for months—that she would help her now is too much.

"Hey, are you okay?" Carol asks and, reaching out, slips her hand under Fay's cot. She grabs Fay's hand and squeezes it. Carol's hand is cool to the touch. Fay concentrates on that and her cough turns fitful and then stops altogether. Carol's hand doesn't move, it just holds hers, lightly but there. *The boys she sits with in the hospital must love her,* Fay thinks. *She knows how to touch with-out ownership.* It's a rare talent. Fay can't remember the last time someone held her hand and didn't want something else from her. Yes, she can. The last night she was home. She was on the couch with Dickie. Carol's index finger mindlessly strokes the top of Fay's knuckles.

They both realize at the same time that the shelling has stopped for the night. They stay where they are anyway, Fay's hand still securely in Carol's. Some of the night insects start up outside. They sound like an electrical wire on the fritz.

"God, I miss the sound of cicadas," Carol whispers. "Don't you?"

Immediately, Fay hurts from the missing. The suddenness of it overwhelms any defenses she has worked hard at installing and the memories seep, then flood in, as if an entire wall of sandbags is gradually swept away by an overflowing river. The nights they rode around in Johnson's pick-up, and he cut the engine and they listened to the ocean before he started in on her, fumbling with her buttons. The pier that she dove off every morning for a long swim, her few minutes of quiet, alone. Fay misses everything in this moment. Even the crummy mobile home and Mrs. Swenson, her nosy next-door neighbor. But those are just the warm-up act. Fay misses Dickie. The sounds of his metal braces in the middle of the night as he goes to the bathroom. He could never make it through the whole night. *Click squeak. Click squeak.* Sounds that used to upset the hell out of her are the sounds she now craves. Dickie nodding his head at everything she uttered, like every word she spoke was brilliant and necessary. She misses crawling into bed with her son and Dickie automatically rolling over in his sleep, one arm finding her waist. The smell of him. Boy smell. The sugary sweat smell that only boys have. She'd fall asleep immedi-ately, in an unguarded way that she could never muster when she was in bed with Johnson. With him she kept expecting an alarm clock to go off. She hasn't slept through one night since arriving in Vietnam, but she could sleep through the entire night like this, under the cot, with Carol's hand holding hers, her fingers lulling her into a dreamless sleep.

"Maybe we should have a bake sale," Carol says seriously. Abruptly, she lets go of Fay's hand and slides out from under her bed. Fay feels the immediate absence of Carol's hand as if her own has been amputated. Carol has a plan now. "We have a lot to do," she says. Fay hears her dusting off her pajamas.

No, Fay thinks, *come back. Don't go.* She's surprised when her eyes fill. *Jesus, what's happening to me?* She brushes at them and sniffs hard.

"We could sell brownies." Carol lights a lantern that throws the whole hootch, its utter smallness and fragility, into high relief.

Fay crawls out. "I'm getting some water. Do you want any?"

Carol waves her off. "It'll only make me pee." As Fay goes through the door, Carol says, "We've gotta get our hands on some of that grass everyone is stoned on. We'd sell a bazillion brownies that way."

Fay quickly looks away at the comforters. For once she wishes she were Carol. How easy her life would be then. How easy it would be to think, like her roommate does, that everything could be solved by the Cross credo: *A touch of home in the combat zone.* How easy it would be to go through life saying things like "bazillion," or "criminy." How easy.

Chapter

FOURTEEN

The next morning the B-Ks and A-Ks are hyped up as if they've been on an Easter candy binge for the last twenty-four hours. As Fay stands beside her tank, wrapping a long rusty chain around her ankles, the children stare at her. Fay feels uneasy, like she's about to go into an abandoned coalmine holding a flashlight on the fritz. Chuck isn't around, but she can't stop thinking of him.

As Fay stands in front of her tank, she feels as if she's gone back in time. She's not thirty-one, she's nineteen again. She will never get a leg up on Chuck. Without her passport, she's powerless. He can tell her what to do, when. Why the hell did she give it to him?

She takes much longer than usual to finish her preparations, kneeling down and splashing some water on her chest, pulling her hair into a ponytail, trying to settle her nerves. *I was drunk. Jet-lagged. I never would've given it to him otherwise. Ginny was the one who should've said something. Stopped me.* Fay shakes her head. It's too late now for the blame game. She must do something. The when and how of it are front and center in her mind.

"You all right?" Ginny whispers. For Fay's sake, she stalls for time, making a show of straightening out the remaining chain on the floor.

"Uh huh," Fay tells her, mechanically. "Let's go."

Ginny handcuffs Fay's hands together. Fay's thoughts about

Chuck are momentarily interrupted by the sensory overload of Ginny's hands briefly touching her wrists as she clicks the handcuffs shut. Ginny's bottom lip is slightly moist. Fay almost reaches up with her handcuffed hands to wipe it. Then, Ginny winds the chain around her.

When Ginny moves away, Fay cracks her knuckles. Some of the kids let out moans. She is making them wait too long. She remembers how it used to be when she loved to plunge into the tank. Despite what most people believe, it wasn't suffocating. It was liberating. Here, the tank would say, as she lowered herself in. This is what you have. This is your ceiling. Know your limitations. Feel your feet on the floor. Where the sides are. This is all there is until you decide to leave. The parameters never changed. In Key West, the water might have been hotter or cooler depending on the time of day or the season, but it was always just water. Time moved slowly and quickly at the same time. It's been years since she's worried about her timing, about the water.

Don't be fooled, the tank says to her now. You could drown.

She slips in from the ledge at the top. With her eyes closed, her body sinks under the weight of the chain through the water, feeling the bubbles fly past her face as they always do. If you're not focused, this is the moment for panic. The bubbles always remind you that you're underwater, bound by metal cuffs and a chain wrapped around your body. That you might be insane for doing this. Whatever you do, keep your eyes closed, and concentrate on escaping.

She doesn't. She doesn't keep her eyes closed.

And then she's in trouble.

Even through the murkiness, Fay can see the kids are looking at her, their mouths are Os, endless vacuums of teeth and air. *They're watching you.* This thought makes her hesitate before she slides her index finger under her bikini's waistband. One second in a tank is a year out of your life. She flexes her torso away from the children's eyes. Another two seconds wasted. *They think you're going to die. They want you to die. They know what you are. They know about Dickie. How you left him.* Under her waistband, Fay's fingers find the tiny key to the cuffs and then . . . it's gone. *Shit. The fucking key.* She swivels with the chain too fast, stirring up the water so that whirlpools around her camouflage the tiny silver key drifting toward the bottom. *You're dead. Stop thinking!* Ginny starts to pound on the side of the tank now—Fay can hear her singing loudly, "Ninety-nine bottles of beer on the wall." The kids believe this is all part of the act. Bent over into an impossible contortion with the slack chain cutting into her sides, Fay spies the key. Another minute passes as her fingers chase it around the floor. It drifts away every time her fingers move toward it, like a feather in the wind. Finally, she corrals it. Her eyes are blurring as she slips it into the latch. Something's not right. *How long have I been in?* she's wondering as she unravels the chain. Her knees start to buckle. She's not done getting free and clear of the chain. *Push off, push off,* but her feet are still on the bottom, the chain wrapped around her ankles, no air left in her lungs. She's taken too long.

There's no thrashing like you'd expect from the movies. No frantic movement. It seems quiet, a relief actually.

The kids. You can hear them yelling, louder than they've ever done. *Go to hell,* you think. *Leave me alone.*

And then. There are hands. Strong hands, like two hooks, grabbing hold of your shoulders, pulling you up. Hands that won't let go. Hands that yank you out, even as the heavy chain, still wrapped around your ankles, drags after you through the water like an anchor. A dead weight dislodged from its mooring.

The hands belong to a man. His face is that of a distant cousin: familiar features that you can't put a name to. "Who are you?" you try to say but nothing comes out. You black out.

When you wake up, you're on one of the cots in the burn unit. It's a question of bodies: The burn unit is underutilized at this moment. You stay in the hospital overnight, but they need the bed. They don't have room for an escape artist who messed up in her act.

Tina and Ginny help you up. On your way out of the building, you see Hands again. He is carrying a stretcher from a flying crane, saving another life. He rushes past you, not noticing that you are alive and on your feet, although Tina and Ginny are your crutches. There's someone else who needs his attention now.

"Wait, wait," you tell Tina and Ginny, who are steering you away from the bodies on moving litters. They don't hear you, however, above the clamor of new patients crying, the machine-gun screeching of their mothers running through the ward, telling anyone who'll listen the facts of what has happened.

Too late.

He's gone.

"He's a limb maker," says Ginny. His strong hands come from years of molding thermosetting resins and wood into fabricated legs and arms. Fay imagines he's Geppetto and Jesus rolled into one. Because of him, children with no legs walk again. Those without arms learn to pick up coins with a hook they move with their holstered shoulder. It doesn't matter if they're from the North or the South. In Qui Dao hope is not limited by geography, by lines of demarcation. She understands the limb maker treats them all the same. It's not for him to judge who is friend or foe. He's here because of his hands. Hands that once set broken bones and stitched cuts in medical school now repair lives. These are the hands that saved Fay. All she can think about are how those hands felt on her: strong, secure, able to twist a goodbye into a hello.

●······●

She hasn't been back in the tank for three days. When she thinks about it, she envisions a coffin, six feet under a mound of dirt the color and consistency of broken brick. One night she dreams that Chuck picks up the tank and, turning it over, dumps out the water on top of her as she's sleeping. She wakes up, her clothes—the same ones she's had on for three days—drenched, not by some strange manifestation of her dream, but from sweat.

Within the dark safety of Carol's comforters, Fay grips her cot. A steady rain thrums against the tin roof of their hootch. Ginny and Tina try to get her to eat a mealy chicken leg they've scrounged from dinner.

"It's not Shake 'N Bake, that's for sure," Tina says.

Fay fakes nibbling it to get them to leave. As soon as they do, she puts the greasy leg on the dirt floor and, over the next hours, watches as ants make a picnic of it. It slowly looks like some bone that's been dipped in chocolate jimmies.

For the first few days after her near drowning Chuck leaves Fay alone. He doesn't want a dead escape artist on his hands. That wouldn't go over well with the PFCers. Ginny is forced back into the show, her shoulder fixed enough to slowly angle her arm around her neck and body into semi-knotted positions.

"I'll do your slot too, Babydoll," she tells Fay. She expands her act into a longer show that includes Jimmy and Timmy, their bodies becoming one screwed-up human pyramid.

Tom Thorne in a drenched yellow rain slicker also stops by. "Come on now," he says when he sees that Fay is still in bed. "You won't get anything done that way." He sits on Carol's cot, the rusted springs creaking, the thin mattress straining under his weight. A puddle forms by his construction boots. Fay wonders if it's possible that a missile could come cleanly through one of the comforters and strike him dead where he sits without doing any other damage. There's so much death here. Yet the people Fay wants to die, don't. One of her neighbors in Florida was struck by lightning through the living room window as her husband sat next to her on the couch, watching *The Ed Sullivan Show*. That's the kind of pinpoint precision Fay wants now.

"The boys will be waiting for you when you're ready," Thorne says in his most reassuring voice on his way out.

The private show will have to wait. Four days have passed since her fuckup in the tank. That's what Fay calls it to herself. She finally struggles out of the cot to a standing position. She's dizzy from not eating, but she makes it to the hospital. Hands is nowhere to be seen.

Inside the clinic, Fay finds the physical therapy room where a small girl, maybe five years old, is walking toward a floor-length mirror. A PFC therapist shadows her in case she falls. The girl is watching herself walk in the mirror, her face grimacing, her fake leg stuttering along. Other children, who are patients, stand on the sidelines, smile and call out to the girl, whose nametag says Ha, "Walk! Walk, Ha!" For a moment, Fay remembers how a few years after Dickie got sick, she called out to him: "Just walk to me here. Come on, Dickie, you can do it. Getting you better is 90 percent attitude." He would try and fail, try and fail, falling to the ground within two steps. After the third attempt, Fay stopped asking, but Dickie wouldn't give up. "Here I come," he'd call out and then crash again before Fay could reach him fast enough. He'd only stop when his arms and legs had bruises.

Ha struggles all the way to the mirror where she plants a kiss on her own reflection and giggles, pleased with herself. Immediately, she is hugged by the other children and the PFC therapist, all of them laughing and congratulating her on her miraculous feat. Fay sees Ha's face beaming as she is embraced, in turn, by each child.

Why hadn't she consoled Dickie like that every time he tried? Fay thinks. The thought is so loaded, so heart-wrenching that Fay has to turn away from Ha and the group. She needs to find Hands.

Down the hall in the prosthetics shop, there's a crowd of Vietnamese men. She watches from the doorway as they huddle around a PFC worker who's drawing crude pictures of limbs on a small blackboard nailed to a ladder. Makeshift wooden shelves along the walls are littered with plastic limbs, just lying there, waiting for their new owners to lose a leg, an arm. Seeing them, Fay immediately wants to get out of there too: The room is too filled with what's missing, what's gone, fake replacements for what can never be retrieved. It looks like a graveyard for broken mannequins. She wants to go back to the other room in spite of the memory of Dickie that it has. At least in that room hope prevails, the limbless walk again, the living dead rise. The prosthetics room, however, reminds her of the hopelessness attached to being an organ donor: You're just waiting for something bad to happen. She has to stay positive. She has to stay focused. A man who saved her once could do it again. There's no telling what he's capable of. Wannabe heroes, Darwin used to tell her, are the easiest marks. They always want to help someone out. She has to find Hands.

At the blackboard, the PFC worker is describing how something called a SACH foot works. Using a chalk stub, the worker writes S-A-C-H. In English and then Vietnamese he says, "Solid" and points to the 'S' on the board. He underlines the 'A.' "Ankle." Circling the 'C,' he recites, "Cushioned," which is followed by "Heel." The class comes to an end and the Vietnamese students file out, shaking their heads over the novelty of it all.

Hands has been up front in the corner the whole time, but

Fay couldn't see him through the crowd. When almost everyone is gone, he moves over to a table where a Vietnamese apprentice is pouring a liquid out of a ripped-in-half soda can. The apprentice, who looks like he's sixteen, pours the thick gel into a funnel that sits on top of a vinyl mold in the shape of a human calf. Hands runs his fingers along the leg, massaging the liquid downward through the supple mold. As the thickness fills and curves the vinyl sleeve into a fully formed calf, Fay stares at his long fingers slowly moving up and down the prosthesis. She remembers those same fingers on her shoulders and for a moment she can feel those hands pulling her up again.

"You should be in bed," Hands calls across the room, startling her. The apprentice empties the soda can, jiggling it a little at the end to get every last remaining drop of gel out.

"What's that?" Fay asks.

"Polyester resin." He touches the apprentice briefly on the shoulder, who lowers the empty can and funnel. "Are you hungry?" he asks Fay. Without waiting for her response, he starts to walk out of the room. She ends up following him, so light-headed she feels like she's just stepped off the swirling teacup ride at a carnival.

Outside, it's pouring. "Here," Hands says, opening an umbrella. Fay doesn't know if she should grab his elbow or not; her usual guidance system is so off-kilter. She ends up holding onto him when they start to slide around in the mud. They walk across the courtyard to the administration wing. A steady wind carries the overwhelming smell of rotting mangos to them. In her fasting state, Fay almost gags on the sugary smell. Hands doesn't say a word the whole time. They head into the administration building. Inside, in a small room, is a long table at which twenty staff—Americans and Vietnamese—are sitting and chowing down bowls of rice with squid and yams. The place smells like a *nuoc mam* factory. In front of each person, there's a small bottle of Coca Cola with a straw sticking out of it. There's a paper plate with a tower of stale cookies. It looks like a child's birthday party. Everyone is talking in Vietnamese, jerking chopsticks from bowl to mouth, the squid, yams, and rice pinched and flung and chewed as the sticks swing rapidly back and forth to the bowls. They're all talking, but Fay can't really hear voices. Everything's muted like the sounds are passing first though a thick pillow before they get to her. Hands sits down at the far end, motioning for her to take a place next to him on the bench. When she slips into the spot, her hearing returns with a flood of sound that's startling. Someone nearby continues to suck on his straw although there's no Coke left in his bottle. Someone else speaks in the fast, high-pitched voice of an accident witness. Two chipped bowls are placed down in front of her and Hands. The smell of the *nuoc mam* envelops her. Suddenly she feels nauseous.

"It's very good," Hands says, motioning with his chopsticks to her bowl. Fay places her fingers on either side of it and immediately knows the rice is already getting cold and the *nuoc mam* is going to taste thick and fishy, like cod liver oil. That's not stopping Hands, who is wolfing down what he's been given. He's got his bowl raised all the way up to his mouth so his chopsticks don't have to travel as far. Fay remembers how Dickie used to eat cereal like that when he was maybe five or six, as if he was worried he'd never get the chance to eat again. Watching Hands, she can imagine what he was like as a child. That's not a good sign. When you start to see a man as the child he was, it usually means you'll end up being asked to sacrifice something.

"You need to eat," Hands says. He's staring at her, his bowl clean and on the table. That's it. There are no seconds, no more entrées. His eyes drift down to her bowl and then up to her eyes. He does it slowly like he's stealing a glance at her legs. "I can't leave until you eat," he says quietly as if he's admitting a dark secret to her.

"Here," Fay says, pushing her bowl toward him, but he nods his head no.

"You're the patient, I'm the doctor." He smiles. "I've got at least ten patients waiting, but I'm sure they'll understand."

There comes a point when you've forgotten why it is you've stopped eating. Whether it was ultimately a failure of faith in yourself or in the world around you, it doesn't matter. Sooner or later the reason's logic, its profoundness, vanishes, sunk by the weight of it, and you either go on fasting out of habit, or you get distracted by something else, something lighter than those dark thoughts you originally had. You turn toward that distraction, like a plant moves toward the sunlight. Before you know it, you've raised your chopsticks, and you eat.

Chapter

FIFTEEN

Hands has a name. Jarvis Pelham.

Fay learns this right before he kisses her. She's almost done eating, *cleaning her plate* as Johnson used to say, when Jarvis runs his fingers through his Jim Morrison hair. He's not as pretty as Morrison. His nose, for one thing, looks like it's been broken a few times. It's flatter than it should be and has a rough bump near the top. Whatever happened, he'd been smacked pretty good. His voice is gentle, though, at odds with that nose and the whole untamed look about him. Studying his face and then hearing that voice is like watching a ferocious lion lick a cub.

"Thank you," he says. She's busy finishing the last gummy mouthful so she can't say anything in response. Standing, the limb maker says, "I'm Jarvis Pelham," and then he leans over and quickly kisses her. It's awkward, the timing is off what with Fay still chewing, and he's there and then gone so fast that she doesn't have time to change anything about it. As he walks away, she's still swallowing her food, that's how fast he was. *Who kisses like that?* Fay thinks. *Who kisses someone with a mouthful of food? Someone who is impatient?* Fay shakes her head and smiles to herself. *Someone who hedges his bets.*

"Oh, I like him all right," Carol from Nodaway tells Fay after she returns from the PFC meal. "Who wouldn't? He's handsome, despite that nose. He's really nice to the patients."

Carol takes down one of the comforters to wash it. Somehow, she's gotten permission to use the laundry up in Eagle Hill, Camp Beecher. Fay lies on her cot, tired out from her first foray outside.

Carol hugs the blanket to her chest. "He had the shit kicked out of him by the Viet Cong. They ambushed him one night outside of town." She shrugs as if she's told Fay he gambles too much.

The news makes Fay sit up. "So?" she says slowly. She wants to keep Carol talking. She knew the first time she saw Jarvis's nose that there was a story behind it. At least she was *hoping* there was a story behind it.

"How come they let him go?" Carol asks brusquely, ramming a tack back into the now empty wall. "Why didn't they nail his ass?"

Fay stands and walks over to the doorway. The rain glitters as it falls. It reminds her of one of those beaded doorway curtains. A breeze is coming in and she gathers her hair on top of her head. Her neck tingles. It's a neurological injury, a consequence of her contorting her body in extreme positions in the tank. The tingling often happens when she jams on the car brakes to avoid colliding with a car in front of her. It's a sign to be careful. At the doorway, she sees Chuck stride across the Pit wearing his rainproof duster, leading a small furry monkey who's on a leash.

Fay waits a beat, and then turning to Carol, asks, "What are you getting at?"

Carol folds up the comforter and puts it on a pile on top of her cot. Then she walks over to another hanging one. "All I'm saying is . . . one night he's gone. The next morning he's back here, his face a mess. The next week he's back on the floor, working on patients as if nothing's happened. The bandages weren't even off yet."

"Maybe he told them he's a pacifist and worked here," Fay says as evenly as possible. She's sure, however, that there's more to Jarvis Pelham than this. He's probably not who he pretends to be at all, at least she hopes so. Carol unpins the next comforter.

"They'd let him go if he told them he worked here and helped *their* children. He must've told them," she tells Carol, who shakes her head in disbelief.

"Why was his face bashed in then? Second of all . . ." Carol holds up two fingers. "What was he doing outside of town? He rode his bike home. Why didn't they steal the bike after they walloped the shit outta him?" A third finger joins the other two, like a Girl Scout pledge. "I don't care if he was Ho Chi Minh. They don't let *anyone* go." She calmly folds another comforter for the laundry pile. "Unless he's playing both sides."

Fay's pulse quickens with every piece of information that Carol feeds her. If Jarvis was out at night, he was up to no good. He was probably playing both sides. This seals it for Fay: Jarvis is the one she needs.

The next morning, Fay is back at the tank, preparing to do a practice run. She needs to work to make money, no matter how little. There's not much choice in the matter. Ginny has already coiled the chain on the stage. Chuck is there also, making sure Fay goes through with it.

"Since when do we have sick days?" he says to her. He gives her a quick smack on her butt as he walks by. "You need some meat on you," he calls over his shoulder.

"Don't listen to him, honey," Ginny mutters, handing Fay a tin cup of Vietnamese coffee. "He's just worried he picked up rabies from that dog he screwed last night."

After not eating for so long the coffee is too strong for Fay. She drinks it anyway. Ginny always shovels in the sugar the Vietnamese way to cut the taste.

"You all right?" Ginny asks, searching Fay's face for an honest answer.

"Never better," Fay tells her and, handing back the cup, she slips past her toward the tank. The kids aren't there yet; the show's not for another four hours. She wants to take a quick dip to get back on track. Carol's news about Jarvis has given her something to latch onto. She wants to return to her routine.

The water is swampy-looking, from sitting stagnant for four days, the surface thick with dead beetles, like a pond in backwoods country. It's the same kind of pond Fay brought Dickie to when they were traveling. He'd sit in the mud close to the shoreline to cool off after the day's heat at one fair or another. For years he begged Fay for swimming lessons, but she couldn't get past the image of Dickie flailing away, his deadweight legs trailing in the water, his body eventually being dragged downward from gravity's pull. She'd slept with a lifeguard one time and knew from him what the result would be. "If he can't keep his hips on top of the surface, he loses flotation," he'd said. "If he loses flotation, well . . . you do the math."

In the distance, the high mountains are cloaked with the densest mist Fay has ever seen. Living in the Keys, she was used to an ocean fog rolling in for a quick morning cover. This fog she's seeing now is more along the lines of a National Geographic photograph that Dickie showed her one time while they were in the waiting room at his doctor's office. "Check out the gorillas," he told her that day. She hears his voice all the time now. What had caught Fay's eye wasn't the gorillas, though, it was the mist surrounding those apes and the trees they squatted by. It was eerie, supernatural, as if it had risen from beneath the dirt, bringing with it the buried souls of people. A mist like that could suffocate you before going back to the hell it came from.

"Maybe you should wait on this," Ginny says, her fingertips on Fay's elbow. A week ago, that would've sent her to her knees. A week ago, she might've given in to what she really feels for Ginny. Today it just seems as if Ginny is holding her back from what she must do. Ginny has never understood how Fay has to use men like Johnson or Chuck or now, Jarvis, to get someplace else. She could never use Ginny for that. She could never *use* Ginny. Full stop.

"I'm fine." She shakes Ginny's hand off and then suddenly the mountains entirely disappear from view under the encroaching cloak. "Help me with the bugs." They both climb up and perch on the mini plywood platform at the tank's top. Beetles form a black lid across the water. They're shell-against-shell, no room for them to move their back legs, to navigate the surface, to graze on gnats. They're drowning in their own imprisonment.

Fay wants to tell them, "I know the feeling." Instead, to keep it lighthearted, she says, "I should've been a juggler." Ginny doesn't laugh. She's flipping the beetles out with a small stick.

"Look, Vietnamese water polo," Fay adds, but Ginny still doesn't laugh. Fay doesn't really want to be cracking jokes, she just can't stop herself. Her nerves are shot. The tank no longer is a silo to her. It's a coffin. Yet, the absurd thought remains that Jarvis can fix everything somehow.

"Carol thinks Jarvis is some kind of spy," Fay says, trying out the words, wanting to know if Ginny knows anything, watching her face, which suddenly relaxes.

"Carol? The woman who pins up comforters in a closet of plywood while *bombs* are falling? Now there's a reliable source." Ginny retrieves the chain so that she can loop it around her.

"I'm going in first without it," Fay says and slips into the water to avoid having Ginny touch her again. In the tank, she keeps her face above the swampy surface for a moment. There's nothing Ginny can do except drop the chain back on the platform with a clunk.

The water feels warmer to Fay, thicker, as if those days that it sat untouched have allowed it to gel into something more substantial, something you can seemingly count on. For a moment Fay isn't sure if the water is safe or not.

"What's the matter?" Ginny asks.

Her head still above the surface, Fay looks across the field toward the compound. There are medical personnel striding with purpose across the far courtyard. A skinny Vietnamese father carries his wounded son toward the outstretched arms of a rushing nurse. Fay thinks how everyone but her is doing things that actually matter. Actually saving lives.

"Two minutes," she says. Before she can give it another thought, she closes her eyes and goes completely under. She waves her hands back and forth in the water so that her filled lungs don't act as buoys and spring her to the surface again. The warm water moves and eddies around her hands, her fingers. Fay thinks about the man carrying his son into the clinic. How many miles had he carried him? That's been the problem all along. There's been nothing at stake. Sure, she wanted to get home, but really, what had she given up for it? All she'd done so far was whine about it, try a bit of attempted robbery on Chuck's trunk, and then a slight nick on her leg. An air bubble escapes through her lips. Then another. Ginny bangs on the side of the tank. Time's up. Despite what Fay warned Dickie never to do in the tank—to think because if you think you're as good as dead—Fay allows her thoughts to turn to Tom Thorne, to the bridge blowers. And then her thoughts float to Chuck. Suddenly, all of them have become one. And what's Jarvis Pelham's story? Before she can think that through, her body intuitively senses that the time limit is being breached, and her hands switch automatically into survival mode, pulling and pushing at the water to propel her upward. As she surfaces and is finally able to breathe in air, she knows what she must do.

Fay waits for Jarvis in the dark, crouched under a plastic tarp covering old bicycles that lean against the house he shares nearby with the other PFC workers. Although it's around four in the morning and the monsoons haven't let off, there is traffic on the street: waterlogged bicyclists starting out early for a long ride to another town's market and drenched walkers making their way home from the bars and restaurants where they wait on and bus tables. Unlike Fay, they have no curfew. They are free to travel as they please, as they risk. Free to live and die as they please.

At last she sees him. Head bowed under an umbrella, he's walking the fast walk of someone who has been up all night and can't wait to get home. Throwing off the tarp, she stands as he reaches the front door.

"Come inside," he hisses at her, and for a minute she's worried that he's mad at her. She shouldn't make him angry; she knows that much from Chuck and Johnson, from the marks she's conned. You can appeal to their sympathy, to their wanting to protect, their sense of loyalty. But if you anger them, you lose everything.

Inside he cups her face in his strong hands and says, "You could've been seen," and she realizes the best of all possible things has happened. He isn't mad. He's concerned for her safety.

"I had to," she says, leaving it to him to wonder what that something is that she had to do. Guesswork keeps them hooked. It's the wanting to figure it out before anyone else does that keeps the audience's egos invested.

"You're soaking," he says, touching her wet cheek. "Follow me," he whispers, and Fay does, down the hallway and into a small room where Jarvis somehow finds a kerosene army surplus lamp and, striking a match, lights it, sending the room into high definition. Fay takes it all in from just inside the door: the twin bed, the solitary wooden chair and small table on which there are books, a non la, a half empty bottle of Wild Turkey, two dented tin cups, cleaned and turned over on a dish towel, and a game of solitaire that Fay immediately calculates is stalled permanently. There's no play left for any of the four columns of cards. Fay records everything and knows more about Jarvis Pelham in that moment than she could learn by talking to him for an hour. He's a loner and lonely. The cards tell her he's the type of man who doesn't give up easily, a man who finds it difficult to accept defeat. A man who believes in the underdog, in miracles. Yet, he's a lightweight. Someone who isn't totally comfortable drowning his sorrows. Someone who can walk away from a half bottle, taking the time to wash out his cup so that's it ready for the one or two drinks he'll have the next day when he returns to his lonely room. Her eyes go back to the non la and she imagines herself standing in front of Jarvis Pelham, naked except for that bamboo conical hat on her head. She'll be able to get him to do whatever she pleases. She hasn't felt this good since she left Key West.

Behind her, Jarvis closes the door without a sound. At the table, he unscrews the bourbon, pours two drinks into the tin cups. "This will warm you up." He hands her one and drinks his in one long drain. He can't pull it off. He coughs. *Good*, Fay thinks, and throws hers back easily, knowing that she'll be able to match him drink for drink and then some. If there's one thing she can do, it's go head-to-head.

He splashes out two more and these they drink as quickly as the first, only this time after he coughs, he touches his battered nose. *That's his tell*, she thinks, making a mental note of the gesture. Every mark has a tell, every card player a revealing gesture.

"I wouldn't have come but I didn't know who else I could turn to."

As he cups his hand around her neck and pulls her toward him, Fay imagines that those bridge and tunnel guys won't know what hit them. She's already imagining herself as she boards a plane for The World, for home, for Dickie. Strapping herself in. Looking out the window—no she won't do that. She won't look back.

Jarvis unbuttons her shirt like he's making a surgical incision:

quickly and efficiently. With her shirt still on, his index and middle fingers carve a line straight down from under her chin until he reaches the exact middle between her breasts. In spite of herself, Fay feels as if she's been cracked open. It's been so long since anyone touched her, she shudders inadvertently from the sheer skill of it. Maybe she was wrong about him. Maybe he won't be so easy after all. He's a physician. He's been trained to keep his emotions flat-lined. And there was that oddly timed kiss at lunch, as if he wanted to keep her off-balance. Now she wonders if it was too obviously calculated and a bit too heavy-handed. Like a boy who pretends to yawn so that he can throw his arm around the back of your chair in the movie theater. He's younger than she is by a couple of years. He might not have hit thirty yet. He must've come here straight from his last residency.

"Cold?" Jarvis whispers and begins to kiss her neck.

Because her neck is the first place that he kisses her, Fay lifts his head away from it by grabbing his thick hair. He tries to return to the same spot as she knew he would, they always do, but she's resistant, wrenching his head away by yanking harder this time on his long locks, making sure he knows she's not messing around. The first step to controlling them is this: Whatever they want, make them think it's more important to them than it really is.

"You can't have my neck . . . yet," she whispers. Then she sucks his nose, his broken, battered nose, gently into her mouth. It's meant to confuse him—it's a Chuck move—and Fay can tell by the way Jarvis's body stiffens that it's worked. He doesn't know if he likes it or not. There's something soothing about it and yet, at the same time, it seems somehow perverse and maybe a kind of punishment.

He pushes her away, but more gently than she expected. Another sign that maybe she was right after all, he wants to be nice to her. She can use that. "Anyone can be nice," she used to tell

Dickie. "But few take advantage of it." Jarvis's hands reach out and start to knead her stomach like he's massaging out a knot. Every nerve on Fay's skin is alert now, but no longer out of pleasure. Duty has kicked in, years of conning men into doing something that was, in the end, only for her gain. Her built-in radar readies itself for picking up on the slightest physical hesitation that might show a weakness, a soft spot, a hole in a tooth where the filling has broken down.

She grabs his shirt on either side of the buttoned front and with a wrench, breaks all of the buttons off in one fell swoop. It's an old shirt so it doesn't take much to make it useless. Jarvis moans and Fay can tell that he's into the more experienced woman thing. He wants *her* to show him around. She pushes him onto the twin bed with its perfectly pulled up sheet, the corners of which are folded and tucked in hospital style. *I'm going to have to break him of that*, she thinks.

Afterward, he falls asleep immediately, although he's a light sleeper and wakes up as soon as she moves off the bed. She ticks this into her memory like the date of a birthday. She knows from her father that doctors are notoriously good sleepers. Years of residency, on call twenty-four hours a day, trains them to fall asleep at the slightest opportunity and to sleep heavily for those few minutes they're able to grab between emergencies. Jarvis doesn't have that same ability. Something keeps him on the surface. Something is eating at him.

"Where are you going?" he murmurs and tries to sit up, but she pushes him down, ordering, "Go back to sleep." Before he can protest, she's shimmying her clothes on, slipping through the bedroom door, and is gone.

Chapter

SIXTEEN

At the next show the kids in the audience are subdued, quiet. It's like they don't know how to behave without the rain coming down. One boy in the front row keeps jerking his shoulder up and down, still getting used to his new harness. All the others are just sitting still. After her night with Jarvis, Fay feels refreshed, although the eeriness of the silent children now threatens to put the kibosh on that. They're still waiting to see if she'll screw up again in the tank. Maybe they like seeing someone else struggle for a change. *We'll see about that*, she thinks.

On the platform she waves her hands down the front of her body and then down her sides to show that there are no tricks here, just a woman in a bikini that says stars and stripes forever. One of the children shouts out something in Vietnamese, but the voice is too high-pitched, the words too fast for Fay to understand. Ginny raises her right hand and, leaning down from the waist, picks up the chain on the plywood. The children start clapping, at least the ones with two hands. The ones who can't simply shout on top of each other.

"Focus," Ginny mutters under her breath as she wraps the chain across Fay's midriff. Today she's measured it perfectly. There's enough give so that the beginning link is easily married with the end link by Fay's waist. The children start to murmur.

They don't really want to see her get into trouble. Ginny clicks the lock on the chain. Smiling, Fay pretends to hold her nose between her cuffed hands. She plunges feet first into the water. The last thing she hears before she goes under is the children yelling out, "No! No!" They are *hers*. She's back on top.

That night, around eleven, she heads for Jarvis Pelham's room before he gets there. Fay wants to catch him in the act of coming home. *This must be what a wife feels like when her husband is cheating*, she thinks as she waits, and laughs at her own joke. She needs to discover what his routine is. She's certain he has one if what she and Carol from Nodaway suspect is true, that he's playing both sides. She needs proof, though. Proof that will give her something to barter with. He seems a careful man. Will that be his downfall? In order for a scam to work you must be flexible, ready for anything. You can't be rigid. If she can follow him and see who he meets at night, she can persuade him to help her. Those bridge and tunnel guys—Chuck—will be there watching her in Long Bihn, mesmerized by what they're missing from home. Their wallets will be chock full. What else do they have to spend their money on? All Jarvis Pelham will have to do is have a small group of his Commie friends bust into the officers' mess and, surrounding the dazed bridge and tunnel guys, demand their money. Chuck will try to protest and confront them. Fay knows this as surely as she believes she'll be seeing her son soon. Jarvis's friends will shoot Chuck as a sign that they mean business and won't take any guff. Fay will simply stay in the tank, looking increasingly alarmed, until the Commies leave.

Sneaking into Jarvis's room unnoticed is easy. She knew the front door would be unlocked. The building is operated by the pacifists. They trust everyone.

Once inside his room, in the dark, she pours herself a glass of the bourbon to keep herself awake. Then she gets undressed, crawls under the sheet, and waits.

Two hours later she can hear his sandals running lightly on the road leading to the house, the soft sucking sounds of his rubber soles sticking to mud, and then the door closing quietly behind him. Like Fay, he doesn't turn on any lights. He walks straight to the booze. She hears the bourbon sloshing into the glass, hears him drinking it down too fast—one swallow so she knows it's a short one—and he pours another. *What have you been up to?* she thinks, but asks, "How was your day, honey?"

He wants her neck again and once more she won't let him. Her neck has become holy. It's the forbidden fruit of Eden. Fay can feel it every time he groans when she yanks his head away. "Goddammit," Jarvis mutters. He gets up and pours himself another drink.

"Thanks." She holds out her glass in the darkness.

A rumbling starts up in the distance. It's midnight and they're naked and nowhere near a bunker. So, Fay does what she learned from Carol from Nodaway. She takes Jarvis's hand and says, "Under the bed. Now!" As soon as they are both safe under there, Fay angles her face toward his and in her most soothing voice says, "Was the hospital busy, honey? I looked for you, but you weren't there."

She wants to press him a bit, see what makes him uncomfortable. Dig a thumb behind a shoulder blade. Then they hear something else. Rain. It hasn't been missile fire at all. It's thunder. It's a freak storm. The monsoon should've been over by now.

Jarvis rolls out from under the bed to look out the window, but it's too dark out to see anything. Fay crawls out from underneath the bed and gets on top of the sheet again.

"Hey, remember me?" she says. Jarvis turns from the window. The rain is deafening. "Come here."

When he returns to the bed, he tries to move on top of her, but she quickly flips him over and straddles him, slipping his dick into her. She loves the fullness of that initial insertion, the hardness coupled with her own interior softness forming a cuff. The sheer control of it. She starts to move slowly. A sound escapes him. A mewing sound that she can tell he'd prefer to keep hidden from her. She stops moving. Leans over and kisses his face softly again and again, inching her way toward its center. Before Jarvis can stop himself, he tugs on her hips. He wants her to keep moving.

"What happened to your nose?" she murmurs as she grazes his nose with her lips and starts up again. Slowly. She kisses his nose each time on the down movement. Pulling him up to a sitting position, she directs his face to her neck as she bobs up and down. She finally lets him kiss her neck and he lets out that mewing sound again. Immediately after he comes, she whispers, "What happened to your nose?" She lies down on top of him, making sure that he stays put.

He begins to hesitantly tell her his story in general terms. How he was captured. How they broke his nose with a big stick.

"I don't really remember very much," he tells her.

The generalities irritate Fay. She starts to feel the crush of time now that she's stopped fucking him. He could be dead by tomorrow and she'll be left with nothing to barter with. She'll be one of those people on *Let's Make a Deal* who have traded in a sure thing, a new stove, for whatever is behind the curtain where Carol Merrill is standing, only to find out that there is nothing behind the curtain but a game of Twister.

"Somehow I don't believe you," Fay says and, pushing off his chest, quickly swings her legs over the edge of the mattress, her back to him.

"I don't." His voice breaks a little like he's about to cry. "I woke up under the same exact tree where they got me."

Fay looks at him over her shoulder. "See, you do remember some things. Look, whatever you did to get out of there, it's okay," she says softly, facing him. "And whatever it is you promised you'd keep doing now, that's okay too."

He sits up. "What are you talking about?"

"You just better be more careful. If I've figured it out, someone else will. This has to be our secret." She rests her hand on his inner thigh.

"I have no idea what you're talking about," he says defensively. Standing, he walks to the table and pours a drink. Fay reads his agitation to mean he needs more coaxing, that he's unable to come right out with it. Dickie couldn't lie for a hill of beans either. She'd end up confronting Dickie with what he'd done and as soon as she did, Dickie would fold, admitting everything, relieved as all get out.

"I want to meet them," she tells Jarvis and, sliding off the bed, joins him by the table.

He spins around to face her. "Who?" he asks, although Fay can see even in the dark that his face is registering something she wasn't expecting. Distaste? Horror? What she hinted to him is starting to worm its way through his face like some kind of parasite. Still, she won't be diverted from what she wants.

"I have a job for them." She taps his nose. "The next time you meet them, I want to go with you."

"You think I *meet* them?" Jarvis's voice rises.

Fay's hand drops. She steps back. "Shit. Goddammit."

Trudging along the rain-swept road back to the compound, she's passed by a black sedan driving in the opposite direction which then abruptly stops a few feet past her. The gearshift is thrown into reverse and the car backs up, keeping pace with her. She's wearing one of Jarvis's rain ponchos—it's orange, hard to miss.

The rain is coming down so fast it's like you're looking through a waterfall. The car means nothing to Fay, her thoughts are still focused on her total fuckup with Jarvis. She left as soon as she realized she'd read him all wrong. He wasn't collaborating with the VC. He wasn't a spy. He wasn't going to help her. She couldn't even ask him for a *loan* now, let alone to help her with the bridge and tunnel boys. He'll want nothing to do with her. She's been on a losing streak for eight months and this is the hand that has finally shut her down.

The sedan's passenger window is rolled down and there's Chuck, and driving, Thorne. It was only a matter of time before they formed a merger.

"Wanna lift?" Chuck shouts to her. "We've cancelled the show."

Fay stops. Her feet in her flip-flops are soaked and stained from the water running off the orange-red clay dirt. It looks vaguely like blood to her. The car idles next to her in the drenching rain. In front of the car, an old man crosses the street, the non la on his head soaked and collapsing.

Thorne leans forward over the wheel. "Have a drink with us."

Fay shakes her head, starts to walk away.

"We're on for this Friday," Thorne shouts after her. "Three o'clock on the strip."

Halfway home, Fay slips on the wet clay, falls to one knee, but quickly struggles to her feet to keep going. She wonders if she were mugged, would she feel as beaten up?

Chapter

SEVENTEEN

Thorne is waiting on the tarmac. The C-130 is in the distance. Crouching behind a row of empty oil barrels that sit outside the hanger, Fay watches him. She's not ready yet to begin the journey to Long Bihn, not ready to commit to what might be a disastrous show in front of those bridge and tunnel guys. She hides as if she is playing hide and seek with Dickie.

A few men run around the plane, shouting instructions at each other, while dry asphalt streams down a metal trough from the plane's cargo doors to the bed of a dump truck. Thorne is dressed in an extra-large green poncho that's flat against his heavy body, as if he's prepared for another freak storm.

The last of the asphalt trickles into the truck. Someone drives the truck away. It flies past Thorne as if he's a statue. He doesn't budge. Sitting where she is, hidden, Fay knows she has a choice here. She can turn around right now. Go back. Find another way. But there is no other way. Her whole life she's wanted a different life, and each time it's ended worse than it started. Will she choose correctly this time? This one time?

She stands, comes out from behind the cans. Chuck is there then, striding to Fay like they're old friends. That very morning, he confronted her in her hootch. Carol was gone because the boys in the field must be entertained. Fay had just returned from the mess hall where she hadn't been able to get down anything except weak tea, her appetite jangled by wondering what Jarvis would do and the thought of doing a show naked for the bridge and tunnel guys.

When she walked through the hootch door, Chuck was already sitting on her cot, furiously shooting peanuts into his mouth. "You wanna tell me something, sweetheart?"

Fay bent over, ran a towel down her legs as if they were sweaty to ground herself. "The tank water's gonna need replacing. The trees are dropping all kinds of shit into it."

"I was thinking something else." Another peanut flew from his fist into his mouth. "That friend of yours, Thorne is it? He's got some funny ideas."

"I was going to tell you." Nervous, Fay rubbed her hair with the towel. There was something in the motion that kept her calm despite Chuck's presence and her rising conviction that nothing was going to go well from here on out.

"Uh huh." Chuck smiled. His gold tooth seemed to gleam more than ever. Standing, he moved closer to her. "When was that?"

Fay lowered the towel. "I wanted to think about it. They want me butt-naked."

Immediately, Chuck grabbed her arm hard and Fay was instantly jammed up, unable to move. "I know what you're up to," he spat. He shoved her away and laughed. "I know when you miss a breath. Sabe Chiquita?"

She wondered if he *could* hear her breath then, the jumpy inconsistency of it as her heart clattered on and on, hooves on pavement. Then, suddenly, Tina was there, calling "You hoo," a hula-hoop resting on her neck like a pearl necklace over her yellow slicker. Wonderful, stupid Tina.

Without a word, Chuck started to walk toward the door, but then he stopped. "They better be prepared to pay for it," he warned before he left altogether.

Now Chuck is on the tarmac, making sure of that. Despite

the warm weather, he's wearing his big black duster coat, which he'd won in a card game in a small town in Nebraska. Fay always thought he looked ridiculous in it. Like he was in search of a lost horse. He's waving his arms at Thorne, stressing some point that undoubtedly is about money. Thorne shouts to the crew of men on the tarmac. They run over to an army convoy truck, normally used to hustle grunts to hotbeds of activity, and haul out Fay's empty tank from the back. Then, they carry it, like a coffin, toward the C-130.

The officers' club at Long Bihn is not what Fay expected. It's brightly lit for one thing. Rows of fluorescent lights, running off a generator, cover the ceiling. A bar is set up alongside one side of the cement block building, a waist-high docking station with men perching on stools. It's an oven in there, the heat contained and stagnated by the sheer number of men. Fay knows immediately that there are more than the agreed to thirty officers in the room, knows that word has leaked out, that she has chosen the wrong street once again. She can't see past the bar. There must be two hundred men.

Chuck shoves and curses his way through the crowd. Behind him, six grunts carry the tank over their heads. Thorne brings up the rear, the men clapping his shoulders overly hard, which doesn't deter him. He grabs Fay's elbow and steers her forward through the men who are already too close, already shouting and catcalling and getting up in her face with big smiles and winks and whistles. She's being crushed to death. Smothered. Voices shout. *Come on baby. Show us what you got. I'm the man of your dreams. Give it to me.* Fay feels as if she's swallowing herself: her head, her shoulders, her breasts being consumed so that every part of her ends up hiding in her belly. She's become one of those rain ponchos that you fold and fold, finally tucking it into a pouch made from itself.

But Thorne doesn't lose his grip on her elbow as he miraculously pushes them through. And then there's a clearing. A rope, thin as a ribbon, marks the "stage area." It's tied at each end to the handles of two mops stuck in metal buckets filled with cement. It couldn't hold a flock of lambs back. Fay takes it all in: the tank installed on the edge of a plywood platform, high enough for everyone to get a birds-eye view. Chuck holding a fire hose, filling the tank in record time. Through a side double door, more grunts bully their way into the crowd by rolling in a wooden scaffolding—the type used by interior painters. At the two ends of the scaffolding, a series of rungs can be used to climb up. The scaffolding is at the height of the top of the tank. The name of Thorne's construction firm is imprinted in large block lettering on the side of it.

"You all right?" he shouts into Fay's face. She barely notices him. She's retreated. Left the premises. Someone else can take over now.

"The price has gone up, Thorne," Chuck yells, joining them. "Where's the goddamn security? My livelihood needs to be protected here."

"Where are the seats?" Fay asks, but her voice falters and no one can hear her over the shouting. Thorne is removing her jeans jacket. There's such a racket Fay can't think straight so she doesn't even realize what he's doing. It's as if she's been drugged, the clamor is so loud and disorienting.

"You'll get your money," Thorne barks at Chuck.

The crowd presses against the thin rope. They raise cans of beer, plastic cups, and fists to her, shouting God knows what. The officers' club has become Babylon, a hundred radios turned to different stations. Two grunts enter the roped off area and drop Fay's chain on the ground. Although it's still crazy noisy, Fay hears the familiar sound of the heavy metal links clunking against the floor and there's something in that sound that finally wakes her out of her stupor. A grunt falls over the rope, jostled by his friends.

"Get him the hell out of here," Fay shouts.

Using his thick leg muscles, Thorne practically shot-puts the grunt in the air. He's revved up, his strength doubling with adrenaline. Shoving his index finger and pinky into his mouth, he lets out a shrill whistle. The noise of the mob drops off a cliff.

"That's better," Thorne says. He holds up his hands. "Gentlemen, please conduct yourself with the integrity you were not born with," he says loudly. A few of the grunts whistle at him.

Fay and Chuck stand side-by-side below the tank. She won't get up on the platform just yet. She wants to see what she's dealing with. The front two rows are the important ones. They can stop a surge and set the tone. Twenty or so officers have found their way up front, forcing the grunts to back up. *Good*, Fay thinks. Her eyes go down the line of officers, measuring their faces for signs of aggression, for a tightness spurred on by adrenaline and their not having fucked their wives or girlfriends for the better part of a year.

"Gentlemen," Thorne shouts, "you have no idea what you're about to witness."

Fay notices that a few of the officers are as old as her father. They are lifers who are here because they know how to take down a bridge with the least amount of ammunition, how to hunt down the most agile tunnel rats. They may have a daughter her age. *Good.* Most of the officers, though, are around Fay's age or younger.

"I bring you the queen of the carneys!" Thorne shouts. He holds up one hand high in the air. The group starts to clap. Fay brushes her hair away from her cheek.

"I bring you the female Houdini!" There's a return volley of collective shouting from the men.

Fay isn't listening to Thorne. Instead she still focuses on each of the men in the front row, waiting until each smiles at her before moving on to the next one.

"I bring you Woman in all of her glory!"

The crowd roars now. They have won the jackpot.

"No one's gonna lay a finger—" Chuck yells in her ear, his fingers lightly touching her shoulder. Although the rest is cut off by the uproar, Fay hears the important part. She chokes on the unexpected sweetness of it as if she's bitten into a bruised fruit that looks rotten but tastes sugary. Her eyes well. She is overwhelmed with gratitude. It's a feeling she's hardly felt in her life and not for a long time for Chuck. It confuses her. There's too much going on, though, for her to stick with it for very long. The men are getting more riled up. Two of the officers, a pair of the older ones who could be her father, are clapping their hands over their heads and jerking their pelvises to the rhythm. Quickly the clapping floods through the room, picking up more and more converts as it crescendos toward the back. The men's hands swing up from their hips to above their heads as if they are doing half-jumping jacks, their hands smacking together to a thunderous clap. Fay can't take her eyes off the two officers who started it, their exaggerated thrusting pelvises. They're whistling teapots. The heated air before someone raises a fist and hits his wife.

Chuck calls over to her, but she can't make out what he's saying. He's already busying himself with the chain, coiling it like a garden hose over his shoulder so that it can be brought up to the top of the scaffolding. Thorne's voice is in her ear, saying, "You ready?" and mechanically, Fay begins to take her clothes off. She unsnaps her hot pants and slides the purple velour waistband past her slim hips. She'd bought them in Woodstock, New York, when the Humans had been putting on a show in nearby Poughkeepsie. They'd reminded her of Jimmy Hendrix. Now they just look trashy, like something you'd see a prostitute wearing.

Thorne steps in front of her, his bulk blocking the best view. There's some loud booing at that, but he flashes his best smile at the boys and pretends to steal a glance at Fay and the boos seem to flip into more jovial, good-natured shouting and yelling, the kind you'd hear at a football game. When Fay, naked, moves from behind Thorne to the scaffold ladder, a deafening silence falls. It reminds Fay of the quiet in the bunkers every night right before the shit starts falling.

"Fay! Get the hell up there!" Chuck's voice reaches her. The volume is turned up again. A plastic cup hits the tank and bounces off. The clapping starts anew, whistles come one on top of another, like harsh mating calls in the jungle. Fay's Scotch-taped the lock's key to her pubic hairs. It snags and tugs as she climbs the scaffolding rungs upward. Chuck is right behind her, with the chain. Fay wonders how she would've done this without him, and she laughs at the novelty of Chuck coming to her rescue. *Chuck, for God's sake.* What had she been thinking?

Thorne has moved to the side for a better view for himself. The clapping and catcalling is full force now. The two officers have stopped their gyrating, their heads angled back so they can take her in, but that seems more troublesome to Fay, something *really* to be scared of. She'd rather have them busy, moving, than focused so intently on her, studying *her.* They are expert watchers. Through binoculars, they observe the enemy march slowly over a bridge, waiting until the right moment of maximum exposure and then blowing them to bits without so much as a sigh. As they take her in, Fay is certain they can see her entire history. *They know about Dickie. They know she will do anything to make it right again.* Her stomach tightens. As she stands naked on the platform, her fingers tremble against her thighs. Despite the pressing heat of the room, her nipples are painfully hard, and she fights a tremendous urge to cross her arms. *Give them a little of what they want. Not everything. Just a little*, she hears Darwin's encouragement. Her body relaxes a little, but not much. She can't look at the two officers anymore. They've assumed the military poses they take right before they're about to give the command to blow the bridge: crossed arms, stiff chins ready for the final nod, the go-ahead. Attack, attack. *Don't look.*

Suddenly, Chuck's face is three inches from her own. He winds the chain around Fay, loose, as if he's always been part of the act, knows the importance of it being kept slack so that she can easily reach the key with her handcuffed hands. Chuck knows his business. The thought of that settles her down some. They're professionals. They know what they're doing. When he clicks the lock shut, he leans in and winks at her.

"After this is all over, we'll get us that fishing boat I always talked about. We'll go home." He glances to the crowd and then back to her. "Piece of cake, Chiquita," he shouts into her face. But then he turns away, takes in the full crowd below, and Fay knows immediately he's already thinking of what happens after. How will they get through that crowd again? *Will* they?

"Can't be worse than Detroit," she lies, and forces a smile. He smiles back, his gold tooth almost blue in the fluorescent lighting. She knows they both have the same image in their mind's eye: Marjorie half-man, half-woman, being dragged from her booth by a bunch of speed-freaked college boys, her clothes being torn, Chuck and the others spilling out of the tents to save her. Marjorie lost her voice for two weeks from screaming so wretchedly. Chuck ended up with a broken jaw.

He rubs his jaw now with the memory and nods his head in the direction of the boys. "Fuck 'em. They're a bunch of pansies," he yells in her ear and starts to help her hop over to the lip of the tank, her body a cocoon of chain links.

And then, she's in. As soon as she's submerged in the water, her heart slows. *This is what you have. This is what you are.* She smoothly angles herself around, away from their eyes. The level of noise outside rises, but she doesn't care. They're angry. They paid their money and they want to see full frontal dammit. *Fuck you,* she thinks, her eyes closed, her fingers already pulling the key free, the sting of her small hairs being wrenched, a wake-up call. She slips the key in the gate and the handcuffs spring open. She turns around to her audience and opens her eyes. She must stay focused, on patrol, for the next few minutes. An officer is grabbing the sides of his head with two massive hands, his mouth dropping open. Fay imagines him doing the same gesture when explosives blast his convoy truck to kingdom come.

In the water, she shimmies her shoulders out of the chain. The men begin to shout numbers, counting the seconds. Thirty. Thirty-one. Thirty-two. For the moment, they are back in this together. They don't want a dead woman on their hands, not after the bridges they explode, the villages they demolition. They're her brothers now, her boyfriends, her husbands. Forty. Forty-one. She maneuvers around, takes her time unraveling the chain past her breasts. Let them get their money's worth. The chain floats from her chest. Her excitement from the show being almost finished makes the water feel colder on her nipples. Her breasts have always been her come-on feature, full and upright, beckoning. Sixty-one. The men are stomping their boots so hard on the ground below that the tank shakes on the cement blocks. They're pulling for her. Sixty-seven. *They're good boys.* She swipes the chain past her hips, her dirty blond thatch. Eighty-one. *Dickie. I'm doing this for Dickie.* Down past her thighs, tight against each other and shaking in anticipation. Ninety-three. Her slender ankles. One foot slips out, then the other.

She's free and clear, surfacing out of the tank in just a minute and a half. Chuck thrusts his hand at her and she takes it. He yanks her so hard that she practically catapults onto the scaffolding. Shaking her hair, the water in her ears slides and she's greeted with a tremendous rush of noise, an overwhelming shouting that rips at the seams of the building and rattles the bottles of booze at the bar. Anarchy erupts. The men suddenly feel how hot the room really is; their shirts are sticking to them, the air is suffocating. All that money, over in two minutes. We've been gypped. On the scaffolding, Fay is wet and naked and every man in the place is taking her in, their goodwill flying out the door like feeding bats. Chuck quickly wraps her in his duster.

That ratchets up the level of hysteria. A couple of grunts, chests the size of refrigerators, break through the rope. They quickly move to the rungs leading up.

"Thorne!" Chuck yells from the center of the platform where he holds Fay, his head pivoting this way and that, scoping out an escape route. "Thorne!" He lets Fay go, readying himself because Thorne is nowhere to be seen. Fay scans the crowd. Her legs are shaking. She can't stop them from shaking. *Fuck.* For a split second she looks at the tank and imagines jumping back into the safety of the water.

The first grunt grabs the top of the scaffolding with his fingers. His face, covered with acne from the horse he's been shooting up for the past five months, appears like a jack-in-the-box. But Chuck is already there, stomping on his thick fingers. The grunt screams as Chuck kicks him in the face. He falls back on the uniform below him. The two men lose their footing and slide down to the crowd below.

"There!" Fay screams at Chuck. "There he is!"

And Thorne *is* there. He's working his way down one side of the room with his construction team. There must be fifty of them and some MPs to boot, each of them carrying baseball bats courtesy of the US of A. Thorne must've had them waiting outside.

Over the months he's become the master of being prepared for trouble: defective cement that won't harden in the overwhelming heat, the Vietnamese stealing his trucks for the black market. He's solved it all. Another stream of his guys, baseball bats in their hands, comes down the opposite side of the room. The two lines of his thugs shove every grunt toward the center, squeezing them from both sides toward the middle, like a funnel, displacing their leverage and forcing them to fight against themselves. There's nowhere for them to go but out the front doors. They're smashed and turned and pinned against each other, their bodies moving uncontrollably against the mob's thrust.

The crowd by the scaffold is diverted momentarily by this spectacle behind them. Chuck grabs Fay, hustling her to the ladder. The waxed oilskin of his duster rubs painfully against her nakedness. One side tugs especially with a heaviness as she rushes down rung after rung. Suddenly, something yanks at her ankle from below. She slips. Her bare feet hit the ground and she's swallowed whole by the steel arms of a grunt, no taller than she is but who has a neck as big as a fence post and he's yelling into her face. Instantly, Chuck is there, pulling and beating on the grunt, who won't let go. He punches the shit out of the grunt, who's hanging on for all he's worth, crushing Fay's rib cage. The duster has become a strait jacket. *I can't breathe, I can't breathe,* and then they're free and Chuck is dragging, half-carrying, her to the double doors on the side, thrashing and kicking with his heavy motorcycle boots at any stray bodies lunging at them. The doors crash open. They're through. She's thrown into a jeep, and Chuck is stepping on it. A few raving uniforms slam against the back of the jeep as Chuck jams his boot on the gas. One of them jumps on the running board next to Fay, screaming "Aiiiiiiiiii!" She slaps him so hard he falls off. Another one lands on the roof, pounds it with his fists. Chuck slams on the brakes, ejecting the guy so fast he can't even get his hands out in time to break the fall. Immediately, Chuck guns it, narrowly missing driving over him. He speeds off into the dark night, the last of the grunts falling away, too slow to keep up with an army jeep used to dodging incoming. Finally, they're alone, speeding into the night.

"Shit!" Fay yells, the crowd's noise still crushing her ears, making them pop and dive bomb in the silence like she's been at a rock concert all night.

One hand on the wheel, Chuck reaches over and, grazing Fay's breast, slides his hand into the right interior pocket of his duster. When his hand comes out, it's gripping a fat white envelope. He places it under his left leg, as far away from Fay as possible. Still, she sees the twenties, the green American money sticking out because there's too much for the envelope to contain. Her stomach rolls. Chuck makes a quick turn onto another street, taking them away from Long Bihn.

"You did all right tonight, Chiquita," he says, not looking at her. "You did a-okay." When she doesn't say anything, he glances her way, sees her staring at the envelope and smiles. "Don't you worry now. Chuck'll take care of you." Then he smiles his gold tooth smile that says you're fucked, baby.

Chapter

EIGHTEEN

Thorne was true to his word: He gets Fay back in three hours. It's six o'clock at night when the C-130 lands on the tarmac back at Qui Dao. Fay feels as if she's been gone for a year.

"That was a doozy," Thorne said when he joined them on the plane. Fay was already strapped into her seat by then. She was still wearing Chuck's duster, her clothes in a ball on the seat next to her. She tried to pass a xu across her knuckles only to lose it somewhere on the floor between the seats.

Right before they landed, Chuck handed her a wad of bills folded over to give the appearance of wealth. Fay didn't have to unroll them; she'd used the fold-over trick herself before. The outside bill was a twenty. Inside she knew she'd find mostly ones. Still, she counted them. Her eyes started to itch and tear. How much was a human life worth? Apparently, one hundred fifty dollars. Fay snuffed hard. *I'll wire it to Dickie tomorrow. At least I can do that.* It was the first time she'd seen it in terms of sending money home to Dickie rather than keeping it for her own escape. She didn't yet realize its true meaning: that she'd finally given up on getting out of there before her one-year contract was up. That she would stay in Vietnam for four more months. Yet, the simplicity of sending the money home and not worrying about who to kill or how she can score a seat on a getaway plane was comforting to latch onto. It was a plan for tomorrow. She didn't want endless hours on her hands. She didn't want to battle a mental slideshow of grunts grabbing at her, their multiple hands hurting her.

Unbuckling her seat belt, she slipped the duster off her shoulders and started to dress. She picked up each article of clothing—the red lace panties and matching strapless bra, the hot pants, the halter top—and dressed quickly, trying to squeeze some feeling of protection out of them. She threw the duster across the aisle at Chuck, but he tossed it right back.

"You might need it when we get off the plane," he told her, as if she was still naked and he was kind and hadn't just cheated her.

Fay leaned back in her seat and buckled herself in. The thick strap chafed at her neck. The metal waist buckle dug into the front zipper of her hot pants. Her naked arms felt too cold. The crushed duster on her lap scratched at her bare thighs and the halter top around her neck was too tight. It was like she was wearing someone else's clothing. She'd changed identities. She wasn't sure who she was, but one thing was for certain: the person she was, that Fay was no more.

The next day after the show, as Fay walks through the Pit, she sees Ginny in the distance, waiting outside Fay's hootch. While once that sight would've comforted or even excited her, now it depresses and makes her feel tired.

"Why didn't you go inside?" Fay asks, trying to derail her. She'd rather smother herself in the mud than face any questions from her at this moment.

Ginny blows out a fistful of smoke. "Where have you been?"

Fay looks her straight in the eye and pretend-sighs. "What are you, my mother?"

Ginny flinches. *Good*, Fay thinks. *Get her on the defensive.*

"What are you doing here anyway?"

"Tina borrowed a car," Ginny says. "We're leaving in five."

"Where?" Fay asks.

Ginny stares at her and takes another drag on her cigarette. "What do you mean, where? Paris." She smirks. "Where the hell do we usually go?" She walks away, shaking her head, and for a second Fay sees her father doing the very same thing, shaking his head at something ridiculous she's said, something so obvious that it merits no words, just a scornful head shake. She feels the same way now as she did then—cut down and silenced—and she's surprised by how much it hurts her.

"Meet us at the gate," Ginny calls back over her shoulder. Her shorts are hitched up her ass and her tanned legs look just right in her red cowboy boots. She could be strolling down any Main Street.

They're off to Happy Bar in a borrowed VW bus that usually carries thirty children crammed into the back, but now holds three women driving on roads that are flash flooding. Another freak shower passing through. The wipers are too thin to keep up with the rain. No one can see through the windshield. Ginny is driving, a lit cigarette in fingers that loosely hold the steering wheel. Too loosely for Fay's tastes. Now that she's certain there's no way out for her, it's important that she stay alive for the remaining four months. She's gone from killer to survivor in one afternoon. In the front passenger seat, Tina starts to sing "A Hard Day's Night," which makes them even edgier and Ginny snaps, "Shut the hell up." The VW hits a pothole and the underside makes an ugly chucking sound like the bus has either broken something, or it won't make it out of the hole. But it does.

"Jesus Christ," Ginny mutters.

"Do you want me to drive?" Fay asks from the back seat because Ginny's a reckless driver in the best of circumstances and now her cowboy boot is pressed whole hog on the gas pedal. She's not slowing down one bit for the flash flooding.

"No, I don't want you to fucking drive," Ginny barks. "Turn on the radio."

When Tina turns on the radio, it's that idiotic blond bee-hived woman, the one on the Army station who talks about the storm as if it's her long-lost lover coming home. "These clouds are going to stick around for a while, I can promise you that," she says in a sultry voice.

"No shit, Sherlock," Ginny says and presses down harder with her right foot, and Fay sees that they're in for it. Suddenly, up ahead the road is not there anymore. Now there's a pond. The only way to get through to the other side where the road has to be is to gun it and hope for the best.

"Hold on," Ginny says as if the road has only a few dips and swerves. It's more like the bottom's dropped out and they no longer have seats under them because for a second they're airborne, and then just as suddenly they smack down again hard. The bus hits the water and it becomes a tidal wave that fans up and over the VW's snub nose, hitting the windshield with a smack that's so loud they all jump.

"Stop!" Tina cries out, but Ginny with her face pressed up against the glass is doing the impossible: She's ramming the car through the two feet of water that has swallowed the road, *their* road. Where the hell is the road? Suddenly, Fay yells, "There it is, there it is!" pointing and screaming the way, and sure enough it is, and it looks dry compared to what they've just been through, although it's covered with enough water and mud to stop anyone in their right mind.

When they arrive at Happy Bar, they head straight to the bar and each order a double Scotch, bypassing the Mai Tais for now. Van gives them the drinks on the house, saying, "Rain very bad." They click each other's glasses and Ginny says, "You got that fucking right."

No one offers a toast. They suck down their drinks like they're alcoholics jumping off the wagon, not wanting any holdups like pleasantries. *We're alive*, Fay thinks, and that's enough for now. She looks around the bar—it's the first time she's done that since they entered—and there's no one else there, only them. The place is empty. Even the reporters are gone because there's nothing more boring to report than rain. It seems like a party has been called off and the three of them and Van the bartender didn't get the notice.

Chapter

NINETEEN

After the Long Bihn show, Fay avoids Jarvis and, as much as she can, Ginny also. Jarvis is easy to avoid. He never tries to find her and when the MPs didn't pick her up that first week, she assumes he won't tell anyone about her curiosity about the Viet Cong.

She tries to lie to Ginny that she needs to do her laundry or take a nap, but Ginny finally corners Fay after a show. "You avoiding me?"

"No," she says, coiling up her chain.

"Good. Then you're coming with me and Tina for drinks. We'll get you in a half hour."

After their fourth Mai Tai at their usual table, Ginny asks, "What's going on with that doctor of yours?" and Fay almost spits out the sip she's just taken. The weeks have wiped out any thought of Jarvis and what had happened with him.

"What do you mean?" she says as nonchalantly as she can manage after four Mai Tais.

Ginny, with her gaze fixed on Fay, says, "You know what I mean."

"What do you mean I mean you mean," Tina repeats drunkenly, weaving her way back to their table.

"Shut up, Tina," Ginny says and zeroes back on Fay: "You're gonna be in serious shit if you don't stop it now."

Fay grabs Tina's pack of Pall Malls, hits one out against her palm and slips it in her mouth. *What does Ginny know? Maybe she's known everything all this time. Her fuckup with Jarvis, Long Bihn, what she intended to do.*

"You don't even smoke," Tina whines and tries to grab the cigarette back, but Fay snatches Tina's lighter and turns away in one quick motion. "Don't be wasteful," Tina wails.

Fay lights it anyway. "There's nothing going on."

"That's for sure," says Tina, looking around the bar.

Ginny leans in, pushing their empty glasses aside so that there's absolutely nothing between them. Nothing to stop her from grabbing Fay's hand.

"It's okay, Fay. There's nothing to feel guilty about."

For a moment Fay wonders if somehow Ginny knows that it's all gone to hell in a piss bucket. Maybe Chuck has told her everything about Long Bihn.

"I made a mistake," she says quietly.

"Don't I know it." Ginny sits back in her chair. She points her cigarette at Fay. "I'm the one who talked you into coming here, aren't I?" She takes a sip of her drink. "It was pure selfishness. Now he's stuck with that asshole."

Fay looks like Ginny's just kicked her hard in the shin.

"Wait—you're talking about Dickie?" she says slowly. The two friends stare at each other trying to figure out what the other is thinking, what the other knows. Ultimately, they have to look away because they're both carney girls, and you never know who's a mind reader.

"We're always left with the assholes," Tina says into her drink. She looks up. "Hey Vanny, let's have a torpedo."

Van brings her a mug of beer with a sidecar of whiskey. Tina raises the shot glass full of whiskey.

"Here's to the good time I must have had," she says to no

one in particular. Dropping the filled shot glass into the beer, she quickly downs the drink. She barely slides the empty mug back across the table before her head slumps to her chest.

"So, where *have* you been?" Ginny asks Fay with an expectant look.

This isn't any good, Fay thinks. Ginny's not letting go of something, yet Fay can't sort out what she wants exactly. *Why did she ask me about Jarvis if she really wanted to talk about Dickie?*

"You look different," Ginny tells her.

"This place isn't exactly a beauty salon," Fay snorts, thrown off balance by Ginny's switching topics left and right. She downs her drink.

"I didn't mean you don't look good," Ginny says defensively.

Fay doesn't believe her. She hates that Ginny keeps bullshitting her lately. In her experience false compliments are just a stone's throw away from full-on lying—she remembers the quack that tried to sell her a lotion that he promised would bring Dickie's legs back to life. "Two months and he'll be running around the house again," he'd told her.

Fay stands up, grabbing the VW keys off the table. "I'm leaving. You two can come or stay. The choice is yours."

They pile back into the dirt-encrusted van that looks like it's competed in a desert road race. Fay slides into the driver seat this time, although she's having trouble finding the windshield wipers to clear the window. Too many drinks. They've blown it. It's past curfew, nine o'clock at night, and the trick will be to somehow get home as fast as they can and not be stopped or shelled or drive off the road because they're so trashed.

Fay doesn't start the car right away. There's too much mud on the windshield.

"Damn it," she says under her breath. She gets out to wipe off the window with a mango leaf she pulls off a nearby tree. When her back is turned, Ginny scoots over into the driver's bucket seat and, turning the ignition, yells to Tina who's lying down in the back seat, "Quick. Lock your doors." Tina's so drunk she assumes they're being attacked, that Charlie is trying to break in, so she hammers down the lock on her back door. Then she passes out.

"Open the door," Fay shouts through the window at Ginny.

But Ginny slowly backs up the van, leaving Fay curbside. Fay runs to the other side and yanks on the passenger door, but that's locked too.

"Ginny! Open the goddamn door!" she yells but now Ginny's struggling with the mechanics of shifting into first. She grinds a few gears in the process, her hand slipping off the small ball on the stick from too many Mai Tais.

"Ginny!" Fay screams again. Somehow Ginny gets the van moving, driving it slowly enough so that Fay can catch up on the driver's side. The window is rolled down a crack.

"What's going on Fay? Huh?" Ginny shouts through the glass. "Are you back with Chuck?" The van sidles a bit in a rut to the left. Since it's curfew thankfully there aren't any vehicles on the road.

Fay gives her the finger, which practically makes her stumble on the street, it throws her so much off balance. "Ginny! For God's sake! It's curfew, you jerk."

"What've you been up to?" Ginny yells louder.

Tina sits up in the back and says, "I think I'm gonna be sick."

"Oh, for God's sake," Ginny says, but she pulls the van over. "Wait! Wait!"

Tina gets out just in time to throw up Mai Tais all over the muddy road. Fay makes a mad dash for Tina's door. She jumps in the van before Ginny can close off that entrance to her. They have to get home. They're in deep shit. There will be snipers waiting for them on the main roads. If they're lucky they'll be found by MPs, who will lock them up for the night for breaking curfew.

Fay crawls from the back seat between the two front seats and falls into the front passenger seat. She rolls down the window. Breathing heavily, she puts her head out the window. It looks like she's going to get sick too, but then she lifts her head and says, "You're my friend, right?" and for a second Ginny's eyes well up. Immediately, Fay can tell that Ginny wants to say she's sorry. Such a place doesn't allow room for apologies, though, because if it did, when would they stop?

When Tina's done being sick, she throws herself into the back seat of the van, wiping her mouth on her sleeve.

"Fay, what's really going on?" Ginny asks.

"I'm fine, thanks for asking," Tina says. "Who's buying the next round?"

Fay forces herself to smile and shake her head. As she often does, Tina's broken whatever weirdness had descended on the van.

"It's dark out," Tina says.

"The back way," Fay says and Ginny nods, stepping on the gas. They've only gone the back way—small dirt roads indistinguishable from walking paths that only the locals know—one time when the Citroën wouldn't start, and Van took pity on them and gave them a ride back to Qui Dao. Still, they have more of a chance that way than risking the main roads.

"Well, this is an adventure," Tina says as Ginny takes a left onto what starts out as a dirt road that can fit four people across.

Is this the way Van took them? Fay can't remember. The road quickly constricts into a narrow path with swiftly encroaching trees and tall grasses that start to graze the sides of the bus. Before they know it, they're committed. The thick vegetation makes it impossible to turn around. Instantly, the path is too curvy to back up. To do so could end in their veering off, crashing perhaps into a tree, or worse, getting stuck and not able to move the van at all. The grasses, as high as the roof, are beginning to stick to their windows. They stick and let go, stick and let go. Ginny keeps her foot steadily on the gas pedal, although they all hear the bald tires losing their purchase, can feel the slight tug of hesitation as the rubber sticks to mud and jungle. The path gets rougher, a bit bumpier, like they're driving over metal pipes here and there.

"I'm sick!" Tina wails from the back. "Have pity, mother of God."

They begin to hit more and more of those pipes. *What are they?* Fay wonders. *Bamboo offshoots?* The engine revs in desperation.

"What *is* that?" Fay asks, though her stomach is sinking with the knowledge of exactly what it is.

"Roots," Ginny says. "They're fucking mangroves, Fay. We're in the goddamn mangroves!"

They're driving over exposed roots. The lane is suddenly lined with mangrove trees, and branches begin to slap repeatedly at the windshield.

"*Ginny*," Fays says slowly, but Ginny isn't listening. She's hunched over the steering wheel, concentrating on what little the bus headlights are showing her, hoping to God she can continue to find the path and not drive off into a rice paddy because where there are mangroves, there's swamp.

Chapter

TWENTY

The branches hit the van and each time you want to yell, but you don't because you're not really breathing and in order to yell you have to breathe. You're waiting for the windshield to smash or at least get one of those spider cracks that grow and grow. The trees multiply as if they're giving spontaneous birth. The soft grasses are gone. What you wouldn't give to be back there now. You're surrounded by a web of trees that leaves the slightest room for the VW to maneuver around. How much farther can you go? *Think of it as an obstacle course*, you tell yourself. *Ginny's a good driver. She'll get us out of here.* But it's so dark you can't see the trees till they're practically on top of you, knobby, ancient branches striking out as if they're angry you've been out so late. *Thwack. Thwack.* The VW bus snaps off branch after branch, the windshield wipers carting away hundreds of clipped fruit, small white pustules that remind you of candy-coated almonds. There are leaves upon leaves, their brown speckled undersides pinned to the windshield from the wetness.

You're being buried alive by the jungle.

You're in for it now. You've chosen another shortcut you thought was the best decision and look at the shit you've ended up in again. You'd think you would have learned your lesson by now. You try to think of other things, other times when you've been driving and in deep shit and you survived. *Smack!* A branch snaps off, gets stuck on the sole surviving wiper, and then that cartwheels off.

You realize your whole life has been jumping out of speeding cars and living to tell the tale. How many times have you taken your life for granted? You aren't a religious person. You can't remember the last time you prayed. Yet now you are willing to make a deal. *Let me make it out of here. Please.* Your hand touches the fat roll of money that you have in your jeans skirt pocket. *Please. Let me wire him the money so he knows I'm thinking about him. I'll never leave him again. I'll be the perfect mother. I won't make any more mistakes.*

The bus hits a mangle of roots and stalls. Coughs. Stops dead.

"Goddammit!" Ginny yells. She bangs the steering wheel. "Fuck me!"

They're in the swamp.

Chapter

TWENTY-ONE

inny tries the starter. Nothing happens.

"That's not good," Tina says.

"No shit Sherlock," Ginny says.

Fay hoods her eyes with the palm of her hand and presses her face against her window. It's cave dark. "Look, it has to be low tide. These are mangroves. If we're going to do something, we have to do it now."

"I don't know, Babydoll," Ginny says, her face against the windshield.

"We can't just walk," Tina whines.

Fay squeezes between the bucket seats, crawls over the back seat, and scrounges around in the stored mess. She finds a flare, the kind you'd use in Kansas when you get a flat tire and the horizon is flat and empty for miles. She finds a roll of masking tape. A poncho. That's it. Not enough to fill a Boy Scout survival kit.

"Let's go," she says because she must keep moving.

"Are you out of your mind?" Tina asks, but she opens her door. They might just leave her. She's always been the disposable third in this threesome.

Fay climbs back over the seat and gets out. "Ginny, come on," she whispers before following Tina and closing the door quietly behind her. For a minute, Ginny stays where she is.

"Ginny, I swear to God we'll leave you here," Fay whispers harshly before Ginny reluctantly opens her door.

No matter how hard they try, they can't avoid the sucking noises their shoes and flip-flops make as they walk. It sounds like the seals of vacuum-packed jam jars being repeatedly broken. They walk as lightly as possible on the muck. The North Vietnamese hide punji sticks in the swamp, sharpened sticks of bamboo that can tear into an Achilles heel in a second. The mangroves are on top of each other now. Single file, Tina trips over a root and catches herself before she hits Ginny's back, avoiding further disaster. Nobody talks. The three of them know that while the day belongs to the Americans, the night belongs to VC. The mangroves are ominous shadows that seem as if they'll come to life any second, their roots becoming legs that will stomp them to bits or catch them in strangling neck holds. The night is windless, the air dead.

Fay leads the other two as close to the path as she can without actually being on the path. The only chance they have is to do the unexpected. Anything that could draw attention had to be discarded at the bus. Fay made Tina remove her silver wig and put on the camouflage poncho over the white T-shirt she's wearing. Ginny covered her flaming hair with mangrove leaves taped to her head with the found masking tape. She looks like a crazy peasant rebel. If they were in any other situation, the three of them would be laughing their asses off.

Fay holds up her hand, halting them, and after listening for a moment, leans over and pulls off first one flip-flop and then the other. The sodden ground feels like wet sand under her toes although she knows it's much more dangerous than that. There are leeches. Punji sticks. She sees a snake, a shiny flash in the dark scuttling across the wet muck. *Is it poisonous?* She can't think of that now. She walks forward, the sandy mud releasing her heels with a *phut*. She wonders if there's a way to tell if there are any punji sticks in the ground in front of her. *Do their sliver points stick out?*

When she hears Ginny and Tina's shoes still making noise, she whips around. Ginny will probably be the most reluctant to remove her shoes because her cowboy boots have been with her longer than anything. Fay stabs in the air at their feet. Behind Ginny, Tina whispers, "Leeches," and shakes her head no. The leaves of a tree on their right rustle. A branch snaps. More rustling. Someone or something is there. There's no place to run except deeper into the trees. Each of them searches frantically for somewhere to hide. Branches, heavy with leaves, bend. A monkey—grey with a fringe of bushy whiskers on its cheeks, like an old religious friar—suddenly appears on a branch near them. "Spies!" Tina cracks, and Ginny claps her hand over Tina's mouth. The monkey seems as startled by them as they are of it. It doesn't move for a second, just bares its long yellow teeth at them like it's grimacing, and then it bounds further up the tree where they can't see it.

Every monkey Fay has ever seen around the compound has been chattering or screeching, but this one disappeared without a sound. Before she can wonder what it means, she's diverted by Ginny wrenching off her cowboy boots. Fay points her finger toward Tina's feet and then turns and starts walking away. Finally, Tina yanks off her go-go boots. To keep their hands free in case they're attacked, they hide their shoes in the swamp brush so that the enemy can't easily come across them.

Tina follows the other two women. She's angry that she had to leave her favorite boots behind. Underneath her feet the muddy swamp smells like leftover fish in a garbage can. In the muck, her pace slows. The distance between her and Ginny widens.

Fay pushes back some mangrove branches, holding them until Ginny can put her hand on them. Ginny, however, forgets to do the same and the branches swing back in front of Tina, slapping her face. She gives them the finger and, swiping the branches to the side, she ducks through.

Up ahead, Ginny follows Fay off the path around two trees, sloshing through ankle-deep water rather than stay on the muddy ground. They motioned frantically to Tina to do the same. Instead, Tina picks the straighter path between the two tree trunks.

A trip wire instantly sets off a bouncing betty, and the explosion tears and hurls her body in ragtag pieces through the air, littering the swamp. Fay and Ginny are catapulted twenty feet into trees. Leaves cut loose by the explosion rain down on them. Ginny's shoulder is wrenched out of its socket. She screams as coucals, their bright orange wings flapping against their black torsos, dive and spin away. Flocks of glossy ibis swoosh off, squawking. Fay crashes face first, smack into a pileup of roots. Her cheek splits and cracks, like an egg. Her front teeth are snapped off like twigs. The right half of Tina's torso thuds on its side a hundred feet away in the mud, her leg still moving up and down. One side of Tina's blown-in head is down on the muck, her eye socket empty and torn, her Japanese wave tattoo shredded. In the trees, monkeys—a pack of forty of them squealing like bats—jump and swing hysterically through the dense growth, shaking loose hundreds of the white mangrove fruit, pelting the women below.

"God!" Ginny's voice screams. She knows immediately her shoulder is shit again. The pain severs her body. "Shit! Fay?!" Ginny yells, grabbing her shoulder, but her face is turned against a tree and the words come out mangled and indecipherable. She rolls over to her good side onto the mud. At eye-level she sees a shredded swatch of the camouflage poncho in the mud. "Tina?!"

Ginny calls. Using her one good hand, she struggles for a root, yanking herself to a sitting position against the tree. She looks around but doesn't see anyone else in the dark. Branches are down. Ripped leaves and white fruit cover the area, but there are too many mangroves to show the damage. "Fay?" Ginny cries out again.

Fay can't breathe. She wants to answer but can't. She spits out a shard of tooth. She slowly turns over onto her back, sliding down roots. Her face is wet with swamp gunk. Stunned, she raises her hand, wipes the mess on her cheek and realizes it's not entirely swamp. Suddenly, her taste buds return. She can taste a metallic wetness soaking her numb, splintered lips as she wipes them.

"Ginny!" Fay mumbles, breathing hard. The pain is lacerating. Opening her mouth feels like she's ripped her cheek down an important seam. She spits out blood and cradles her cheek with her hand, her pinky pressed against her lips as if that will staunch the blood gushing. Within seconds, her forearm is wet, the spaces between her fingers pipelines for the blood flow.

"Fay?" Ginny yells. "Tina?"

Fay struggles to sit up. "Ginny!" she manages to scream in spite of the ricocheting spasm that's seizing her face.

There's only one sound they hear in reply: leaves rustling. Not from the wind. Not from a monkey or a bird, or from Tina. Lots of leaves. Moving. Toward them.

The sheer fright of it propels Ginny to a standing position and then she's wrenching Fay up, shouting at her to come on. Despite the pain, they stumble away as fast as they can. Holding each other, staggering and tripping, they lurch to the perimeter of the swamp where they watch in horror as VC race toward them from several directions like a pack of wolverines. The enemy are yelling directions to each other, squeezing the distance between them and the two women.

"No!" Ginny wails as she almost drops Fay in the swampy muck, but somehow keeps them both on their feet to continue their sad imitation of a race to the finish. They reach the edge of a swampy field. Fay tries to shout something. She can't form the words. Her bashed-in mouth is no longer working. With Ginny's arm around her waist hauling her along, Fay tries to tell her, "Wait. Do you hear that?" All that comes out is jabbering nonsense. She has heard *something*, however. Over their pursuers' bloodthirsty cries, Fay can hear the not too distant *whup whup* sound of a chopper.

And then there it is. An American Huey. Speeding toward them. Before Fay and Ginny can think about jumping up and down, machine gun fire begins to hit the underside of the chopper. The VC are giving them a fight. Fay hears a loud whoosh and seconds later the Huey's rocket hits pay dirt, the Willie Pete exploding on impact near the VC, now running as fast as they can away from the women and the burning white smoke engulfing them.

The chopper sets down in a grassy area of the swamp, the whooshing air from the blades flattening the knee-high wet grass. Fay sees Jarvis hop out of the cab before the pilot. He runs and runs, the pilot behind him. She and Ginny stumble through the swamp grass, weeping uncontrollably, their faces burned beyond recognition. The sight is a deadbolt to both men, stopping them twenty feet away. Jarvis's hand automatically rises, his face wrenched into a horrible rictus.

"Sweet Jesus," the pilot gasps.

"Help us," Ginny wails as Jarvis's fingers reach through the white smoke still trailing through the air, toward the scorched flesh of the women before him.

By the time they carry Fay and Ginny back to the chopper, the American back-up arrives in the form of a F-4 Phantom cruising in at six hundred and unleashing a cannon that just for the hell of it blows one section of the mangroves to smithereens.

Jarvis lowers Fay as gently as possible to the chopper floor but, even so, she screams the scream of a calf being branded. "Get Tina," she wails.

"We don't have time," Jarvis yells over the rotators.

"Motherfuckers," Ginny shouts. It's what she's been yelling ever since they found her, and the pilot threw her over his shoulder and raced for the chopper.

"We've got to go," he shouts as he jumps into his chair now. It's only a matter of time before the Americans are answered by more VC. The Americans took out the scouts, that's all. The full Communist artillery is streaming through the mangroves. This is their backyard. Their land.

The pilot punches it and they're up, in spite of the impossible angle they're rising at. "Hold on, we got incoming," the pilot shouts.

The enemy has arrived, crawling out from their tunnels, their backdoors that fool the Americans every time. Machine gunfire wings the Huey, the chopper serpentines through the air. The F-4 is jammed up too, the VC launching portable mortars at the plane. Fay and Ginny are crying from the Willie Pete that's left a large mess of embittered nerve endings biting, clinching and twisting. They have no skin left. Their clothes are partially gone, fried right off their backs; in other places the material is still there, stuck to their open wounds. The air scorches their bloody burns. Jarvis tries his best to make Fay comfortable in the back on a pile of surplus uniforms. Her cheekbone has been obliterated. Her skin is flayed. Fay's face is bleeding, but it isn't. When she touches it, her fingers are covered in what looks like raspberry jam. Unable to stop himself, Jarvis looks away.

"Promise me you'll wire him this money," Fay murmurs, although it comes out as if she has guppies swimming in her mouth.

She tries to reach into her pocket, which isn't there anymore, there's just her skin, and her hand keeps falling from her lap onto the metal floor. "The money," she repeats.

She knows Jarvis can't decipher the inhuman sounds that she's making. The chopper dips and angles away from something and Jarvis is almost thrown from his knees to the floor. His hands shake as he forces Fay to sit up. A constant, low moan escapes her lips. "I know, I know," he tells her, but Fay wants to tell him he doesn't have a fucking clue.

Ginny is another story. Ginny's shoulder must be set right. There hadn't been enough time to do so out in the swamp. Jarvis props Ginny up, against the side of the Huey.

"Motherfuckers!" she screams at him.

"Hold on, girl," he says. Hands trembling, he grasps Ginny's hand. With his foot against her shoulder, he yanks as hard as he can, popping it back in. Ginny shrieks, the immediate and then gone pain of it leapfrogging over all the other pain she's feeling. She's had it with this fucking country. She starts to laugh and cry at the same time. "*Fay*," she wails. Once a shoulder dislocates, it's forever inclined to pop out again, like a broken jack-in-the-box. This is the end of Ginny's career as a contortionist. Then, because the shoulder is taken care of, the burnt mass of pain around her face and body overcomes her and she wants to run as hard as she can, shrieking from one end of the Huey to another.

"Don't move," Jarvis says, holding her down.

He crawls back to Fay. "We'll be there soon," he tells her and squeezes her hand. Her face has swollen to twice its size already. Her bloody mouth is set firmly. The pain is so sharp, so lacerating around her entire face, the burning coolness of ice, that she's afraid to move anything—her mouth, her cheeks, her eyes, her chin—for fear that her skin will fall off. *Where's that noise coming from?* It's a low moan like a bass beat underneath Ginny's cries.

Fay realizes it's coming from her own mouth, those low sounds, and she wants to stop but she can't. It's like when she gave birth to Dickie, the moans coming out of her like clockwork, with each rising labor pain and push push push. And the doctor saying, any minute, any minute.

"You girls have stirred up a hornet's nest," the pilot calls over his shoulder. They can see their friends, the F-4, looping around them now. It's hard to know what's real, what's happening because everything is at warp speed. The slide projector is all gummed up and the same slides are juddering: mountain, river, jungle, mountain, river, jungle.

And then they're free. The F4 has taken care of whatever it was attacking them. Immediately, the noise drops away. The dark, silent night comes inside with them, into the back of the chopper, through the wide cargo doorway that fits a coffin perfectly.

It's January 30th, the Vietnamese lunar New Year, so the pilot, hyped up still from the firefight, shouts back, "Happy New Year's Eve," but almost immediately they all hear the chopper's radio spewing reports of the massive destruction being unleashed by the Viet Cong below them. There is no safe place for them to land and yet to stay in the air is certain death.

In honor of Tet, the Vietnamese lunar New Year, the North and South had agreed to a twenty-four-hour peace pact. The North Vietnamese, wearing poker faces, had their fingers crossed behind their back the entire time. It begins with Nha Trang. The Viet Cong are a tidal wave, building in momentum. Seventy thousand Communist troops move secretly and simultaneously to Hoi An, Da Nang, Qui Nhon. The North Vietnamese unleash their furor in one stupendous lash-out on this New Year's night. They move through each village and leave a wasteland.

"Doc, I'm going to need your help up here," the pilot yells back as the reports drone on and on, but it's too late. Out the left side they see them coming in the distance. Silver and beautiful to look at, the enemy planes rush toward them in tight formation.

"Shit," the pilot says.

Jarvis lifts up his head. "Dear God."

Fay turns her face to the chopper's side opening and sees the planes swarming in. Automatically, her right hand extends to Ginny, who grabs onto it. In that moment, they understand so much. Everything really. They understand they'll never fly in another plane. Never see another child with a stumpy thigh or wrist. Never perform at all again. Never taste another Mai Tai. Share the same pillow. Celebrate their thirty-second birthdays. Never get back to The World. This is all they have left. This is it. This moment.

"I always loved you," Ginny says, crying, and Fay thinks, *Dickie. My son.* She raises her burnt hand as if she can stop what must happen, her destiny unfolding, her fingers stretched as far as they can go without snapping off.

..... ●➤

Chapter

TWENTY-TWO

The pilot yells, "Hold on," and the helicopter snaps a ninety-degree turn, a turn so steep even Fay can tell they're not going to make it. An explosion shot-puts her sideways into another soft pile of army uniforms. Someone cries out "We've been hit," and there's a speeding toward the ground, endless and yet hardly any time at all. Seconds really.

And then nothing.

A jumble of slides. She's picked up, heaved over a shoulder, her face a painful mess as it rocks roughly against a belt or a softer patch of material. He is running, breathing hard. Her leg. There is something radically wrong with her leg. Swamp smells. Mud and leaves. Water. Then, the back of her shirt wet from the soft ground underneath. She tries to flip over, to push her face into the cool wetness, but is held back.

He's running again, her head a pendulum, each step a jolt of searing pain. She cannot stand another minute. Stop, she tries to say. Stop.

His voice, murmuring, "You'll be okay now." Other voices. Vietnamese. She is swaying softly. Dreams of being in a hammock stretched between two oak trees. Dickie cradled in her arms.

She's awakened by the *phut phut* of sandals in mud. A glimpse of a small woman, a non la on her head. She passes out again.

Hard ground against her back. A woman very close to her face smiles with blackened teeth. She pats Fay's shoulder. In a torrent of Vietnamese, Fay recognizes one word. Safe.

Darkness descends. The glare of lights that is quickly extinguished. Her face covered with cool, wet leaves. She sleeps.

When she wakes fully up for the first time, she's in an empty room of white. One hand and one ankle are in leather cuffs strapped to metal bed railings. The other hand is tied up in some sort of noose around her neck. In a heavy cast, her other leg is pulled toward the ceiling on a pulley. She is spread-eagled. Every limb is swaddled in gauze. *I'm in a fucking nut house*, she thinks. She angles her face to get a better view of the leather wristband and suddenly there is only pain again. Searing, ripping pain. Every nerve on her face in the open air feels like exposed wires. Her moment of relief is gone. Her hands automatically try to lift for her face, but they're immediately stymied, held back by their restraints. She wants to claw at her face, to scratch so the unbearable itching will be relieved. It feels like a stew of poison ivy, chicken pox, and the biting of a hundred red ants. She's thrashing, knows somewhere it's useless, but can't stop writhing anyway. If she could only rip the handcuff off. *God! Escape escape,* the thought pounds in her head even as two American military nurses and a doctor rush in and ask her in English to calm down. Even as she feels the pinch of the needle in her arm. *Escap*—

Fourteen months, fifteen days, four hours, and thirty-five minutes. That's how long it takes to rebuild a face from scratch. Twenty-one surgeries. Fifteen cases of Silvadene cream. Four hundred and sixty-one stitches. Thirty skin grafts. One set of false teeth. All those months in Vietnam and she's finally gotten her wish: She is home again. Back in The World. On 68th Street in

Manhattan at the Weill Cornell Medical Center. The best burn center in the country. As they roll her gurney through swooshing glass doors, a nurse repeats softly next to her, "Sweet Jesus, sweet Jesus," like a rosary prayer.

When the surgeons are done, she is a mishmash of scar tissue, white and pink countries on a molded relief map. They don't allow a mirror near her, not until they think she is ready.

When she finally sees her reflection, sees what she is left with, what she's become, she can't cry. The sight is too shocking. It's past crying. Some of them look away—embarrassed? Ashamed that this was the best they could do? One of the nurses coughs dryly.

A doctor touches Fay's shoulder, saying, "Mental preparation aids the healing process." And she immediately remembers reciting to Dickie, "Getting you better is 90 percent attitude, 10 percent luck." The things she didn't know before. They are endless. Now she's the one in the room who's ashamed. Ashamed that she thought she knew so much and here she finds out she knew nothing at all. Her platitudes were nothing more than the lies that snake oil salesman spouted when he sold her that witch lotion to bring Dickie's legs back to life.

"Shut the light off when you leave," Fay tells them. When the group of white coats exits the room, they remind Fay of penguins, slowly shuffling forward with heads bowed, a long journey ahead of them.

The next morning as the usual painkillers start to wear off, she opens her eyes. Although her vision is a bit pill-induced blurry, she makes out a stocky man standing at the foot of her bed. He isn't wearing a white coat.

"I bet I'm lookin' pretty good to you now," Chuck says and smiles his gold-toothed smile. He throws a dirty, rolled-up newspaper on to her lap. "You see that? This is leftie territory, Senorita. That was their reading material in the waiting room. We got to get you out of this hellhole, *comprende?*"

In shock, Fay's hands begin to shake so violently she picks up the newspaper just to steady them and have something else to look at other than Chuck. *How the fuck did he find her? No, don't think of that.* She tries to focus on what he's tossed her: *The Village Voice.* The front page is column after column of anti-war articles. *Don't think of the days, the months it must've taken him to track you down. He'll stop at nothing.* She flips through the newsprint, barely seeing any of the words. She doesn't stand a chance. *Wherever you go, he'll always find you*—this thought is cut off by the page now in front of her. Both of her bandaged hands drop to the dirty ink, a smudged photo. The words are swimming as she makes out that there's some kind of photography show at a nearby gallery. It's the photograph that grabs her attention. *It's him. Him.* Her heart twists. It feels like it's wringing itself out, as her fingers smooth the creases, slowly wiping away the dirt on her son's face, as if he's just come home from the playground.

"Watcha got there, Chiquita?" Chuck says, taking a step toward her.

Fay catches herself, closes the newspaper, looks up with her best phony smile with her new fake teeth, and says in her most truthful voice, "Nothing—I'm just so happy you've come."

When she finally gets out of the Weill, it's been almost thirty-six months since she left him. No matter. She'll find him. He's in the same city as her for God's sake. The photograph was taken in an art gallery that's ten blocks from the Weill Center. How hard can it be? She's sure the newspaper is a sign. They'll escape to Alaska. She'll find Dickie, lose Chuck, and they'll make their way north on all the SSI money she's been accumulating in the hospital. The

Alaskan icy air is an attraction. So is the remoteness. Chuck will never find them there. She's sure Dickie will love the glaciers and seals, the stars blanketing the sky in the night, glittering lights assuring them that all's well. They'll find a cabin somewhere they can call their own. Dickie would love that too.

"Are you out of your fucking mind?" Chuck tells her. "He's probably dead or living the high life in Mexico. Not our future, Chiquita. I'm buying us a charter boat."

She says she needs his help. She cannot do it on her own. When Chuck continues to put up a fuss, she tells him, "You found me. And look, we're back together again. We're just like Elizabeth Taylor and Richard Burton." Fay's lost almost everything, but not her touch.

"One month. Then, I'm getting us that boat we always talked about."

They don't find him in a month. All they find out about is the photographer who's dead. No one knows anything about a boy named Dickie. The show has long ago been taken down. Now, paintings of baby bottles adorn the walls. The gallery owner is smartly decked out in a Chanel skirt suit. When Fay shows her the dirty page from the *Voice*, the woman says, "That's Pete. Pete Smith. I never heard of any Dickie."

"Where's Pete then," Fay asks, but the gallery owner only shrugs and says, "Your guess is as good as mine, honey."

"We'll have to go back to the Keys," Fay tells Chuck the next day. "Start back at the beginning and trace his steps."

They're in a Horn & Hardart, drinking their bitter morning coffee. She notices that Chuck's hair is grey, that sitting next to her he's shorter than she remembers. He looks like he's a retiree fresh off a tour bus, waiting for his grandchildren to come pick him up. "We have to start at the beginning," she repeats.

Chuck winces. Fay hopes it's because he's just swallowed the bitter coffee, but then he deep sixes that notion by reaching over and giving her a good one across her still sensitive face. It happens so fast none of the other diners notice or if they do, they stick to their own troubles. They're not going to interfere with a man and a freak show.

Fay tucks herself in, lowers her jaw so he can't see it trembling, sniffs hard to steel herself.

"That's my price," she insists quietly, staring straight ahead at the automat shelves. "I'll stay with you and I won't give you any trouble. That's my price," she repeats. It's not much to start her new life on, but she's started on less before. At least, she knows what she has to do. There is Dickie and there is nothing else.

Retrieving the torn-out newspaper article from her vinyl bag, she uncreases it. Over the months, the photo of Dickie has been smoothed into a charcoal drawing, all dark smudges and lines. She can see how much he's grown, how his chest has filled out, how his mouth is no longer on the verge of a smile, but grim and determined, like a coal miner's. It's his mouth that makes her heart ache. *What has she done to him? Will he forgive me?* Her fingers touch the dry, lifeless paper, the closest thing she has to her living son.

For the first time in her life, she can't lie to herself, can't tell herself that the next place will be better, that Chuck will love her, that she will be a perfect mother. From this moment on, she will see herself as she really is. She runs her finger across Dickie's hair. From this moment on, she will never lie again to her son.

Part Three

DICKIE

◆●‧‧‧‧‧●◆

Chapter

TWENTY-THREE

Of course, I killed Johnson. I'd had enough of his needling and beatings. They call that a mind-fuck in Province-town, the only place I know where intellect is measured by how many times you can fit a sexual reference into a sentence. Whatever you call it, I'd had enough. That day when Johnson threw me in the tank was it for me. Some kind of neural synapse snapped in my brain; the right no longer controlled the left. Anarchy prevailed.

I reached up with my handcuffed hands and latched onto his like I was a dying man. Then I yanked with all my might. He wasn't expecting it. The shock of hitting that water handicapped him far worse than my legs did me. I could hold my breath for close to two minutes by then. I was betting on the surprise factor. Even more, what I'd suspected turned out to be true. Johnson had grown up on a dairy farm in upstate New York. There were no lakes nearby, no ocean, and no time for playing in some school friend's pool. Johnson couldn't swim.

When he fell in, it was as if he'd been jet propelled to the bottom. It was so fast he even kicked over the ladder. I'd given it all I had to heave him in there. The water made a loud noise, like when someone does a cannonball, and then he was next to me, only his face was at the bottom and his ankles were by my head. I took advantage of that too. And the narrowness of the tank. I grabbed his ankles and slammed him repeatedly against the Plexiglass.

He kept trying to right himself, wrenching his waist around, slapping at my ankles and legs a few times, but it was no good; my braces were like armor. He'd already started to panic, which is the one thing you don't want to do in the tank. If you panic, you automatically breathe in, and either your mouth or your nose opens. A big bubble rushed past me, then some others, and that was that. The key to the handcuffs had fallen from his fist to the floor of the tank. I unlocked the cuffs and, pushing off the sides, went to the surface just in time.

I had to get out of that tank fast. Then what? I hadn't thought it through. Perched on the shelf and gasping for air, I decided it was the stupidest thing I'd ever done. *Why didn't I poison him, inside the house, while he was lying on his bed?*

Soon, Mrs. Henderson, our next-door neighbor, would be coming home. What would she make of the body floating in the tank next to her carport? Without any more hesitation, I grabbed the sides and, straining every muscle in my upper body—Fay was right, it is the upper body that counts—I threw myself over the side of the tank, landing hard on my side on the ground. It was still raining, thankfully, and the ground had become soft sand with give. The fall knocked the wind out of me, my braces rattled, but that was it.

Now what? I could say he slipped. Hit his head or something. I had the TV turned up too high. I hadn't heard a thing. I sat up on the sand and looked at the tank. Johnson looked like one of those fetuses in a mad scientist's lab jar: plastic, unreal. After his lungs had filled with water, his body had drifted downwards, his cheek coming to rest against the bottom, his neck folded under his shoulders as if it were broken. His back was curved against one side. The bottom of his T-shirt bulged out with water. The buoyancy of the water made one bent leg tap against the wall. I could see that his eyes were wide open. *Shit. What have I done?* A wave of nausea hit me, and I wrenched my shoulders around so I wouldn't have to see him. The street was deserted. *I can't stay here,* I thought.

There was more bad news. Johnson had *carried* me out to the tank. My sticks were still inside where he'd scooped me up. *Dammit.* I crawled my way to the house, my legs swinging back and forth along the sand like an alligator's tail, dragged down by my braces and the exertion of having just drowned a man. Breathing heavily, I heaved myself up the back plywood steps.

I made my way to the kitchen. There were my crutches in a heap on the floor. I grabbed them and stood up. Immediately, I felt faint. A voice started to thrum inside of me: *Get out of here.* Jerking down the hall, I went into my room, grabbed Fay's postcard from under my pillow, and threw on a dry T-shirt. I was almost out the door when I thought, *Money. I need money.* In the kitchen, I snatched at Johnson's cigar box so fast I bobbled it, but then caught it. I scooped out every cent. Seventy dollars and fifteen cents. It wasn't much, but it would have to do.

The next thing I knew I was on Main Street as if nothing had happened, except my right eye kept jimmying over my shoulder, like I had a nervous tic. God, the strain my nerves were under. A man doing the final walk on death row wouldn't have such nerves firecrackering off. I hadn't exactly prepared for this. I crazily half-expected to run into that school administration woman who had been dogging me. *Maybe she was following me right now.* As I passed people on the street, they seemed to stare at me more than usual.

Obviously, I needed to get out of town. Fast. That much I did comprehend. The quickest way was a bus. At the depot, I checked the board. There was a bus leaving for Miami in twenty minutes. I bought a ticket, reluctantly handing over three dollars and pocketing the seven cents the ticket agent gave back to me.

My shorts were still wet from the tank, so I quickly found the nearest men's room in search of something to dry them. It was stifling hot in there. I grabbed a handful of paper towels, went into a stall, and frantically patted down my shorts. To calm myself, I counted one-one thousand, two-one thousand, all the way to twenty-one thousand. My body started to shake as if I was cold. The numbing effects of my adrenaline speedball were wearing off. When I walked out of the stall, I couldn't look at myself in the mirror. I finally forced myself to take a peek, but I saw someone I didn't recognize. A young boy stared back, his face grim and determined. He reminded me of someone who had been busing tables for ten hours at a place where none of the tourists leave tips. Whose eyes were hard and whose jaw kept doing this weird thing, moving around as if he was grinding the hell out of it.

By the time I opened the bathroom door and swung my way out, the bus driver and the other passengers were already in the bus. I plopped down in the first empty seat midway toward the back. I heard first gear. I took a deep breath and felt my breathing slow.

That soon changed. As the driver cranked it into third, the shakes started again. Lying across the two empty seats, I reached down and pulled my legs up into my stomach. I began to cry. Let me be clear on this: I wasn't crying for Johnson or what I had done to him. No, in that moment, with the crusty velour of the bus's seat pressed against my wet cheek, I realized I was alone. Now and forever. Until I found Fay again. That was a lot for anyone, even more so for a boy of fifteen. I had, as they say in Provincetown, fucked myself royally.

Chapter

TWENTY-FOUR

L ying might not sit well with me, but I'm good at it. That's something I picked up watching Fay. Her face was the same, lie or not. As unreadable as a street sign in the night. At first when I realized the depth and breadth of her lies, I was embarrassed. How many years had I swallowed her truth benders and come back for seconds? How stupid could I be? Then I was pissed. What kind of mother lies to her only child, and a lame one at that? Once that anger took hold, it settled in my chest. Sometimes if I think of her now, twenty-five years later, I find it difficult to breathe, the resentments choking any good will toward her.

But I'm exactly the same as her. Just this morning I told a woman on a checkout line at the P-Town A&P that my accident, as I called it, happened while I was diving. She took in the perfect V of my shoulders to my waist and was immediately convinced that I'd once been some kind of competitive swimmer. It's times like this I'm grateful that I've kept up my two hundred sit-ups a day and that I've replaced my kitchen counter routine with a bench press and weights.

"I'll never forget what it was like," I said to the woman, and glanced down at the one item I was buying, a box of tissues, giving her the sense that I may be still weeping about it. I told her that the *accident* happened twenty years ago, when I was twenty and competing in a college championship. That I guess I wasn't made to handle that kind of pressure. She gave me a look that's usually reserved for battered children.

"You look awfully familiar," she said. "But I've just moved to town, so I doubt that we know each other." I get that a lot. And every time it scares the shit out of me. I'm not on an FBI poster at the PO, but it stops me every time. I stood there, holding my breath, calming myself down, reminding myself that I *worked* at the PO and that's one of the first stops for anyone moving to Provincetown or any other town. You start and end there. On Day One you fill out the paperwork to have your mail delivered, or you rent a box. The last day, before you get in the car and cart your stuff to some other place, you're filling out a yellow forwarding card.

So, she probably did see me before at the PO. Now I took *her* in. Dyed blond hair, which I usually try to avoid. Too much like Fay. I could tell, though, by the oversized sweater she was wearing over her jeans that she was hiding a too soft stomach. I like that. Tight stomachs mean they know what they want and how to get it. Not my type. I glanced down. No wedding ring. Although sometimes it's easier if they're wearing one. The line in front of us moved and she began to unload her grocery basket onto the belt. Ten packages of Weight Watchers dinners. Someone who ate alone.

"How do you and your husband like it here?" I asked her.

She flinched. *Divorced*, I thought. "It's just me," she said. It always amazes me how much strangers will confide in me simply because I'm seen as handicapped. My legs are sturdier than they were as a kid and I don't need braces anymore, but I still stutter along, one foot not entirely sure of itself until the other swings down and is placed on firm pavement. I still depend on my sticks too, although my forearms are bigger from hauling myself around all these years.

"Not much fun, is it?" I told her.

She opened her mouth to say something, but the cashier asked her for money. I slid my tissues down closer to the woman. I could've gone in the express line, but that moves too fast. Conversation requires time.

"You finding your way around alright?"

"It took me a week to find the laundromat," she said, laughing, and grabbed her two plastic bags full of frozen dinners. She turned partway to leave, then hesitated.

"Believe it or not, water's scarce here," I said quickly. I paid the cashier and got back my change.

"How can that be? We're surrounded by it," the woman said, laughing harder.

I laughed too. "Damned if I know."

"Is that all you have?"

I hesitated and then raised my sticks. "I have to pick and choose what I get."

She gave me that charitable look again. "Can I drive you somewhere?"

I smiled. "That would be great," I said. And then I told her the lie I tell everyone. "By the way, my name's Pete. Pete Smith."

We made our way to her small station wagon, walking so close to my Mustang in a handicapped spot that I could've reached out and touched the still warm hood.

Three hours later I'm walking as fast as I can from her rented apartment up Bradford Street. "Pete!" I hear behind me. It's my housemate, Spin. His real name is Anthony Spiga. I don't know who gave him the name Spin, but it's better than Anthony Spiga. Spin's smaller than me, wiry from his head to his thin feet. He's usually dressed in a wife beater, tight cutoffs, and some Converse high tops, one purple, one yellow. It's not my style, which is khakis and a nice pressed shirt. Evidence that I came from a good home. People who live here think we're lovers, but we're not. We're not even friends. I stick to the A&P and women who are in town only for a short stay.

"Where have you been?" Spin asks as he walks next to me.

"Nowhere," I tell him.

A quick image of Mary—that was her name—flashes in. She's pulling on a robe as fast as she can, but I'm already at her door.

"Are you sure you don't want to stay for dinner?" she's saying.

"Who was that blond woman I saw you driving with then?" Spin asks. This catches me off guard.

A bicyclist blows a sharp whistle as he races by us.

"Who is she?" Spin asks again, but I'm ready for it this time.

"I don't know what you're talking about. It wasn't me."

After Spin and I get in my car and I drive us home, I draw a bath almost to the top. As soon as I lower myself in, I let my head sink under. I hold my breath for as long as I can. Keeping my eyes open, I watch the water's surface manipulate the overhead fixture into rolling waves of light.

When my trailer burned down last year due to faulty electrical wiring, I moved in with Spin. It was the first time I'd lived in a home that didn't have wheels or cement blocks underneath it. His house is a small purple Cape off Commercial Street, the main street in Provincetown. The west end of Provincetown, where we live, tends to be quieter. There are fewer guesthouses and bed and breakfasts. Most of the condos and small cottages have been owned for years by the same people. Our neighbors on one side are two sixty-year-old men who wear matching outfits whenever they go out. Sometimes I see them leave in sweatshirts that boast taglines like *Don't look at me. I'm with him.* On our other side is a fifty-year-old lesbian who complains daily about her lack of a lover, but who insists every day on wearing the same muumuu dress made of a fabric that should be covering a couch.

We are perfect roommates. Spin, for all his lack of fashion, is an obsessive compulsive. Every windowsill houses orchids that normally would only be seen in hothouses in Florida or the jungles of Brazil. These aren't the ordinary ones you see in northeast garden stores at Christmas time. Spin's orchids are purple stars with pink tongues the size of your thumb, or they have cascading yellow pods that quiver as you pass. There's not a speck of dust or a nick on them. The rest of the house is the same. He can't go to sleep at night until everything—dishes, the Sunday paper, throw blankets on the couch—is tidied away. And I always leave rooms looking as if I've never been in them. Comes from those years with Fay, moving within thirty minutes' notice.

His house was bought and paid for like everything else Spin owns, by what I call his pharmaceutical entrepreneurship. Out back, in what used to be a garage, he's got a lab—"the still"—that would rival any biotech firm on Route 128 near Boston. My philosophy has always been it's best to put yourself front and center to avoid suspicion. Spin agrees. Small-town cops tend to think the drug trade originates only where foreign languages are spoken, or in some abandoned brownstone in Harlem. Not in a garage that is painted fuchsia, surrounded by beds of irises.

I'm not about to judge him for the profession he's chosen. How could I, given what I've done? It's not like he has a lot of options; he's a high school dropout. Growing up in Revere, Massachusetts where the mob still has dibs on the far back booths in Lorenzo's, Spin knew two things: He wanted to date Vinnie, not Veronica, and he had to move to a town where that was the norm, not another reason for murder. Yet, he couldn't leave it all behind. The art of selling drugs had been passed down from his father and uncles like other families teach their offspring about the family textile business. All the same, I'm glad he doesn't sell to children or teenagers. His trade is delivered to gay men who are here for the weekend and want a boost in their dance step. The big seller is X, which Spin informs me was widely dished out by psychiatrists to troubled couples in the seventies. It's known as the love drug and although I've never wanted to try it, I can see why others would.

I still enjoy a nice-sized joint myself. The last vestige of my time with Johnson, I guess. Well, not really. There are, of course, other lingering effects of my time with him.

On the bus to Miami, no one took the seat next to me, so I remained lying down. My sticks leaned against the back of the seat in front of me, within a finger's reach. Road travel usually lulls me to sleep, but my nerves were too jangled for that. I stared at my hands that were clasped next to my knees, and it seemed as if they were larger than usual, like they could rip open a coconut with a twist of the wrists. A flash of those hands gripping Johnson's skinny ankles dropped into my head as if it were a bowling ball. *No, don't think of that*, I thought, and shut my eyes so tight I saw only an explosion of white lights. The bus's engine suddenly seemed louder than it should, as if somewhere along the line we'd dropped the muffler. Underneath my cheek, the seat's velour felt increasingly like it was covered with a layer of crushed peanuts. I slipped one hand between my face and the filthy seat and sniffed hard. *The important thing is you're getting away,* I told myself. *No one knows you. Or what you've done. You can do this. Stop worrying. But what if they found me? What if the school administrator reported that I was missing? What if the FBI was waiting for me at the next stop?* I kept my hand balled up, the knuckles jabbing painfully against my cheekbone. *Don't be stupid. That school administrator saw you. She thinks you're sick. They probably haven't found the body yet. The body. Jesus.* And with that, I thought of Johnson again. It was hard not to. It was like trying to hold your breath. After a few minutes whether you want to or not, your mouth opens and lets in air. *He deserved it,* I told myself. *He would've killed me. I was only defending myself.* This was the beginning of my lies about what I'd done.

Four hours later, when we were pulling into Miami, I couldn't fathom that I'd actually killed someone. *There must be some mistake. Maybe he'd only lost consciousness. Maybe he was still alive. Maybe I'd left too fast.* Soon that logic disappeared too, like water swirling down a drain.

Nevertheless, en route, I'd formed a plan. "You can do this," I heard Fay's voice urging me on. She was right. In a way, she'd raise me to do just this: disappear at a moment's notice. I'd decided the best thing to do was to switch up my mode of transportation. "Cover your tracks," Fay said. That made me think, in turn, of trains. After the bus arrived in Miami, I made my way quickly to the nearby train station. *Now where?* I thought. Staring at the arrival and departure board, I scanned down the list of destinations. "Think big, Dickie," Fay was saying. "Big is good. We can get lost in big." One thing was for certain: I had to go north. Away from Florida.

I saw the Tamiami Champion was leaving in two hours for Penn Station in New York City. I almost ran to the ticket booth, my braces making hideous noises with the strain. Ten minutes later, I was $45.22 poorer, but relieved I had a plan. We'd arrive at Penn Station the following morning by noon. I couldn't afford a bed in the sleeper car, but there was Fay again, telling me, "You don't want to fall asleep anyway. You need to keep an eye out." Once on the train, I told myself I'd at least have a roof over my head, a seat, and I'd be on my way somewhere far, far away.

I didn't know anything about New York City. Then I remembered I didn't know anything about the forty towns that Fay and I had lived in at one time or another. "It's all the same," Fay would say. "It doesn't matter if you're in Vegas or Tuscaloosa. There are people who want attention, beds to sleep in, and a supermarket that never fails to disappoint." Thinking of Fay calmed me down again.

After buying my ticket, I found an empty bench to lie down on. The curved wood, like a ship's hull, cradled my back. Every so often the station's loudspeakers crackled an indecipherable message.

I woke up with a start, my left cheek damp with spit against the hard wood of the bench. There were more people in the station. *God, don't tell me I missed the train.* I looked at my watch: thirty minutes to go. Relieved, I sat back against the seat and glanced around, composing myself. Most of the benches had at least one person on them. But diagonally across from me was a sight that nearly made me scream out. A man was sleeping with his back toward me. He was wearing an old railroad jacket. His hair was in a familiar buzz cut. *Johnson.* Automatically, I moved as fast as I could and took a seat on the farthest bench across the waiting room. I peered around the rows of benches between us. He didn't stir. *Could it really be him? Could he have somehow survived and, what's more, found me?* I watched him for twenty minutes. By now, they'd announced "all aboard" for my train at least two times. He was near the double doors that led to the platform. Slowly, I clicked my way toward the doors. I gave him as wide a berth as I could as I passed him. Just as I almost made it, he stirred as if sensing a shift in the air. I froze. His face turned toward me as he rolled over on the bench. Grey motorcycle mustache. Scar running down his left cheek. *It's not him. It's not him.* Hurriedly, I picked up my pace to the train. Stick, foot, stick, foot. *It wasn't him.* I kept repeating this to myself as I hurled myself up the metal steps, into the train, down the aisle and into a seat that faced backward so that I could keep an eye out for anyone coming out of the station. *It wasn't him.*

But in a way it was. After that, Johnson rode next to me the entire way to New York. He was my travel companion, providing an unceasing monologue that accompanied the scenery we passed. I had killed him. With my own two hands.

Across the aisle sat an elderly couple who were traveling to visit their daughter in the Village, or so I overheard them tell the man sitting in the seat facing me. He was dressed in a black suit that looked like it had been ironed too much. An undertaker's uniform. Or so I imagined, and then I was right back to seeing Johnson floating in the tank, the cod-like whiteness of his face and arms matching the white of his undershirt. The woman of the elderly couple kept turning in my direction. Now I think she was probably just taking in the view outside of my window rather than her own because the scenery on my side was much more captivating: towns staggered along the ocean, bays curving in and out. But then, all I could think was that she knew who I was, had seen my photograph already on television, and as soon as the train stopped, she was going straight to the nearest pay phone and dial the police.

Hours of such torment engulfed me as the train hurtled along. The one time I got up to go to the bathroom, I convinced myself that when I returned to my seat Johnson would be there, waiting for me. "You think you could kill me?" he'd say. "Think again, boy." I waited behind the bathroom's metal folding door, paralyzed, sweating even though the bathroom felt like the inside of a Frigidaire. Still, I hesitated. *He's there, I know he is.* Finally, a loud knock came at the door, and I was so startled I dropped one of my sticks. It hit against the sink with a clang. Several more rapid knocks. I managed to pull myself together and open the door with difficulty. A small boy was outside, his hands cupped on his crotch. "I gotta go," he whined and pushed past me and my sticks into the bathroom.

I went up the aisle, preparing for the worst.

Johnson wasn't there. He was dead. My seat was empty.

Chapter

TWENTY-FIVE

As much as I try not to get involved, I'm worried about Spin. He's HIV positive and while he's always been wiry, now he's shading into the land of the skinny.

"Have you been dipping into the still lately?" I ask him this morning. We're eating breakfast in the backyard—currant scones that Spin has baked. The man is a constant source of surprise. There are also two mugs with a mellow blend of coffee.

He stops mid-chew, the scone filling out his cheek like a chipmunk with a nut. "No," he says, mouth open, food showing. Spin's table manners leave a lot to be desired. I try not to sit directly across from him most days.

"You feeling okay?" I press on, although that old voice inside my head is saying, *Back away. You don't need anything extra.*

He swallows. His Adam's apple seems like a big goiter to me. *When has he gotten so wraith-like?* I wonder. *And where was I when it had been happening?* I pride myself on picking up on the slightest changes in people, and here it was right in front of me and I'd been clueless. What else had I been oblivious about?

"I'm all right," he says, confidently, but then blows it by looking away too quickly. He's been keeping it from me. We share a house and he bakes me scones in the morning, but we really don't know very much about each other. Well, I know a lot about *him.*

We've only ended up together because I can't commit to anyone and no one wants to commit to him.

I'd met Spin through the PO. He had a mailbox at his house, but every day, around two in the afternoon, he'd stop in to buy something: a couple of stamps, an overnight box, one time a magnetized pad of paper that you could stick on your refrigerator. I could tell he was gay by the way he swung his hips and did his twirly Qs on Commercial Street. I watch how people walk all the time. You can tell a lot about people by what their gaits are like, their posture, whether they keep their eyes on the pavement. Seeing him in the PO, I figured that Spin probably had a hard time picking men up, not that he wasn't the type to try. He just doesn't have the GI Joe good looks that are mandatory in this town. He dresses like them, but he can't quite pull it off. It's like a middle-aged man trying to dress like a skateboarder. His hair is all wrong. No matter how he grooms it, it's the inside of an electrical box.

At two, the lunchtime rush is over, and the PO is usually empty. Spin and I got to talking one day about whether it rained more in Provincetown than Seattle. It seemed that way from the downpours we'd been receiving that week. After that, every day he came in we said a few lines of dialogue back and forth, not meaningful enough to qualify as conversation, more like a drive-thru interaction. Then my trailer burned down. I told Spin about it, which was unlike me, telling someone something that was directly about my life. But I was distraught. The fire had destroyed the small possessions I owned, most importantly that one postcard from Fay that I'd grabbed after killing Johnson, and the pair of her handcuffs. They were also the last evidence of my life before I ran away. I didn't tell Spin about *that*, of course, but he must've sensed something.

"You could move in with me," he said, brightly. "I've got a second bedroom."

With my trailer gone, I needed a place to stay. It was either that or live at the PO, which I didn't think would go down so well. I moved into Spin's the next day.

Now at the patio table, he gulps down his cup of coffee in one go, as if he's going to be late for work. There's a part of me that wants to ask him again about how he's feeling, to force him to tell me the truth, but that other voice is back, the one that keeps me alone, but safe. That voice is louder than ever, progressing into a five-alarm fire stage. *Don't say a word*, it shouts. I let him gather our crumb-filled plates and dirty coffee cups together and walk toward the house. Spin's having a hard enough time as it is. He doesn't need me poking into his business. He doesn't need me telling him how sick he's starting to look. All that would do is point out to him how he's never going to be accepted by the men he pursues: dark-haired, strong jaw-lined boys whose bodies ripple as they strut through town. The truth is I have the same genetic flaw as Fay: We're experts at excusing ourselves as soon as anyone demands some sort of *involvement*. We're very good at coming up with satisfactory explanations of why we can't do something for someone else. That safety mechanism kicks in now. I convince myself that getting Spin to open up about being sick is as foolish and cold-hearted as asking an amputee if he misses his legs. Why open that wound for him?

So, I watch him walk into the house and slide the screen door behind him. *Say something*, I think. *Call out to him*. I don't. I hear him blow his nose—a loud honking noise that sounds like geese flying south. I feel him staring out the kitchen window at me. I close my eyes and turn my face up to the sun, trying my damnedest to feel its warmth.

On the way to New York City I'd figured out that I needed a new name. I'd always liked the name Pete—it sounded like the name of a happy kid. I knew my last name had to be a name that thousands of other people would have. Like Smith. So, Pete Smith it was.

With my new name, I stood on the corner of the busy intersection at 34th and 8th. *Where should I go?* I walked by a city cop who was struggling with a drunk. Yesterday, being so close to the police would've sent me running, but here in this crowd I felt somewhat safer. For a blissful moment I saw myself as others would see me: a blond haired, blue-eyed boy who perseveres. Already I was breathing easier than on the train. I walked along, my pace slowing, taking in how many people there were. It was bigger than I'd hoped for. A tornado of noise and visual stimulation. At any other time in my life I would've been overwhelmed by such confusion, but as I made my way along the street, a brief feeling of relief came over me. In a place like this, I would be a blemish on the landscape, nearly invisible. Money or not, somehow, I would have to make this work.

Although by then, my hunger really kicked in. I hadn't eaten in almost two days. Suddenly, my confidence began to ebb. The overcast city looked like all the colors had been bleached out of it. I felt my fingers trembling. How would I get through the day, let alone a week, a month? The only thing to do was turn myself in. I shook my head. *You can do this.* I kept walking.

I remembered that night when Fay and I were coasting away from yet another man's trashy mobile home. The unsuspecting man was still sleeping at home under a jumble of blankets. Fay told me, "I wish I was a Catholic."

I laughed. "Why?"

"They believe there's an end to our suffering," she said soberly.

Life *was* suffering—I certainly knew that now. However, given the choice between suffering in prison or freely in the city, it was better to take my chances.

My shorts and T-shirt might've been fine down South but now I was in the North in October, where the temperature was twenty degrees colder. The smell of roasting peanuts from the vendor carts teased my empty stomach. I kept walking down 8th, not knowing where I was going but just wanting to be doing something. Hundreds of people were on the streets, scattering in different directions like bees streaming out of a honeycomb. The collective energy of the crowd and the colder air rejuvenated me. I stiffened my arms and swung myself along.

At West 47th, there was a line of policemen cordoning off a large building. Radio City Music Hall. A line of limos were inching their way through. Ordinarily I would've wanted to see what all the fuss was about, but not now. Not now when a policeman was the last person I wanted to come up against. I quickly pivoted down 47th with my head down.

Thirty minutes later, I ended up at the YMCA, which was in a cold limestone building on East 47th. According to the flyer I received at the front desk, it'd been donated by the Vanderbilts. I comforted myself with the idea that I'd tell Fay when we were together again about how I stayed with the Vanderbilts in New York City. There was one giant room on the second floor with rows of cots that cost ten dollars for the week. I paid for one night.

During the night I awakened from a nauseating bitter smell and found a grizzled old man's face not two inches from mine. When I screamed and nearly poked his eye out with one of my sticks, he moved on, but I knew right then I had to get out of the Y as soon as possible.

The next morning, I walked the ten blocks to the New York Public Library on 5th Avenue. If there was one thing that I was good at, it was finding my way in a new town. I needed to get my hands on a city map. A library would have one for free, along with newspapers. I also wanted to make sure my name wasn't in some headline already. Along the way, I saw a dirty Mets sweatshirt that had been discarded on the sidewalk with a baseball cap. I picked up both and threw them on so assuredly it seemed as if I'd been the person who'd left them.

Inside the library I read the *Daily News*, scanning first for news of Vietnam. It was disheartening: The Commander of the Forces, General Westmoreland—Westie—was sending more troops. *Why, if we were winning as much as they said we were?*

Next to me at a long table in the library's newspaper room, a man was surreptitiously ripping out pieces of another newspaper. I could see they were from the classifieds. With a red Bic, he was circling some of the job ads. When he caught me staring, he shrugged, and then, standing, slipped away, leaving the tattered newspaper.

I too needed somehow to make some money—my savings were rapidly approaching zero—and I desperately wanted to find a place to stay. After searching through the *Daily News* and finding nothing, I picked up the weekly *Village Voice* and sat down at another of the long tables. The *Voice* had news that the *Daily News* didn't: Senator McCarthy was expected to announce that he was running against Johnson because he was opposed to the war. There was a running tally of wounded versus killed.

I could no longer pretend. The war was not going well. Who knew when Fay would come home? *Don't think of that,* I told myself, and quickly flipped the pages to the back. In the classifieds a small box ad caught my attention: Artist model needed. Must be handicapped. No experience preferred. Room and board. A phone number was provided. Well, I was certainly handicapped. Fay had always told me that my face and blond hair should've been in magazines. Every other job was out of my league. I was hardly an accountant or a truck driver. I coughed loudly to cover the sound of the paper tearing and slid the ad into my pocket. Then I made my way to the public phones.

Chapter
TWENTY-SIX

One day, I come home from the PO and find Spin curled on the sofa underneath a pile of blankets. It's late June, hotter than it should be for this time of year. There's an empty, dirty glass on the coffee table. The house is stifling. All the windows are closed, all the doors shut tight. My line of vision catches on three yellow petals scattered on the wood floor.

From the walk home, there are two dark ovals underneath the arms of my postal service blues. The whole way I'd envisioned a tall glass with clinking ice cubes and gin and tonic. Seeing Spin now, I don't want to stay a minute longer anywhere downstairs. Something's not right here, but I don't want to know what that something is.

Spin is staring at the television, but the volume is turned down so low you can't hear any of the words. I glance at the wood stairs leading to the second floor where our bedrooms are, however, it'll be suffocating under the eaves that barely miss my head. Besides, what if he follows me up there? Without a word, I head past him on the couch, through the living and dining room area, straight for the slider and the patio.

"Where are you going?" Spin asks. His voice is small, helpless. The blankets are drawn up to his chin.

"It's too hot," I say back. I slide open the glass door. The hot air outside feels cooler than the hotbox I'm in. There's a breeze that flattens the wet spots on my shirt against my skin, chilling it for a second. *Better already*, I convince myself. Both sticks lower onto the flagstones in preparation for stepping through the open door. Although my back is to him, I hear Spin moan and rustle under the covers. Automatically, I glance over my shoulder. I can't help myself.

He's pulled the covers tighter around him. "It's cold in here," he says in that small voice again. I know he wants me to ask him if he's sick, to see if he needs a glass of ginger ale or aspirin. *Stay out of it*, the familiar voice says. Without a word, I swing my way through and close the slider behind me. *It's not your problem.* I angle a lounge chair on the patio so it's not exactly with my back to the house, but it's not exactly welcoming either. I worked all day. I should be able to come home and relax. *He probably just caught a twenty-four-hour bug.* Leaning my head back over the top of the plastic chair, I close my eyes. Maybe in a bit I'll drive to the beach, sit in my car, watch the tourists from Kansas driving in with their RVs, their hands pointing through rolled-down windows at the wide ocean before them.

"The ocean always makes your problems seem small," Fay told me as we drove along the Atlantic City coastline, away from Roger and his tears and his apartment above the game arcade.

It sounded so stupid when she said it, like something you'd read on a Chinese fortune cookie, and I was mad at her then for making us leave once again.

"He was nice," I said, looking at her. I knew she'd hate it that I said that, but I did it anyway.

The ends of the tie-dyed scarf wrapped around her neck were blowing out the window. Her jaw was set hard and for a moment I didn't think she heard me, but then she glanced my way and said, "We don't do nice."

● ······ ●

When I dialed the number in the classifieds, a man answered, "Hello?" as if he was surprised. I told him why I was calling, and he asked me to meet him in two hours at a luncheonette called Horn & Hardart's on 34th and 8th. I didn't mention that I was fifteen years old, of course. The idea of going back to the Y for another night helped to steady my nerves enough to walk the nine blocks. I had no choice really. My shorts and found sweatshirt were all wrong for a job interview, but there was nothing I could do about that either.

Against the walls in the luncheonette there were machines with vertical metal slots that swooped around every time you hit an olive green plastic button. If I'd felt more at ease, that machine would have kept me entertained. I'd never seen anything like it. The slots held liverwurst sandwiches on white bread, plates of macaroni and cheese, cherry pie slices, and apples. On the wall was a huge banner that said, LESS WORK FOR MOTHER. The place was packed with people taking a midafternoon coffee break.

I'd arrived early, so I stared at the food items. "I can help you carry it to a table," an older woman suggested. She had on a pale green uniform and a little paper hat and was standing by a metal cart full of used plates and bowls. I splurged on a cup of chicken soup and turned to scan the room for an empty seat, the woman now holding my soup in her hands. The man had said he would be wearing a white carnation in his coat, which had almost made me laugh because I'd a sudden image of a clown with one of those fake flowers that squirt. I didn't expect to see him, I was still thirty minutes early, but then I saw him on a stool at the window counter. He was turned sideways so I could see the very large and startlingly white carnation in his lapel. He had on a wool overcoat although it wasn't *that* cold out and the restaurant was very warm.

He was a lot older than I'd expected, with a tremendous head and in profile, a sharp beak nose. A shock of bristly black hair stood up on his head like porcupine needles. An empty seat beckoned on his other side.

"How 'bout this one?" the woman said, holding my soup and standing near an open table.

"That one," I told her. I pointed in the direction of the seat next to the man.

I swung my way over to him and slid onto the open stool.

"There you go," the woman said, setting my soup down, which drew the man's attention away from what was in front of him: several close-up black and white photographs of hands, a pocket watch, and a cup of grayish tea. Sometimes people would look at me but act as if they weren't. Usually their interest was piqued by my sticks or braces and wanting to appear polite they'd look away quickly, or they'd sneak glances out of the corner of their eyes. It annoyed the hell out of me. This man, however, gazed at my legs with empathy—no pity, no surprise—as if he once walked with braces himself and was now healed.

"Good day," he said, nodding at me. His right hand was fingering the edge of one of the photos. "Isn't she beautiful?" he asked and slid the photograph over to me. It was a close-up of a pair of hands, palms up. The hands, although small like a female's, were gnarled and curled like an old man's.

"Yes," I lied. The man smiled shyly and slipped the photograph in with the others. I weighed telling him that I was the one who'd called, but something made me hesitate. *Check him out first*, Fay warned. I began to eat my soup. It had as much chicken in it as a bouillon cube. The man kept moving the photos into different layouts on the counter, first this way, then another. All the photographs were of deformed hands. Sometimes he'd pick up the pocket watch and place it so that it barely touched one of the photographs. From the inside pocket of his overcoat he withdrew a perfect blue jay feather and placed that on top of the photos as well. He never stopped smiling. Whatever it was he was doing was giving him immense pleasure.

"Stories need to be told," he said quietly, startling me. I didn't know if he was talking to himself or me, so I didn't respond. "Where are you from?" He swiveled his stool in my direction.

"Washington," I lied, taken aback. *Had he figured out that I was the one who had called?*

"Ah," he said, settling himself better on his stool. "Did you know that Washington has more birds than any other state in the union?"

"No, I didn't know that," I said truthfully. I couldn't even remember if Fay and I had ever *been* to Washington. I slurped a spoonful of soup. The photos were unsettling and made me nervous. I thought of the ad again: *Must be handicapped.* I glanced down at my braces and oxfords from which you could see my turned feet fighting to get out. I looked again at the photos. My fingers began to tremble on the spoon.

Then a group of young girls, maybe thirteen years old, dressed in Catholic school uniforms—plaid, pleated skirts and blue toggle coats—passed in front of our window. We watched them as they jostled each other. Neither of us said anything for a few minutes—by now my soup was getting cold—and then the man said, "I see we both appreciate the same things in life." Before I could object, he added quickly, "There's nothing wrong with appreciating beauty. No harm extended."

Not knowing what to say, I fell into his odd manner of speaking. "No harm received," I said.

He smiled shyly.

Maybe it would be all right. I couldn't go back to the Y. I swallowed another mouthful of soup. *Tell him,* I thought. *Tell him you're the one.* I cleared my throat. "I called you."

"Ah, I thought so," he said. His eyes flitted to my sticks leaning against the counter between us. He smiled thinly again. "I have a house in Queens, a very nice house, though small, which has recently become emptier than I wish it to be. My mother, you see, has passed. An empty house is no good." He leaned in closer to me. "It rattles."

More nervous than ever, I picked up my spoon again. I'd no intention of having another sip, but I needed to stall him. There was obviously something very wrong with him. *Listen to how he talks for Chrissakes. Look at those photos.* What other options did I have, though? He hadn't yet said a word about the artist model part either. Suddenly, I thought something else about what that actually might mean. *How could I have been so stupid? These photographs were only of hands, but what if he shot other body parts? What if he wanted to take a picture of me naked?* Why hadn't I thought of that before? I'd been so thrilled at the idea of a job and a place to stay that I hadn't stopped to think. And now other obstacles rushed over me. *You can't afford company. Remember? You're on your own whether you like it or not.*

As if he were aware of my stalling, the man cleared his throat and went on. "I have a crushing deadline"—at this he rubbed his forehead. "An exhibit. In less than one month." He looked me up and down again. "Yes, you will do nicely. However, I demand cleanliness of anyone entering the house. And there is just one other thing." He waved me closer with his bony fingers, lowering his voice.

In spite of myself, I leaned in.

"You must under no circumstances enter the basement without me." I didn't know if I should laugh because it was something out of the horror comics I used to read in Key West—*The Fiend in the Cellar!*—or I should yell for help. He immediately shook his head. "No, no. You must not think there is anything salacious about what I propose. I have nothing to hide, only things I wish to *preserve.*" His fingers worried a photograph's edge. "I am an artist and my darkroom is in the basement. I am very particular about who shall see it when."

"What would I have to do?" I asked nervously.

"Don't worry about that," he said, glancing again at my legs. "I simply want to take some photographs. It will be painless. You will have your own room and three meals a day." He coughed slightly. "And some pocket change."

A strong urge came over me to tell him yes. *No.* I couldn't have anyone knowing me. I couldn't live with him. But neither could I live at the Y again and I was low on cash.

"Why don't you tell me your decision after you finish your soup? You must allow me to buy you another cup. I am very sure that that one is too cold. And it was my fault, my nattering on, that has hindered your finishing it. Besides, you'll find the tomato infinitely more palatable."

With that, he stood and walked to one of the automats. Plunking in the necessary coins, he got me another soup, this time a wide bowl. When he slid it on the counter in front of me, I looked down and saw a bowl full of what looked like blood. I stared at that dish as if a severed foot rested in it.

"When was your last meal?" the man asked quietly. When I didn't answer him, he took out a package of two saltines from his overcoat pocket. "Here," he said, gently. "These will help."

His soft voice almost made me cry. How long had it been since someone had been nice to me? Had served me a bowl of soup? Despite my wanting to go it alone, a flood of missing Fay washed over me then. I was fifteen years old and without a friend in the world.

"Allow me," the man said. Taking the package of crackers from my hand, he broke the Saltines into pieces and sprinkled them on the soup. "Go on." He motioned toward the bowl.

I swallowed a spoonful, the hot soup warming me considerably. The plastic spoon still trembled noticeably in my hand.

"My dear boy," the man murmured. "I know you're afraid."

Startled, I almost dropped the spoon in my soup.

"Who isn't?" He sipped his grey tea. "But," he said, drawing in a breath, "you have nothing to fear with me. Your secrets will be safe with me."

This time the spoon fell. A wave of soup splashed onto the counter.

"Dear me," the man said, immediately wiping up the mess with a paper napkin.

Not knowing what to do, I glanced over my shoulder at the door.

"What a rude man you must think I am." He continued mopping up the spill. "Here I am prattling on to you and I haven't even told you my name. Laurence. Laurence Jones." He gave me another barely there smile. "Perhaps you've heard of me?"

I hadn't. I swallowed another mouthful of soup, praying for Fay to tell me what to do. But she wasn't saying a word.

"And yours? I promise that will be the only question I ask you."

That sounded good to me. Since Fay wasn't saying anything to the contrary, I cleared my throat and answered, "Pete. Pete Smith."

...... ●◗

Chapter

TWENTY-SEVEN

Last night I eventually grew tired of sitting on the patio, so I left Spin sick on the couch, and after getting a pizza to go from Spiritus, I drove to the beach. I was parked and taking my first bite of a slice when I remembered that Spin loves Spiritus pizza. In spite of his compulsive cleanliness, he doesn't mind the extra oil that drips orange onto your paper plate. After that, I couldn't eat another bite. I ended up throwing the whole thing out in a trashcan in the parking lot. When I went home, three hours later, he was asleep, exactly where I'd left him, curled up on the couch. Or maybe he was just pretending to be sleeping. This morning before I left for work, he was still there, though. The blankets had been pitched to the floor. He looked small.

When I come home from work later, I'm relieved to find the front door wide open, curtains on the windows blowing like laundry airing on the line, and the couch empty. Must've been a twenty-four-hour bug like I thought. The house is quiet. *Good.* I'm in the kitchen mixing a gin and tonic when I hear someone on the stairs. A moment later and Spin's in the kitchen with me, looking pale, but he's dressed up in what is usually his club-hopping Friday night outfit. It's Tuesday. Six o'clock in the evening. He smiles, flexing his skinny arms in his sleeveless white T-shirt. His thumbs are hooked in the waist of his black leather pants, like

237

he's some sort of cowboy except he's wearing the purple and yellow high tops on his feet.

"Where are you off to?" I ask him, surprising myself. That nasty voice immediately launches: *What do you care?*

He opens the refrigerator door, takes out his rack of Chinese herbs, and, removing one of the vials, drinks down its amber contents. It's supposed to dilate your veins and give you a heightened sense of energy. He downs a second and third in quick succession.

"Isn't that dangerous?" Again, I surprise myself. The familiar voice is shouting now to shut the hell up. *Go about your business.*

"The show must go on," Spin says, closing the refrigerator door.

"Shouldn't you stay home?" I ask. "You seemed a little sick last night." I take a sip of my drink, crunch down on some ice to stop myself, but it doesn't work. "I could go and pick up a pizza," I offer. It's as if someone else is saying these words, not me. Someone who cares.

He pitches the three empty ampules into the trash one after another. The can is empty and when the glass vials hit, we hear them shatter. I flinch with each burst of glass.

"You're jumpier than a speed freak," he says. "Don't wait up, honey." He steps toward me, kisses me quickly on the cheek, and then pirouettes out of the kitchen.

The front screen door slams.

I lean against the counter. HIV hits some people slowly, like some deep philosophical realization. Others go downhill fast. How many of the men Spin cruises tonight will have it? I look around at the kitchen, which as usual is spotless. That dirty glass on the coffee table last night must've bothered him no end. *Why hadn't I cleaned it up when I saw it? Would it have killed me?* The dish drain is empty, the rubber mat underneath scrubbed clean. The black stove shines back your reflection if you hang your head over it. Inside the six cabinets, each shelf has been covered with black self-sticking vinyl. *You don't have to leave,* I tell myself. But it's no good. I run my fingers down the rims of the dinner plates, first shelf, second cabinet over from the refrigerator. I don't actually do this because I remember every item, every cabinet. Inside the silverware drawer corralled forks are next to the knives, and two rows of spoons: soup and then teaspoons. When I'm done reviewing every cabinet, every drawer in my mind, I turn off the light and go upstairs to my room. I lie down on my bed with my Postal Service blues and my shoes on. It's no good. It's never been any good. I memorized every kitchen, every room of every crappy trailer and mobile home I'd ever lived in. And by daybreak, Fay had us packed and in the car.

After I finished eating my tomato soup at the Horn & Hardart, Laurence and I rode the subway together out to Queens. We practically ran for the LL train from the D. As I sat down, I asked him breathlessly, "Aren't there other trains?"

"Other trains?" Laurence asked, confused.

"I mean, if we had missed this one." I wasn't saying this to needle him. I wanted to know where we were going, how often the trains ran, what trains would take me where, just in case I had to make a quick escape. Fay taught me to always find out what public transportation was available as soon as you visit a new town.

"You never know if you'll need it in the middle of the night," she'd cautioned.

"Why? We have a car."

"You can never have enough back-up plans."

"I *always* take this train," Laurence said peevishly and, offering no explanation, he looked away. The subway windows rattled as we came through a turn that brought us a fingernail away from a blackened wall. Laurence was a complete stranger and yet, I knew I shouldn't ask him anything further. I stayed silent, worried that I'd already irritated him.

Laurence Jones lived on Fulton Avenue, a busy thoroughfare in Queens saddle-stitched with small frame houses, one of which had been his mother's. Although she'd died two years before, if the dust covering most of the objects was any indication, everything was exactly as she'd placed them. Walking quickly through the living room—sagging couch, scalloped end tables with framed photographs and cheap figurines of boys in lederhosen and girls in bonnets—I followed Laurence into a bedroom.

"You can stay here if you'd like," he said. "It was my mother's room." The twin bed was covered with a blue chenille bedspread that was tightly stretched to all four corners. And then I saw why he hadn't been thrown by my braces. A wheelchair sat in a corner, by a small window.

Everything was neat in the room, simple. Quiet. I liked that immediately. Picking up a corner of the lace curtain that covered the bottom half of the window, I looked out onto the backyard where a small crab apple tree stood. *How many hours had his mother sat at this window?* For a moment I felt safe. A family had lived here. It was a real home.

It was getting darker outside, although it was barely late afternoon. The outline of the gnarled tree was framed by the heavy grey sky. Suddenly, it looked silly in the small patch of yard in this Queens neighborhood. This was crazy. Soon snow would be on the ground. Where could I go then? Where could I hide so that I'd never be found?

"I can have that put somewhere else," Laurence said quietly from the doorway. I dropped the curtain I'd been holding and lowered my stick to the floor again. He pointed at the wheelchair. "I'm sorry it's distressed you," he said. "I don't like it either. I don't know why I've left it here. Bad memories." He sighed and tugged at his coat lapel. "I'll move it right away."

Now I felt awful for coming. I didn't know Laurence, but he seemed to be a nice, if odd, man. What right did I have coming into this innocent man's life and home?

"Please don't go to any expense on my account," I said, my voice breaking. Whether he picked up on that, I don't know. He smiled as if he was afraid to show his teeth. I sensed right away that I'd embarrassed him.

"Expense? No, no. We wouldn't want to do that." I had no idea then, but that was Laurence's attempt at a joke. He was notoriously close with his money, using the same teabag over and over, darning socks that had so many holes they were useless even as furniture dusters. Not that he was poor. Months later, I would catch him one morning retrieving an old cigar box, like Johnson's, from under a floorboard in his bedroom. He'd pull out a wad of bills from his pants pocket, shove it in the cigar box, and put everything back again. But I didn't know any of that yet. Now he paused and looked at me with an astonished expression that seemed to say: Who are you?

"I'll wheel it out of here then," he said, more forcefully. Taking a hold of the wheelchair, he began to push it out of the room, but then stopped to give me a once-over. "I think you might fit some of my clothes. Yes. You must take a shower, dear boy. Your days as a gallivanting hobo are over, I'm afraid. Dinner will be in one hour," he said over his shoulder as he and the wheelchair went down the hallway toward the living room.

I told myself that if I was going to leave, now would be the time to do so. Then I looked at the tidy single bed, the soft chenille coverlet. The bedroom doorknob had a lock. *Maybe it wouldn't hurt to stay one night. Just until I made a plan.*

"Please don't be tardy," Laurence called out as he disappeared from view.

●·····●

Dinner that night was what I'd always imagined real families ate every night: roast beef, mashed potatoes, skeletal green beans that glistened with butter. Within twenty-four hours, I'd realize it would be the only time Laurence would cook such an elaborate meal.

Before dinner I'd gone to the bathroom for my shower. He'd left a neatly folded stack of his grey flannel pants, a grey button-down shirt, a belt, boxer shorts, and socks on the toilet. The pants were too big for me, but I could roll them up and the belt would at least keep them from falling down. Locking the door, I took a quick shower, happy that I could finally scrub myself clean, but still uneasy enough not to linger.

Now I stared at the full dinner plate in front of me and I almost started to cry I was so grateful. I glanced around the oven-warmed kitchen, my hands resting on the Formica table, and told myself, *I've made the right choice. I'll be okay.*

"Don't be shy," Laurence said as he helped himself to the roast beef.

I dug in.

"That's a good boy," he said, slivering the meat on his plate.

Later that night, when I went to my bedroom all my previous fears unfortunately rushed in again. The room looked smaller, more like a possible trap. I made sure I locked the door even though Laurence had been perfectly pleasant throughout dinner, talking mostly about his mother who had had no aspirations other than to take care of him. "Unconditional love," he said, his fork raised in the air with a green bean speared on its tines. "Do you know what I'm speaking of?"

I knew I didn't know squat about that.

I'd just stripped down to the boxers in the bedroom and turned toward the bed when there was a soft knock on the door. My stomach seized immediately. *Here we go*, I thought. My hand automatically touched the doorknob but then retreated. *What did he want? Maybe I'd imagined the knock.* Then, through the door, his voice: "Peter, please open the door."

I backed away. "I'm asleep," I said, trying to keep my voice steady.

"I have pajamas for you."

"That's okay," I said through the door, my voice pitching higher at the end in spite of myself.

"Dear boy, it's not a question. Please open the door."

Mollified by his saying "Please," I leaned over, unlocked the door, and backed up as fast as I could in my braces. I crossed my arms over my naked chest. He walked in, his arms straight out bearing a set of old man's pajamas that were boxy and striped and slightly mothball smelling. He placed them on the end of the bed.

"Where are your old clothes? I'll wash them," he said in a no-nonsense voice.

I hesitated. If I needed to run out of there in the middle of the night, I'd want my clothes. Who knew if there was still any evidence on them from Johnson? "That's okay," I told him.

He frowned.

When I still didn't budge, he shrugged. "Have it your way then." He walked through the doorway and before closing it, said, "Well, goodnight."

"Goodnight." Then I leaned over and clicked the lock tight.

········●➤

Chapter

TWENTY-EIGHT

y Timex, lit up in acid green, reads one fifteen in the morning. There's a slight breeze that's so warm it makes my bedroom in the eaves feel hotter. I've already counted the twenty-three dropped ceiling tiles. Lying on top of the bedcovers fully dressed, I run through the words I can create from Andersen, the manufacturer of the windows Spin installed a year ago. Besides the obvious—*an, and*—there are *sender* and *denser*. The one syllable words—*rend, nerd, and, sand.* One eighteen on the Timex. The roll blinds hit against the window sashes from the breeze, each time sounding like a slap. One nineteen.

Finally, there's nothing to do but pull on my khakis and button-down. I slip my feet into my oxfords, which feel brittle. When I tie a knot on the first one, the shoelace breaks. Holding the frayed shoelace seems symbolic of something.

By the time I walk down Commercial and into the A-House, the bartender is yelling last call. The bar is still packed with men who look as if they've been manufactured on an assembly line: white taut shirts, butt-hugging jeans, work boots. A disco ball, a holdover from the seventies, spins in the center of the dance floor. My eyes take a few moments to adjust to the semidarkness and that roving beam.

The dance floor is still jammed. A female voice sings over and over "I Will Survive," her voice and a steady thump blasting through the speakers. I find a dark corner. There are several bodies in front of me, watching the dancers. One of the dancers is Spin. *Okay, you can go home now. He's fine.* Spin gyrates on the edge of the dance floor, seemingly dancing with several men near him, but I can tell he's on his own out there. For one thing, none of the men so much as glance in his direction. Everyone else dancing seems to have clasped hands in the air, and they are jumping up and down in sync. Spin's hands are not holding anyone's. His rhythm is slightly off as his fists pound the air. Every time the light cuts across him, the sweat running down his face glistens. *He shouldn't be here. I shouldn't be here. Why did I come? To check on him? Okay. He's fine. Now go home.* Then he tries to sneak his hands on the waist of a Ken doll near him. Ken isn't having it. He immediately pushes Spin's hands off and says something to him, which I can't hear. He turns his back to him, facing someone else that could be his twin. The two Kens continue to dance, but it's obvious they're also moving away from Spin, leaving an empty space on the dance floor.

"Do you want a drink?" A beefy man with nipple rings and a leather harness straddling his chest jerks his head in the direction of the bar. He's as out of place in this sea of white T-shirts as I am. He's crept up on my left side without my knowing. That's not good. I'm losing my protective radar with each passing day.

"No thanks," I say curtly, angling my body toward the dance floor. I don't want Spin to see me, but I want to get rid of harness man. I've seen him in the PO before. During the day his wardrobe is more like a car salesman: short-sleeved, button-down shirts, shiny polyester pants that end in sensible shoes.

"I know you," he says loudly in my ear. I can smell the hours of beer on him, like wet, rotting leaves. For a minute, I stand completely still—frozen by those words I dread. *I know you.* It's been twenty-five years, but those three words still have the force of a pickax splintering a bed of rock. I shift my right stick forward, preparing to leave. He puts his hand on my shoulder.

"You're my candy man," he says beerily into my face.

Maybe he's been out to Spin's house to pick up some product, I'm thinking. Suddenly, I feel as if I can't breathe, the weight of him is too much.

I shrug his hand off. "I'm afraid you've mistaken me for someone else," I tell him and immediately am transported back to the day that I said those same words to someone else when I lived with Laurence. What would Laurence think if he could see me now? "My dear boy," he'd say, wagging his head from side to side. "What a debacle. What*ever* would possess you?"

My breathing constricts further. *Get out of here.*

"Wait," harness man calls after me. "I didn't mean to upset you."

Outside the air is damp, saturated with humidity and ocean moisture. I can feel the forearm cuffs of my sticks sliding with sweat. "Stupid. Stupid. Stupid," I mutter to myself, gulping air, willing myself to calm down. My breathing gradually slows. The shock of my going there, however, starts to settle in. Why had I gone? I realize that I wanted to see for once where Spin spent his nights—what it was that would compel him to leave the house when just yesterday he was sick with fever. At least *he* knew what excited him. Great. Well, I'd seen it now. The overwhelming loneliness of it. I'd never be able to forget the image of him rejected and separated from everyone else.

I push along the middle of Commercial Street, through the weaving men and women who, like me, haven't stayed after last call. The sound of a clicking engine from behind forces me to veer closer to the curb on the street. Cars can barely move five miles an hour on Commercial during season because the crowds are so thick and unruly. An older Mercedes convertible inches past me, the back seat overflowing with men in drag. Barbra Streisand, Cher, Diana Ross, and Judy Garland are blowing dramatic kisses as they drive by, the top rolled down.

"Pete!" I hear a voice shout behind me.

I quicken my pace.

"Pete!"

Dammit.

"Where've you been?" Spin asks when he runs up to me.

I pick up the pace again, practically killing myself. "Out."

"Hey, where's the fire?" he says, which stops me. He realizes that's a poor choice of words what with my trailer burning down last year. Giggling, he murmurs, "Sorry." His T-shirt is plastered to his chest. His hair is a frizz ball and he's breathing hard from running full-on to catch me. He rubs the palm of his hand across his forehead, then wipes it across his leather pants.

"It's hot, isn't it?"

A string of Mardi Gras beads lies broken by my feet. One of the beads shines by the curb.

"I said slow down, not stop," he says. As if released from a spell, we both start walking again. "This flu sure sticks with you."

"Maybe you should've stayed in then." As soon as I say the words, I regret them. *Shut up,* I tell myself. *Go home and go to bed.*

Spin laughs. Not what I expected. Then he throws his arm around my shoulders. Again, not expected. He has a hard time keeping it there with me chugging along, but somehow he does it. The longer his hand remains on my shoulder, the harder it is for me to break away. The harder it is to ignore it.

"What are you on?" I ask.

He laughs again, like he doesn't have a care in the world. "A new batch. You should try it, Petey. Might loosen you up."

I stop walking.

"I'll share with you," he says earnestly.

"I'm not interested. Do you mind?" I stare at his hand on my shoulder.

"Oh," he says and drops his hand. "I didn't mean anything."

I start to walk, and he follows me. My impulse is to apologize, but something else is taking over now. I'd been foolish checking up on him. Of course, he was all right—he wouldn't have gone if he hadn't been. *But what about the next time? And the time after that? Are you going to follow him every time he gets sick?* I feel him fall behind another step or two in back of me. He can't keep up the pace. I hear Fay's voice, the one I hate. The one that told me when I was a kid, "We don't do nice." The same voice that says now: You're not equipped. You know that. He's *sick*. Are you going to take *that* on?

We're two houses away from his, the only sounds are my sticks creaking and the soft squeaking of Spin's sneakers. There will be an endless stream of times, now, of sickness. By the time I swing open our gate I've made up my mind.

Not being in the Y, I slept dreamlessly that first night with Laurence. In the morning, I dressed in his clothes again, made the bed, and left the pajamas on the chenille bedspread, folded exactly in the same way that Laurence had given them to me. My own clothes I hid under the bed.

I found him in the kitchen, still at the Formica table as if he'd spent the night there. A white box of glazed doughnuts sat in the middle of the table next to a small pile of paper napkins that said Happy New Year! with brightly colored illustrations of party hats and blowers. I was startled to see the kitchen wall clock read ten thirty.

Laurence stood up and tapped the box of doughnuts. "Are you hungry? You should eat one of these." He was dressed completely in black, his shirt buttoned up to his Adam's apple. We looked like twin Jehovah's Witnesses. Only he reminded me of those stick figures kids would draw, skinny with hair standing straight up from the head. He walked over to a closed door on the other side of the kitchen. A sign was hanging on it with an illustration of a traffic light; the green was lit up. Underneath it read, "GO." He flipped it around and it became a red traffic light with "STOP" across the bottom. He opened the door.

"We're already getting a late start," he said, and glanced at the doughnuts. "You must eat quickly, I'm afraid."

My stomach immediately pitched, but I grabbed a doughnut, ate it in two bites, and followed Laurence down the steps to the basement.

"Please close the door behind you," he called up from the bottom of the steps.

"I'm sor—" I began to say.

"There mustn't be any more conversation." He put his index finger to his lips.

In the basement there were two rooms with cement flooring and walls. One was his darkroom where he developed all his photographs. It was small and windowless with rope strung from one end to the other. Photographs were clothes-pinned to the lines like counterfeit money. On a long table, large rubber dishpans were lined up as if for washing. One of them was half full and covered with Saran Wrap. I looked down and saw a murky reddish-purplish liquid.

"Don't ever touch that," Laurence said next to me, the room so close I could feel his breath on my neck. "It is very . . ." he hesitated. "Unstable." I instantly backed away.

Above the dishpans, which later I found out were called tanks, though they looked nothing like that, was a shelf full of plastic bags holding white powder, with labels that said Panthermic 777 Developer.

The other larger room had a couple of stools, a hung backdrop of silver paper, an antique chaise of worn black velvet, and a large chair that looked exactly like what I imagined a king's throne would look like: scrolled wood covered in chipped gold paint, wide curved arms, and feet like an eagle's talons. A small round pillow perched on the seat. It had an embroidered message: *Queen for the Day.* By the left wall was a large black oil tank that seemed out of place. In the center of the room perched on top of a metal stand was a black boxy camera with a large bellows and an accordion front, ending in two lenses. There were several lights similar to spotlights, aimed slightly upwards at black umbrellas that were opened and hanging from the ceiling by fish line.

I took it all in, the doughnut roiling in my stomach, and had a tremendous urge to race up the steps as fast as my sticks would take me.

"Sit please." Laurence bent over the camera.

Slowly, I moved toward one of the stools, but he said, "No. There." Without looking, he pointed toward the throne.

"It says it's for a queen," I told him.

Silent, he pointed to the throne again.

When I sat down, I couldn't look at him. I stared numbly at my oxfords, wishing I was anywhere else but there. I heard him move the camera stand, its metal legs scraping against the cement floor. It wasn't as if Laurence had threatened me in any way, but it felt as if he *might*. Unlike the day before when he was "nattering" on, now he was quiet, but because I didn't know him, I took his silence as a bad sign. Maybe the thing about me not letting him wash my clothes had pissed him off. I picked at the flannel on my thigh.

"You will need to take those off, I'm afraid," he said quietly. "But please leave on your braces and shoes. For the time being."

I could hear my heartbeat thumping in my ears. I swallowed

but my mouth was dry. My fingernails scraped the flannel. As my eyes lowered to the floor, I shook my head. No. There was the sound of footsteps, and then suddenly, he was crouching in front of me, his hands holding onto the curled ends of the throne's arms.

"You should leave on your boxers, of course," he said. "I'm only interested in your legs."

Without waiting for me to answer, his hands reached out and began to unbuckle my belt, which was really *his* belt. "Everything is going to be fine," he whispered. "You liked staying here last night, didn't you?"

"Cut it out!" I said, shoving his hands away.

He stood up. "I don't think you understand. These photographs are for an exhibit I am completing for a well-known art gallery in New York. I don't have time to waste. If you cannot do this, simply say so, and you can be on your way and I will find someone else. No hard feelings."

That made me look up at him. My fingers halted their clawing. His giving me the option made it seem less threatening, less likely that it was anything more than what he said it was. He said I could leave. No hard feelings. I thought of the warm, clean room I'd slept in and then of the hard cot at the Y. Of the roast beef he'd served me last night. *He's not asking you to be naked for God's sake. He just wants to shoot your legs. A couple of clicks of the camera and you're done.*

"Okay," I said quietly. Taking a deep breath, I stood and began to unbuckle my pants, letting them fall to my ankles.

"Wonderful."

I sat back down and slowly pulled the pants over my braces and then my shoes. I turned my head away, embarrassed. I'd never let anyone but Fay and maybe Johnson ever see my legs bare, without my Boy Scout shorts. Without my shorts to divert your attention, you'd focus on how pale and thin and crooked my legs were. How they still turned inward at the ankles. The braces looked like cages, torture devices, my oxfords and black socks ridiculously out of place.

"Magnificent," Laurence said.

Staring at the dirty cement floor, I shook my head, surprised that my eyes were welling up. *Don't cry,* I told myself. *Crying's for fucking sissies.* That helped. But when Laurence began to click the shutter once and then again and again, now adjusting the lens closer, now moving the camera nearer, I began to shiver, not from cold or fear, but from an overwhelming feeling that I was doing something that was wrong. It didn't matter where I'd end up or what I did—this is what would define me from then on. I looked down at my legs and my braces and thought, *This is who you are. This is all you are now. Get used to it.*

"Good," Laurence murmured. "Good. Trust me. Look up. Look up."

I did. I stared ahead, straight at the camera, my hands gripping the chair's arms, my lips pressed tightly together to stop them from trembling. But it was no good. I couldn't stop shaking, no matter how hard I concentrated. Above the camera's lenses was a thin metal plate that read GOWLANDFLEX. I began to form words out of the nameplate on the camera. Land. Flex. Wand. Flew. Now. Go.

"Magnificent," Laurence repeatedly crooned as he clicked away.

But every time he said it, I felt myself get smaller. It was as if I had gotten a job cleaning my high school's toilets and, scrub brush in hand, was being watched by every beautiful girl I'd ever wanted. After that, they'd never look at me the same way again.

Chapter

TWENTY-NINE

'm not going to leave Spin tomorrow, but I have to start preparing for it. I sit on my bed at night and in the darkness listen to rain thrumming against the roof. *You've gotten too comfortable*, I tell myself. The problem with living in actual houses is that you get spoiled. How can you willingly go back to a trailer on wheels? Rain on a shingled roof sounds comforting, on metal it's threatening. But I have to leave. And soon.

The next morning, I make my way downstairs. The house smells like cinnamon. Through the back slider I can see that Spin is already at the patio table, a coffeepot and plate of cinnamon swirls in front of him. I turn around and, without a word, walk out the front door.

From then on, I start eating all my meals out. I make sure I do my laundry when he's working in the still. After work, I stay out late at night, usually sitting in my car at the beach, listening to a talk show. I feel better listening to those people calling in, who are in far worse shape than Spin or me. A woman relates the story of how she lost her job, she's drinking too much, and her kids hate her. *She has it bad*, I think. Or at least that's how I'm rationalizing what I'm about to do. *Spin will be fine*, I tell myself. *He owns his own home. He's got money, his own business.*

"Hey, stranger," he says to me a week later. It's seven thirty in the morning, a Saturday, and I've tried to slip out the front door again, but this time he's waiting for me in the La-Z-Boy.

"Muffins will be ready in a few minutes," he says, and smiles. It's his hopeful smile, the one I've seen countless times when he asks me to go somewhere with him.

"Sorry. I'll have to take a rain check," I say stiffly.

"You working overtime?" he asks, his voice sad now.

I nod my head. Somehow that doesn't seem like lying to me.

"Maybe I'll see you later, then?"

I nod my head again.

The morning's dense fog hasn't lifted yet. The damp air chills my short-sleeved arms. For a few minutes, as I walk down Commercial, I can't see four feet in front of me. Perhaps I'll simply disappear in the enveloping fog. The idea appeals.

By the time one month turned into two, Laurence and I'd settled into a life of sorts together. Every day he took photographs, either of me or some other handicapped person who answered his new ad. He ran it weekly in the *Voice*, but now offered $1.40 an hour—the minimum wage in 1967—rather than room and board.

"Why don't you let any of them stay?" I asked him once. I hadn't yet gone to the second floor of the house where Laurence's bedroom was, but there had to be more than one room up there given the layout of the first floor.

He looked at me with amazement. "You are the entrée. They are the dinner mints."

Entrée or not, it never got any easier, no matter how many times he took my picture. I quickly learned the art of zoning out, erasing any thought that came as soon as it came. *Don't think. If you think, you're dead,* I repeated silently. Fay's mantra.

When I wasn't his subject, Laurence had me assist him, covering the lights slightly with colored cellophane paper, or loading the Swinger, a white plastic camera that allowed him to take instant Polaroid photos. Sometimes he photographed me with whomever showed up that day, sitting us in different poses. That was the hardest: leaning my head on the shoulder of a stranger, such as the woman who had an angry red birthmark the size of a teapot covering most of her face, or the man who'd been born with a flipper instead of an arm. *I'm not you*, I'd think to myself. *We're not the same.* But as the weeks went on, I had a harder time convincing myself of that.

Laurence *was*, though, like me in some ways. He was a horrible insomniac, hardly able to sleep for more than a few hours. Every night I could hear him padding around upstairs in his bedroom, then making his way on my floor to the basement door and stairs. One morning, I stumbled my way into the kitchen, having spent another sleepless, tiring night.

"Are you ill?" he asked me. When we weren't in the basement, he was surprisingly caring toward me, especially if he was concerned that I was sick. I'd decided it was the camera that made him unkind. When he was photographing me, he turned into one of those fathers at a Little League game, with a constant tight-lipped expression that said you can do better than this.

"Do you not feel well?"

Shaking my head, I slumped down at the kitchen table. He had a box of sugar doughnuts on the table and a cup of half-drunk tea in front of him. He drank tea all the time and it was the first thing he offered to his many artist friends who perpetually stopped by. Regardless of how many visitors or tea drinkers there were, he used the same tea bag over and over, dunking it into each cup as its boiled water turned lighter and lighter brown. By the time he got to the last person's cup, the water was barely the color of faded newsprint.

"Would you like some tea?" he asked me now.

"You don't have any coffee, do you?" I rubbed my eyes.

"Are you not sleeping? Is the bed not good?"

"I'm not a good sleeper."

At this he grimaced as if I'd said the ugliest thing possible and turned toward one of the two refrigerators in the kitchen. One held food and the other, rolls of film. Some of the kitchen cabinets stored brown envelopes with his photographs, filed in a mysterious order known only to him.

What was no longer mysterious was whether Laurence was going to try any funny business with me. The day before, a young blond woman had rung the doorbell. She was one of Laurence's students from Brooklyn College where he taught in addition to selling his photographs through Gallery 180, the art gallery that represented him. The young woman followed Laurence upstairs to his bedroom. I heard the door close, then the woman's muffled laughter. They didn't come downstairs for hours. That night at dinner, after she'd left, I asked him who she was, and it was one of the few times I ever saw him really irritated. He spat out a Balzac quote about every sexual involvement meaning the loss of a masterpiece. He didn't look happy when he said it.

Drinking our tepid tea on a morning in the second week, Laurence had asked me nervously, "I don't think school would be a very good idea, do you?" He seemed relieved when I agreed. I lied and told him that I'd been spending the last few months reading independently and had worked out my own system of learning. I left out the part about being on the run.

He clapped his hands. "Marvelous. We shall be our own lyceum then. We must get you a library card!" he exclaimed.

From then on, after our photography sessions, I made regular visits to the local library.

"How I wish I had your freedom," Laurence would call out as I left the house. He seemed heartsick when he said it.

I realized very quickly that Laurence being at the Horn & Hardart's that fateful day when I'd arrived in New York City was a rarity. He very seldom journeyed into the city. At twelve every day, we took a lunch break and walked to the nearby Woolworth's. As he did the first day that I'd met him, Laurence always chose a spot facing a large glass window that looked out onto the street. As we ate our lunches—a steamed hotdog in a damp bun for me and a piece of coffee cake for Laurence—we watched as young girls, out for lunch from school, walked in.

At Woolworth's, the draw was one particular girl whom Laurence always hoped to see. He called her Apricot Angel. She lived in our neighborhood and was about fourteen years old, going on twenty. She and two other girls made up what Laurence referred to as his groupies, although they'd never recognized him or paid any attention to him. There was nothing lascivious about how he watched them either. I had the distinct feeling that he examined them as an anthropologist tracked aboriginal tribes. Laurence studied them as art objects, nothing more. He even gave them all names based on the colors they wore. Apricot Angel was partial to orange. Chocolate Brownie wore every shade of brown you'd see in the woods. Snowflake Princess dressed only in white, although her ski jacket and matching skirt seemed to turn grey as the weeks passed.

One day I was in the front room of the house reading the horror stories of H.H. Munro when there was a banging at Laurence's front door. He was busy downstairs in the darkroom, developing a new batch of photographs that featured a husband and wife who were midgets. Apricot Angel stood alone on our front stoop. In her hands were a nub of a pencil and a small pocket memo book. The wire spiral on top was partly torn out of the pages.

"Wanna buy a subscription to the *New York Post*?" she asked me, loudly snapping a piece of gum.

I looked at the pocket memo book, which clearly had doodles all over the cover, and stick drawings of people hanging from gibbets.

"You work for the *New York Post*," I said. It wasn't a question.

"Uh huh," she replied and blew out a bubble that burst. Pink strings and gummy pieces flattened against her lips. With her free fingers, she peeled them off, sliding them back into her open mouth. For a second I saw her tongue, pink and small, like a snail.

"That doesn't look like an official subscription form to me," I said, motioning with my eyebrows.

"Is your creep of a father home?" she asked and snapped her refurbished gum. She eyed me up and down, her gaze finally fixing on the stirrups of my braces that poked out from underneath a pair of Laurence's grey wool pants before disappearing into my oxfords.

"Anything else?" I said. Before she could answer, I closed the door in her face.

I didn't tell Laurence about it. He was too gaga over her and wouldn't have believed me anyway. What would I say? That I didn't like strangers taking an interest in me?

A few afternoons later, however, Apricot Angel with her entourage strolled into Woolworth's while we were there.

"Oh my," Laurence murmured.

Apricot Angel was wearing a decidedly different outfit this day, dressed as a burlesque dancer. At least she was wearing a beaded black dress and matching headband under her small orange ski jacket and matching orange wool hat. The two other groupies were dressed as witches, with pointy rubber noses, the color and surface consistency of pickles. It was the first week of December, five weeks after Halloween.

Laurence lowered his teacup onto the saucer where his used tea bag sat folded in a paper napkin, ready for him to take home. We watched as the three of them began to circulate around the store's luncheonette, holding out orange boxes, the size of school milk containers, that said UNICEF in bold black letters. There were mostly bank clerks and secretaries at that hour in Woolworth's, using their half hour to wolf down watery macaroni and cheese, or a greasy grilled cheese sandwich on white bread. You could hear each of the girls say in a bored, mechanical voice, "Care to donate?" or "We're collecting for the starving children in Africa," and each time it would be followed by a *ka-plunk* of a coin being pushed through the slot. I was astonished by the number of people who fell for it.

"We must give them something," Laurence whispered to me, as if what he was saying was treacherous or unthinkable. It *was* unthinkable, given his normal skinflint ways, and I quickly stopped his hand as it reached into his coat pocket for his wallet.

"Don't. They're only going to keep the money for themselves," I said close to his ear.

He pulled away from me as if I had stuck my tongue in his ear, his face sheer disappointment. "My dear boy," he said, loudly. "Where did you get such a horrifying notion? They are angels of mercy."

To prove his point, he took out a single dollar bill and two quarters. When the threesome arrived by us, he slid one quarter into each of the orange boxes that Chocolate Brownie and Snowflake Princess held out.

"Can you spare it?" Chocolate Brownie muttered, walking away.

"Big spender," Snowflake added, following Brownie out of the eating area.

Laurence acted as if he hadn't heard them. He pushed the folded dollar bill through the slit on top of Apricot's box.

"Doncha live on my street?" she asked, staring at me.

"Yes, yes, we do," Laurence gurgled.

Normally, her recognizing me would have sent me into a tailspin. But Laurence's ebullience over her spurred on a sense of ownership that had been growing within me the last month. Yes, posing for the photographs was hard, but it was a known factor. I was fed and clothed, had a halfway decent bed, and I was going to keep it that way.

"You," I said pointing at her chest, "live on *our* street." My hand pressed against my chest.

She gave me a wide, cold smile and then began to chew a wad of pink gum, rather loudly. "You're the one who closed the door in my face," she said.

Confused, Laurence immediately turned to me.

I locked onto Apricot's eyes, which narrowed immediately.

"I'm afraid you've mistaken me for someone else," I told her.

She laughed meanly. "Why do you talk like that?"

"Dear girl, are you quite sure—"

"Like what?" I asked her, cutting Laurence off, something I'd never have done before because he was, after all, the roof over my head. But this girl was pissing me off now. Who did she think she was? Well, I would show Laurence *exactly* who she was.

"Like you got something up your butt." Her jaw was moving rapidly, working that gum.

"Young lady, I'd like to say—"

But whatever Laurence wanted to say, Apricot Angel waved him off. "That's okay, pops." And leaning closer to me, she blew out a bubble as large as a fist and quickly let it pop, right into my face.

"My goodness!" Laurence cried.

I was so startled I couldn't say a word as she sucked the deflated balloon back into her mouth and shouted, "Happy Halloween!" Then she skipped off in search of her friends.

"My stars," Laurence said. "I didn't know we were going to have such an adventure today. Wasn't her outfit splendid? I wish I had my Swinger with me. She *is* a spitfire. I do believe she has her eye on you, my boy."

I kept my lips cemented together, holding in words that would've certainly resulted in Laurence reconsidering whether he wanted to keep providing shelter for me. Apricot Angel was going to be trouble. No doubt about that. Given the choice between having her to live with or me, I knew exactly whom he'd choose. How long would it be before he'd grow tired of me and want a new subject? Sure, she wasn't handicapped, but maybe his next series would be on teenage girls. Apricot Angel was the type who glommed onto the suckers of the world like Laurence. And she'd know a liar too when she saw one.

During the second week of December, Gallery 180 held the exhibit of Laurence's work. He'd invited all his subjects to attend the opening night's cocktail party—we were each supposed to stand near our photographs—but only the midgets and I showed up. They'd previously told me that they'd been married for ten years and lived on Staten Island. He was going to night school to become an accountant. She was hoping to land a fairy role in an off-Broadway production of *A Midsummer's Night's Dream*. They left the gallery after thirty minutes, claiming it was too crowded and they were tired of staring into a sea of stomachs.

The room was dimly lit, although several strobe lights swept repeatedly across the room, lighting up real faces and then the faces in the photographs. The effect kept everyone off center. You couldn't get a grip on where exactly you were in the large room. Several people bumped into me, misjudging their distance. Whether that was from the lights or the champagne they were downing in black plastic cups, I couldn't have told you. I began the evening next to a vast wall that had two dozen photographs of my legs and feet, ending in a half-dozen close-ups of them without my braces and shoes on. After the first pale-faced, black-clothed visitors gaped at the photographs and then at me without saying a word, I moved through the crowd to the photographs of the birthmark lady. I pretended I was a visitor too, a fake smile on my face as I stared in mock admiration of her supposed self-confidence. I remembered, however, how she had cried uncontrollably and for what seemed like a very long time at the end of her photo session. She'd told me it was the first time in her life someone had made her feel beautiful. Laurence, who had been making a show of putting away his camera, had ignored her tears, only saying, "I dreamt that I was John Lennon again last night." He often began to recount his dreams whenever he was uncomfortable with whatever was happening around him.

Now as I stood in front of the birthmark lady's photographs, I found him at my shoulder. "You're supposed to be over there," he said petulantly. "By *your* photos."

I shrugged. "It's too crowded. Besides, none of the others are here."

"But *you* are," he said, irritated. "You must earn your keep, my dear boy."

I flinched. Visibly. That's what Johnson had said before throwing me into the tank. *You're gonna earn your keep for once.*

"What is it? Are you feeling faint?" Laurence asked, suddenly concerned. The strobe whisked across his face and jet-black hair.

"Yes," I lied.

"Here." He surprised me by slipping a twenty-dollar bill into my hand. "There will be taxis outside."

I swallowed. "What about the exhibit?"

"We can't have you fainting in here, can we?" Rubbing the top of his bristly hair, he looked around as if he were searching for help. "Go home immediately."

I hesitated, confused by his sudden change. But when he repeated "*Go*," I left and got in a taxi. It wasn't until the taxi pulled up to Laurence's house that it dawned on me what he meant by that, "We can't have you fainting in here, can we?" Maybe he hadn't been concerned about me at all. Maybe he'd simply been worried that I would steal the attention away from his precious photographs.

Every night after dinner, while Laurence was developing his latest rolls of film in the basement, I read or I did my old kitchen counter routine, which I'd returned to as something to do in the evening hours when I was alone.

"Oh, my dear boy," he cried the first time he caught me doing it. "Watch the sugar!"

In spite of his initial doubts and worries that I would injure myself, or break his mother's precious flour and sugar canisters, I think he enjoyed watching me. "You *are* strong," he said as I swung back and forth, picking up my right hand, then my left on the two counters.

If only you knew how strong, I thought to myself countless times. Although life had settled down for me at Fulton Avenue, my inner turmoil had not. At night, with Laurence in the darkroom, I lay on top of the chenille bedspread in his mother's room, wondering when it would come to an end. When would I make a mistake? I examined my hands routinely as if checking for dirt and realized with a crushing sense of defeat that maybe the last person they'd ever touch in my life would be Johnson.

Something would happen. It always did.

Chapter

THIRTY

The days I love best in Provincetown are the ones in January when the sky is that brilliant blue and the wind whips in from the ocean. It's like a belt snapped into the air, stinging our faces and the backsides of our legs, making us feel alive. During the hot summer days, however, the scorching sun at the beach seems to get on everyone's nerves as the afternoons progress.

The gay boys are the worst. At four, the ones who haven't gotten lucky all day in the dunes start to whine about whether they should go to yet *another* T-dance, or that they're tired of being the only ones who buy the beer or cook the dinners every night, or who do all the social activity planning. They start to search for somebody to pick on. You can easily find these men in the crowd: sunglasses slightly lowered on their noses, their eyes flitting around for prey.

This never stopped Spin though. Every day at three he'd take his break from the "lab," stopping in at the PO on his way to the beach. My shift would end shortly after. "Just going for a walk," he'd say. "Wanna come?" I'd tell him no and that was the end of it.

But when he stops by the PO this afternoon as I'm leaving and asks me, I can't turn him down. Knowing that I'm plotting to move out, I feel as if I owe Spin something. I don't like it either. As I sort out what it is exactly that I owe him *for*, he notices my hesitation. "Please," he says quietly, looking around us on the PO steps. I don't know who he's looking for—no one's out there but us.

"Don't make me beg," he whispers.

I try to avoid going to the beach whenever I can. It's not that I don't love the ocean or the sight of a pretty woman, in a bikini the width of dental floss. The beach is a painful reminder of what I really look like. Sand is not exactly a steady surface for a guy with two crutches. It takes us over an hour to walk what everyone else does in a half hour or less. We've drawn more stares than if we were buck naked.

"Well, he's *driven*," I hear one of the gay boys say about me as we pass by.

My white Brooks Brothers is fully unbuttoned. I'm drenched in sweat. Added to my khakis I'm wearing my heavy oxfords. Not exactly beach attire.

Spin snaps out our blanket in the dead air and smooths it over the hot sand. He practically hops up and down he's so happy. Unfortunately, his thin chest looks even scrawnier against the wide expanse of sea and sky. He has the physique of a boy who builds sandcastles. He's still wearing his backpack, which adds to the schoolboy illusion. His wiry hair is frizzier than ever near the ocean.

Throwing my sticks down, I find a spot on the blanket and sit.

"Aren't you hot with that shirt on?" he asks as he unshoulders his pack. I know what he wants. He wants me to lift the curtain and wow the audience. My small, rippled waist leading up to the broad shoulders, the muscular arms—this is what he has to offer as bait to the sharks circling around us. This grieves me no end. Not because I feel like a freak attraction. No, I mourn for Spin who must depend on me, someone lower than him in the food chain.

He lies down next to me on his stomach, facing me, his eyes closed, his toes tapping against the blanket. Right away I notice it. A purple lesion, the size of a dime, on the back of his thigh. Normally it would be hidden by his shorts, but he's cut this pair too high up.

I look away, watching two men in the water. They stand on tiptoes, grimacing against the cold water inching up their thighs as they slowly move deeper and deeper.

It's no good. I'm drawn back to that lesion. Maybe I hadn't seen it correctly the first time. The glare of the late afternoon sun often transforms the beautiful into the ugly: a sunburn in a dark club looks healthy, on the beach it's painful to look at. Maybe it's not a lesion at all. Maybe it's just a spider bite or a mysterious grape stain.

It's a lesion. The more I stare at it, the more it seems to throb with the heat. *Should I tell him? What will happen if I do?* That second voice of mine kicks in: *Don't tell him. It's not your problem.* But that second voice is weaker ever since I went to that club the other night and witnessed him all alone in that crowd.

The two men are up to their waists now. With their palms they lightly brush the top of the surrounding water.

"Take off your shirt already," Spin murmurs. "You look like a geek. Everyone's looking at us." This is, of course, exactly what he wants. But does he? If he knew that angry sore on the back of his thigh was uncovered, would he still want us to be noticed?

"Spin," I finally say.

He opens one eyelid.

"Roll over, will you? I can't talk to you that way." I notice a man to our right. He's by himself, stretched stomach down across a thin white hotel towel no bigger than a dishtowel. In a Speedo, most of his body lies directly on top of sand. He's watching us.

"Roll *over*," I say more urgently. There's nothing that I want more in the world at this moment. Still, he doesn't move. I take off my shirt and that does the trick, he immediately turns over. Fay used to say you can't expect an audience to give you what you want until you deliver the goods.

A half hour later, Spin starts to flip his body again, but I stop him this time with my hand on his shoulder. I've never touched him before. Several times I've gone out of my way to avoid doing so. Touching someone is open to interpretation. You can get yourself in a shitload of trouble. Given the circumstances now, though, I don't care what message I'm sending before I grab his shoulder, other than *don't move*. He immediately stares at my fingers on his bicep.

"Don't do that," I say quietly.

"Do what?" Still looking at my hand, he smiles. "Oh."

Our letters have crossed in the mail. He's imagining what he wants to do with my hand.

"There's a lesion on the back of your leg," I tell him, keeping my voice low.

"What do you mean?" His smile falters. He tries to lift his head, but I'm still holding him down by the shoulder.

"It's on the *back* of your leg."

"Shit," he says and closes his eyes. "Shit. What am I going to do?"

At first, I think he means now, this very moment, but when his eyes open a second later, they've dulled from their usual dark blue to ash and they're wet.

"How long?" I ask him. He doesn't answer me. He doesn't have to. Somewhere in me I know. I look at the ocean. It's empty now. The sunbathers around us are gradually pulling their stuff together, umbrellas are folded down, sand chairs gathered. For them, it's time for T-dance where they'll show off their glistening bodies, dancing with wild abandon, proud of how full of life their bodies are. How good their lives are. How much they're loved.

Grabbing my shirt from the blanket, I place it on Spin's chest. "Here. Put this on around your waist." Something about doing that makes me feel better.

His fingers massage the collar for a moment before he sits up and ties the shirt around his waist. "Pete," he says so quietly that I know more is coming. "I've wanted to tell you—"

"You know Sally at the office?" I say fast, interrupting him from whatever it is he wants to tell me . . . it can't be good. I don't wait for him to answer my question. He knows it wasn't really a question anyhow. Of course, he knows Sally.

"There's a trailer available for rent," I barrel on. "Where she lives. I'm supposed to take a look at it at six tonight. You know I've really appreciated you letting me stay at your place temporarily."

It's all a lie, of course. I hate myself for saying it. But there it is. How can I take care of a dying man? Look what happened with Laurence. I don't know the first thing about taking care of anyone, other than myself. I don't know the first thing about sickness or death. For all my experiences, not one of them has prepared me for this. In fact, my life has prepared me for just the opposite. Fay had gone off and died by herself, away from me. Just like a cat will up and leave its warm home where it has lived for eighteen years and find an out-of-the-way bush to crawl under and die. That's what I'm used to. *Be a fucking cat*, is what I want to yell at Spin in this moment.

"Well, that's great," he says, forcing a smile. "That sounds perfect." He ties my shirt tighter. I want to slap him hard to make him angry. It would be easier for me then. Fay used to have a routine with the men she'd been with. As soon as she got tired of them, she'd do something awful—once she worked it out so that some poor jerk had found her in bed with his sister—his *sister* for God's sake. Fay would get them to yell and punch walls, so she'd be justified in packing our bags and driving us away. I want Spin to grab one of my sticks and smack the living daylights out of me. *Better yet, take the goddamn sticks with you, so I'm left on the beach unable to go home until a park ranger comes and takes pity on me. Let me fry in this fucking sun.* But Spin isn't angry, or at least he's not showing he is. He knows I'm leaving when he needs me most. He knows he will probably die alone and in pain. Still, knowing all this, he says in the gentlest voice possible, "We should get going then. You don't want to miss your appointment." He stands and then starts to pull the blanket out from under me.

Christmas Eve at Laurence's house was fast approaching. In November, he'd told me how excited he was that I'd be with him this year. Before his mother died, it had been a favorite holiday for him, but after her death he hadn't so much as lit a candle, let alone a tree. "This year will be different," he claimed.

He seemed to be endlessly entertained by all the lights on the houses on Fulton Avenue, pointing out the uniqueness of the decorations where I only saw the same old beat-up crèches, the same standard red, blue, and green lights in the shape of large teardrops. That changed on December 20th. That morning, Laurence awakened unusually energetic. He requested that we make a journey into the city. It had been a long time since Laurence had taken a trip into the city, other than for his exhibit. We hadn't ventured farther than Woolworth's.

"I'm in the mood to wander," he said mysteriously. We ended up at Grand Central Station, one of his favorite places. Unknown to me, however, that was the day *The Village Voice* was publishing a review of his exhibit. He, of course, knew about it. Opening night, the *Voice* had sent over a photographer and the art critic David Seardon. Now, seeing a copy of it on a newsstand in Grand Central, Laurence hesitated, as if from second thoughts, and then began to rifle through it, his hands visibly shaking. He was too tall for me to catch a look over his shoulder, so I tucked in at his elbow. It had the ghastly title of "Stolen Lives." There were two photographs: one of the midgets sitting together on the throne and another of me standing next to the girl with the face birthmark, holding a hoe, like a reproduction of *American Gothic*.

Laurence quickly read the text, his index finger weaving down the page. "This is *abortive*," he whispered. I read the first sentences: "No wonder American Indians thought photographers could steal the souls of their subjects. Laurence Jones has shamelessly stolen the souls of the most challenged among us. He believes this is art. Shame on him."

"You gonna buy that or just make it dirty for my next customer?" a man who looked like a pug dog—big rheumy eyes, smashed nose—growled from behind the small counter.

"I am being asked to pay for my own suicide," Laurence muttered as he reluctantly plunked down the money. He rolled up the newspaper and jammed it into his overcoat pocket. "They have taken what's beautiful and made it ugly," he said as he walked away.

We went home immediately. We'd barely been in the city fifteen minutes.

Whether he read the entire article, I've no idea. I never saw it again. He fell into a deep depression after that, only dressed in his ratty bathrobe, barely left the kitchen table, no longer shaved.

Christmas Eve arrived. Finally, I forced him with much begging to leave the house to get a tree. I wanted to celebrate: President Johnson was pushing for an end to the war. He'd gotten Saigon to agree to the Paris Peace Talks, which were scheduled to happen in early spring. Like a boy scanning the sports pages about the Mets, on my weekly library trips I'd read with hope and anticipation every newspaper article on the prospect of a peace treaty being signed by the end of the coming year. Maybe everything would turn out okay. Fay might be coming home soon.

How would she find me though? This idea troubled me no end. I knew she'd return to our mobile home in the Keys. But what would she think when Mrs. Henderson ran out to greet her, bursting with the sordid details? There was no way Fay could know where or how to reach me. Queens would not be on the top of her list as potential places of where I might be. Queens wouldn't be on the list at all. That didn't stop me, however, from imagining otherwise. Fay would somehow follow my trail. She'd chat up the ticket agent at the bus depot in Key West. She'd check out the trains. During the weeks leading up to Christmas, I'd lie on my bed, my daydreams about Fay tracking me more and more outlandish, until I'd be startled by the fact that the sun had gone down and I was immersed in darkness.

Laurence, of course, knew none of this. I hadn't told him about Fay yet. If I started, I knew I'd tell him everything. *Everything*. No, I couldn't tell Laurence. Besides, now I was obsessed about getting the perfect, real Christmas tree, something I'd never done before.

On Christmas Eve he awakened, again depressed and agoraphobic, saying he couldn't be expected to actually *celebrate* Christmas, claiming on top of everything else—his mother's death, the monstrosity of living after those who love you pass to the other side—that he had had "helter-skelter dreaming" the night before. Helter-skelter dreaming. This was not a good sign. Laurence's faith in his dreams was as unshakeable as his daily photography sessions. They were not to be trifled with.

"This isn't some whimsy that I can simply overlook," he said matter-of-factly as he sat at the kitchen table, still in his bathrobe. It was three o'clock in the afternoon. I was ready to go get the tree, already dressed in my black wool overcoat, another Laurence hand-me-down.

"Dreams are a serious business, my boy." He sipped his watery tea. "And mine are inevitably telling me something that I should pay attention to."

"Oh, really?" I said in a slightly mocking tone.

"Yes," he said affirmatively. "They *are*."

I slumped down at the table, making sure I caused a racket with my sticks knocking against the table.

"I swear I have never had such a headache," he said, rubbing his temples.

"What was it about?" I said, referring to his dream. I picked peevishly at a button thread on my coat. The two months I'd lived with him in relative safety had begun to change me back to what I'd been before Fay left for Vietnam: a teenage boy who desperately wanted a normal home, a normal life.

"Which dream?" he asked. "There were many . . . skittering around like deranged cockroaches." Closing his eyes, his fingers fluttered at the air.

It seemed that we would be there for the rest of the afternoon. I unbuttoned my coat.

"I thought you *liked* Christmas," I said, frustrated. "What about the lights and the Madonnas?"

The telephone rang, another bad sign. The tree sellers closed at five o'clock on Christmas Eve. They had trees of their own at home to decorate. The phone would only hold us up more.

"Don't answer it," I blurted out, but it was too late. The receiver was already in his hand. It was Clea Stevens, the owner of Gallery 180. *Mrs.* Stevens, as I was instructed to call her from the first week I'd lived there, was an ambivalent cocktail: One minute she was praising Laurence as the next Cocteau and the next she'd be at our kitchen table, sighing, "I don't know, Laurence. Maybe the public isn't ready for all of this."

"Yes, Clea, I'm aware that it is almost Christmas, but *my*

dreams," he whined. I went into my bedroom and closed the door, defeated and miserable.

A little while later, I had almost given up hope of ever having anything remotely like a real Christmas when I heard footsteps outside my door. Laurence found me lying on my bed, my overcoat still on because it was so cold in the house. Surprisingly, he was dressed: black pants, one of his grey cotton shirts peeking out from the lapel of his dark threadbare overcoat. His face looked more ashen than ever. He seemed on the verge of collapse.

"If we are going, we should leave soon," he said, wringing his hands.

I pushed myself to a sitting position and, reaching for my sticks, stood. "Thank you so much," I gushed as I followed him through the house.

He stopped immediately, almost knocking me down. "Dear boy," he said. "You should thank Mrs. Stevens, not me. She is your fairy godmother. This is all *her* idea."

By the time we got to the corner where they sold the trees, there were few left and those had lost most of their needles. The trees were piled willy-nilly against a chain link fence, in front of what used to be an old gas station that had shut down years ago. Two rusty gas pumps still stood on a blacktop strewn with broken glass, mostly from cheap liquor bottles. A boarded-up building sat to the right, its whitish paint covered with graffiti. It was hardly the perfect setting for some yuletide spirit, but it was close to where we lived, and it was the only place open.

"They're not in very good shape," I groused, mostly to make Laurence feel bad for delaying us. It probably wouldn't have made any difference if we'd arrived earlier. It was Christmas Eve after all. Every other family had had their trees for weeks. But I wanted to make him *think* it would have made all the difference in the world. I might've experienced a lot for a boy of fifteen, but I could be a pain in the ass when I felt things weren't going the way I wanted them to. Nothing had ever gone the way I'd wanted with Fay and I hadn't showed her one raisin of my frustration. Look where *that* had gotten me.

Laurence didn't seem to hear me. His gloved hand was fingering a needleless branch on a three-foot tree that wouldn't have satisfied even a dog dying for a pee.

"They're not in very good shape," I repeated, stubbing one of my sticks against the stump of another tree. It was roped up and lying on its side in the rubble as if it had been lassoed, tied to a tailpipe, and dragged there.

"Bewilderingly so," he replied, his fingers still massaging his sad tree. It was as if he were willing the tree to grow its needles back. His pale face looked like a chiseled ice sculpture against the overcast sky. Suddenly letting go of the tree, he rubbed his temples with both hands.

"Do you have a headache?" I asked hurriedly. If so, I'd have to act fast. One of these trees was better than none.

"Just a little pressure," he said. Closing his eyes, he added, "It smells like snow, doesn't it?" When I didn't say anything, his eyes opened. "You have to close your eyes in order to smell it." So, I closed my eyes and when I did, a crisp dampness was instantly all around me.

"You smell it?" Laurence asked, and I nodded my head. "This tree is lovely, really." Opening my eyes, I saw that he'd retrieved the tiny tree and was twirling it around by holding onto its topmost point. He was smiling. What had gotten into him?

Carrying it, he walked toward the makeshift table where you paid. A banner was strung across the chain link fence: Girl Scouts of America Christmas Tree Sale. Then I realized what had changed his mood.

"Look," he whispered to me. "It's our little Apricot Angel. Did you know she was a scout?" he asked as if Apricot Angel and I were friends. She was wearing her orange wool hat and matching mittens. She cupped the mittens near her mouth and blew on them.

"Let's go," I whispered urgently to him. "These trees are too expensive."

But it was too late.

"Hey," Apricot Angel called out. She was standing next to someone I took to be her troop leader, a woman who looked as if she'd never laughed at a joke in her life. The woman's breasts were so big she couldn't zipper her coat up all the way. Apricot Angel appeared unbelievably bored. She was chewing another piece of gum rather noisily.

"Hello, my dear," Laurence said, spinning the tree in the air like a top.

"Five dollars," the troop leader said.

Laurence took a step back. "But surely that cannot be the price of this little tree."

Apricot Angel snapped her gum as loudly as a cap gun. Laurence jumped. He let the tree drop to the ground, positioning it so that it leaned against him. He wiped his brow.

"Five dollars, mister," Apricot Angel repeated and then gave us that dreadful, fake smile that made me want to slap her.

"My goodness," Laurence mumbled and, reaching into his pocket, retracted a five-dollar bill folded into a swan. Apricot Angel grabbed it before he could have any second thoughts. She passed it to the troop leader without so much as a glance. The swan was lost on the both of them. The troop leader shoved the bill deep into the recesses of her blue parka and zipped it half-closed again. The whole transaction had taken less time than it takes to say Merry Christmas.

"We should go." I was embarrassed for Laurence, for us,

although I couldn't have said why. What's more, I hated that it was Apricot Angel who'd made me feel this way. Angry, I pivoted around to start the journey home.

"You're that artist fella, orangeja?" the troop leader asked, which made me turn back immediately.

"Someone told me you take pictures of stupid people," Apricot Angel spoke up. Her gaze was fixed on me. I felt Laurence waver next to me and the tree nearly slid off him to the ground, but I caught it just in time with my stick and leaned it back against his waist.

"Charlene, that's a terrible thing to say to the nice man," the troop leader said and smiled at us, the same smile that Apricot Angel—*Charlene*—had shot at us.

"We should go home," I repeated, this time more forcibly and I actually started to walk away. This was a risky move on my part. It meant that I was depending on Laurence to follow with the tree. Thankfully, he did, cradling the tree in his arms like a baby although he didn't walk so much as stumble along next to me.

"Merry Christmas," Apricot Angel called after us in a grating voice. Neither of us said anything back.

Laurence, mortified, trudged along next to me. "Such coarseness," he said as we walked up the steps to the house. He fumbled in his pockets for the keys. "My heart is broken."

He went straight to the backyard, still cradling the tree. Despite how cold it was, he sat down in a vinyl lawn chair underneath the crab apple tree. Our pitiful Christmas tree hung across his lap, looking more like a broken stick than ever.

He didn't come in till after I drifted off to sleep, wrapped still in my overcoat. Before dawn I woke up to a colder than ever house. I looked out my bedroom window. A thick softness of snow had fallen during the night, covering the Christmas tree which was still on Laurence's now vacant chair. A large black bird perched on the end of it. It was the biggest crow I'd ever seen. *I wonder if Laurence knows what one crow means*, I thought, and got out of bed.

He was asleep in the kitchen, his head resting on his arms on the table. There was an unfinished letter to his right, left off mid-sentence and addressed to his mother. Something about the world being a prison. I left him where he was and went to retrieve our tree.

That afternoon, when I asked him what the crow's appearance meant, he shook his head gravely while staring at his slippered feet. "You say it was big?"

I nodded my head. "With its wings out, it was as big as my chest."

His hand massaged the rough stubble on his cheek. "That was a raven," he said solemnly.

"Yes, but what does it mean?" I asked impatiently.

"Death, my dear boy. Death."

Chapter

THIRTY-ONE

After I drop Spin back home from the beach, I find a mobile home in Wellfleet to rent that afternoon. Not in Sally's trailer park, of course. That was a lie. It's in back of a falling down house with grayish curtains, several windows boarded up, and a black garbage bag fluttering in the breeze that's caught on a bush in the front yard. There's a second, smaller trailer two car lengths away from mine that looks like it should be left at the town dump. The man who owns the property and lives in the house in front is a notorious boozehound and wife beater. It serves me right. Having to listen to someone used as a punching bag every single night is honest retribution for what I've done to Spin. I move what I own—my clothes, two boxes of books, and a futon—within thirty minutes. Spin is nowhere to be seen as I pack everything with the help of the two gay men next door. They lift the futon onto the Mustang's roof and rope it down, tightening the nooses by pulling on the ends of the rope with their entire weights.

Somehow, we found our way through Christmas without Laurence ending up in the hospital for electric shock treatments. Nevertheless, it was bleak. There was a tree but no ornaments, other than some paper cutouts of triangles and circles I'd crudely managed out of old newspapers. There were no presents. He never got out of his bathrobe. Throwing his overcoat over that, he left one of the kitchen windows open for the entire day, a sprawl of birdseed cast across the table, a few abandoned birds hopping in and out as if it were a drive-in. "I cannot breathe in here," he said as if that explained it. While he barely left the kitchen table, I spent the day on the couch, wrapped in as many clothes as he'd lent me, staring at the Christmas tree and wishing I knew how to fix things. In spite of myself, I had grown fond of Laurence, but I didn't have a clue what to do for him, how to make everything right again.

At one point during the day I went into the kitchen to check on him. His index finger was slowly inching some birdseed toward one jittery sparrow. A teacup sat in front of him with grayish water in it. I asked if he'd like some tea. He looked at me as if I'd asked him to dance.

"My dear boy, what do you think *that* is?" he asked, tapping the lip of his cup. I made my way back to the couch and stayed there for the rest of the day.

A week passed. Still, Laurence's mood didn't improve. It was as if we'd moved into a funeral home, everything cold and austere, a deathly hush following me everywhere, and Laurence at the kitchen table, as shadowy and solemn as a funeral director. The food refrigerator became emptier. I could walk to the store, but how would I get the bags of food home with my sticks?

We began to subsist on nothing but weak tea and stale doughnuts that he had boxes of still. Laurence was content with this, of course. The simplicity of it appealed to him. There was nothing to disturb him from his misery at the kitchen table. He rarely went down into the basement anymore. No one came either; he'd stopped running the ad. One morning I walked into the kitchen to find on the table a few of his photographs that hadn't made it into his exhibit. Laurence held one in his hands, with his face close to the surface as if he couldn't see it.

Not thinking, I blurted out, "Are you going to do something with those?" at which point he picked up a pair of scissors and cut it in half.

After that, I became driven to lift him out of his sadness. I kept the teakettle full of fresh water. He'd stopped bathing weeks before, but I made certain that the bathroom was spotless, his shaving brush and razor placed on the right side of the sink as he liked them. Then, one day I came up with a different plan. I pretended to happen upon his many envelopes in the kitchen cupboard. Pulling out the one that I knew housed the photographs of me, I said innocently, "What's this?" He smiled wanly and with his bony hand, motioned me over to the table with it. I almost kissed him for it.

"It's cold," he said, shutting the window for the first time in days. We spent the day going through each of them in intimate detail, which I was only able to do by pretending they were someone else's legs, not mine. "You were my best subject, you know," he said wistfully.

For a few days afterward, his mood steadily improved. It was like watching an alcoholic recover. One morning he stayed in the bathroom for over two hours, lying in the empty tub first fully clothed in pajamas and bathrobe, and then in the afternoon, finally taking the leap and actually undressing, filling the tub with water, and taking a long bath. Suddenly he was dressed again, grey shirt buttoned to the top, black creased pants, polished wingtips.

"We need food," he said, and I did kiss him for that, lightly on a very cold cheek.

We'd survived and with each passing day that Laurence appeared to be on the mend, my memory of the previous awful month weakened and then was forgotten. It's what I'd done all those years with Fay.

By now it was the end of January. The days were near zero and

Laurence let me turn up the heat. "Just a smidgen," he told me. Everything augured well, as he would've said. We'd only to get through February and then spring would be on its way. He liked the spring. It was a time of hope, he said. Soon, the sugary smell of his mother's hyacinths from the backyard would drift into the kitchen, bringing with it memories from better times.

I woke up on the first day of February with a feeling of anticipation. I swung my sticks out into the kitchen. Laurence, fully dressed, sat at the table with a newspaper. The kitchen was warm: the window was still closed, and the oven was on.

"Shoo shoo," he said to a crow that perched on the outside windowsill. He rapped the newspaper against the glass and the crow flew off. "I've already been to the store and gotten us coffee cake!" he exclaimed, cheerily raising the newsprint in front of his face. I looked at the paper's headlines facing me, and I let out a horrible scream as if I'd cut off my hand. "VC Bomb Saigon," the headlines read in blocky bold letters. "Thousands of Americans feared dead on Tet."

Chapter

THIRTY-TWO

onths have gone by now and I rarely see Spin. He almost never comes into the PO anymore. Or maybe he picks times when he knows I won't be there. That's what I'd do. I sort the mail and sell stamps to tired year-rounders who are crossing off the days on their refrigerator calendars to when they can leave for a month in Belize.

My nights are worse. Weeks of quiet in my trailer have suddenly been replaced by a nightly ten rounds of the most godawful violence you've ever heard under one roof. My landlord, Buzz Harpur, is on a nonstop bender that he takes out on his poor wife. I lie on my futon bed, pillow uselessly over my head, mentally shouting at Mrs. Harpur: *For God's sake, leave!* Every night I think of Spin and how this is what life must feel like for him. He and Mrs. Harpur are soul mates, their lives made more painful by men.

One day I realize that it's November because there's been another mass stranding of pilot whales in Cape Cod Bay. I read all about it in the *Provincetown Advocate*, which someone has left in the bathroom at the PO. Whales swim unaccountably into the Bay some Novembers, get trapped in the shallow waters, and end up stuck in the sand, where they die. Some thirty pilot whales have washed up down by Herring Cove. Divers from the Cape Cod Stranding Network, wearing cold-water survival suits, have been working feverishly through the night, trying to push the heavy whales back out into the ocean. These particular whales travel together in social groups called pods. I learn that once a whale is born into a pod, it never leaves willingly. No matter what happens, they stay together. This makes me think of Spin, and then I realize that while I might think of him every night when Mrs. Harpur is having the shit kicked out of her, it's been at least three months since I've actually seen him.

When I leave the bathroom and return to my station at the front counter, I ask Sally, "Hey, have you seen Spin lately?" She doesn't look at me when she shakes her head no. *Is that because she's heard I abandoned him and is disgusted? Or does she know something about Spin? Maybe he's gotten worse.*

"I'm taking lunch," she says, closing down her register.

The rest of the day is interminable. Finally, at four, I'm able to leave. I walk down Commercial as fast as I can, swinging my sticks out in quick succession. How many times have Spin and I walked down Commercial Street together over the years? Hundreds? Most of the time I've been embarrassed by his prancing, his constant lookout for something that was out of his league anyway. Now I realize I'd give anything to see him twirling down this street.

His house looks dark even for a November day. I ring the doorbell although I know the door won't be locked. Nobody comes right away. Maybe the doorbell is broken. I knock. I wait for a good five minutes. Silence. Then something shifts in the air, as if the barometric pressure has dropped, but the air temperature and humidity are exactly the same. He's on the other side of the door. I feel him. I know it as surely as if I can see him.

"Spin," I say quietly. "Spin, open up." There's a click of a lock and then the door opens. Thank God I hadn't seen him at the PO. I wouldn't have recognized him. The man who stands before me is bald, weighs maybe one ten, and leans heavily on a wood cane.

"Pete," he says, his voice like his body, a shadow of its former self. It's breathy now and soft. "Come in." He waves a bony hand—the one not clutching the cane—toward what had been the living room, but which now is obviously his dying room. Blankets are tossed and tousled into a knotted web on the couch. The coffee table is covered with dirty glasses, used tissues, and a cereal bowl full of what looks to be a mound of pharmaceuticals. Trays of uneaten delivered food—the kind that shut-in seniors receive—are waiting for someone to pick them up. Blinds close off every window. The television, on low, is set to a religious channel that we used to watch for laughs. Pushing aside a slew of discarded *Advocate*s on the La-Z-Boy recliner, I sit down. Spin collapses onto the couch and immediately curls onto his side in a fetal position, his feet jammed against the web of blankets. I shift my weight to stand again, so that I can straighten the blankets for him, but he holds up a hand.

"I'm good." Again, his voice is full of breath. His eyes are cloudy. His head swivels and he watches the religious program intently. The main speaker is someone who's recently been written up in the papers as having had sex with a prostitute named Geechee. Now this man is on his knees begging his congregation for forgiveness. Spin doesn't crack a smile.

"Why are you watching this? We used to laugh at it, remember?"

He doesn't take his eyes off the TV. We sit watching the stupid show for ten minutes. Finally, I can't stand it anymore. I make a move toward the trays of food for something to do.

"Leave it," he says, his voice more adamant. His eyes never leave the television.

"Look, this place is a wreck," I say. "Let me at least clean up."

"I'm fine."

The show finishes with a choir singing, "Take Me to the River." His eyes close. "I need to sleep now. Please close the door on your way out." His bony hand reaches out and, grabbing a couple of pills, he pops them in his mouth and dry-swallows them. He crunches his body even tighter, a corner of a blanket gripped in his hands.

In desperation, I look from one window to another. Every orchid is a shriveled stalk of brownness. The wood floor is littered with brittle, curled petals.

I clear my throat. "At least let me take the plants out," I plead. *When was the last time I begged for anything? The one time I begged Fay to take me with her? Not to Vietnam. That I hadn't been smart enough to do. No, where was it? St. Louis? Hoboken?*

"You're better off not showing what you want," Fay had said over my whining. "There's more of a chance people will give it to you that way."

"Leave it. I like *them*," Spin says and starts to cough hard.

I immediately take a step toward him, but he holds up a hand. "No! Stay away from me!" he shouts, his cough ratcheting. "Get out! Get out! I don't want you to see me like this!"

There's nothing to do but leave. I stumble my way out the door and click it closed behind me. As I pole my sticks as fast as I can away from his house, I can still hear him coughing. My breath catches. Rounding the corner on Commercial, I'm hit full-on by the stiff November wind propelling off the ocean. The sheer will of it almost knocks me over.

For years I wondered why that day in Laurence's kitchen, I was so certain that Fay had died when I read that headline. She would've said it was because of our blood bond. "Blood is thicker than mud," she used to say. Whatever it was, I knew when I read those headlines that Fay was dead.

My grief was sudden and deep. Blubbering, I told Laurence everything. I had nothing to lose now. He was all I had.

Amazingly, all those months, he'd never asked me one thing about my past. Well, maybe not so amazingly. He hadn't wanted anything interrupting our lives and taking me away from him.

"Oh, my dear boy," he said quietly while I told him about Fay, the Amazing Humans, Ginny, and even Tina. "Vile man," he muttered when I finally got around to Johnson. Laurence was on the floor with me at this point. His overcoat was splayed around him as if he'd been shot and fallen down. I sobbed on and on, spewing everything like a psychotic rant. I don't know how he followed what I was saying. I kept skipping back and forth over time as if it had all happened in one day.

"It's amazing you're alive to tell the tale. We'll go away," he said, rubbing his hands together. "We'll be like Jimmy Cagney on the lam," letting "lam" roll slowly off his tongue. We both knew that was out of the question. He'd barely left the house in months. Still, I appreciated him saying it, and it made me stop crying then.

"Really?" I said, rubbing my cheeks.

He patted my thigh. "You need some tea," he said and got up slowly. He went over to the kettle and turned a burner on.

"You're not going to tell anyone, are you?" I asked, sniffling as I stood. He looked at me like I'd swallowed a spoon. I sat down at the table, worn out.

He busied himself with getting two teacups from the dish drain. "What I don't understand . . ." he began but didn't finish the sentence. Instead he lifted an already used tea bag from a spoon rest on the stove and dropped it into a cup. "Well, what a monstrosity," he finally said. I didn't know if he was referring to the bombing or to Johnson again, but it didn't matter. He'd said the same thing the day after the *Voice* review of his exhibit came out. That relieved me somewhat. We'd gotten through that. Maybe this would be the same.

I was wrong. Not about us surviving together. About what he thought the monstrosity was.

He carried the cups over to the table, sat down, and made a show of dunking the same tea bag into the second cup of water.

"Your mother." He fixed me in the eye. "Why in the world would you care what happened to *her*? After all, she dropped you in the drink. It sounds to me like she had *you* do what she couldn't do herself—get rid of that odious man forever. And you, a mere boy. Her hit man." My face must have registered shock or at the very least dismay because he quickly added, "No, my dear boy, no. She does not deserve your loyalty. Not in the least. Trust me. Your mother was no mother at all. *I* know. I know what a *real* mother is. Yours was . . . she was . . ." He lowered his voice to a whisper. "A monster. It would be best if she *were* dead."

We never spoke again of what I told him. At least not directly. In the days that followed, Laurence became more protective, asking me if I needed anything and making me three meals a day, even if it was nothing more than canned soup.

"You have to keep your strength up," he kept saying. Later on, I realized this was exactly the sort of thing he needed to pull himself out of his own depression. He secretly loved when people needed him for something. It had thrilled him when young female art students would visit and he could send them on their way with a photograph in their hands, or a bit of advice. Although he'd stopped inviting them the past month, now he invited them every week. He wanted everything back to normal for both of our sakes, or as near to it as he could get, living with the knowledge that he was harboring a murderer.

At first, I was angry with him for blaming Fay. Who the hell was he? He didn't know Fay at all. But he chipped away at my already fading loyalty to her by slipping in stories about his own mother every night while we ate dinner. Stories that would indirectly prove to me how often and deeply Fay had failed me.

Like when he was eleven and he and his mother had been caught unprepared in a snowstorm. His mother carried him all the way home from the subway because his sneakers were soaked, and his feet were frozen. "Not once did that dear woman complain about her own frostbitten feet," he told me gravely. He recounted how she'd worked two jobs—as a receptionist for a dentist and cleaning offices on the weekends—and did sewing repairs at home so he could go to art college. How after his father died suddenly from a heart attack when Laurence was thirteen, she told him that he'd never have to worry about her remarrying.

"She used to say, 'I loved your father and I love you. That's more than enough. I'm grateful, not greedy.'"

And his Christmases. No wonder he'd loved that holiday. Every single bit of it that I'd begged my mother for and hoped for every year, Laurence's mother gave unasked to him. The outside lights that they strung up together—his mother on the ladder and Laurence unspooling the never-ending roll of colored bulbs. The tree dripping with tinsel. The dinner of brown sugared ham and sweet potato casserole with marshmallows and bowls of peas and corn, and "more pie than you could finish in a night." The presents wrapped the night before with ribbons, their ends scissored to perfect curls. Even the television switched to that ridiculous fake log burning in a phony fireplace with that cheesy music playing in the background.

"She was my number one fan," he said longingly at the kitchen table and then gave me a meaningful look. "She would've done anything for me. That's what mothers *do*." He hesitated, wanting to make sure I got the full import of whatever he was going to say next. "Or at least *good* mothers."

These stories wore me down over the months that followed. I began to question more than ever what Fay had or, more accurately, *hadn't* done for me. Why had I hung on to some childish hope that she'd come back and our lives would be miraculously different from what they'd always been? There comes a time when most teenage boys naturally start to separate from their mothers. Living with Laurence, I began to separate from the mother I never had. Fay didn't become a ghost. In some ways, she became even more real to me. I saw her for what she was. The doubts about her that had wormed in and stalked me from Key West now hardened into resentment and then hatred in Queens. They lurked inside of me, waiting to be exposed.

When I realized that Laurence wasn't going to turn me in to the police, I convinced myself that his knowing that I killed Johnson made our bond stronger—that he'd be tied to me forever. We were in it together against the world. The frequent visits by his artist friends and the art students, however, disrupted that fantasy. Yes, he would keep my news a secret between us. It would be something that we alone shared. But he obviously needed to surround himself with company.

Then, one afternoon something else dawned on me. Andy Warhol, who was on friendly terms with Laurence, paid a visit— he'd found out about the *Voice's* review and had been thrilled and intrigued by it. Warhol had been to the house before. While I hadn't known who he was at first, afterwards Laurence made sure I did by handing me a folder he'd created of newspaper clippings about Warhol's Marilyn Monroe prints.

This particular afternoon, we were all having tea in the front room and Andy, who was next to me on the couch, said, "You have beautiful hands." I stared down into the teacup that I was holding on my lap and murmured a quick thank you.

"They look *so* strong," he added.

At that, Laurence nearly dropped his cup on the carpeting. It rattled precariously against its saucer, luckily saved.

"Oh my, Laurence," Andy said. "That was *close*."

"I had the most troubling dream last night," Laurence said, his face drained of color. The dream involved trees with branches that gave birth to popsicles, not leaves. His words, however, were lost on me. What did his dropping his cup mean? Was he nervous that Andy would somehow divine what my hands had done?

Warhol left within the hour, but every minute he stayed was torture for me. By the time he stood to leave, my thoughts had shifted to something much more frightening. Maybe *Laurence* was afraid of those hands and what they could do. Maybe he'd started to doubt that any story about his mother would change me, the core of me. Maybe he ultimately couldn't be my protector. I was damaged goods. Maybe he needed to protect *himself*.

After that, I was glad that we had such frequent visitors. They'd calm him, I reasoned. He'd see that life would simply go on as it had before. That my news hadn't changed that. That he had nothing to fear. In addition to the visitors, I was grateful he was spending hours again in the basement. Perhaps he'd return to his old self.

While he now knew a lot about me, I'd kept one thing secret from him, however. One thing for myself. My name. It was silly really, considering how much he did know. But that day with Andy reinforced that I should keep my real name to myself. I superstitiously believed that if I told Laurence my real name, I'd invite something into our home that would stay uninvited. That whatever bad spirit had found Fay would find me if I so much as whispered the words.

"The apple doesn't fall far from the tree," I whispered anxiously one day as I stared through my bedroom window toward the snowbound crab apple tree out back. I wasn't talking about the garden.

Chapter

THIRTY-THREE

"Did you hear? Spin died last weekend," Sally tells me this morning, startling me so much I miss a customer's open hand and her change clatters all over the counter. "It's in the *Advocate*," she adds.

After work finishes, I head for the town library. Stephanie, the librarian, waves at me from behind the checkout counter. Spin used to say she was the only person in town who wasn't a direct descendant of someone on the Mayflower. She was *on* the Mayflower.

"Where do you keep the *Advocate*?" I ask her.

Her snowy hair is as usual piled on top with two pencil nubs sticking out. Her eyelids flutter with the weight of fake eyelashes. She points me toward the back.

There's a hard knot in the back of my throat the size of a walnut. It's June. *All that time, by himself, in that house with those dead orchids.* Regret isn't something I allow very often, not even with Johnson—that was another lifetime, another life—but regret is what washes through me now. *Why hadn't I tried again? Brought him a pizza? It wouldn't have taken much.*

I find the *Advocate*. It's not much of a write-up. A few lines remarking about his love for orchids and that he was to be cremated. Nothing else about his life. I photocopy it anyway. That night I cut it out and tape it up on the bare refrigerator door. *Look what you've done*, I tell myself. *Take a good look.*

•·····•

I stayed with Laurence through three springs of smelling his mother's hyacinths. There was a new photography exhibit of people who owned strange pets: bats and armadillos, a woman who had raised a python somehow in a Brooklyn brownstone. The show wasn't reviewed at all.

I became familiar with the elevator ride of Laurence's moods and managing our daily needs when he was incapacitated. On those days that we needed food I had it delivered from a nearby grocery store. One morning I was waiting for a delivery in the front room, rereading *The Castle of Otranto*, when a knock came at the door. Apricot Angel was on the front stoop, our usual box of canned soups, glazed doughnuts, and Lipton tea in her hands. We were eighteen by then. It was a warm spring day, around Easter. I noticed that the buttons on her blouse were straining across her chest. She was giving me the once-over too. My arms were bare because I was wearing one of Laurence's undershirts, which was a bit too small for my broad shoulders. Luckily, he was in the basement.

"Just leave it on the steps," I said gruffly through the screen door.

"How come I never see you in school?" she asked and smiled that fake smile of hers.

"It's Easter break."

She shook her head. "I don't mean now. I mean *ever*."

My mind was spinning. *Here we go*, I thought. What I'd been waiting for. Dreading, really. I stared at her, my anger mounting that it would be her, that she'd be the one to bring everything to an end. Stupid Apricot Angel.

As luck would have it, she was one of those people who are uncomfortable with silence. She turned her head and watched a Corvette speeding by. I kept staring her down, telling myself to keep my mouth shut. She bit her lip. I could tell she was trying to salvage the conversation. She wanted to say something that would keep me there. Maybe she was unwilling for me to have the upper hand. Or maybe she liked my arms. I didn't know and I didn't care. All I cared about in that moment was how I could end the conversation without drawing more attention to myself.

"You must go to that private school—what's it called?" she asked. Fay had been wrong after all. Give people time and they *won't* let you off the hook.

"*Maybe*," I said, stalling.

She gave me that fake smile again and I hoped for a minute she was going to drop it.

"What's it called?" she repeated, smiling more broadly, and I realized immediately that I was wrong about that smile. It meant exactly the same thing it always had: You're dead.

Surprisingly, I knew the name of a private school. I'd read in the newspaper about a very posh school called St. Andrews in Manhattan. The Mayor's son went there. So did one of the Rockefellers.

"St. Andrews," I told her and tried to appear bored by the whole thing. I leaned further over my sticks pretending I was getting tired.

"I'm leaving for Busch Gardens tomorrow," she said, startling me by switching topics.

"Oh yeah?" I said in a weary voice. I looked right past her shoulder at the street so that she'd get the hint.

"My whole school's going. Bet that private school of yours isn't."

"Aren't you a little too old to be doing that sort of thing?" I couldn't help myself. That anger I'd felt at first had now receded into simple envy, not because she was taking this trip with her friends at school, but that she *went* to school. And she was headed to Florida where I could no longer go.

"You're jealous," she said back.

I snorted. "I went to Busch Gardens tons of times. It was in my backyard for Chrissakes," I lied, not thinking. I was sick of her believing she was so superior.

A different smile appeared now. One that was totally genuine. "Oh, so that's where you're from," she said slowly, working everything out. "Flo-ree-da."

I didn't say a word. I couldn't. All I could manage was to keep staring at her without my lips trembling and that was torture. I pressed them together, folding them in slightly.

"Where in Florida?" She didn't wait for me to answer. Instead, she put her index finger to her lips and tapped them as if she were a great thinker. "Backyard, huh? So, what was that, like Daytona *Beach* or something?"

If I wasn't so nervous, I would've laughed at her geographical stupidity. At least she was miles from where I'd actually grown up. "Yeah," I said quickly. "My father was a race car driver down there and after he was killed, I moved up here with my uncle." I glanced back over my shoulder to make her see the connection to Laurence. I could still feel my lips quivering.

Frowning, she said, "Where's your mother then?"

"Dead," I replied as coldly as possible. "I don't like to talk about it, really." Her face immediately sagged. She knew I was lying but she also knew she'd lost, at least today.

I glanced back over my shoulder. "Coming," I shouted, although no one had called me. I shrugged to suggest there was no hard feelings but now duty called. "I've got to go," I said and shrugged again. I turned as she was saying goodbye, leaving her and the box of food on the steps.

"Don't you want me to bring in the food?" Her voice came through the screen door.

I stopped and turned for a second. "No thanks. My uncle will get it. See you." Then, I walked slowly down the hallway into the kitchen. Hidden from view, I leaned against the kitchen counter and waited until I heard her Dr. Scholl's sandals clatter down the cement steps. My whole body was shaking by then. *You're okay*, I told myself. *She doesn't have a clue. She's fishing. So what she thinks you're from Daytona?* But for days afterward I kept going over everything she and I had said to each other.

By that third spring, Laurence's visitors also began to take me aside and ask me if Laurence was feeling well. He had a morbid fear of doctors, but Clea Stevens's husband was a physician and Laurence allowed him to make a home visit.

I had no idea if anything was seriously wrong with him. He didn't look healthy, that much I could see with my own eyes. But who would after being housebound for months at a time? We never discussed how he was feeling except sometimes he would report a reoccurrence of his old headaches.

Other things preoccupied me anyway. That run-in with Apricot Angel unsettled me. Not just because she might find something out about me either. I couldn't stop recalling how her shirt was pulled so tightly across her chest. At night, in bed, I imagined every button, that small air pocket that formed where her shirtfront gapped. It'd start off with me being sexually aroused, but always end with me feeling more alone than I'd ever felt. And although Laurence and I never talked about it, I could sense that my confession was still on his mind. I caught him staring at my hands one day when we were eating breakfast. Another night, while I was doing my kitchen counter routine, he looked up from a newspaper and asked me, "My dear boy, is that still necessary? You're as strong as a Greek gladiator." I took them as further signs that he was afraid of me, as if I were a boarder who refused to move out.

With my mind elsewhere, it came as a surprise, then, when Dr. Abbott, Clea's husband, took me aside during his house visit and asked, "How long has he been having trouble urinating?"

I stared at him blankly, slightly affronted. Years of Laurence's verbal prudishness had rubbed off on me. "What do you mean, sir?" I asked.

Shaking his head, he walked away.

By the end of the week, Laurence was scheduled for prostate surgery at Mt. Sinai Hospital. He was operated on during a sunny day in July. Early the morning of the surgery, the surgeon stopped by his hospital room to make sure Laurence's vitals were on board. However, Laurence refused to sign the waiver for when he'd be under anesthesia.

"I'll be fine without anything," he told the surgeon. He didn't look fine. He looked as if it was a good thing he was lying down.

"It's not up for discussion," the surgeon replied, glancing over in my direction and motioning with his head toward the door. I followed him out of the room into the vast hallway that smelled of disinfected death.

"Look, son, is he compos mentis?"

"If you're asking me if he's sane, then yes," I snapped back. Hospitals made me nervous. There were too many people in uniforms, too many needles they could inject truth serum drugs with, and too many wrist restraints on the bed railings.

The surgeon raised one bushy eyebrow. I wondered what Laurence would've made of *that*.

"How serious is it?" I asked him.

"He'll be fine," he said, and then tapped me on the shoulder with his clipboard and walked away. *What did that tap mean? Was it like a wink, a ha-ha, a not a chance? Was it a better-fend-for-yourself sort of tap?* I watched him walk down the hallway and suddenly I began to realize what all of this might mean for me. If Laurence was really sick, if, say, something happened while he was on the table, then what would happen to me? Surely, he wouldn't leave the house and everything in it to me. He was too fond of Clea and several of his art students. Even, God forbid, Apricot Angel. I'd gotten huffy with the surgeon, but there had been times when I wondered if Laurence *was* sane. I'd made the best of a situation—*how much longer could it last?* I asked myself in that hospital hallway. *You've had a good run,* I thought. *Don't push it. Who knew if when he was under anesthesia, he'd suddenly blurt out what he knew about me?* As these thoughts cycled through my mind, I was suddenly in the elevator, pushing the button for the first floor. Then I found myself exiting the building. Before I knew it, I was sitting in the back of a cab headed to his house for a quick pit stop. It was as if I always knew it would come to this: packing a bag again—this time one of Laurence's suitcases that he never used—with his hand-me-down clothes. Pulling up the floorboard, three over from the door in his room, and grabbing five hundred dollars from his old cigar box. Running my fingertips lightly across the stuffed envelopes in the kitchen cabinet. One last time. Standing in the doorway of my bedroom and whispering, "Thanks for everything." And then, finally, slamming the waiting taxi's door shut and not looking back.

I told the cab driver to take me to Port Authority, the bus terminal. The first bus going north was to Boston, and from there it would finish the trip in Provincetown.

"Provincetown?" I repeated back to the ticket seller. "Where's that?"

"It's on the ocean," her muffled voice told me through the plastic window. "What's not to like?"

I stayed on board until the driver kicked me off. The bus had stopped near an enormous pier. When I swung down off the last step, the salt air stinging my eyes, I stared and marveled at the wide expanse of ocean and realized how much I'd missed the ocean over the last three years since Key West. Sailboats slipped by, propelled by a breeze. The parking lot was crowded with station wagons with fins and Volkswagen buses decorated with flower power decals. To the right was Commercial Street where the stores were now small, rundown fishing houses, their shingles chipped, a few swinging on nails in the breeze. I breathed in the air that smelled of fish. Someone was frying something in one of the houses. *Okay*, I thought. *This can work.* I looked at that ocean and imagined myself becoming a stowaway if I had to, leaving America for good.

I found a cheap rooming house on Pearl Street that was run by a guy whose name was Carl, but whom everyone called Bogart because he grew pot plants as high as my waist in every bathroom and in the basement of the house. Plant lights were strung up everywhere, which gave the place a weird purplish glow. Using some of Laurence's money, I paid Bogart to put me in touch with a guy whose name I never got but who forged a spanking new Social Security card and driving license for me. Although I was nineteen and old enough, I'd never actually driven a car.

"Pete Smith, huh?" the nameless forger said one moonless night as he handed me the cards on the sagging porch at Bogart's house. He was wearing black aviator glasses.

"That's right," I said, pocketing the cards. "Pete Smith."

Chapter

THIRTY-FOUR

After finding Spin's obituary at the library, I call in sick for a week and a half. Sally stops by, bringing a meatloaf that I know I'll throw out as soon as she leaves. I have until the end of this week to get back to my job, she tells me. She hands me a Post-it on which she has scrawled: Nunzio and Camarano LAWYERS Revere. ABOUT SPIN. There's a phone number.

"One of them keeps calling at work," Sally tells me. "Says he was trying you here, but you never answered. I told him I wasn't having any luck either. That you must've gone off on one of those fancy-pants cruises."

She takes in the pile of dirty dishes in the sink, the obit on the fridge door.

"Stop feeling sorry for yourself and get your ass back there. We're not going to hold your job forever," she says before she slams the trailer's screen door. That's Sally's idea of kindness. The pull-up-your-bootstrap kind. How can I just go on, though, with business as usual? I've been doing that my entire life and I'm tired of it.

"You get up in the morning and you get through your day. By nightfall you're ecstatic," Fay used to tell me. What kind of fucking life is that? I ask her now, sitting alone at the fold-down kitchen table in my trailer. I'm sick of Fay and everything she taught me. I'm angry. I have been for a very long time. If I had a photograph of her right now in my hands, I'd rip it to shreds.

Unread mail and papers are starting to form into furniture within the trailer. Without realizing it, I've created a miniature Fulton Avenue. Before I can stop myself, I stand and kick at one of the towers of unopened mail. I swing my stick at another pile, sending it flying. Breathing hard, I turn to the sink and those dirty dishes, but before I can throw them against a wall or on the floor, I hear the Harpurs start to argue next door, followed by a loud crash. That snaps whatever is in me. Grabbing my keys, I go outside, the first time in weeks. As I drive down Route 6, I tell myself I'll go into P-Town. At least I can stop by the A&P and pick up some groceries. The simplicity of it calms me down. *Just groceries. Nothing else. Get in and get out. No complications. You've got to focus on getting back to work.* I tell myself this even as I'm thinking what a great story it would make to tell some lonely woman in the checkout line that my only friend has died, and I'm so depressed I can't go to my job. For once I wouldn't be lying. But thinking of that, I only feel worse. Those days are over. I can't keep making the same mistakes, I tell myself as I pull into the parking lot.

All the lines, even Express, are long—summer season is at full throttle and vacationers are stocking up on paper plates, hamburgers, and watermelons. I stand behind a stocky man who only has a twelve pack of beer corralled against his hip like it's an unruly child. The A&P doesn't sell beer, but the liquor store next door does. Although he's at least in his sixties he looks like he could take out the cash register with one punch. He has the physique of an aging bodybuilder except he's sporting a wild beard that covers the bottom half of his face. He keeps swinging around and glancing down a nearby aisle, then scanning to the left toward the fruit and vegetable section, and then back again at the aisle. I notice that his belt buckle is a skull and crossbones. He makes a sound like he's spitting through his teeth. One of his front teeth is gold.

"She said she was going for shampoo," he snorts. "I'm gonna

kill her if she makes me go through this line again." The way he says it makes me wonder if he's serious.

The line moves along and then he's at the conveyor belt. "Goddamn it," he says, throwing the beer down on the belt. "I already paid for this," he tells the checkout guy who's still ringing up the woman who's in front of him.

"Honey, relax. We don't sell beer," the checkout guy says, rolling his eyes. "Fifteen eleven," he tells the other customer.

"Go in front of me," the man tells me, but then he yells out, "Jesusfay, where did you go? Alaska? I'm holding up the line here."

At first it doesn't register. Maybe it's the way he mashes the two words together. Jesusfay. Like one of those ministers on the TV religion program that Spin and I used to watch and laugh at together.

A woman pushes past me. Long blond hair, teased out and over like one of those heavy rock bands called Twisted Sister or Cinderella. That long hair shields her face from me, like someone who is shy or on the run. She slips in next to the man in front of me, and dumps hot dogs and buns, cans of tomato soup, boxes of Saltines, and can after can of Chef Boyardee Spaghetti & Meatballs in a pile on the conveyor belt, instantly reminding me of my childhood more vividly than a photo album.

"Jesusfay, you said you needed shampoo," the man says. The words separate and sift through. Jesus. Fay. My heart seizes like someone's reached in and grabbed it and is holding it completely still in some kind of wrestler's death grip. Her back to me, I scan down from her hair to the flip-flops on her feet. She's wearing a cropped purple T-shirt and tight aerobics pants, her body is compact, small. It can't possibly be her. I need to see her face to be sure.

"What's that?" says the woman, pointing to a bottle of shampoo that rolls down the belt. And then, turning away from him, she faces me. Her face is a mishmash of scar tissue. It's a child's sculpture: half of it globbed-on mashed potatoes, the other half silly putty with an unnatural shine to it. Her eyes are red-rimmed, and sunken in next to everything else. It's past ugly. It's hideous. Her arms are covered in a similar patchwork. *It's not her*, I think. *Thank God.*

"You want to say something, don't you?" the woman says. She's talking to me. I force myself to look back at her. She gives me the same once-over as I gave her, piece by piece, my face, my hair, my broad shoulders, my sticks. Then her eyes come up to my face again.

"Oh," she says. Her mouth stays open, like she's going to say something else, but nothing comes. Something about her mouth is odd, but I can't put my finger on it. The A&P feels like the air conditioning is on the fritz and my heart still has that death grip on it. Strangely, the pink splotches that are quilted on her face now look like they're being drained of their color.

"Thirty-three forty-eight," checkout guy says, and the man says, "Jesus Christ, what'd ya buy?" and the woman is staring at me and, in the space a plane could land in, she finally says something.

"Dickie? Shit. Is your name Dickie?"

My plastic basket crashes to the ground, scattering my frozen TV dinners on the floor. There's no way that this is my mother, the woman I haven't seen in twenty-five years, this woman who's asking me my name. She's dead. *Dead.* There's no way I can stay there either, with this woman whose name is Fay but who looks like some ghoul from one of my childhood horror comic books. Head down, I pivot and pole out of there as fast as I can, feeling sick to my stomach.

"Dickie, wait," she yells, and then she's behind me, chasing after me through the automatic doors. "Stop," she shouts next to me, like I've snatched her purse. She runs in front, heading me off in the parking lot and, putting up her hands, forces me to come to a standstill. "Stop. Jesus." She bends over at the waist, not out of breath but like she has a pain in her side. For a moment I think I should make another break for it, but the shock freezes me where I am.

Fay rights herself. "I can explain—Jesus, this is incredible. I mean, running into you here," she says, her hands waving in the air. "You think you've seen it all. We only got here this morning. Do you know how long I looked for you?" She laughs nervously. "Christ. I can't believe this." Her voice is still Fay's voice. Older, though. Worn out.

Before I can stop it, my eyes start to tear. I turn my head away, forcing myself to concentrate on something, anything. It's too much to take in. *There. That motorcycle that's illegally parked. It's a fucking Harley—*

"Dickie, listen to me. I looked. Okay? I looked for you. I went back to Key West."

Suddenly, I feel her fingers on my chin. *No.* I jerk my head away but I'm unable to say anything. I'm afraid that if I open my mouth, something unreal—bats or a shrieking parrot—will come out of it. I feel like I'm going to throw up.

"What the fuck are you doing, Fay?" I hear behind me and then the man who was with her in the store is there, two bags clutched to his chest.

"You remember Chuck, don't you?" Fay says. "It's Dickie, Chuck. *Dickie.* Can you believe it?"

"You're shittin' me, right?" Chuck says. "Dickie? Christ, is that you, boy?" Chuck pushes the bags in Fay's direction and reaches out. Before I can stop him, he's grabbing me in a tight hold. I automatically shove him as hard as I can. He almost falls to the blacktop.

"Hey!" he yells, stumbling. "What the hell—"

"Keep your fucking hands off me!" I yell.

"Listen to this punk, Fay," Chuck says, catching his breath.

"You're lucky I don't beat the crapola out of you." He raises his fist like he's about to start right away, but then he laughs, a gold tooth shining in the sunlight. He drops his hand. "Nice seeing you, kid. Let's do it again in another thirty years. Let's go," he tells Fay.

But she shakes her head. The bags rustle against each other. She pushes them back on him, saying, "You go ahead. I'm going to have a cup of coffee with Dickie."

"No," I tell her. "No fucking way." I sound like I'm fifteen years old again, not forty. But I don't move. For the life of me I can't figure out why I'm staying. Part of me wants me to run away as fast as I can. The other part is rooting me to the spot. It's like watching a sink hole swallow up a nearby house and knowing you'll be next at any second.

"Don't talk to your mother like that," Chuck says.

"Go on," Fay urges him. "I'll be there in an hour."

Chuck's got the two bags clamped against his chest again. His body sags briefly. "One hour," he finally says. He adjusts the bags, shoring himself up. "You don't want me looking for you." He walks toward a battered pickup truck and gets in, drives away. Fay and I watch him, not saying a word.

"I have to go," I finally say when the truck takes a right out of the parking lot. "I have to go back to work."

"It's five o'clock."

"Night shift at the PO." I start to walk away.

"All I'm asking for is one coffee."

"I don't think so," I tell her, turning around. "It's been twenty-five years, Fay."

"You think I don't know that?" She glances toward a passing convertible full of pretty boys.

"I don't have anything to say to you."

She smiles at that. "After twenty-five years?" she asks in her seductive voice. "*That* I don't believe."

I look down at the blacktop. There's a ground-in bottle cap by my right foot. I stab at it with my stick. "What happened to your face?" I say as harshly as I can.

"See?" she says softly, surprising me. I look up at her—which is exactly what she wants me to do. "There's so much to talk about," she adds.

We walk to Spiritus because parking is difficult during the summer on Commercial Street and I know it'll be dark inside in the back booths. I don't want to see her face again under the glare of lights. Everyone is at T-Dance at the Boatslip, leaving Spiritus empty except for the beautiful teenage girls who serve behind the counter. They're older than Laurence would've liked—in their late teens—but they have the stunning, full faces of Renaissance virgins that he adored, although their heads are masses of dreadlocks.

"Can you get this?" Fay asks as we walk into the cool darkness. She raises her hands. "No pockets."

I buy her a cup of coffee, but don't order anything for myself. I can't think of putting anything into my stomach. In the back corner, none of the wood booths have people at them. I sit down at one, on a bench against the wall, making sure that I'm near the end so Fay can't sit next to me and also ensuring that I'm facing the front. She slides in on the other side, her back to the girls at the counter.

"This is unbelievable," she says, shaking her head. She stirs her coffee in its Styrofoam cup. "I mean not in a million—"

"What are you fucking doing here?"

She sips on her coffee and grimaces. Again, her mouth looks odd, as if it's not comfortable with itself. "I was looking for you, of course," she says sweetly and for a second I almost buy it because she looks and sounds so honest. Then she laughs. "No, it was just dumb luck. Chuck has a charter boat. We came for season. Shit, Ginny would get a kick out this. Look at you. You're even more handsome than I expected."

"Is she here too?" I ask and immediately old remnants of envy rise up from a tamped down earth for the way Ginny could move her legs into weird positions, for how close she was to Fay.

"She's dead," Fay says matter-of-factly. She takes another sip of her coffee and winces. "Hot," she says.

"How?"

I think I see Fay's eyes tear, but she glances away and when she turns back to me, they're dull. "We fucked up. It's a long story," she says and stares off again, this time watching two customers, an overweight woman and man who have walked through and are checking out the outdoor tables in the back fenced-in eating area. Their faces are painfully red from staying in the sun too long.

"Amateurs," Fays says, staring at the couple. "I was burned badly. My face. Obviously. My arms. Pretty much all over. My mouth was bashed in," she continues on, now looking at me. She taps on her front teeth. "They're false." She stirs her coffee. "We were in a chopper," she says and sips her coffee, thoughtfully. "Do you remember what Tet was?"

Immediately I'm transported back to Laurence's house, to his kitchen. He's holding up the newspaper and there I am, screaming and falling to the kitchen floor.

"Yes, I thought you were dead."

My stomach has settled down. I can't believe I'm sitting here with Fay and yet, at the same time, it feels completely, strangely natural. For so many years I've heard her voice in my head. And yet, the face across from me is not Fay. It's a ventriloquist's dummy with Fay's voice. Still, somehow, it's her. I imagine briefly that we'll try to patch our relationship back together again. Each of us with our shitty lives. Suddenly, in spite of myself, I want to know about everything that happened to her. Where she's been all these years.

Fay is smiling that awkward smile again. "No, I didn't die. Almost. But not quite. We weren't even supposed to be where we were. It was just luck they saw us. They were on their way to Camp Beecher where there were causalities when they saw the explosion." She glances around again. "Listen, do you think we could go for a drink somewhere?"

She says it like she's asked me if I could buy her a Danish. I almost tell her yes, but a self-protectiveness surfaces and shuts it down fast. It's not like I'm holding onto an adolescent grudge. It's deeper than that. I stopped expecting she'd find me many years ago in Laurence's kitchen when I was convinced that she was dead. But even dead, she remained close to me. I never thought of her as a stranger. I do now. Maybe it's because the face I'm looking at isn't Fay's. Then, something else emerges. It hits me that quite possibly I don't want to sit in any bar with her, not looking like this. P-Town is small. Someone might see her with me. It's the same feeling an adolescent boy has when his mother wants to drop him off at school. Only I would've loved it if Fay had done *that* for me when I was a kid. I see myself for what I've become: a man as scarred as his mother is. Someone who can't get past his past.

"No, let's just stay here," I tell her, lowering my voice as if that could make it better. For me. For her. I don't know, just better.

"In the dark," she says. "Right?"

I feel ashamed, but that doesn't last because Fay stands and I'm afraid she's going to insist. She surprises me, though, as she always could. She walks up to the sunburned couple, who are now sitting in a booth at the front, and asks them for a cigarette. I lower my chin, keeping my eyes on her, imagining what the couple is thinking as this horribly disfigured woman bums a cigarette. Fay saunters back to the table, a lit cigarette gripped firmly between her scarred lips, and sits down.

"Anyway," she says and lets out a cloud of smoke, the cigarette bobbing in her mouth. "The chopper was shot down. Ginny"— she pauses. Her eyes well up but then, she shakes her head and continues. "And this guy, this doctor I knew—" She pauses again and waves at the air with her cigarette. "Shit. Well, he didn't make it either. The pilot carried me for three miles until we were found by some South Vietnamese and then recon. I was in bad shape. My leg was broken by the crash. He carried me the whole way. He was a good man. So was that doctor."

When she says it, I can't help myself, I start to laugh. "You wouldn't know a good man if he hit you in the face," I tell her, laughing meanly. Fay stares at me, the cigarette tilted in her uncomfortable mouth. She takes it out and flicks it between her fingers. The ashes fall right on the table.

"All these years," she says, slowly, "wondering how you turned out. When the chopper went down, the last thing I thought of was you. I was going to wire you money. I told myself that if I lived, when I got home I'd look for you. I did, for two years. *Two years*. I tracked you to that gallery. You know, the one that had the photographs of you in the *Voice*? When that didn't pan out, I dragged Chuck back to Florida. You know how hard *that* was? What I had to pay—" Here her voice catches. She shakes her head quickly like it's a nervous tic. "What I'm still *fucking* paying for? And this is what I get. A fucking smart mouth." Her face winces and for a brief moment her eyes look like they're getting wet again, but then that same steeliness shades over them. It's like watching a metal grate slamming down over a storefront.

Still, my resentment and anger are so deeply ingrained in me that I'm not moved by any of it. I'm not even sure I believe her.

"Oh, come on. It's not like you ever ended up with a 'good

man.'" I do finger quotations in the air between us when I say those two words. I think of Johnson. The last, the worst of the bad men.

Fay stands up. As if she's reading my mind, she says, "I'll have that drink now and you can tell me all about the man I left you with. Remember him? Johnson? He drowned, right? That's what Mrs. Henderson told me. I paid a little visit to Mrs. Henderson. Remember her? Because no matter how bad it got over there, I knew I had to get back no matter—" With this, Fay's voice breaks entirely. She turns away toward where the pizza ovens are. She raises her hand up to take a drag of her cigarette. It's trembling ever so slightly. After she blows out a plume of smoke, she turns back to me. Forces a smile. Then, she puts a hand on her small hip and sighs, staring off to the side.

"The thing is, Dickie, I can't exactly work anymore." The words come out fast then. She can't get them out quickly enough. "Chuck's okay—shit, he's the only one who'll have me. But Chuck thinks in terms of ownership. Always has. Always will. He's got it in his thick head that because I look like this, it's okay to smack me whenever he wants. The charter boat business isn't for me, though. And I wouldn't need him if I had my own money," she adds matter-of-factly.

"What are you talking about?" I say although I know damn well what she's talking about. She'll keep her mouth shut if I give her enough money to go away. I have no idea what she knows about Johnson, but this much I'm sure of: She knows that he's dead and I was probably the last person who saw him alive. Knows he wouldn't have gone in that tank on his own. My hands are gripping the edge of the table, the tips of my fingers are white blotching into pink.

"I'd like that drink now," Fay tells me and, dropping the cigarette on the floor, stamps it out. "I'm in the mood for some good Scotch. Nam taught me there's nothing like twelve-year-old Scotch to make you forget how shitty life really is."

"Sit down," I tell her, trying my best to keep my voice even. I see Fay for what she's always been: a survivor who will do anything. Leave her child. Move in with an abusive man. At dawn, get in the car, turn the ignition, and drive away, without a backward glance. How could I possibly have thought she'd died? People like her grow old. They survive hurricanes that take the roofs off houses, men who beat them, choppers going down. Those years of waiting for her, hoping that she'd find me. I was so stupid. Laurence was right. She *is* a monstrosity. I feel overwhelmingly tired. I rub my face with both hands. When I drop my hands to the table, Fay is still standing there, eyeing me.

"Hey, you all right?" she asks me with her sweet voice. She slides into the booth again and reaches her hands toward mine resting on the table, but I move mine away fast. "Listen, I know I haven't been a good mother. I know—"

"Shut up," I tell her, angrily. "You don't know a damn thing."

Fay hesitates and then she says, "I don't need much. SSI covers my weekly. I just want to get a car—it can be used even." Her voice has started to rise, the words racing a bit. She's panicking. She's afraid she won't get anything. Staring at her new patchwork face, I realize she's not the same. She's something she never was. Desperate. For the first time ever, I feel sorry for her.

"A car, nothing special, and a small trailer. Remember our trailer, Dickie, when it was just you and me? It was okay then, wasn't it? You always wanted a house. Remember?" She forces a laugh, hoping it will ease the strain. Her fingers have found my hand and are lightly touching my knuckles.

I look down at my sticks. My entire life has been crap. Fay. Johnson. Spin. No, Spin was my fault. Spin's gone. It's too late to do anything about that. But I can do what Fay asks now. Somehow there is a connection between the two.

"I'll get you the car and trailer," I tell her, looking up at her.

"Go to Race Point this time Friday night. I'll be there." I take a breath and force myself to say, "After that don't ever come back here. I don't want to see you again."

Fay's mouth opens, but she doesn't say anything. I start to walk away but then I stop and turn back to her.

"How much?" I ask her because I can't stop myself. I have to know. I have to know how much I was worth to her all those years ago.

"How much?" she asks, confused.

"How much were you going to wire to me?"

She hesitates, glances away, putting her fingers on her bottom lip. "A hundred and fifty."

As soon as the words are out of her mouth, I leave. I move through the double open doors and out onto Commercial Street, which is teeming now with happy, drunk people. They've left T-Dance and are on their way to stand in lines at The Lobster Pot or Mojo's. Everyone is laughing and dancing, their arms around each other. Halfway up Commercial, I realize I'm going in the wrong direction. I don't care. I don't even care that I'm crying. I just keep walking. This is what Spin must've felt like. No one should know how much people think they're worth. Now I do.

At five o'clock on Friday night, I pull away from a used recreational vehicle lot in Orleans, a ten-year-old Scamper pop-up trailer hitched to the back of a used Chevy Cavalier. The passenger door of the Cavalier is dented in. It was the cheapest one on the lot.

On the way to Race Point I almost turn around several times. I imagine switching out the Chevy with my Mustang and driving through the night. West maybe, through Ohio and into Michigan. Maybe stopping for a few days at a campsite on Lake Michigan. I could live in the Scamper until I got myself sorted out with a new job, a new life. Some place where I didn't know anyone. Other than stopping for a few traffic lights, however, I keep driving on Route 6 until I see the signs pointing to Race Point Beach. I've lived in P-Town for over twenty years. I know every street name, every corner. Whenever I pass the street where Spin and I lived I think about him moving here to escape his past and setting up a home for himself and eventually, for me. Maybe that doesn't exactly qualify as history or roots but it's the closest thing I've ever felt to permanence. Ultimately, I've realized I'm not Fay. I don't want to leave. That was what she was good at, not me. Every time I'd ever left some town or state, I'd been forced to do so. No more.

When I pull into the parking lot Fay is already there. She's pacing by the tall dune grasses that shimmer and bend in the evening sun. Something about those grasses lowers my blood pressure. They've been here since the Mayflower docked. They're not going anywhere either.

By the time I'm out of the car, Fay is by the hood, smiling.

"I was afraid—"

"Here." I hold out the keys. "In the glove compartment is the registration. I signed the back. You bought the car from me for a dollar."

She laughs and takes the keys. "Isn't that a bit much for *this* car?" she tries to joke.

I fix my eyes on her, not saying a word, a strong urge coming over me to hop back in the car, gun it, and leave her standing there. I imagine watching her in my rearview mirror, her solitary figure getting smaller and smaller until I can't see her anymore. The opposite of what my side mirrors promise me: *Objects are closer than they appear.*

A woman appears over a nearby dune with two boys who plunge down the steep sand, pretending they've landed in a space shuttle on an unknown planet. "Wait for me," the mother calls.

They don't. They run to their station wagon, arguing who gets the front seat.

"Dickie, thank you for this," Fay says, waving at the car and the trailer. "It's great, really."

I give her the smile I've given a hundred women in the A&P.

"I'm not doing it for you," I tell her.

I hear her breath catch. Then she turns away, tapping her false front tooth, and watches the mother throwing a beach chair and wet towels into the back of the wagon. The family gets into the car, rolls down their windows, and drives off. I want to believe that I've hurt her. That maybe she's thinking about the times I rode shotgun with her. All the times we loaded up the old asthmatic station wagon and drove off with the trailer swinging behind us. The times we drove through state lines before dawn, with her promising this town will be better, you'll see. I want to believe that she enjoyed my company as much as I did hers. That we were in some way like that family driving off, glad to be with each other, shouting out suggestions for where we could eat dinner that night, knowing full well that there was just going to be Saltines and tomato soup. I want to believe, but it's too late. Maybe if I hadn't met Laurence and heard his stories about what a good mother is. Maybe if Fay had found me sooner. She didn't, though.

"Well, so long then," she says, like we simply met for a coffee or a quick swim. "I'll send you a postcard care of the PO." Then she sits in the car and starts the engine. Her other hand gives a short wave out the window, and the Cavalier with the trailer in tow cruises away. As she turns left onto the exit road, a taxi, which I'd arranged beforehand, passes her on its way into the parking lot.

Somehow, I knew in the end that she wouldn't even ask me how I'd get home. She'd be too anxious about leaving before Chuck found her. The taxi stops in front of me. Would she have stayed if I hadn't been so cruel to her? Had she expected our time together to be different? Expected to drive me home? To be invited in for a cold one before hitting the open road? To hug and wish each other well before she started her next adventure? Maybe even asked me to come along?

Fay doesn't answer the questions this time in my head. It's Laurence's voice, loud and clear that I hear. "I'm afraid my dear boy the answer is a resounding no. Now, I think we need that cup of tea."

······●◆

Chapter

THIRTY-FIVE

Here's a knock on my trailer door. At the same time my telephone rings.

I haven't been answering my phone for weeks. The phone stops ringing. I stare at the Post-it that lies before me on the table. ABOUT SPIN all in caps is Sally's way of driving home the point.

The phone rings again. Just like it has every morning and afternoon. I know who it is. I know what Nunzio or Camarano will say. A walnut comes into my throat again, as it has every day for the past several weeks. Only this time, my eyes sting. *Maybe you should answer the phone. Just to be certain.* I shake my head. I'm not ready yet.

Another knock comes at the door. It's too soft for Sally. She's more of an open-the-goddamn-door kind of gal. A third knock comes, still soft but more of a rat-a-tat-tat. Whoever it is, isn't going away. I shove the Post-it into my pants pocket and move toward the door.

A small girl stands there with a half-dead flower in her hand. It's a sorry excuse for a daisy. The usually white petals have liver spots. Her blond ringlets touch her shoulders. She's wearing a jumper and the wool material is so coarse that I find myself wanting to scratch my chest just from the looks of it. Why the hell is she wearing a jumper like that in July? She holds out the flower so that I'm forced to open the screen door and take it. She keeps the door open with a bony knee. The phone starts ringing again.

"Your phone is ringing," she tells me.

"I know."

We both stand there, not saying a word until it stops. Almost immediately I feel it: the lack of air to breathe. The walnut back in my throat. My stomach feels like someone is pulling it out, hand over fist. Same as it has since Sally dropped off that damn Post-it.

"My mother and I live there," the girl says and points to the brown and tan trailer that has seen better days and too many downhill lives. The screen in a corner of the door has pulled loose and curls downward. The wooden steps are swaybacked in the middle. In one of the jalousie windows is a large sticker of a fire-man that says Cat Finder. I've seen this girl from my windows. I've done my best to avoid her and her mother, who from a distance looks like a child herself.

"What's your cat's name?" I ask, hoping this will divert her from whatever it is that's brought her to my doorstep.

She scrunches up her face as if she's trying hard not to cry. I've made a mistake, I can see that right away. Finally, she says, "We had a cat, but now she's in heaven. What's *your* name?" she asks. Her eyes stare at my sticks. They're too interesting for a girl of five years old not to be distracted by them.

"What's yours?" I reply, hoping for an easy diversion. There are five-year-old children who have the attention spans of fleas. They're the ones who swing on the PO's queue rope for corralling people into a straight waiting line.

I slip my hand into my pocket and finger the Post-it. *What were you thinking, Spin?*

"Stella," she says, interrupting my thoughts, and there's something about a pipsqueak like her having such an older woman's name—*A Streetcar Named Desire* comes to mind, sultry nights breeding sex—that I almost laugh.

"What's so funny?" Stella asks. She puts a hand on her small hip.

My smile fades. "Nothing. That's a pretty dress you're wearing."

"It's ugly," she says with a shrug. "Can't you walk?" she asks me. Any second now she's going to ask me about the accident, whether a car ran over me, or something like that. They always do.

But *she* doesn't.

"Were you born like that?" she asks.

"No," I say back, startled. I take my hand out of my pocket. Maybe it's because of Spin's lawyers calling me and my holing up in this tin can for so many days, but with the door open I can feel a shift in the breeze as we stand there. The wind is coming off the ocean now.

"No, I was sick once and—"

Her penny eyes get bigger then.

I have the impulse to tell her the whole damn thing, how I got polio when I was two years old because of Walter Winchell, because Fay made a terrible decision. But I swallow it whole, like some kind of espionage secret written on a piece of paper. I swallow it before it can live another day. I look up at the tie-dyed sky. The sun will be down in thirty minutes. Soon, there'll be crowds of people pouring out of T-dance in P-Town. Four hours later, they'll find themselves parked on a bench in front of Spiritus Pizza, alone. It's the same thing every night during season. Nothing changes except occasionally the faces. Day in, day out. Every night people end up alone. Why do people live like this? Why did Spin? Even whales know that the best way to survive is to stick it out in their pod.

"Do those hurt?" Stella asks, pointing at the cuffs that grab my forearms.

I shake my head no and am surprised to find my eyes smarting. Thunder sounds in the distance. Somewhere over the ocean the moisture and heat are circulating into a storm. They're predicting high winds along the entire national seashore. The television news starts every evening with a spiraling graphic that spits out the words, Hurricane Watch. Some people—the *seasonals*—have taken to putting strips of masking tape in big X's on their windows. The aluminum frames will creak, do their best to hold back the swell, but when push comes to shove, those windows are going to shatter under a force too large to hold back no matter how much tape you put on them.

The phone rings again.

"Answer it," Stella says. And maybe because she says it so authoritatively for a kid, or maybe because she takes the flower back out of my hand, or maybe I'm just sick of hearing it ring, I pick up the receiver.

"Hey, how long have you lived here?" She pulls on the hem of my shirt. I don't think anyone has ever done that to me. Now I know what it feels like. It's not what I expected. It's not annoying in the least. You're wanted, it says. Pay attention.

"You are the executor and sole beneficiary," Camarano is telling me on the phone. His voice is rushed like he's calling me in between appointments, and he needs to make this quick. "Would Thursday at two be convenient to review everything?"

Stella tugs at my shirt again. "How long have you *lived* here?" she asks again.

I cover the phone's mouthpiece. "Not long. But I may be moving soon," I whisper, and realize that it's true. A flood of relief mixed with guilt washes out of me. Spin. He knew what he was doing the whole time. We'll be ending up together after all. Within a few weeks I'll be living again in his house. Only now it will be *my* house. I wonder if the orchids will still be there. If there's any chance I can bring them back to life.

"Thursday at two then?" Camarano asks.

"Yes," I barely manage to get out before I hang up the phone.

"Hey, mister, why are you crying?" Stella asks.

It's all I can do to shrug my shoulders. I rub my eyes. *Spin. Anthony. Whatever your damn name was. Well, you certainly had the last laugh, didn't you?* He knew I wouldn't be able to sell the house. Maybe I could've in the past, taken the money and left. I can't now. He knew me better than I thought. He knew that what I wanted most my whole life was a home without wheels.

I look down at Stella, the unmarked beauty of her small round face. What Laurence would have called "the magnificent sense" of her. He would've turned her name into Stella Bella without so much as a wink. By now in the conversation, he would've invited her in for some stale doughnuts and milk. Maybe he would've given her one of his photographs of the midgets. Later on, he would've called Clea Stevens and held her captive on the phone for hours, talking about his newest find, his Stella Bella.

Stella tugs on my shirt again. "Hey," she says softly. She's not here for Laurence. She's here for me. "Does your mother live here too?" she asks.

I let out a short bark then. I shake my head no.

Then the sound of a screen door slamming catches her attention.

"Hi Mama!" she bellows. "This is—wait." She turns to me. "What's your name?"

I watch a lankier, grown-up version of Stella strolling across the dirt from their trailer to mine. She's carrying a metal pan. She's smiling and good-naturedly saying she hopes her daughter hasn't been a pest. She's been meaning to introduce herself.

"I hope you like brownies," she says at my steps. She raises the pan.

Stella stamps her foot. "He hasn't told me his name!"

"Dickie," I say, looking from one to the other. "Dickie Stonewell."

····•●

ACKNOWLEDGMENTS

Many thanks to Brooke Warner and She Writes Press for giving this story the green light, and to Samantha Strom for her project management and Anne Durette for her editing prowess. Thank you, Gerilyn Attebery, for the exquisite cover.

Also, to Bennington College where, as part of my thesis, I first wrote the short story from which this novel later sprang. My thesis advisors, Maria Flook and Martha Cooley, offered invaluable advice on that initial story, which focused only on Dickie. Thanks also to my Bennington writing group allies—Alden Jones, Ricco Villanueva Siasoco, Andrea Graham, Oona Patrick, and Sarah Johnson—and Christine Destrempes, Ailish Hopper, and Maria Flook for faithfully reading several drafts as only true friends would. To Joy Johannessen for her excellent editorial advice on a prior version and to CB Lee for her incredible insight and suggestions, especially on Fay's journey in Vietnam.

I am grateful to the Vermont Studio Center for a residency when I needed it most and where I also met the artist Sara Lee Hughes. I am indebted to her for the years of friendship and for her many encouraging letters and vividly rendered drawings of my character Laurence Jones that cheered me on.

Thank you to my brother, Richard, Wendy, and my nieces, Jessica and Nicole, who provided an unwavering home of support and respite over the ten years it took me to finish this story.

Several books were helpful as I was researching for this book.

Specifically, *In the Combat Zone: Vivid Personal Recollections of the Vietnam War from the Women who Served There* by Kathryn Marshall, and Stanley Karnow's *Vietnam: A History*, an old copy of which I was fortunate to find just waiting for me on my father's bookshelves. I am deeply grateful to the American Friends Service Committee (AFSC) for opening up their archives to me several years ago while I was researching a rehabilitation hospital that they operated during the war in Quang Ngai, Vietnam. More information about the AFSC and the vital and compassionate work they do can be found at www.afsc.org. Qui Dao, the rehabilitation center that figures so predominantly in Part Two, is purely fictional, although the statistics concerning patients were kept as close to fact as possible. AFSC's Quang Ngai hospital moved and impelled me to show the heart-wrenching consequences of war on children.

Similarly, the character of Laurence Jones is fictional, however there are a few elements that I loosely wove in based on the diaries of the artist Joseph Cornell. For instance, Cornell did name girls he came across by their clothing, including an "apricot angel" who wore orange. And he did allegedly feed birds on his kitchen table and reused his tea bags past their prime. While he had prostate surgery, he actually died later from heart failure. However, Laurence Jones is in no way meant to be a factual representation of Joseph Cornell. For that I encourage you to go to the source, *Joseph Cornell's Theater of the Mind: Selected Diaries, Letters, and Files*, edited and with an insightful introduction by Mary Ann Caws.

Finally, the manuscript for this story would have remained locked away in my desk drawer had it not been for the artist Fiona Sinclair who gently urged me to give it the light of day. I'll spend the rest of my days thanking her for that and the wondrous, creative life she gives us every day. You are my heart. You are my home.

ABOUT THE AUTHOR

Photo credit: Sylvia Stagg-Giuliano

Randi Triant is the author of the novel *The Treehouse*, selected as an ultimate summer read by *AfterEllen*, and the psychological suspense novel *A New Life*. Her short fiction and nonfiction have appeared in literary journals and magazines, including two anthologies of writing about HIV/AIDS, *Art & Understanding: Literature from the First Twenty Years of A & U* and *Fingernails Across the Blackboard: Poetry and Prose on HIV/AIDS from the Black Diaspora*. She lives in Massachusetts.

SELECTED TITLES FROM SHE WRITES PRESS

She Writes Press is an independent publishing company
founded to serve women writers everywhere.
Visit us at www.shewritespress.com.

The Fourteenth of September by Rita Dragonette. $16.95, 978-1-63152-453-0. In 1969, as mounting tensions over the Vietnam War are dividing America, a young woman in college on an Army scholarship risks future and family to go undercover in the anti-war counterculture when she begins to doubt her convictions—and is ultimately forced to make a life-altering choice as fateful as that of any Lottery draftee.

Don't Put the Boats Away by Ames Sheldon. $16.95, 978-1-63152-602-2. In the aftermath of World War II, the members of the Sutton family are reeling from the death of their "golden boy," Eddie. Over the next twenty-five years, they all struggle with loss, grief, and mourning—and pay high prices, including divorce and alcoholism.

Tasa's Song by Linda Kass. $16.95, 978-1-63152-064-8. From a peaceful village in eastern Poland to a partitioned post-war Vienna, from a promising childhood to a year living underground, *Tasa's Song* celebrates the bonds of love, the power of memory, the solace of music, and the enduring strength of the human spirit.

In the Shadow of Lies: A Mystery Novel by M. A. Adler. $16.95, 978-1-93831-482-7. As World War II comes to a close, homicide detective Oliver Wright returns home—only to find himself caught up in the investigation of a complicated murder case rife with racial tensions.

Things Unsaid by Diana Y. Paul. $16.95, 978-1-63152-812-5. A family saga of three generations fighting over money and obligation—and a tale of survival, resilience, and recovery.

Trespassers by Andrea Miles. $16.95, 978-1-63152-903-0. Sexual abuse survivor Melanie must make a choice: choose forgiveness and begin to heal from her emotional wounds, or exact revenge for the crimes committed against her—even if it destroys her family.

Pieces by Maria Kostaki. $16.95, 978-1-63152-966-5. After five years of living with her grandparents in Cold War-era Moscow, Sasha finds herself suddenly living in Athens, Greece—caught between her psychologically abusive mother and violent stepfather.